2/23

Hayner PLD/Large Print
Overdues .10/day. Max fine cost of
item. Lost or damaged item: additional
$5 service charge.

the
Sandcastle
Hurricane

Center Point
Large Print

Also by Carolyn Brown and available from
Center Point Large Print:

The Sunshine Club
The Hope Chest
Hummingbird Lane
Miss Janie's Girls
The Family Journal
The Empty Nesters
The Perfect Dress
The Magnolia Inn
Small Town Rumors
The Sometimes Sisters
The Strawberry Hearts Diner

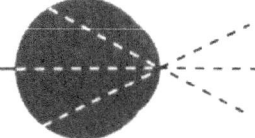

**This Large Print Book carries the
Seal of Approval of N.A.V.H.**

the
Sandcastle
Hurricane

CAROLYN BROWN

CENTER POINT LARGE PRINT
THORNDIKE, MAINE

This Center Point Large Print edition
is published in the year 2023 by arrangement with
Amazon Publishing, www.apub.com.

Originally published in the United States
by Amazon Publishing, 2022.

This is a work of fiction. Names, characters,
organizations, places, events, and incidents are either
products of the author's imagination or are used
fictitiously. Otherwise, any resemblance to actual persons,
living or dead, is purely coincidental.

The text of this Large Print edition is unabridged.
In other aspects, this book may vary
from the original edition.
Printed in the United States of America
on permanent paper sourced using
environmentally responsible foresting methods.
Set in 16-point Times New Roman type.

ISBN: 978-1-63808-571-3

The Library of Congress has cataloged this record
under Library of Congress Control Number: 2022946192

This book is for my grandson
Seth Lemar Brown.
Sometimes a memory sparks
a whole story. Today I'm remembering
Seth helping the younger grandkids
build a sandcastle and dig
an enormous hole when we had
a family reunion at the beach
in Florida.

Chapter One

Who in their right mind would name a hurricane Delilah? That's just asking for trouble," Ellie Mae fussed as she put the final screw in the plywood covering the last door on the second floor of the Sandcastle Bed-and-Breakfast.

"That's better than Jezebel or Lucifer. I understand that the names they give them aren't random, and they come from a list that is put together years in advance." Tabby wondered at the same time if hurricanes should be given names of the infamous rather than common folks.

"The last one that created havoc in south Texas was named Ida. That sounds like an old-maid aunt's name," Ellie Mae said as she finished the job.

"If there's another one this fall, it will be named James. The names are switched back and forth between female and male to keep things equal," Tabby said with a giggle.

Ellie Mae tucked the drill and extra screws into a tote bag, slung it over her shoulder, and started down the rickety old wooden ladder that had been propped up against the railing around the balcony. "Well, then, I hope there's not another one this year, because your ex-husband does not deserve any glory—not even the negative kind that folks talk about for years to come."

"You got that right." Tabby felt a surge of anger thinking about any notoriety that man might get.

James had always been a good provider, and a good father, but he believed that the man's word was law in the family, and he had no reason to discuss his decisions with her. His attitude had been the final straw that had broken the old proverbial camel's back and caused their divorce two years before.

"Be careful!" Tabby glanced over the side of the railing, tracking Ellie Mae's movements. "Neither of us would win a contest for gracefulness, Eleanor Mason Landry."

"I will, Tabitha June Landry." Ellie Mae set her feet on the ground and gave her cousin a thumbs-up. "Why are we second-naming each other?"

"Probably because Aunt Charlotte does when she's either scolding us or worried about us," Tabby said as she threw a leg over the railing and planted a foot on a ladder rung. "And I could hear her voice in my head saying, 'You girls be careful on that ladder. It's as old as Methuselah.' "

"You sounded just like her. I didn't think she'd ever leave Sandcastle," Ellie Mae said with a smile. She grabbed both sides of the ladder to give it some support but let go briefly with one hand to scratch her nose.

"Don't shake this thing. I'm already afraid of heights, and . . ." Tabby gasped as the ladder began to weave. She stopped midway up.

"My nose was itching," Ellie Mae yelled over the sound of the wind.

"Scratch it later," Tabby said in a no-nonsense tone. "And I figured Aunt Charlotte would breathe her last right here in Sandcastle, but she seems to love living in Colorado."

A rush of salty-smelling wind heralded Delilah's arrival and whipped Tabby's dark brown hair across her face. She eased down the ladder a rung at a time, afraid to push her locks back and even more scared to look down.

The ladder wobbled once more, and she sucked in enough air to explode her lungs. "Did you have to scratch your nose again?"

"Nope. The wind is really wicked. Hurry up before it carries you and this ladder away," Ellie Mae shouted.

Dammit, Tabby thought as she stepped down again and cursed the wind for blinding her with her own hair. Santa Ana must have left this ladder behind back at the Alamo before Texas was even a state.

Dark clouds blotted out what little sunshine was left as they rolled toward the shore. Tabby looked up to see the tops of the trees all blowing toward the north. She could hear at least one limb of the old oak in the backyard moaning before it cracked. There would be a mess to clean up when the storm passed on through, for sure.

"If we survive this hurricane, I might give you my share of the B and B and move to Colorado with Aunt Charlotte. I thought tornadoes were the evilest thing on earth, until now," Ellie Mae yelled over the noise of the rushing wind. "We need to figure out a way to put that last piece of wood up from the inside of the window; then we won't need to climb down this rickety old ladder."

From the sound of her cousin's voice, Tabby could tell she wasn't far from the bottom now. "If that had been possible, Aunt Charlotte would have already figured it out. At least we only have to go down this thing one time."

Lightning streaked across the sky in a long, ragged line, and a clap of rolling thunder followed. Tabby fought the urge to let go and cover her ears. She forced herself to keep a tight grip on the sides of the ladder and hoped she wouldn't end up with dozens of splinters in her palms. She glanced over her shoulder to see more lightning flash behind Ellie Mae, turning her into a momentary silhouette.

"Just four more steps and you're on the ground," Ellie Mae said. "You could jump from there."

"Not . . ." She let go with one hand and instinctively covered one ear when the thunder rolled so close that the noise rattled the ladder. "Going to . . ." She quickly got a grip on the edge of the ladder again. "Happen!" she yelled above all the mixed sounds of the weather, the angry surf, and the creaking tree limbs.

"Hurry up, woman. I can feel the rain and see sheets of it coming right at us," Ellie Mae said. "Those waves are taller than me."

"That's not very tall." Tabby glanced down at the ground and then at the surf not a hundred yards away from the B and B. "But then, that's a good sign."

"How can you be so positive about everything?" Ellie Mae asked.

"I've wallowed in a negative world too long. When I moved down here, I decided I was leaving all the bad behind and just dwelling on the good," Tabby answered above the rush of blood pounding in her ears. "Let's be thankful for everything, including a drill that didn't run out of power and even this rotten old ladder."

"The little things, huh?" Ellie Mae asked.

She'd barely gotten the last word out when the next rung on the ladder snapped in half. One second, Tabby was only a couple of steps from solid ground; the next, she was grabbing for anything to break her fall. With her hands outstretched and catching nothing but fistfuls of air, she landed on Ellie Mae and sent both of them to the ground.

Everything seemed to happen in slow motion, and then poof! Just like that, she was struggling to catch her breath, lying flat on her back, staring up at a mass of black clouds. A mop of her own hair was in her face and mouth, trying to choke her to death as she struggled to fill her lungs with air. When she opened her eyes, Ellie Mae was pushing her off, sputtering and trying to catch her breath all at the same time.

"Not"—Ellie Mae rolled over and sat up—"graceful . . ." She inhaled deeply.

Tabby was staring up at the angry black clouds with lightning bolts shooting out of them and thunder rolling close behind. "Is that what drums sound like in heaven?" she asked between gasps for air.

"Not funny!" Ellie Mae gasped. "You knocked the wind out of me."

"It's either laugh or cry! Are you hurt? Did I break any bones when I fell on you?" Tabby sat up and checked her arms and fingers. Everything seemed to be working just fine.

Ellie Mae shook her head. "Only if pride is a bone. How about you?"

"Nothing broken, but I'd hate to have to take all those boards off the windows by myself when Delilah passes over. Thank God you're not dead." Tabby stood up and took a couple of steps to be sure she hadn't sprained an ankle. "I might have a few bruises—but, girl, you're the only woman I know who can burn ramen noodles in the microwave. If I'd died, it'd be my fault that you starved to death."

Ellie Mae got to her feet. "I'm glad you're not dead, too. I can only live on ramen noodles so long before they start to gag me."

Tabby tipped the ladder over and brought it to the ground, "According to Aunt Charlotte, clumsiness is the Landry curse, but then, we also got strong bones from the Landry DNA. We'll have to buy a new ladder to remove the window coverings when this is over. I'm not going to trust a single one of those rungs on this old thing ever again."

"Tough or not, you better get your skinny butt in the house or else put some rocks in your pockets." Ellie Mae picked up the tote bag she had tossed on the ground and got a firm grasp on the other end of the ladder. "Tabby June Landry, you are *not* in Texas anymore."

Tabby bent against the wind and headed around the east end of the house. "You are not in Texas anymore, Dorothy."

"Same story. Different name," Ellie Mae told her. "And, honey, as tall and thin as you are, this wind could carry you away and set you down in Montana."

Tabby glanced over her shoulder and sent up a silent prayer that when Delilah passed through, the old stone building would still be standing, and her peace wouldn't be destroyed—again.

Rising out of the rocky and sandy beach right across the East Bay of southeastern Texas and the Bolivar Peninsula, the Sandcastle Inn had a stone seawall in front of it that had been built with the same gray stones as the house. With twelve-foot ceilings in every room, the inn stood like a tall and proud sentinel keeping watch over the small beach town of Sandcastle. A wide porch wrapped all the way around the first floor and provided a catwalk for the rooms on the second story. Three of the bedrooms faced the Gulf of Mexico—or "the ocean," as Aunt Charlotte called it—and two had a view of the old barn at the back of the property. The house had been home to generations of Landrys, was on the registry of historical homes, and had survived more than one hurricane.

Tabby was only five feet, seven inches, which wasn't all that tall, though it seemed to Ellie Mae like she towered above her. She felt like that about most people since she had to stretch to measure an inch over five feet. Tabby was exactly—to the day—ten years older than Ellie Mae and had always been her younger cousin's idol.

And still is, Ellie Mae thought as she helped fight the wind and carry the ladder around to the back of the house. They really should take it out to the edge of the water and hurl it out to the storm gods.

Hey, now! Aunt Charlotte's voice popped into her head. *That old thing might wind up in the Smithsonian as a relic someday.*

Other than having the same birthday and sharing a sassy old gal, Charlotte Landry, for an aunt, not a single thing about the cousins would testify to the fact that they were related. Tabby was a tall brunette with dark brown eyes, compliments of her Hispanic mother, Gloria. Ellie Mae was a short curvy woman with strawberry blonde hair and mossy green eyes, just like her Irish mother.

"Ever notice that neither of us looks a thing like the Landry side of the family?" Ellie Mae asked.

"Just goes to prove that God is merciful," Tabby said with a smile.

Together, they maneuvered the ladder to the barn out in the backyard. According to the historical marker hung up next to the B and B's front door, the place had begun as the home of Rufus Landry, a prominent boatbuilder. The property had been passed down from generation to generation. Now it belonged to Ellie Mae and Tabby.

Rufus Landry's boats had been built somewhere in a warehouse that had long since been destroyed by time and previous hurricanes. When they were ready for the final touches, each one had been brought to the barn to be painted in a dust-free environment. The huge stone building was bigger than the house and, just like it, had withstood a hundred years of whatever the weather could throw at it. The wide barn doors had been left open when the cousins brought out the ladder earlier that day, and now they flapped in the wind, slamming back and forth against the stone walls and threatening to break into splinters.

"Think Delilah will be strong enough to rip these doors off their hinges?" Tabby asked as she set her end of the ladder on the weathered wood floor.

"I hope not." Ellie Mae looked up at the loft, where she'd built a playhouse as a little girl when her parents had left her with Aunt Charlotte for a whole week one summer while they went to a conference.

"I got my first kiss from a boy in this barn," Tabby said, "and it wasn't from James."

"I should hope not," Ellie Mae said. She gave the barn another glance and headed outside. "You didn't meet him until you were in your junior year of college. I'd be disappointed in you if you hadn't kissed a guy before then."

Tabby drew in a long breath and said, "Well, far be it from me to disappoint my baby cousin in any way."

"You're riding high on that positive wagon, aren't you?" When she slipped outside, the wind hit her in the face and brought a fine mist of salt air with it. With so much heartache in her cousin's past few years, she wondered how in the world she could draw even one happy thought from her heart.

Tabby followed her, and together, they managed to get the doors closed and locked. "I was thirteen when I kissed a boy the first time. How about you?"

"Fourteen. His name was Elijah, and it was on the front porch of our house in Conway, Arkansas." Ellie Mae jogged to the back porch and held the door open for Tabby. "Age before beauty."

Tabby swatted at her as she dashed inside. "Delilah isn't supposed to be here until midnight, but she's sure tellin' us that she's on the way. Just knowing that ninety percent of the town has evacuated and being in this dark, creaky old place makes for an eerie feeling, doesn't it?"

"As a little girl, I wondered if this place might be haunted." Ellie Mae shivered. "There's been a lot of Landrys come and go in it. Do you think their ghosts are still hanging around, watching to see what we do with the place now that we're here? And who's going to fill our shoes when we get ready to retire? We're the last of the family, you know."

"Guess you'd better have some kids so the almighty Landry name doesn't die with us," Tabby said.

"Why me? You can still produce little Landry babies." Ellie Mae picked up a flashlight from the hall tree in the foyer and turned it on to illuminate their way into the kitchen. When the gold house phone hanging on the kitchen wall rang, it startled her so badly that she dropped the light, and the house went dark again.

"I'll try to get it working again if you'll fumble your way into the kitchen and get that phone," Tabby said as she picked up the flashlight.

Ellie Mae knocked over a chair on the way across the kitchen floor, but she grabbed the receiver on the third ring and said, "Hello?" and then, "Well, crap! I missed Aunt Charlotte's call!"

"Are you all right?" Tabby yelled.

Suddenly the kitchen was filled with light, and Tabby was standing at the end of the table. "I thought you'd fallen."

Ellie Mae shook her head and righted the chair. "One for one. You fell off the ladder, and I knocked over a chair, so we're even on the clumsy chart today." Ellie Mae barely got the words out when her cell phone rang. She slipped it out of her back pocket, saw that the call was from Aunt Charlotte, and hit both "Accept" and "Speaker."

"Hey, what's going on in Colorado? I've got you on speaker with me and Tabby. We just finished covering all the windows and the front storm door, and this house is pitch black."

"It's beautiful up here. We've got our first snow," Charlotte answered. "But that's not why I called you, Eleanor Mason. I had to call both lines to get you."

Ellie Mae rolled her eyes toward the ceiling. "Why did you second-name me?"

"I do that when I need for you to pay close attention to me, and this is so important that I'm not giving you girls a choice. You just have to do it," Charlotte said. "The assisted-living center there in town has been evacuated. I know a couple of the ladies who work there, and one of them called me with a big problem. Four of the old folks there don't have family to take them in. Nearby nursing homes and hotels are full, and there's quite literally no room at the inn or anywhere else in South Texas. I don't know anything about them other than there's two women and two men, but I told my friend that they could stay at the B and B for a couple or three days."

"But . . . ," Ellie Mae stammered.

"I know the second floor isn't all prettied up like you girls want it when you get done repainting and redecorating, but it's better than nothing, so give them each a room. The fifth bedroom is Alex LaSalle's. He always stays with me when there's a hurricane because he knows how to take care of the well and the generator, and he's a damn fine cook." Charlotte's tone left no room for argument. "Tabby June, you let him help you in the kitchen, because for the next few days, you are going to have to fix three meals and about two or three snacks a day. I've got to go now. My neighbor is here, and we're doing yoga."

"Yoga?" Ellie Mae asked.

"Yep, we got this program on the television that teaches us the basic stuff. Folks down in Sandcastle always lose power when tropical storms or hurricanes hit, and most of the time, a big storm will knock out the cell towers for your phones," Charlotte reminded them. "The old house phone will work if the storm doesn't snap the lines from the pole to the house, but the last hurricane knocked that out, too. I'm so glad I'm not there right now."

"But, Aunt Charlotte, we aren't equipped for five extra people," Ellie Mae argued.

"Sure, you are," Charlotte said. "There's enough staples in the pantry and the basement to last at least three months, and the two freezers are full of food. The old folks will only be there for a few days until the power gets fixed and whatever damage is done to the assisted-care center is repaired. Y'all will do fine. They're older than I am, so they'll probably just eat and sleep. Bye now." She ended the call.

Tabby groaned. "I didn't sign up to run a nursing home."

"It's just until the storm blows over," Ellie Mae answered. "Maybe three days at the most. But the rooms on the second floor will be full, and our redecorating will come to a halt."

"We wouldn't have time to do much, anyway. We'll be busy cleaning up the damage. The way the trees are creaking in this high wind, I'll be surprised if some of them aren't uprooted," Tabby said after a long sigh.

"Just think about all the cleaning and laundry." Ellie Mae sat down in a chair and laid her head on the table. "At least we haven't started stripping all of the ugly wallpaper."

Tabby pulled out a chair across the table from Ellie Mae and sat down. "Even when the B and B is reopened next spring, I'd only planned on making breakfast and maybe keeping a fruit bowl and cookies out for a nighttime snack. I hope she was right about this guy who's coming to help out being able to cook. What did she say his name was? My brain stopped listening when she said four old people were coming to stay here."

"Alex something or other." Ellie Mae raised her head and drew her dark brows down. "Alex . . ." She frowned. "Alex LaSalle. That's it."

"Sweet Jesus!" Tabby said.

Alex LaSalle had helped Miz Charlotte Landry make it through more than one hurricane, but those days were over now that she'd moved north and given the Sandcastle B and B to her two great-nieces. He hadn't been by to welcome them to town, but then, he'd been busy keeping up with his job as a fishing guide. Besides, he hadn't seen Tabby in years—not since he kissed her when they were teenagers—and he felt awkward about meeting her again.

Until two days ago, when the prophecy about Hurricane Delilah's arrival had been set in stone, he hadn't had time to do anything but get up at three in the morning, catch and cut bait fish, stock his boat with snacks and beer, and get ready for another trip out into the deep.

He had already boarded up his small two-bedroom house—the place he ran his business out of—and taken all the precautions he could with his boat. He said a little prayer as he slung his old army duffel bag into the back seat of his pickup truck and bent against the wind coming off the water. The curls on the waves would be a surfer's slice of heaven if they had been able to get out there that day, but with the red flags flying on every pole on the beach, not even a seasoned surfer would chance the riptides.

He had just slid behind the steering wheel and fastened his seat belt when his phone rang. "Hello?" he answered without even checking the caller ID.

"Hey, I hear you got a storm coming down

22

there," Charlotte said. "Are you going to ride it out or evacuate?"

"The wind has hit, and the waves are probably taller than I am," he said. "I was just about to evacuate. I've battened down the hatches and said my prayers that my boat survives the storm."

"I need you to go take care of things at the B and B." She told him about the folks from the assisted-living center who needed a place to stay. "I've already called Ellie Mae and Tabby and told them what's going on. Neither of my nieces know jack squat about keeping a generator going or taking care of the well house."

"I'll be glad to hang around and help out, and this will free up a family with three little kids so they can get on out of here this afternoon." Though he wouldn't admit it to Charlotte, he really would like to see what kind of grown woman Tabby had become, too. "I was just talking to my hired hand before you called. He's got family up around Lufkin they can stay with, but the wife works at the assisted-living center and refuses to leave until all the residents have a place to stay."

The wind had gotten strong enough to rock his truck, and he could hear limbs popping off trees all over town.

"That's the very woman that I just talked to. We were on the cookbook committee together at the church," Charlotte said.

"Then you know they need to get out of here in the next few hours," Alex said.

"You go take care of things, then," Charlotte said. "And thank you, Alex. We've ridden out lots of these things, but I'll rest easier knowing you are there to help my girls with this first one."

"You're welcome, but I'll miss you during this time. Seems to me like you still owe me some money from our last poker game." Alex chuckled.

"Seems to me like it's you that owes me money," Charlotte said with half a giggle. "Take care of my nieces. Call when you can."

"Will do, and don't worry," Alex said, but when he looked down, the screen on his phone had gone dark.

The drive from his place to the center took only five minutes, but by the time he arrived, the wind was doing more than just whistling through the trees—it was making a growling noise as if it were angry with the whole world.

He parked and swung open the door to the feel of a fine mist in the air. Delilah was on the way, and she was bringing chaos and destruction with her. Alex hoped that this wasn't the big one that would destroy the old Sandcastle B and B.

Barbara, the center's supervisor, must've been waiting for him, because she held the double doors open. "Charlotte Landry is an angel."

"I've never seen a halo or wings, but she is a sweet old gal," Alex said with a grin.

Four elderly folks stood behind her with luggage, duffel bags, and even a few big black trash bags surrounding them. "Thank you and Miz Charlotte both for doing this," Barbara said. "I'll help you get all this loaded. I think we can get it all done in one load since you have a truck."

"I'm not helpless," one of the guys said in a deep southern voice and hoisted a faded military-looking duffel bag onto his shoulders.

"I ain't either." The other one, much shorter and rounder, followed his lead and carried a couple of garbage bags out to the bed of the truck.

"I'm Maude," one lady said in a prim tone that indicated she usually had every hair in place, but the wind was stirring it up and making it look somewhat like a mop that had dried upside down. She patted it a couple of times, then gave up and rolled a pink suitcase out to Alex's truck and left it beside a rear wheel. She moaned as she hiked a hip into the passenger seat, where she immediately flipped down the visor and used the mirror to try to do something with her gray hair. She wore pale pink lipstick and minimal makeup, and a baby-blue pantsuit that matched her eyes.

"I'm glad we're going somewhere that's safer than the center. They should have built it up on stilts rather than on a concrete slab," she said as she slammed the door shut.

"Oh, yeah," a tall Black man said. "You whine all the time about your knees. How would you climb up stairs if this place was six or eight feet off the ground?" He introduced himself to Alex. "I'm Frank, and this here"—he pointed to the shorter man—"is Homer. Thanks for rescuing us."

"I do not whine," Maude declared with a dramatic sniff.

Alex marveled at her ability to continue the conversation through a closed door.

"No, you plain old gripe." Homer chuckled. "And a house on stilts might help in a flood, but not so much in hundred-mile-an-hour wind."

"Oh, hush!" Maude snapped at them both. "You're just like Cleo, always wanting to argue with me."

The other woman tossed a bright orange tote bag into the back of the truck. "She's talking about me. I'm Cleo, and I'm not afraid of a hurricane," she bragged. "I would have tied a rope around my waist and stood on the roof just to experience the thrill, but Barbara won't leave until we're all gone, and she's got them three kids to get to safety."

"Cleo is wild as a one-eyed loon," Maude huffed. "Always has been and always will be. Don't pay a bit of attention to her."

"At least I've lived *my* life to the fullest and haven't let anyone else control me." Cleo swished the skirt of her multicolored dress to one side and hopped up into the back seat, right behind

Maude. Orange, yellow, and red beads had been worked into a long red braid that hung down her back to her waist.

From the smart-ass remarks and the dirty looks, it was evident to Alex that the two old ladies couldn't stand each other. That should make for an interesting time at the B and B. Usually, he and Charlotte were the only ones in the place when the storms came. He would go over there a day or two before, cover all the windows, and they'd ride out the weather by playing board games or poker, or reading books by the light of oil lamps. This would be different with Charlotte's nieces there, along with two old war veterans—judging from those duffel bags—and two women who were as different as night and day.

"Get on in here, Homer." Cleo's green eyes glittered with mischief as she patted the seat beside her. "I don't bite on the days when a hurricane is supposed to hit. You can sit in the middle, and Frank can have the window seat. Hey, whatever your name is," she said as she pointed to Alex, "do you think I could stand on the roof of the B and B when Delilah hits us? This is my first hurricane since I was a kid, and we lived up near Winnie, so it wasn't like we were right there when it made landfall. I don't want to miss a single bit of it."

"I'm Alex LaSalle," he introduced himself, "and that would not be a simple no but a *hell no!*

You are not standing on the roof, on the catwalk, or even out on the back porch. All of you will be safely inside when Delilah hits us in a few hours."

"Well, rats!" Cleo said with a sigh. "I should have stayed in the center. If this storm is as big as they say it is, that place is going to be demolished. I understand the B and B has withstood a Category 4 hurricane in the past, so I suppose there's not a chance it will be knocked down."

Alex started the engine and eased out onto the street. "I hope the house is still standing and all of you guys are alive and well when Delilah has passed."

"If the good Lord wants that house to be flattened, He'll do it, and He will do it a lot quicker if there's a fool standing on the roof," Maude spat out.

"If the house falls down, you can rest assured that I won't bother to dig through the rubble to find your sorry carcass," Cleo said.

"Hmmph," Maude snorted. "*You* can rest assured that the feeling is mutual."

Holy smoke! What have I gotten myself into? Alex wondered as he gripped the steering wheel to keep the truck on the road. When they passed the gas station, they could see it was boarded up. Both churches—one on each end of town—had wood over the windows, but the steeples seemed to be leaning slightly to the north.

A streak of lightning crashed into the highway in front of them, and what looked like a ball of fire rolled across the road like a tumbleweed in an old Western movie.

"Sweet Jesus!" Cleo yelped. "That's the first time I've ever seen a lightning ball."

"That's a message from God telling you to behave or He'll send the next one rolling right over you," Maude told her.

Homer raised his voice above all the noise. "Don't pay them no never mind. They'll still be fighting when they reach the Pearly Gates. God have mercy if they die at the same time."

"If I have to share a room with her in this B and B place," Cleo said, "that just might come sooner than later."

Homer chuckled and reached up to pat Alex on the shoulder. "Thanks for rescuing us. This is our first hurricane since we moved into the center, and we weren't sure where they'd find a place for us to stay until it comes and goes."

A short man who was almost as wide as he was tall, Homer sported a rim of gray hair around a bald head that he covered with a Dallas Cowboys cap. His brown eyes and round face, plus the striped overalls and plaid flannel shirt, reminded Alex of his own grandfather.

Another strip of lightning zigzagged through the sky, leaving a crackling sound in its wake, followed by more loud thunder that sounded like it was sitting right on top of the pickup truck.

"That one would have parted my hair if I had any." Homer chuckled.

"Gonna be a big storm." Frank practically hugged the window. He wore a long-sleeve shirt buttoned all the way up around his thin neck, and he sat straight and tall. His dark eyes took in everything at once, and Alex figured that if he asked the elderly gentleman what had been said on the fifteen-minute trip, he would have no trouble reciting every word back to him—verbatim.

"Y'all ever stayed at the Sandcastle B and B before?" Alex asked as he made a left-hand turn toward the structure that sat just a few hundred feet back from the beach.

"Nope, but I'm looking forward to it," Homer said. "I ain't been real happy with this retirement-center thing, but what's an old fart to do when he ain't got family? Me and Frank should've gotten us wives when we was young enough to chase them down, but we was too busy in them days, runnin' away from all the women."

"That's right—and then, when we can't chase a woman no more or working at our store tires us out before the end of the workday," Frank said in a deep Louisiana accent, "Homer talks me into going to a glorified nursing home with him."

"I grew up in Winnie, Texas," Maude butted in. "I moved down here after my mother passed away. I've seen the B and B when we come into town on the center's shuttle but never been inside."

"I've never been in the place, either," Cleo chimed in from the back seat. "I retired a couple of years ago and moved into the center just before Miss Prissy Pants in the front seat did."

Before anyone else could comment, big drops of rain dotted the windshield. Alex slowed down and drove right up to the garage doors of the B and B. He parked, got out of the truck, and ran over to push a button on the outside wall. The doors raised, and he jogged back to slide behind the wheel and drive into one bay of the three-car garage that was attached to the inn. An older dark green truck and a burgundy SUV took up the other two spaces.

"We're here," he said, "and from the size of those big drops of cold rain, it looks like we made it just in time. I'll show y'all on into the house, and then I'll come back and get your things for you."

"I hope my room is on the ground floor," Maude said. "My knees won't climb up and down steps all day."

"Besides, she doesn't want to be anywhere near me." Cleo giggled. "If she's seen with me, her halo might lose its shine."

I feel sorry for Tabby and Ellie Mae, Alex thought as he opened the truck doors one by one and helped the old folks out. *They're going to have their work cut out for them the next few days, or maybe weeks, if the center gets so much damage that no one can move back into it for a while.*

They're not the only ones. His grandfather's voice popped into his head. *You are staying here with them, too.*

"You will all be staying on the second floor," Alex said. "I've been here through several storms and hurricanes. The guest rooms are upstairs, but there is a lift chair you can use, Miz Maude. Miz Charlotte used it all the time. Have any of you met the two new owners, Tabby and Ellie Mae, maybe at church or in town?"

All four of them shook their heads.

Alex opened the door into the kitchen, stood back, and let them parade inside. "Then let's make everyone acquainted before we get you settled into your rooms. You will probably have time to unpack and catch a little nap before we serve supper."

Chapter Two

I'm sure not wearing my positive britches right now," Tabby muttered as she studied the old, yellowed paper with a pattern of ivy vines on the kitchen walls. She sighed.

Her younger cousin had always been the go-get-'em one of the two—a leader. Tabby had been a follower, up until seven years ago, when her daughter was killed in an automobile accident. She'd wallowed in negativity for a while but then decided that if she was going to survive losing Natalie, she had to pull herself together and turn her life around. She managed most days, but still, when push came to shove, as far as her daughter was concerned, she had to fight the negative feelings.

From the first day they arrived, she and Ellie Mae had planned to start redecorating the ground floor of the old B and B after they'd settled in. Ellie Mae liked the old wallpaper and thought it gave the place character, but Tabby had been eager to tear the faded ivy right off the walls. She had envisioned painting the walls a light yellow and the burled-oak wainscoting white. Ellie Mae thought they should leave things as they were, and said that the wallpaper might be yellowed, but it was a testament to the era when the house was built. She had even gotten a little teary-eyed at the idea of painting oak.

Now any redecorating would have to wait until Delilah—dang her hurricane soul—blew through town.

Her mother's stern voice popped into her head. *Did you ever consider that maybe the reason y'all can't agree on the redecorating is because you shouldn't be there?* Gloria had tried to talk Tabby out of divorcing James. When Tabby set her heels and said no—at least a dozen times—Gloria tried to convince her to leave her job at the bank and come work for the Landry and Landry Law Firm.

"I would tell all this hideous wallpaper bedtime stories before I would come back to Oklahoma and back to work for you and Daddy," Tabby muttered.

"Are you talking to me?" Ellie Mae turned away from the kitchen window.

Tabby sucked in a lungful of air and let it out in a loud whoosh. "I was fighting with my mother. It's hard to remain positive when rocks are being hurled at you, isn't it?"

"Oh, yeah," Ellie Mae said with a nod. "But it's my dad that gives me more grief than my mother, as you well know."

"You're the lucky one," Tabby said.

"How do you figure that?" Ellie Mae asked. "A parent is a parent."

"You basically only have your dad to gripe at you and try to run your life. I have both parents," Tabby answered.

"Yep, you got that right," Ellie Mae agreed. "We'll have to stand united against them all to ever get through the holiday season with our sanity."

"And you got *that* right." Tabby smiled and pointed toward the window, where hard rain pelted against the glass. "Delilah is letting us know she's on the way."

"I just heard several vehicle doors slam, so here comes the first wave of guests. So paste on your best smile and get ready to work," Ellie Mae said. "I suppose we'll have to make supper tonight for seven?"

"Oh, yeah, we will," Tabby said through a wide smile that didn't reach her eyes. "It doesn't look like any of that smoked turkey we thawed out yesterday will go to waste. We can use it to make sandwiches, and I'll put on a pot of soup to go with them. I can handle the food, but I sure hope Aunt Charlotte wasn't just pulling a joke on us when she said that Alex could cook. I was used to cooking for two or three, but for the last few years, I've only been making food for one—not a houseful—and I can use all the help I can get."

"I can set the table and do the cleanup, but,

honey, you do not want me trying to help with cooking. Those old folks would starve to death." Ellie Mae chuckled.

"They might have a choice of starving or freezing if the generator plays out when we lose power." Tabby paused and then went on. "Hopefully, Aunt Charlotte has enough fuel stored in the barn to keep it going. If she doesn't, remember that one of those freezers is half-full of nothing but different flavors of ice cream, so we'll be eating that for breakfast, dinner, and supper. On a positive note"—the grin changed into a real smile—"our guests are arriving in the middle of the afternoon, so today we only have to do snacks and supper."

"Miss Positive Britches rises again in the midst of what I think of as a nightmare." Ellie Mae patted Tabby on the shoulder. "Do you know how much we can depend on the generator when the electricity goes out?"

"Aunt Charlotte says it'll keep the refrigerator, freezers, and hot-water tank going just fine for several days, but we'll have to use oil lamps, flashlights, and those LED lights that we found in a box in the attic," Tabby answered. "We use gas for cooking, but if the hurricane knocks that out, she says to use the woodstove out in the barn, and she keeps a couple of cords of wood stacked up and covered behind the building."

"Well, thank goodness this hurricane isn't

hitting us in the hot part of summer. Our guests would suffocate in the heat with no air-conditioning," Ellie Mae said.

Tabby took seven mugs out of the cabinet and set them on the counter. "I was hoping that the storm would swerve off to the east and we'd escape with only some rain in our area this year. We've passed the peak, and in only three weeks, we'll be pretty well over the whole hurricane season."

"Guess Delilah is going to break us in as the new owners. Next time Aunt Charlotte calls, I'm going to ask her the name of the first hurricane she endured when she took over the business," Ellie Mae said.

"She didn't just take over the business, girl. She was born in this place and grew up here. She took over running the boat business and taking care of her mother when her dad died. She told me all about it a couple of years ago. When a hurricane blew away the place where the boats were built, she just never started it up again and decided to turn the house into a B and B."

Even though she was expecting it, the knock on the back door startled Tabby so badly that she almost dropped the box of tea bags she was holding.

"Come on in," Ellie Mae yelled out and then gasped when the first person came into the kitchen.

Tabby whipped around to see what had shocked her cousin, and really did drop the box of tea bags. The first woman through the door looked like she should be telling fortunes in a carnival in her flowing multicolored skirt and that fancy, long braid bedazzled with beads.

"I'm Cleo, and I want to thank you for letting us stay here. We would have evacuated with the rest of the old folks, but we don't have family to rescue us, and all the hotels from here to Mexico are full," she said.

"And I'm Maude, who can thank you myself for your generosity," said a woman behind her. "I don't need Cleo to do it for me." She gave Cleo the old stink eye and stuck her nose in the air.

"I'm Homer." A short man with a face as round as his body followed right behind them. His blue eyes and bibbed overalls reminded Tabby of Grandpa Isaac, Charlotte's older brother and Tabby and Ellie Mae's grandfather. Her grand-father had passed away when Tabby was a teenager, but looking at Homer now sure brought his twinkling blue eyes and humor back to her mind.

"Frank." With only one word, Homer's opposite introduced himself. He had thick, curly gray hair and a nose sprinkled with a few freckles. His eyes seemed to take in everything at once.

"We're making tea and coffee for everyone, but first, let me show you to your rooms"—Ellie Mae motioned toward the door leading out into the foyer—"and make you familiar with the place."

"I hear y'all have a lift chair," Maude said.

"I can get up the stairs all on my own," Homer said. "I don't need to be riding in no lift chair. Until last year, when me and Frank decided to sell our gas station and retire, we took care of ourselves."

"And I've wished a million times that we hadn't sold out," Frank added.

"Hello, Tabby and Ellie Mae." Alex smiled at them when he came inside. "It's been a long time."

"It has been a minute, hasn't it?" Tabby wondered if he even remembered that dry, awkward kiss in the barn more than twenty-five years ago as well as she did.

"More than twenty years' worth of minutes, and a lot of water under the bridge, but it's good to see both of you again. Miz Charlotte sure talked a lot about y'all," he said with another smile. "I'm going to start bringing in the folks' belongings. Is it okay if I just put everything in the upstairs hallway, and let them sort it all out?"

"Of course," Tabby answered. "I'll help you bring in their things while Ellie Mae shows everyone to their rooms. Then we'll gather around the dining room table for a snack and a little visit to get acquainted."

Alex headed out into the garage. Tabby remembered the box of tea bags on the floor, picked them up, and then started across the kitchen. The four older folks followed Ellie Mae out into the foyer.

"Have you ever used a lift chair?" Ellie Mae asked.

"No, but it looks like fun," Cleo said. "I'm glad we'll be on the second floor. If the floodwater makes it into the house, at least Maude won't drown."

"What makes you think I'd drown?" Maude snapped.

"You're so uptight that you'll forget to take a breath and your body will sink." Cleo's voice faded as Tabby followed Alex out into the garage.

"Do Cleo and Maude argue like this all the time?" Tabby asked.

"I don't know about all the time, but they sure did all the way over here from the center. The old guys seem to get along just fine, and from what they said about owning a gas station together, I guess they're friends," Alex answered. "Looks like the old gals are a different story. They're going to be a handful, but it's only for a couple of days—three at the most, if the hurricane knocks out the power."

"I wonder what kind of history they've got that makes them act like that?" Tabby gripped the handles of two suitcases and rolled them across the concrete floor. She thought of her father and

Ellie Mae's dad and their constant disagreements. Could these two women be related? "Did they both like the same boy in the fourth grade? Or maybe one of them slept with the other's boyfriend in high school and they've never forgiven each other."

"Have no idea, but I guess we'll learn the art of refereeing in the next few days." Alex chuckled. "Did you grow up to be an author? That sounds like the beginning of a pretty good book."

"Not me. I was the vice president of a bank in northeast Oklahoma until a few weeks ago," Tabby answered. "But hey, if things get slow around here, I just might use what I learn about the people who visit the B and B and start writing books. Lord knows I've read enough to learn a little about how to write one."

Alex hoisted an army green duffel bag onto his shoulder. "Oh, really? And what kind of books do you like to read?"

"Mystery," she answered.

"Me too," he said as he turned and headed around the back of the other two vehicles.

Tabby stole a couple of sideways glances toward him. Hard upper-arm muscles strained the sleeves of his pale blue knit shirt that was the same color as his eyes. The lanky kid who had kissed her more than twenty-five years ago now had broad shoulders and what looked like an acre of chest. His thick blond hair touched his shirt collar, just like it had when he was a teenager, but now there were a few crow's-feet around his eyes.

She helped carry all the baggage to the foyer and wondered what Alex had done from the time he was fourteen until he was forty, other than read mystery books. Aunt Charlotte hadn't mentioned him, but then she hadn't given Tabby and Ellie Mae the low-down gossip on folks in Sandcastle when she made the decision to move to Colorado and bequeath the B and B to them.

"So, you and Aunt Charlotte were friends?" Tabby asked as they stacked up all the luggage and bags at the foot of the steps.

"Yep," Alex answered. "Mostly we were hurricane friends. She needed help to keep the generator running, and then I took care of cleanup and repairs. Neither of us had family in this area, so she was kind of like a grandma to me, and . . ." He raised a shoulder in half a shrug. "She told me I was like the grandson she never had. I hope that doesn't bother you and Ellie Mae."

"Lord no!" Tabby said. "Not one bit. I worried about her having so much to do with this place at her age."

"At her age?" Alex chuckled. "She could run circles around me and not even break a sweat. I didn't believe her when she said she was leaving Texas. She told me she was getting too old to run the B and B, but I was surprised when she passed the business down to y'all instead of selling it."

She must've been waiting for me and Ellie Mae to get to the right place to turn this business over to us, Tabby thought. *She wanted to be sure that James and I weren't going to give our marriage a second chance, and then when Ellie Mae's roommate, Sam, died, she probably thought that Ellie Mae needed a change of jobs and scenery.*

"She said she was tired of fighting the storms," Alex went on as he piled two suitcases onto the lift chair and pushed the button to send them upstairs, and then he picked up a duffel bag and took the steps two at a time.

Tabby grabbed a tote bag and followed him. "It came as a shock to me and Ellie Mae both, but we are grateful for her decision."

"What made you two take her up on the offer?" Alex asked at the top of the stairs.

"Two months ago, Aunt Charlotte called me and said that she had friends who had relocated to a nice little village in Colorado, and they had helped her find a cabin in the mountains," Tabby answered. "She said that she would rather deal with snow than face off with another hurricane. She couldn't sell the B and B. There's something in the paperwork that says it has to stay in the Landry family forever and ever, amen." She took the suitcases off the lift chair and rolled them into the hallway. "If you'll go back down and load the lift chair and send it up, I'll unload at the top and the folks can sort everything out."

"Sounds like a plan to me," Alex said with that same crooked little smile that had caused her to have a crush on him all those years ago. "But what made you and Ellie Mae decide to take her up on her offer to hand this place over to you?"

"Long story short is that we both needed a change, and Aunt Charlotte provided it," Tabby answered. "I'm surprised that she didn't tell you about it, since y'all were good friends."

"Charlotte has never been a gossip, and you can trust her with your deepest secrets," he said as he went back to the bottom of the staircase.

He loaded the lift chair with two more suitcases and sent them up.

"The Charlotte you knew and the one I knew were two different people." Tabby raised her voice just slightly. "What's your story? Why did you come back to Sandcastle?"

"Now that's a long story for another time," he answered. "Maybe we'll be stuck in this place long enough we'll swap life stories."

"Maybe so." She set the suitcases on the floor, pushed a button, and sent the chair back down for Alex to reload.

Maude came out of a bedroom on the left side of the hallway. "Those suitcases belong to me. My room is very nice. I like the yellow-rose wallpaper, and although the bathroom is small,

I do like having a bathroom that I don't have to share with anyone, especially Cleo," she fussed. "She had the room next to mine at the center, and she hogged the bathroom every night. She knew I wanted to have an early bath—but oh, no, she had to do whatever she does with all those creams she uses to prevent wrinkles. Please, tell the lady who owns this place that she is a sweetheart for letting us stay here. All the hotels in this part of the state are full, and besides, they wouldn't have had three meals a day."

"My cousin and I own the place now." Tabby chose the right moment to get a word in edgewise. "But having you stay here was Aunt Charlotte's idea. I'll tell her that you are happy with your room. Ellie Mae and I are both glad to help out." Tabby fought the urge to cross her fingers behind her back like she did when she was a child telling a white lie. "It'll only be until Delilah blows over, and then things will get back to normal." She took three garbage bags off the chair and sent it back down to Alex again.

What's "normal"? the voice in her head asked. *And what if this hurricane demolishes that retirement home—or whatever it's called?*

"Don't even go there," Tabby whispered.

"Go where?" Ellie Mae took the steps two at a time, grabbed the end of a bag, and dragged it to Cleo's open doorway. "This thing feels like it's loaded with rocks, but at least they've tagged these bags with names so we know where they go, and those two old gals won't start a catfight over them in the middle of the hallway."

Tabby checked the tag on another bag and pulled it along behind Ellie Mae. "I was muttering to myself that I hope that the center where these folks live doesn't get much damage, and this is a temporary thing."

"Amen to that. I wonder what the deal is with the two women. They look at each other like they could each kill the other one," Ellie Mae said out of the corner of her mouth. "What do you think Cleo has in this bag? A dead body? Certainly feels like it."

"I wouldn't put anything past her. If Maude goes missing, we might have to check her room and her closet." Tabby chuckled. "Like you just said, I'm glad whoever packed them put name tags on the ties. If Maude opened a random bag and found a dead body, she'd have a heart attack. I'm not sure we could get an ambulance down here from Anahuac right now."

Ellie Mae parked the bag beside Cleo's door and followed Tabby back to where the lift chair was about to reach the top. "Do you think whatever it is has been brewing a long time?" She picked one of the two duffel bags from off the chair when it stopped. "This one looks like military issue."

"And old," Tabby said. "And, girl, whatever is

between them didn't happen last week. That kind of hatred takes a while to fester."

She thought of the way she felt about the drunk driver who had T-boned her daughter's car, killing her instantly. He had died also, but she had no sympathy for him or his parents. At that time, she'd had nothing but pure red-hot anger in her heart. Even now, when she thought about the pain she'd suffered that night—well, she sure wasn't Miss Positive at those times.

Frank came out of his room and hoisted a bag up on his shoulder. "It *is* military, and it's been with me through thick and thin for more'n sixty years now."

Homer pointed toward the second bag. "That one belongs to me. Frank's has got *Tyson* on the side, and mine has *Andrews*. Names are kind of faded now, but then, so are us old men. Time gets us all, but when we were issued those bags, we were young and full of spit and vinegar."

Tabby could see the long friendship in the look they exchanged and wished just once she could have witnessed one like that between her dad and Ellie Mae's. They were like two bulls locking horns every chance they got.

"They went to Vietnam with us," Frank said, "and then came home with us. We call them our good-luck bags, and now that we're old, we're hoping our luck holds out where this hurricane is concerned."

"Not me!" Cleo popped out of her room and grabbed one of the bags beside her door. "I'm not giving in to old Father Time without a fight. When I die, I want to slide into heaven looking like an old swamp witch, all withered up because every bit of my love, fun, and energy got used up."

"Of course you do. You've always been a hippie type of renegade," Maude huffed as she claimed a garbage bag. "Putting our things in garbage bags seems so undignified."

"Oh, stop your fussing," Cleo said. "What our stuff is packed in doesn't matter one bit. They were in a rush to get us out of there. It's not a sin that your Bible is tucked inside that big old plastic bag and not in a gold-lined box encrusted with diamonds."

"You are horrible." Maude slammed her bedroom door.

"Don't mind her." Cleo smiled. "She'll get over her meanness when hell freezes over. Thanks for getting all our stuff up here, and again for letting us stay. My room is nicer than the one at the center, and I'm glad you didn't put me right next to Maude."

"You are very welcome," Tabby said as she took the last of the bags off the chair and set them to the side. Tabby intended to find out what the history between those two was before they left. That just might keep her mind off surviving another holiday season without Natalie.

Alex ran up the stairs and claimed the last two bags just as Cleo disappeared back into her room. "Those would be mine. When I stay here during storms, I'm usually the only one on the second floor, so this will be different. If those two old gals bring out pistols or shotguns, I'm going to take up squatter's rights on the living room floor."

"Do you think Cleo's got guns in that heavy bag?" Ellie Mae whispered.

"I hope not," Alex answered. "Maybe they're like little kids: they're cranky because they're afraid of what's happening and also a little hungry. They might be nicer if we feed them."

"I don't think cookies and cupcakes will help that kind of anger, but it's worth a try," Tabby said. "And speaking of food, Aunt Charlotte says you're pretty handy in the kitchen."

"I can't boil water without someone calling the fire department," Ellie Mae said as she started down the wide staircase. "So I hope Aunt Charlotte was right."

"Charlotte and I both love to cook, and I'm glad to help out in the kitchen—not only with cooking but with cleanup or whatever needs doing while I'm here. What have you got in mind for supper?" Alex asked.

"We're having turkey-salad sandwiches and soup," Tabby answered. "Aunt Charlotte kind of sprang this on us, so that's the best I can do for tonight."

"Yep, she did," Alex said. "I was on my way out of town. Figured I'd go north and then west until I was out of the storm's pathway."

"Thanks for helping out," Tabby said. "Aunt Charlotte had already gone when we arrived a couple of weeks ago. She hates goodbyes, so she left the keys under the back-door mat and was on her way to Colorado. So we didn't even get a crash course in how to handle the generator and well house. After supper maybe we can all three sit down and figure out a menu for the rest of the week. The pantry is well stocked, and the freezers in the basement are full—only partially with ice cream."

"I'll join y'all, but don't expect much from me," Ellie Mae said, covering a laugh. "I am most *definitely*—and underline that last word six times—not good in the kitchen. I can clean and do laundry and know my way around power tools and a hammer, but I don't cook."

"Are you a carpenter or just a fix-it person?" Alex asked.

"Finish carpenter for the last few years. My roommate, Sam, and I did house-framing before that," she said. "Just because I'm short and female doesn't mean I can't use power tools."

"I'm not really surprised," Alex said. "Did you ever hear of the 'goose and gander' law?"

"Oh, yes," Tabby answered. "Aunt Charlotte said that what was good for the goose was good for the gander. That girls need to know survival skills, and boys need to know how to cook and clean."

"That's right," Alex said with a nod. "She said my grandpa was a good man to teach me how to take care of a house as well as catch fish."

"That sounds just like our Aunt Charlotte." Tabby set about making a pitcher of sweet tea. "She still believes that guys and girls alike should be able to do anything. It probably comes from having to take care of herself all these years. I can mow the lawn, put gas in my car, and take out the trash."

"And I can microwave a bowl of soup if I have to, and do all kinds of carpentry work," Ellie Mae added.

"Between the bunch of us, maybe we'll make it through Delilah," Alex said, "but for now, what's on the agenda? The folks will be coming down here pretty soon."

"We'll set out cookies and those cupcakes I made yesterday, and have some sweet tea, milk, and coffee," Tabby said, and then lowered her voice when she heard the lift chair starting down the stairs. "I see you took the second room on the left. Are you planning to buffer between Cleo and Maude?"

Alex reached up to a cabinet shelf, brought down a stack of dessert plates, and took them to the dining room table. "I can sleep through mortar fire. I did a stint in the service, so I mean that literally. I figure if those two women don't share a wall, maybe it will keep down the complaining."

Ellie Mae set seven glasses on a wooden tray and carried them to the dining room table.

"Don't let your clumsy show," Tabby teased.

"I'll do my best if you don't trip me up and then fall on me," Ellie Mae said and then threw over her shoulder, "Hey, Alex, is that business about sleeping that soundly fact or fiction?"

"Proven fact," Alex said with a nod.

"So, you know how to operate our old generator, take care of the well house, and cook, and you've been in the military. Are you a super-hero?" Tabby asked.

"I don't have a cape, and no one ever gave me a title," Alex answered as his face broke out into a wide grin.

"I used to think Tabby had a cape." Ellie Mae headed to the walk-in pantry. "We've got to think about desserts and snacks when we figure out tomorrow's menu."

"Used to?" Tabby winked. "Was I ever a super-hero? And what is this *we* business? Who will make desserts with me?"

Ellie Mae brought out a package of chocolate chip cookies and arranged them on the platter that Alex had set down. "When I was a little girl, you were already in college. We only got to see each other a few times through the years when our fathers would give in and agree to be civil for a few hours—and on Thanksgiving, when we came to Aunt Charlotte's for the holiday. You were always so tall and beautiful, and I felt like an ugly little frog."

"I hope I never made you feel like you were an ugly frog," Tabby said.

"You didn't, but I've always been short and carried a little extra weight and . . ." Ellie Mae paused.

Tabby butted in before she could go on. "Since we're having a moment of honesty, I've been jealous of your Dolly Parton figure."

"For real?" Ellie Mae blushed and was glad that Alex had gone out into the foyer to help the old folks find their way to the kitchen.

Tabby took a couple of long strides and gave her cousin a hug. "Yes, for real, and I'm glad you are here to help me get through this storm."

"Right back atcha." Ellie Mae tightened the hug and then stepped back. "I'll bring the ingredients to you for desserts from the pantry. That will be my job when you are cooking, and I'll do the cleanup when you finish. We're tough Landry cousins who can get through anything as long as we work together."

"That's what Aunt Charlotte said when she turned this place over to us, but I'm wondering how tough we really are right now," Tabby said with a sigh. "We've got old ladies who hate each other, aging veterans, and a hurricane named Delilah that's coming right at us with a full head of steam."

"Plus, a sexy guy that you keep sizing up." Ellie Mae carried the plate of cookies to the table.

"I have not!" Tabby whipped around to put a few more cupcakes on a tray. A crimson blush burned her cheeks, and she was glad Alex hadn't heard what Ellie Mae had said.

Chapter Three

The hurricane hopped right over Bolivar Peninsula, which stretched out along the southern Texas coastline, like the strip of land was no bigger than a matchstick. It didn't even slow down, but probably picked up even more water as it whipped across East Bay and slammed into Sandcastle with all the force that made the weatherman a prophet. Winds snapped trees in half as if they were those little tiki bar–drink umbrellas, leaving them in an undignified, naked, leafless mess.

Ellie Mae was in that limbo state between being almost awake and nearly asleep when a loud pop caused her to sit straight up in her pitch-black bedroom. Her heart thumped so hard that she could hardly breathe, and when she did inhale, she wondered if Cleo and Maude were having a duel after all. She envisioned holes being blown in the wallpaper that she was fighting so hard to keep intact. Now Tabby would have a good reason to strip it all away.

"Sam," she whispered in her foggy state, "what's going on?"

Then she remembered that her best friend and former roommate was not in the B and B, and that the hurricane had probably made landfall—if not right in Sandcastle, then close by. She pushed back the covers, slung her legs off the edge of the bed, and felt along the wall and the dresser until her hands landed on one of the camping lanterns that she and Tabby had distributed to everyone. She got a firm hold on the handle and pulled it up. Bright LED light lit up the room, but it didn't stop the noise outside.

She held up the light, immediately dropped it, and then covered her eyes with her hands. Aunt Charlotte hadn't said a word about the B and B being haunted, but there was a ghost standing right there in front of her in a long white gown and a scary face. She tried to squeal, but it sounded more like a mouse caught in a trap than a real scream.

Tabby reached down, picked up the light, and set it on the dresser. "It's me, Ellie Mae."

When she could catch her breath, Ellie Mae said, "You just scared the bejesus out of me, and what in the hell are you doing with that goop on your face?"

"I'm sorry. I didn't mean to startle you, but I was putting on a cleansing mask when the lights went out," Tabby answered. "I was coming to steal the light from your room, rather than trying to feel my way back to the one that's in my room. My dresser is on the other side of my bedroom, and yours is close to the bathroom door."

Ellie Mae backed up and sat down on the edge of the bed. Heart still pumping like she'd run a marathon and adrenaline racing through her body, all she could do was nod.

Tabby sat down beside her and said, "Let's go to the kitchen and have a glass of milk and some of those brownies that were left over from supper. Neither one of us is going to be able to sleep for a while with all this noise. The wind sounds like it's trying to tear the house down, and I guess those shotgun blasts are really tree limbs cracking and breaking. I'm surprised that the other folks aren't awake."

"Remember what Alex said about sleeping through mortar fire?" Ellie Mae asked. "I expect Homer and Frank could do the same, since one of them mentioned Vietnam."

"I heard you holler for Sam. Want to talk about him?" Tabby asked.

"No. Yes. Maybe," Ellie Mae said, "but I would like a snack, so let's get your lantern and go to the kitchen." Talking about Sam right then was too raw, too intense for her to face without breaking into sobs, and Tabby didn't need that.

"Why do we need two?" Tabby asked.

"In case one of them loses power," Ellie Mae told her.

Tabby followed Ellie Mae through the bathroom that connected their rooms and into her bedroom, where she retrieved her lantern, and together they headed for the kitchen. "It sounds like we should've used that plywood and built an ark instead of covering the windows with it."

"Plywood wouldn't work," Ellie Mae told her. "You got to have gopher wood and lots of pitch for that, but we might find ourselves floating out in the Gulf in this house when Delilah does her dirty deeds and passes on, and wish we had attached a boat motor to the back porch."

When they reached the kitchen, Tabby set the lanterns on the table and lit two oil lamps. She carried one of the lamps to the table. "This should give us more light."

"I can't imagine living like this all the time," Ellie Mae said. "I mean like back in the days before electricity."

"Too bad we can't just light a lamp to get us through dark times that have nothing to do with the sun or light bulbs," Tabby said.

"You're thinking about Natalie, aren't you?" Ellie Mae asked. She remembered the emptiness, the ache in her soul, and the sheer numbness when Natalie was killed, and couldn't imagine how Tabby had even survived the pain.

"Yes, I am," Tabby answered. "Wouldn't you like to have had a light to get you through Sam's death?"

"You have been my light," Ellie Mae whispered.

Tabby swiped a tear away from her cheek and

gave Ellie Mae a hug. "Honey, I couldn't have made it through my dark times without you, either. I just never thought about being a light."

"Me either, until you said that." Ellie Mae poured milk into two glasses and carried them to the table. "I believe this is worse than any tornado I've been through. A tornado passes through really quick. This thing seems to linger on and on. I think Alex was right about being able to sleep through anything."

"Did I hear my name?" Alex appeared out of the darkness.

"Yep, you did." Tabby motioned for him to have a seat. "I thought you could sleep through mortar fire."

"I can, but not a hurricane this bad," Alex answered. "Miz Charlotte and I've endured a lot of storms, but this one is a real bugger. There might not be a Sandcastle left when she loses power and passes through."

"So this is the worst one you've ever seen?" Ellie Mae asked.

Alex pulled out a chair and sat down. "I don't know about 'seen' until we get out and check for damage, but it's sure the worst one I've ever heard."

"Milk?" Ellie Mae asked.

Alex nodded. "Thank you, and I would love a glass. And maybe I'll help you finish off these brownies."

"Not if I get to them first," Homer declared as he joined them.

Blue-and-white-striped pajama legs showed below a red-and-black plaid robe that didn't quite meet in the middle of his round belly. Ellie Mae pictured him with a white beard, little round glasses, and a red suit for just a moment. If they were still here at Christmas, maybe they could rent a suit and he could play Santa Claus for the guests.

Don't even think like that! Tabby's voice was plain in her head.

Once Ellie Mae shook the vision out of her head, Homer was saying, "That's one ferocious storm out there. I bet the wind is pounding us at a hundred and fifty miles an hour."

Ellie Mae poured a fourth glass of milk and set it in front of Homer. "The weatherman said the winds would be at least a hundred when Delilah made landfall. But I agree, it sounds worse than any tornado I've been close to."

"Ain't never been in a tornado, but this is the mother of all storms I've heard in my lifetime," Homer declared. "If a tornado is worse than this, I believe I'll steer clear of them devils."

Ellie Mae didn't even ask if Homer wanted milk—just poured up a glass and set it in front of him. Thank goodness she and Tabby had laid in supplies and gotten extra milk and eggs, even if it was just for the two of them. Charlotte had told them to freeze at least ten gallons of milk because if the roads flooded, it could be days before they could get to a grocery store.

Alex glanced across the table at Homer. "So, you couldn't sleep through the pop when that transformer blew out, either?"

"That sounded enough like gunfire that it made me think, at least until I got full awake, that I was back in the jungle in Vietnam. I was tellin' Frank to run when I come to my senses," Homer admitted. "I don't think I was fully asleep yet, though. Them two old women across the hall snore loud enough to wake the dead. I'll have to drag out my earplugs if I ever expect to get any sleep. It's a wonder to me they didn't scare Delilah away."

"Earplugs?" Ellie Mae asked.

"I still got the ones I used back in the war days when I couldn't sleep for the bombs going off"—he reached for a brownie—"and the snoring at night in the barracks. I've always been a light sleeper. I'm going to like staying here a few days. We couldn't get up in the middle of the night and scrounge around for midnight snacks at the center."

"We want you to make yourselves at home," Tabby said, "but we also want you to be careful on those stairs. Don't be too proud to use the lift chair."

"Don't you go worryin' about us, darlin'."

61

Homer grinned. "The war and the reception we got when we came home knocked the pride right out of me and Frank, so we'll use the chair when we need it. Are you serious about us just helping ourselves to snacks?"

"Of course," Ellie Mae answered.

Their guests should never want for food, she thought, not even if they wound up having to stay a whole week. She made a mental note to keep Aunt Charlotte's cookie jar in the middle of the dining room table, and to be sure it was full all the time.

"Changing the subject here," Alex said. "Do you think things will be back to normal enough that we'll be able to have the Sandcastle Festival the weekend after Thanksgiving?"

Ellie Mae finished off her milk, stood up, and took her glass to the dishwasher. "We came here for Thanksgiving when I was a little girl, but we never stayed for the festival."

Tabby reached for another brownie. "We were only here for the holiday, too. My dad and Ellie Mae's could barely get along for an afternoon. What's this festival all about?"

"It seems like every little town in the state has a festival," Alex answered. "Anahuac has the Gatorfest, Winnie has the Rice Festival, and we have the Sandcastle Festival. Businesses buy a plot of land for one day on the beach to build a sandcastle. The trophy for first place passes from one business to another, and it's a big honor to have it for a year. Second and third place get a ribbon, and even that's a big thing."

"For the past couple of years, me and Frank have gone to the beach to check out the sand-castles and hit the food wagons," Homer said. "We get our shrimp tacos, then we get funnel cakes, and sometime during the day, we have a basket of crab cakes and cotton candy. Then we take a candy apple and one of them big cinnamon rolls back to the center with us."

"Do you walk down here?" Ellie Mae asked.

Frank joined them, sat down at the table, and reached for a brownie. "I take it you're askin' about the festival, and since Homer has his mouth full, I'll answer. We don't walk down here. Something about a patient getting lost a few years ago. Amazing thing is that once we get out of the van, we don't have to have a supervisor."

Homer took a couple of gulps of milk and said, "Frank is right, but we always have a good time there, so I hope they don't have to cancel it. I keep telling the folks that we should build a sandcastle for the center, but can you see Maude getting sand between her toes or working with Cleo? One of them would want the sandcastle to have a steeple or at least an angel sitting on the top. The other one—namely, Cleo—would demand that it have hippie beads hung all over it."

"I can see Cleo getting all up in the middle of the whole event," Ellie Mae said. "So, folks come to the beach and build sandcastles. Is that and the food vendors the whole festival?"

"Oh, no!" Alex held up a palm. "Two blocks of Main Street, or what we all call the strip, is roped off, and vendors also set up tents where they sell jewelry made from seashells and all kinds of things. The vendors rent those spots, too, because it only costs ten bucks to enter the sandcastle contest. People claim a section of the beach and mark their territory with a flag that the festival provides. The castles can get pretty fancy, with lights and all kinds of decorations. You get your picture in the Anahuac newspaper if you're one of the top three winners."

Ellie Mae sat back down at the table. "Has the B and B ever had an entry?"

"Not since I've been back in this area," Alex said. "You could change that this year, if we even get to have the festival. From what I hear going on outside right now, there might not be anything left of Sandcastle when this blows over."

Homer cocked his head to one side. "Sounds to me like it might be moving on north. I hear pounding rain, but the wind is dying down. And if it flattens everything in town, us Texans are a strong bunch of folks. We can and will build back. Maybe not the same way things was, but every town has to have a church or two or three, and a gas station, and in these small communities, folks turn out to help each other."

"I was expecting the storm to be here for days," Tabby said.

"When they come in at more'n a hundred miles an hour, they don't hang around long. Where are y'all from, anyway?" Homer asked.

"I was living in Alma, Arkansas, when Aunt Charlotte called me," Ellie Mae answered.

"And I moved here from Sallisaw, Oklahoma." Tabby took the empty brownie plate and her glass to the dishwasher.

"So you're used to tornadoes instead of hurricanes?" Frank asked. "I'm not sure which would be worse."

"Think of a hurricane as a Class 5 tornado underwater," Alex explained. "It hits, does its damage, and moves on, but always leaves a few days of pouring-down rain and a lot of destruction in its wake. The roar of hundred-mile winds is so much louder than sixty, which is what I'd guess it is now, but it's far from being over."

Tabby shot a smile toward her cousin. "You were right."

"About what?" Ellie Mae asked.

"I would definitely need rocks in my pockets if I went outside right now," Tabby answered.

"We would probably all need to weigh ourselves down—even me." Homer chuckled again.

Frank laughed. "If that wind knocked you on your butt, you'd roll all the way to Kansas."

"Are you sayin' I'm fat?" Homer asked.

"Can you still fit into your army uniform?" Frank shot back.

"Of course not," Homer answered.

"I can, and the pants are even a little bit loose." A crooked grin played at the corners of Frank's mouth. "I tried them on last week."

"The waistband of my military britches wouldn't fit around my thigh," Homer said, "and I've enjoyed every bit of food that put these pounds on my body."

"I can be your witness to that"—Frank nodded —"because I probably ate pretty much the same thing you did every day." He turned to face Alex. "After eating what we did in Vietnam, we made a pact that we would never take good food for granted again. Thank y'all for the company, but now, I'm going to take my lantern and go back to bed."

"Me too," Homer said.

They were reminiscing about some horrible dish the army had served when they were in Vietnam as they left the room together. Ellie Mae wished that for just one day, her father could be that kindhearted—to his own brother, for that matter.

She covered a yawn with the back of her hand. "Do you think that we'll be able to check on damage tomorrow and maybe take down the wood on the windows?"

"Probably not," Alex answered. "The rain will hang around for a while. There might even be hail. We'll need to wait to uncover the windows until it all stops. The tail of a hurricane can be almost as violent as the actual storm."

"Well, on that note, I'm going to go back to bed. It's only six hours until we have to make breakfast." Ellie Mae picked up her lantern and headed out of the kitchen. Before she reached the door, she turned around and said, "Or maybe I should say, until I set the table and *y'all* make breakfast."

Tabby waved her away with a flick of her wrist, blew out one of the oil lamps, and picked up the other one to use as a light to get to her bedroom. She was thirty-nine years old, but she felt a little uncomfortable sitting in the kitchen with Alex. Maybe it was that silly kiss from decades ago or the fact that she hadn't dated since her divorce, but most likely, it was because she was sitting there in pajama pants, an oversize T-shirt, and no bra.

"Are you sleepy?" Alex asked.

"Not really," she answered.

"Me either," he said. "Stay awhile and talk to me."

"What about?" Tabby asked. Had he suddenly

remembered their awkward flirting as early teenagers?

"You could tell me why you left your home in Oklahoma and came down here to the beach," Alex answered. "And then you could ask me why I decided to come to Sandcastle. That way we'd know something about each other—other than the fact that we both know our way around the kitchen and that we had a little crush on each other when we were barely teenagers."

"You remember?" Tabby set the lamp back on the table and pulled out a chair. Getting to know him as an adult put a little spring in her step.

"Of course," Alex answered with a smile. "A boy never forgets his first kiss, especially when it's with a beautiful girl with big brown eyes."

"Oh, really?" Tabby's pulse kicked up a notch. It had been a long time since anyone had complimented her.

"Truth!" Alex held up a palm. "I don't remember us talking too often when we were kids. I was too shy to say much to someone as pretty as you were, and then we shared that one kiss, and when I came back the next day, you were gone."

"But I came back," Tabby said. "You've lived in this town all these years. Yet you didn't come around when I was here."

"Why would I?" Alex shrugged. "You were way out of my league, and by the time I came home after a stint in the army, you were married. Even in that case, trust me when I say that I never could get you out of my mind."

His words rendered Tabby speechless for a moment. When she finally found her voice, she wasn't even sure how to begin a conversation, but she did want to know more about him. "Okay, then, if we're going to talk, you go first."

"Deal," he said with a slight nod. "My granddad lived up in Smith's Point. My dad was killed in a boating accident when I was just a baby. He was a fisherman and so was my grandfather. They were together out on the Gulf when a storm blew up out of nowhere. My grandfather was the only survivor when the boat went down. When I was five, my mother remarried and . . ." He paused and took a deep breath. "Her new husband didn't want to raise another man's son. Truth is, I wanted to be out on Granddad's boat or running barefoot on the docks or the beach all the time. I guess you call it being a free spirit or maybe a wild one, but, boy, did my stepfather *not* like it."

Tabby didn't need to hear his whole life story, but there was something about his eyes as he talked to her—not quite haunting, but a little bit of loneliness hiding down deep in his soul.

"I had pretty much been left to run wild up until then, and though my mama loved me, she knew Atlanta city life wouldn't be right for me. I would never adapt to living in a fifth-story apartment," Alex said. "So she left me with Grandpa when she moved, which was fine by me. Now, your turn."

"But that's only until you were five years old, and you didn't tell me why you came to Sandcastle," Tabby said.

"That was chapter one," Alex said with a grin. "Now you tell me your chapter one, and another day we'll go into chapter two."

"What has Aunt Charlotte told you?" Tabby asked.

"Just that she was tired of hurricanes and that she was giving this place to her two nieces because y'all both needed a big change in your lives. I remembered you from that summer when we flirted with each other, but like I said before, Ellie Mae was just a little girl," Alex answered.

"I see." She scarcely knew how to begin, especially if she was only going to tell things up until she was five years old, like he had.

"Okay, then, chapter one. The Landry family was in the boatbuilding business, and the barn out back was used for the finish painting and detailing." She went on to tell him a little of the well-known folklore. "Aunt Charlotte might have already told you this much, but they made a fortune. Rufus—that's Aunt Charlotte's father— lost his wife when his son was a teenager, and he remarried soon after. Aunt Charlotte was born to his second wife when his son, Isaac, was already a teenager."

"Charlotte just told me that her family was in the boat business. I never knew what that barn out back was used for," he said, "but go on."

"Isaac, who was my grandfather, had two sons. One is my father, Kenneth. The younger one, Jefferson, is Ellie Mae's dad. We are both only children. Charlotte never married but inherited this place when her dad died, because her brother didn't want anything to do with it. I guess there were hard feelings between him and his father because of the marriage to Aunt Charlotte's mother. My dad wound up in Sallisaw, and he and my mother have a law firm there. Ellie Mae's father went into law also, but he moved over to Conway, Arkansas, to set up a practice. Neither of our fathers are real happy about us deciding to come back here."

" 'Back'?" Alex asked. "How can you come back when you never lived here?"

"It was mine and Ellie Mae's favorite place when we were little, and our whole lives, Aunt Charlotte told us that the B and B would one day be ours, as it had to stay in the Landry bloodline. Our folks always came down here for the Thanksgiving holiday; Aunt Charlotte would throw a hissy fit if the family didn't get together once a year. Mama hated having to come to"—she waggled her fingers in air quotes—" 'this boring

71

place,' so there was always tension over having to come. But I loved the short flight in Daddy's little airplane and getting to spend time with Aunt Charlotte." Tabby hesitated and decided that was enough for one night. "And that's chapter one." She was still working through the next chapters, especially those concerning Natalie. She blinked away the tears threatening to roll down her cheeks when she thought about the chapters that would have been in her daughter's life. They would never be written or lived out, and that was so unfair.

"But you've left me with a cliff-hanger," Alex said. "I don't know what happened in your life to make you say yes when Charlotte decided that it was time for you to take up the reins and run this place."

Tabby pushed back her chair and stood up. "That's a very, very long story—maybe even book length. Stay tuned for more, another day."

"I'm holding you to that." Alex stood up. "I'll use my lantern to walk you to your room."

"Thanks, but I have one, too." She blew out the second oil lamp, and the room was only dark for a minute before it was lit up again when she pulled the top up on her lantern.

"I'll walk you to your door anyway," Alex said. "I wouldn't want Miz Charlotte scolding me for not being a gentleman."

He walked her to the foyer and then stopped.

"Which one is yours? Charlotte told me that y'all were turning the office into a second ground-floor bedroom, but what's behind door number one and door number two?"

Tabby pointed toward her bedroom door. "Door number one, right there, is my bedroom. Ellie Mae did convert the office into her bedroom, and we share the bathroom that separates the two rooms, but we don't fight over the time we spend in there, like Cleo and Maude. Thank goodness each of the upstairs bedrooms has its own private bath."

"That sure makes things easier with those two women." Alex lingered in the foyer. "Tabby, I really am looking forward to hearing chapter two."

She opened the door to her room but didn't go inside. "I am, too, and thanks one more time for all you're doing for us."

"You are very welcome. Miz Charlotte is like a grandmother to me, and we had a lot of fun both during hurricane season and throughout the rest of the year as well. Feels weird to say it like that, when these things are so devastating, but we did." He took a step toward the stairs.

Suddenly, she didn't want him to go. "How many years have you been helping her?"

"That, darlin', is a chapter four or five discussion." He disappeared up the stairs with a grin.

She closed the door and flopped down on her bed. Even though her head was on the pillow and her eyes were closed, sleep didn't come for at least another hour.

Chapter Four

When he heard Tabby gasp before breakfast later that morning, Alex thought she had burned herself or that the gas to the cookstove had gone out—but when he whipped around and saw Cleo, he understood why her eyes had gone all wide.

"Happy Halloween, everyone!" Cleo was dressed in a pair of harem pants that looked like they'd been dragged through every color of paint in the world, and a hot pink blouse with one turquoise sleeve and a bright red one. A purple floral scarf was tied around her head, and the ends flowed down over her right shoulder. "With everything boarded up, this is almost like a haunted house, which is wonderful for Halloween. I'll be available to tell all y'all's fortunes in my bedroom throughout the day. No appointments"—she held up a palm—"but first come, first served. If there's a ribbon on the door, it means I'm in session with someone else."

"Have you done this kind of thing before, like maybe for a festival or a party at the center?" Alex bit back a smile as he remembered the "sock on the door" sign in the military. "You certainly look like you've dressed for it in the past."

"My husband and I owned a carnival right up until the day he died two years ago," Cleo answered. "My job was telling fortunes and taking care of all the bookwork and the logistics of moving from one place to another. Sometimes I looked like this. Most of the time, I wore jeans or overalls like Homer favors."

Alex didn't doubt her story one iota. She looked like a fortune-teller and had the spunk of a steampunk teenager.

"You owned a carnival?" Tabby's tone was coated in disbelief. "For real, you actually *owned* it?"

"Yep, I did," Cleo answered. "Ran away from home when I was sixteen and joined it, and later on down the road, my husband and I bought it."

Ellie Mae pushed back her chair and refilled her coffee cup. "That's awesome. You can tell my fortune, but I want to hear that there's a tall, dark, handsome man in it, and that a happy ever after is involved."

Cleo crossed the room and poured herself a cup of coffee. "Of course there is, darlin'. And there might be one in the cards for Tabby, too."

Alex had expected the old folks to spend most of their time napping in front of the television, not telling fortunes. He sure didn't think one of them would have owned a carnival. Now he wondered what kind of stories the other three could tell.

"Then this evening, maybe we can watch a scary movie on television," Homer said. "Frank, you can help me find one—nope, we won't be doing that since we shouldn't use the generator power to watch television. Maybe we can talk about the scariest book we ever read."

Frank sat down at the table. "I don't read scary books, and don't ask me to tell ghost stories, because I don't know any."

Homer headed over to the bar separating the kitchen and the small nook where a table for four was located. He poured two cups of coffee and handed one off to Frank. "I'd have to call bull crap on that one, Frank. We lived through some real scary stories in Vietnam. Some of them would terrify a person more'n anything a movie can show you. They was real, not fake."

Alex made a mental note to ask them more about their war stories the first chance he got.

"And they ain't for tellin' or rememberin'," Frank said.

Alex had heard war stories from some of the guys who had booked fishing trips with him, but very few of them wanted to talk about Vietnam. Maybe it had been because of their reception when they'd gotten back home, but most likely, they just didn't want to relive the nightmares.

And that's why you don't want to bring it up, his grandfather's voice told him. *Some things is best left untold.*

Alex removed a pan of biscuits from the oven and set it off to one side. "Since we got to be inside until this rain slows down, fortune-telling sounds like a great way to spend some time. Maybe we can also decorate sugar cookies to have this evening since we're too old to go out trick-or-treating."

"Who says we're too old?" Cleo asked and winked at Alex. "But I'm game to stay in out of the rain if you and Tabby will make cookies and let us decorate them."

"None of you are diabetic, are you?" Tabby asked.

"I'm healthy as a horse," Homer said, "and all that's wrong with Frank is that he's got a bum shoulder from carrying me out of the forest to the medical tent when we was nineteen years old. It was rainin' worse than this, and there was mud everywhere. He lost his footin' and fell forward in a puddle. He had me on his back when he went down, busted his shoulder on a log, and it gives him fits nowadays. There was Viet Cong all around us." Homer took a sip of his coffee. "I see that dirty look you're givin' me, Frank, so I'll hush now."

"What happened?" Alex asked.

"We was lucky to get out of that situation alive. I limped for a while, and he had to wear a sling, but it was on his right arm, and he's a lefty. That meant we could still carry a rifle and defend our country," Homer answered.

"And that's enough of that story." Frank lowered his chin and gave Homer another look.

"I don't believe in taking a bunch of medicine, so I steer clear of doctors. What I don't know can't hurt me," Cleo answered, "and I love sugar cookies. Can we make them look like black cats and ghosts?"

"Of course you can." Tabby carried a platter of bacon to the dining room from the kitchen. "Let's make them right after breakfast and have the fortune-telling stuff this afternoon."

Ellie Mae got jellies, picante sauce, and a jug of orange juice from the refrigerator and set all the jars on the table. "What are you going to do, Miz Maude?"

"*My* mother and I always made popcorn balls to give out to the trick-or-treaters," she said with a sideways look at Cleo. "She was ninety-six years old when she died last year. I hated living in the house all alone, so—"

"So she came to the assisted-living center," Cleo interjected, finishing the sentence for her.

"I wouldn't have chosen that one if I'd known *you* owned the place." Maude's tone dripped with icicles so cold that Alex could feel the chill all the way across the room. "But it is the closest one to the cemetery where Mother is buried. I can go visit her and keep flowers on her grave."

"You own the center?" Alex dumped the biscuits into a bowl and carried them to the table.

"Yep," Cleo answered with a nod. "It's an investment."

Ellie Mae filled a basket with a dozen blueberry muffins and carried them in one hand and a platter of scrambled eggs in the other to the dining room. "I think that's everything, so we can eat now. Y'all just holler if you want a coffee refill."

"You're sure a pretty bartender." Homer winked.

Frank nudged him. "Stop flirtin'. She's young enough to be your granddaughter."

"I wasn't flirtin'," Homer told him. "I was payin' her a compliment."

"Yeah, right." Frank chuckled. "So, what if the center is demolished, Cleo? What will you do with the insurance money? Build another?"

"With her reputation, she'll probably buy a bar." Maude reached for a biscuit but pulled her hand back. "Mother and I always said grace. Would y'all mind?"

"Not at all," Tabby said. "Aunt Charlotte liked to bless the food, too."

They all bowed their heads, and Maude said a quick prayer. The moment she said "Amen," she put two biscuits on her plate before she passed them over to Homer.

"You were going to tell us why you bought a retirement center, Cleo," Alex said.

Cleo shrugged. "I had to invest in something or the government would take a big chunk of my money in taxes. It provides me with a free place to live. If the place is all blown to smithereens, then I think a bar is a wonderful idea, Maude. Thank you for the idea. I could live above it or in the back room and hire a good-lookin' guy to run the place for me. Alex, you'd make a good bartender. Want a job, if I buy or build a honky-tonk? Is this county dry or wet? Can we even *have* a honky-tonk here?"

"It's not a dry county, but I don't know about liquor by the drink," Alex answered, biting back a laugh. "We'd have to check into that—I'm a fishing guide, not a bartender."

Homer's hand shot up. "I'll be your bartender, and Frank can help me."

Maude's expression went from fairly pleasant to absolutely disgusted. She folded her arms across her chest and glared at Cleo. From the look on Cleo's face and the broad wink she shot his way, Alex had no doubt she was baiting Maude into an argument.

"I wasn't serious," Maude said through clenched teeth.

"You are always serious." Cleo slathered a muffin with butter and took a bite.

"Am not," Maude argued.

"So serious that you'd probably drop dead if you ever smiled," Cleo accused. "And you better get your hands off your bosom or you'll have greasy spots on your pink shirt. We really should be wearing fall colors on Halloween, not pink."

Maude fumed. "I will wear whatever color I want. Mother and I never did like Halloween anyway. It's not a Christian holiday."

"Did you two know each other before you moved into the center?" Frank asked.

"I can't say that I ever really *knew her,*" Maude answered, "but we were acquainted about sixty years ago."

"Well, I knew you," Cleo said, "and I didn't like you then any better than I do now."

"I'll put five on Cleo if push comes to shove," Tabby whispered.

"I'll take some of that action," Ellie Mae said on the other side of Tabby, "but before we do that, I've got an idea." She raised her voice a notch. "Hey, Maude, how about when we get through making cookies and decorating them, you and I make popcorn balls? My nanny used to let me butter my hands and help make the balls after she poured that hot-syrup stuff on them. How many do you think we'll need?"

Alex could feel the tension level lower considerably, and the expression on Maude's face softened. Ellie Mae had done a fine job of redirection. Maybe he had been wrong in thinking that the two Landry women would have trouble handling a house full of elderly people. But then, Tabby had mentioned that her father and Ellie Mae's didn't get along, so perhaps they were used to running interference in arguments.

"There's seven of us, so maybe fourteen so we could each have two?" Maude's tone had changed from bitter to sweet. "I know the recipe by heart."

"I'll butter my hands up good and help make the balls when y'all get ready for that step," Cleo offered. "We used to have a huge Halloween party after we closed down the carnival that night. We'd have cookies and popcorn balls and a big bowl of orange punch. Sometimes"—she winked at Alex again—"I'd spike the punch with just a little tequila."

"Did you do much of the cooking for the carnival folks?" Alex asked.

Cleo turned her head slightly and frowned at Maude. "Not too often, but when I did, I used several of *my* mother's recipes to make what we called pot meals like chili, soup, beans, or spaghetti. The carnival family's favorite was clam chowder and hot yeast rolls right out of the oven."

Alex dipped deeply into the platter of eggs and put them on his plate. He liked to start the day with a big breakfast, but cooking for just one person wasn't any fun at all, so he usually just had a bowl of instant oatmeal and toast. "I guess we've got our Halloween all lined up, then, since we can't get ready for trick-or-treaters coming to the door. Cookies after breakfast. Then popcorn balls and fortune-telling, and maybe we'll play Clue this evening. Charlotte and I used to play board games to pass the time during hurricanes. Who knows, maybe the butler did it in the pantry with a bag of sugar this time."

"Maybe we could just have sandwiches for lunch so we can eat all the cookies and popcorn balls we want," Frank suggested.

Homer clapped his hands. "This is going to be the best Halloween ever. Too bad we won't be here at Thanksgiving. I bet we could put on a spread that would even make Frank gain a pound, and we could build us an award-winning sandcastle that would take the trophy at the festival."

Alex bit back a remark. Holidays were often his best days for fishing trips, especially for folks who didn't have a lot of family to spend the days with. He sure hoped that everything was back to normal by then. He stole a quick sideways glance at Tabby and thought he might wrangle an invitation for leftovers the day after Thanksgiving. He sure didn't want to get in the way of the family gathering if the other Landrys were planning to come to Sandcastle for the holiday.

Sweet angels in heaven, no! Tabby thought and almost choked on a bite of muffin. Having the current residents and her father and her uncle in

84

the same house would be more than she could bear. She had wondered if they would make the traditional trip to Sandcastle for Thanksgiving Day since Aunt Charlotte had moved, but they had told her they were coming.

"Mainly to see if you've had enough of that gawd-forsaken place and you're ready to come back to civilization," her mother had said.

"And because our cook always takes that week off, and your mother wouldn't know how to bake a turkey," her father had smarted off.

An entire month with Cleo and Maude's bickering would cause Tabby to pack her bags and go back to Sallisaw for sure. Not even the angels in heaven could be expected to put up with that much bitterness and fussing. Even when she had to endure her father's and his brother's hateful attitudes, it was only for a day or two at the most—never for a whole month.

Cleo cocked her head to one side and narrowed her eyes. "I believe this house really is haunted. I hear a baby crying."

"That's not a baby," Maude argued. "It's a bird on the back porch. There's no such thing as ghosts—not even on Halloween."

"Birds are flying around in this storm? I don't think so," Cleo said. "It might be the whine of that old coffeepot. We used a big old coffee machine at the carnival, and whoever took the last cup had to put on another pot. We kept it going from dawn until midnight, unless we were traveling."

"Mother and I never had a fancy coffee maker," Maude said with a sniff. "We always used a percolator that we put on top of the stove to brew our coffee."

Tabby pushed back her chair, went to the kitchen, rolled her eyes toward the ceiling, and gave thanks that those two old gals would be leaving the B and B as soon as the hurricane passed through town for good and the rain stopped coming down like "baby elephants," as Aunt Charlotte would say.

"Who all needs a refill?" she asked as she carried the coffeepot back to the table.

All four of the older folks raised their cups, and Tabby poured up the last of what was in the pot in Cleo's mug. She returned to the kitchen, put on a fresh pot, and heard that whining noise very clearly this time. It wasn't a bird, but it could have been a baby, and it was definitely coming from the back porch.

Not more people! she thought as she headed through the utility room. Before she opened the door, she sent up a prayer that no one had left a baby on the B and B doorstep. With two old veterans, a pair of women who hated each other, and an old flame who still made her heart flutter, she did not need an infant in the house. And there was no way she could get a baby to the proper authorities in a storm like this—or even call someone to come and get the poor little thing.

Rain was still pouring down when she opened the back door. She heaved a sigh of relief when there was no basket with a baby in it. She could barely see the gray shape of the barn, but knowing that it was still standing gave her hope that the house hadn't suffered too much damage. However, the huge old live oak that had stood next to the back porch was now uprooted and lying on the ground. When she was a little girl, a swing had hung from one of the limbs, and she'd spent time every Thanksgiving on it. Later, she had pushed Ellie Mae on that same swing. Now it was gone. Maybe the fact that the old oak was gone was an omen that the family really would die out with the two of them.

The tangled roots had been washed clean by the hard rain and looked like Medusa's hair. *Thank goodness it didn't fall on the house or the barn,* she thought as she pulled the door closed—but not before something wet brushed against her leg. She squealed and stepped to the side, just in time to see a Chihuahua dash into the utility room, a full-grown tabby cat right behind it with what looked like a mouse in her mouth. The cat hopped into a laundry basket and laid the mouse down.

Tabby shivered from her head to her toes. There were three things in the world that she hated, and a mouse was both of them. Mice ranked right up there with spiders and cockroaches, both of which also made her skin crawl. In one fell swoop, Tabby was on top of the washing machine with her knees drawn up and screaming for Alex.

She heard a chair hit the floor, and the little Chihuahua hid behind a mop bucket and whined. The animal itself looked like an overgrown rat with rusty-colored fur. His big brown eyes darted around the small utility room as if he was looking for a hidey-hole to shimmy into until someone killed that mouse in the laundry basket. Tabby understood what the poor little thing was feeling.

Suddenly, Alex and all the rest of the B and B guests were crowded into the room. The dog stopped whining and glanced over at the laundry basket. The cat growled and swatted at him, then licked the mouse.

"Sweet Jesus!" Tabby shivered and closed her eyes tightly. "I can't watch her eat that mouse. Throw it out in the backyard, Alex."

"That's not a mouse, Tabby," Alex told her. "It's a kitten, and the mama cat is Julep. Charlotte said she was going to have another litter. Looks like she's brought a newborn kitten to the house. Probably because of this storm."

Tabby opened one eye enough to look down at the wet cat. "Are you sure?"

"Yep, it's a kitten," Ellie Mae said. "She's

having another one. You can come on down off the washer and see for yourself."

Tabby opened her eyes and peeked into the basket. Sure enough, the mama cat now had two kittens, and she was busy washing the second one.

"I hope none of you folks are allergic to them. I can't throw them out in that rain," Ellie Mae said.

"Anyone allergic to cats and a dog?" Alex asked the folks peeking around him.

"Not me," Maude answered.

Cleo pushed Alex to one side so she could get a better look. "I'm only allergic to ragweed, and Maude is, too. That one hunkered down over there in the corner isn't a kitten. That's a Chihuahua."

"That's the little guy who begs for scraps at the back door of the center. Frank and I feed him almost every day. We figure maybe some folks came down to the beach and lost him a few weeks ago." Homer squatted down and held out a hand. "Poor little Duke. As small as you are, it's a wonder that you didn't drown or get washed away to sea."

Ellie Mae grabbed a rag from the mop bucket and dried Julep's wet fur. "Poor Julep. Where have you been hiding these past two weeks? Aunt Charlotte said there was a stray cat that came with the property, but why didn't you come around and meet us before now?"

Tabby slid off the washing machine. She felt a little foolish for thinking that a kitten was a mouse, but dammit! A black newborn kitten was about the same size as a mouse, and that would have fooled anyone.

"Julep is kind of a community cat that lives out in the barn or sometimes under the back porch," Alex said with a grin. "The space under the porch is probably a miniature lake right now, and the barn is locked up solid, so she couldn't find a place to have the babies."

"Julep? That's a strange name for a cat." Maude raised an eyebrow.

"Charlotte said she was drinking a mint julep when the cat appeared on the back porch a couple of years ago," Alex explained. "Looks like these first two kittens are true Halloween cats. They're both black."

"Here comes another one, and it's black, too, but it's got white feet and a little white mustache," Ellie Mae said.

"I hate cats," Maude said, "so keep them out of my room."

"You hate everything," Cleo said. "I'm glad you never had kids, or you would have hated them, too. If we hadn't been moving around so much with the carnival, I would have loved to have had a cat or a dog."

"That was your choice," Maude snapped.

"I'll take care of Julep." Cleo glared at Maude.

"I don't even mind if she stays in my room. I'll give Alex some money to get whatever we need for a litter pan and food, and she doesn't have to be a stray anymore. I'll adopt her and all the kittens she has."

A mint julep or a mojito or even a double shot of Jack Daniel's on the rocks sounded pretty dang good to Tabby when she thought about motherhood. The very idea caused her brain to close that door and think about a good slug of something stronger than sweet tea.

She knew where Aunt Charlotte kept her liquor, and after the guests were all in their rooms that night, she fully well intended to make a pitcher of margaritas—and maybe even drink all of it by herself. She did not plan on taking in four senior citizens—or a dog and a cat with kittens—and all of them living together during and after a hurricane. That was reason enough to break out the liquor.

Maude stooped to pet Duke, and the little dog licked her fingers. "I do not hate children. Mother and I taught the preschool Sunday-school class until the week before she died. I just have never liked cats and never will, so you keep that critter away from me. I'm going to adopt this little guy. He needs someone to take care of him."

"Never say never," Cleo said. "It'll come back and bite you on the butt."

"You should know," Maude said. "You said you'd never come back to Winnie, Texas."

"And I didn't." Cleo toyed with the ends of the scarf. "I came back to Sandcastle and bought the retirement center where you live. Come to think of it, you never even said thank you."

"You might change your mind about cats, Miz Maude," Ellie Mae said, "when you see these precious baby kittens. They're so cute when they get their eyes open and start tumbling around with each other. I hope Duke and Julep can get along."

"It might be a good idea to keep them separated," Frank said. "I've seen him chase squirrels up trees. He thinks he's mean and tough, like *the* Duke. That's why me and Homer named him what we did."

"Never seen him around cats until right now," Homer added. "But seein' as how Cleo is taking the cat and you want to adopt the dog, they might fight as bad as y'all do."

Cleo chuckled. "You probably got that right. I've laid claim to Julep and her babies. Alex, would you please take them to my bedroom? And, Ellie Mae, can you figure out a way to make a makeshift litter box for her until we can go to the store?"

Tabby appreciated Cleo taking charge, but she wondered if the woman wasn't doing it just to show up Maude. She would love to know what their issue was with each other—maybe before they left, she could get them to at least tell her chapter one of their story. She smiled at that idea and wondered when and if she and Alex would have time to share the next portion of their life stories with each other. Part of her wanted him to stick around the B and B for a while; the other wanted the two bickering women to go back to the center. If the latter happened, then it would mean there was no reason for Alex to stay.

"Cleo, do you want us to do that right now?" Alex asked. "Or after we clean up the kitchen and make cookies?"

"Either one, but if Maude even looks sideways at those little darlins, they could die." Cleo sat down on the floor beside Ellie Mae and began to croon to the cat. "You're a pretty girl, and we'll raise these babies together." She reached inside the basket and rubbed Julep's wet fur with a dry towel. "I might decide to buy a house and move out of the center just so you'll have a place to live. Do you want a diamond collar? We could get matching ones, and I could turn into a crazy cat lady who reads books to her baby kittens."

"You've already got the 'crazy' down," Maude muttered and headed out of the room with her nose in the air and the Chihuahua on her heels.

"Looks like you've got a friend," Homer told her.

Maude picked Duke up and held him close to

her chest. "See there, I don't hate everything. This dog loves me." She pointed at Cleo. "If your cats get out into the hallway, I'll turn my dog loose on them, so keep them away."

Cleo raised her voice. "You keep that yappy little critter away from my Julep and her babies."

"You are not my boss," Maude said. "I'll get Duke settled in and then come back down to make cookies. Come on, baby. You can ride in the lift chair on my lap."

"She's only doing that because I want the cats." Cleo giggled and then whispered, "I really do want these cats, but she needs a pet, so I did this on purpose. A pet will be good for her attitude. It'll give her something that needs her and to love."

Tabby was speechless for several seconds. "That was kind of sweet," she finally said, "but you couldn't have made them show up on the porch at the same time."

"Shhh . . ." Cleo put a finger over her lips. "Don't tell Maude that. She thinks I'm an evil witch. Always has and probably always will."

"Why does she think that?" Ellie Mae asked.

"Because I was a free spirit who wanted wings to fly when we were younger, and she was a stick-in-the-mud who was afraid to get on a broom or a magic carpet with me," Cleo answered. "Julep and her babies might be better satisfied in here than up there where that dog can aggravate them, but let it be your idea. Maude will gloat if she thinks she's won a battle."

Tabby nodded. "I'll take the blame, and maybe when the storm is over and the barn is safe, she will want to move her babies back out there. Why would Maude be so mad at you after all these years, anyway? You don't have to answer that if it's too personal."

"No problem," Cleo said with a grin. "She's my older sister."

Tabby's face must have registered shock because Cleo laughed out loud. "Kind of hard to believe, isn't it?"

"Yes, ma'am, it is," Ellie Mae said. "Y'all don't even look alike."

"Neither do you and Tabby," Alex said.

Tabby finally managed to speak. "But we're just cousins, not sisters."

"Well, the short form of a long story is this." Cleo kept petting Julep as she explained. "I'm just two years younger than Maude, but like I said before, I was born to be free. Mother was domineering and had panic attacks if she didn't get her way. That meant controlling me and Maude both."

She stopped and smiled as if she was remembering something special. "The carnival came to Winnie during the Texas Rice Festival, and I went with it when it left. It was love at first sight for me and Lewis, but we couldn't get married until we were of age, and that was a couple of years later. Sixty years ago, the regular world frowned on young people living together, but not so much in the carnival world."

"Some people still frown on it," Ellie Mae said.

"Narrow-minded folks wouldn't recognize true love if it kissed them smack on the lips," Cleo snapped. "Lewis and I had a little travel trailer, and we worked hard, got married, and saved our money. When we were in our thirties, the carnival went to southern Oklahoma, like it did every winter. That was our time to recuperate from the busy season and to repair, repaint, and get the equipment ready to go back out in the spring. That year, the owner took sick and died. Lewis and I scraped all our savings together and made a bid on it. The owner's survivors sold it to us for half of what it was worth, and we worked our butts off for many years to take care of our carnival family."

Tabby waited patiently while Cleo kept petting the cat.

"And Maude got mad at you for leaving?" Alex asked.

Cleo shrugged. "That would be putting it mildly. Daddy died a few weeks after I ran away, and Maude blamed me for that. Then Mama had one of her spells, and Maude had to come home from her first year of college and take care of her. Maude had to go work in an insurance company to support the two of them when she really wanted to be a schoolteacher. Everything from those two catastrophic events to ingrown toenails has been my fault ever since," Cleo said. "You'd think that sisters could find a little love in their hearts for each other, but . . ." She shrugged again. "Evidently, it isn't going to happen. I sent what money I could to help out since I couldn't be there. After Lewis and I bought the carnival, I did even more, but I never even got a thank-you or a note saying Mama had received it."

For the second time in only a few minutes, Tabby was speechless.

"Oh. My. Goodness!" Ellie Mae shook her head. "It's still hard to believe that you two are sisters."

Cleo patted her on the shoulder. "Thank you for that. Maude would probably drop graveyard dead before admitting we're sisters, but I assure you we are. She looks like Mama did, and I'm the spitting image of my father's sister, who always had wings instead of roots, too."

Tabby shifted her gaze over at Ellie Mae. No one would ever think they were related, either, so she could understand exactly where Cleo was coming from—and yet she loved Ellie Mae like a little sister. Did Cleo love Maude even though Maude didn't return that affection?

"I didn't expect that," Alex said.

"Me either," Ellie Mae muttered.

"Please don't tell Maude that I told you," Cleo said. "She disowned me a long time ago, and she sure doesn't like people to know that her sister was involved with a carnival."

"Did either of you ever have a pet?" Alex asked that afternoon when he found himself alone in the living room with Homer and Frank.

"Yep, we did," Homer answered.

"Dog or cat?" Alex asked.

"Dog," Frank said. "His name was Rooster."

"I missed him." Homer's eyes misted.

"Why would you name a dog Rooster?" Alex asked.

"He was named after John Wayne's character in *True Grit*," Homer explained.

"Rooster Cogburn," Frank said with a nod. "Poor old boy was just skin and bones when he came slitherin' out of the forest that day in Vietnam. It was about this time of year, and me and Homer fed him scraps from the mess hall."

"Took us a few weeks to fatten him up, but ol' Rooster got us through a lot of tough times," Homer said with a sigh.

Both of them went silent for a few minutes; then Frank chuckled.

"Remember that night when we'd been out on patrol and Rooster went with us?"

Homer nodded. "If he hadn't been with us, we wouldn't have come back alive. He growled about the time we were about to walk into an ambush and saved our sorry hides."

"Wasn't the first time he sat guard with us, either," Frank said. "By the time we got some meat on his bones, he was part of our unit. Homer was point man, and over there, the members of your company became your family. Homer had to be on constant watch so that he didn't lead any of us following behind him in those sticky hot jungles into a trap, but old Rooster would either stay right by him or else he'd run on ahead."

"He'd lay down flat on the ground if he thought I shouldn't go on," Homer told Alex. "And he wasn't never wrong. I wondered if maybe he wasn't a trained military dog that got lost from another company at some time and nearly starved to death in the jungle before we found him."

Frank smiled at the memory. "He could smell a grenade hanging in a tree or a booby trap."

"What did he look like?" Alex asked.

"A big old raw-boned, floppy-eared hound dog," Homer said with half a chuckle. "In these parts, he would have been trained to track down coyotes, but over there in that place . . ."

"You got to understand," Frank said, his tone all serious, "one time, we were out there in the jungle for four days and three nights, with no sleep except for a quick nap when we could catch it. Rain as bad as what's falling outside was coming down, and we got one meal a day.

We shared what little we had with Rooster, and he was a real trooper about it."

"We had to walk through ten miles of waist-high water, and Rooster swam it right along beside us." Homer's voice had a hollow sound to it.

From both of the guys' expressions, Alex wondered if maybe the dog had drowned by the time they got back to their post.

"We made it back that time, so hungry that even the mess-hall food tasted like heaven," Homer went on, "and Rooster got his own plate instead of just scraps."

"Hell, I would have given him my dinner, if the cook hadn't let us take a plate of that stew out to him," Frank declared. "Our bodies—and his, too—had just taken a beatin' worse than you can imagine. A ten-mile walk through water and two days of trying to get through jungles so dense that a machete had to cut through it, plus—"

"Tell you one thing: when you're over in a place like that, with danger around every corner, the jokes the guys tell are funnier, and mail call is the most important thing of the day," Homer said.

"What else happened on that mission?" Alex asked.

"That's classified," Frank said, "but I ain't wanted to go huntin' since I got back from there. Do you know what immersion foot is?"

"I've heard of it," Alex answered.

"Well, me and Homer both had it by the time we got out of that water, and we were cryin' like little girls. No one teased us about it because more'n half of the squad were cryin' right along with us," Frank said. "It's almighty painful and hard to heal, but we lived through it."

"That pain wasn't as bad as what we came home to face," Homer said. "Folks callin' us names and sayin' that we were murderers. Now *that* was a hard thing to put up with."

"How about you? Did you serve?" Frank asked.

"I did, and I was deployed, but I got sent to Kuwait for a few months in the sand," Alex answered.

"Don't know if I'd like that any better than the jungles," Homer told him.

"What happened to Rooster?" Alex asked.

"We were out on a recon mission, and he took a bullet." Homer pulled a hankie from his pocket and wiped tears from his eyes.

"Went right through his heart," Frank added, his voice cracking. "We carried him back on our shoulders and had a proper funeral for him. All the guys came out and . . ."

"And we all cried worse than when we had immersion foot," Homer said. "Even though he was mine and Frank's dog, the rest of the squad had kind of adopted him for our mascot."

"Hey, you guys ready to come decorate cookies?" Tabby called from the kitchen.

"Yep, we'll be right there," Alex replied, raising his voice above the rain still pelting the roof.

"I'm sorry about the reception you got." Alex stood up. "My grandpa talked about his cousins coming home from that war and was so ashamed of how they got treated."

Frank laid a hand on Alex's shoulder. "Thank you for that, son. I'm just glad none of y'all since then have had to put up with what we did."

"I'm just sorry that we didn't get to bring Rooster home with us." Homer sighed again as he pushed up out of the recliner and headed to the kitchen.

Alex thought about a big old red hound dog that would probably be sixty years old now. Would the little Chihuahua live to be an old dog? He looked across the room and forgot about the dogs—Tabby was wearing a bibbed apron, and flour dusted one of her dark eyebrows. He wondered if Homer and Frank ever regretted not having a wife who would decorate cookies with them.

Do you? Charlotte's voice was back in his head.

"Every day," he whispered.

Chapter Five

A dozen cookies cooled on racks set on the counter. Another dozen were in the oven, and a third panful was ready to be baked. Ellie Mae was doing the math in her head—thirty-six cookies, seven people—but Cleo beat her to the punch.

"That's only five cookies for each of us. We better make at least one more pan," she said. "I can eat a dozen all by myself."

"That's not the truth. You're too skinny to eat a dozen cookies," Maude argued.

"I can eat an elephant a bite at a time," Cleo told her. "I might be planning to hide half a dozen in my room for later."

"I like the idea of hiding some in my room, but what if I don't like elephant?" Homer asked.

"You'll love it," Frank said with half a grin. "Today it will taste like sugar cookies and popcorn balls. Are y'all making them with just a sugar coating or with caramel, too?"

"With caramel," Maude answered. "That's the way Mother and I made them for the kids every year. I missed doing things with her when she died." She cut her eyes to Cleo.

"Then bring on that elephant," Homer said with a broad smile.

Why can't my dad and his brother get along like Homer and Frank? Ellie Mae bit back a sigh.

Because they never had to go through tough times together. That builds character and teaches people to depend on each other, Aunt Charlotte whispered softly in her ear.

Ellie Mae thought about the years she and Sam had lived together as roommates. True enough, it was an unusual situation that most folks didn't understand, especially her father and his parents, but it had worked for them. Sam was Black and had been her best friend since they were in high school. It just seemed natural to move in together after they had both graduated and gotten jobs as carpenters at the same place. The first time she met him, she'd been intimidated by his size— six feet, four inches tall; wide shoulders; what seemed like an acre of chest. She could have sworn he was a football player or a bodybuilder, but he was neither. He had learned a bit about woodworking from his grandfather and loved it.

She was deep in her own memories when Cleo's voice brought her back to the conversation.

"What did you and *your* mother talk about when you were making popcorn balls?" Cleo asked.

"Those were private conversations," Maude answered.

Ellie Mae had always envied people who had siblings, but not anymore. If sisters acted the way Maude and Cleo did toward each other, then she was glad she'd never had one. She'd always had a great relationship with Tabby—somewhat like she thought sisters might have. Sam, however, had always been like a brother. Ten years they'd shared either a trailer, an apartment, or a house. He had died three weeks ago, and she was still in denial—the first stage of grief.

Tabby had always been there for her and had understood when she refused to go to college to study law. Sam had been there when Ellie Mae cried over her boyfriends or cussed about her parents, and he hadn't fussed at her when she was in one of her Jesus moods—when not even Jesus could have lived with her, according to Sam. On those days, he made his famous bacon-wrapped chicken and homemade macaroni and cheese for her.

He bought three pounds of bacon at a time, she remembered with a smile.

As she stirred orange food coloring into a small bowl of icing to decorate the cookies, she thought of the fact that he'd declared macaroni and cheese a vegetable. Maude had chosen a seat at one end of the table and had Duke in her lap. Hopefully, with Cleo all the way at the other end, the two sisters would just snap at each other and not come to actual blows. Frank and Homer had taken the same places they'd had at the breakfast table, leaving plenty of room on the other side for Tabby, Alex, and Ellie Mae.

The last time she had decorated sugar cookies had been when she was fourteen, and they had been shaped like Christmas bells, Santa Claus, and wreaths—not ghosts, witches, and cats. That was the same year that her father, Jefferson Landry, had caught her kissing a boy on the front porch. The next week, her mother, Dara, had left. For years, Ellie Mae had thought that her mother was either ashamed that she had given Santa Claus a pink beard or that she had kissed a boy. Either one might have caused her mother to catch a flight back to Ireland.

"Y'all think we need any other colors?" She didn't want to remember those days or the bleak ones that had followed, when her father barely acknowledged that she was living in the same house with him.

"Orange, black, white." Maude pointed to each color. "We've got pumpkins, ghosts, quarter moons, and bats."

"And black cats," Cleo finished for her.

"They aren't black until we decorate them," Maude argued. "You can decorate those since you're all into the voodoo stuff, and besides, I don't like cats."

"You already said that," Cleo told her. "Only *old* people repeat themselves."

Alex brought the cooled cookies to the table. "Okay, folks, have fun. And Cleo, I'd have to disagree with you on that statement. Sometimes I repeat myself, and I'm not old. I'm only forty."

"That means *old* is setting in, but you can fight it, darlin'," Cleo told him. "Just keep young thoughts in your head."

Alex tapped his forehead with his forefinger. "I'll try to remember that."

Frank picked up a ghost shape. "My mama used to let me do this when I was a little boy. I still miss her, even though she's been gone for more than twenty years."

Alex pulled out a chair and sat down across from Frank. "Was she from these parts?"

"Not really," Frank answered. "She came over here from down in the Louisiana-bayou country and married my father. He and his family lived in Cotton Holler, a little community that a hurricane wiped completely out and that was never rebuilt. We never did have a post office, but we had our own school up until I was a freshman. That was the year they bused us down here to Sandcastle. Mama wasn't happy about us coming to the white people's school, but if I was to get an education, then that's what I had to do. Homer saw that I was scared out of my head and took me under his wing."

Homer chose a cookie shaped like a cat and smeared on a layer of black icing. "His folks had a little café up there that had the best chicken-fried steak in the whole world. My daddy used to drive us up there after church on Sunday, and we'd eat in their café and then bring home one of his mama's pecan pies. I'd talked to Frank a few times when we were up there at the café, so I knew him already."

"Those were the good old days." Frank's smile said that he was remembering those times fondly. "Mama ran the café and took care of the hirin' and firin'. Daddy worked for a rice company over near Winnie and helped out with the café on weekends. I worked there after school and on the weekends, and as much as my folks wanted me to step up and run the business after I graduated from high school, it just wasn't what I wanted to do with my life."

"You must've gotten that Louisiana accent from your mama," Ellie Mae said, and wished again that she could have a conversation with her father and Uncle Kenneth where one of them said something nice about the good old days or each other.

Frank didn't answer for a while, but then he said, "Guess I did. Wish I'd have gotten her patience, too."

"Don't let him kid you," Homer said. "He's got the patience of Job. I'm the impatient one of the two of us."

Frank kept his eyes on what he was doing, but

he smiled. "Don't mistake patience for pure old laziness."

"He's also humble." Homer held up his cookie for everyone to see. "Look, my black cat is done!"

Ellie Mae brought the last of the cooled cookies to the table, sat down on one side of Alex, and picked up a quarter-moon shape to work on first. With a long table separating them, the two feuding sisters gave each other long, cold glances. Ellie Mae was familiar with those stinky looks, as she had called them when she was younger.

Across from her were two old friends who could almost finish each other's sentences. Then there was Alex and Tabby. From the vibes Ellie Mae got flowing between them, she suspected there was history. Could he be that boy she'd kissed in the barn all those years ago?

Such a lot of history right there around the table. What made people tick? she wondered. Why was there so much animosity between her father and uncle? Why couldn't they see past the color of Sam's skin and accept him as her friend?

"I'm going to eat Homer's cat first. He's put lots of icing on it," Cleo said.

"My nanny at the time—I had more than a dozen through the years—said there couldn't be any eating until all the cookies were decorated," Ellie Mae said. "My mother thought my cookies were ugly, the last Christmas that I had with her. Decorating Santa with a pink beard might have been the beginning of my rebellious streak." If Ellie Mae ever had children—which was doubtful at this point, since few men were interested in a woman who wielded a hammer better than a hand mixer—she would teach them to be individuals and not let what other people thought affect them.

"How long has it been since you talked to Aunt Dara?" Tabby asked.

"She calls on my birthday," Ellie Mae answered, "and Christmas, and she never, ever forgets to laugh about my ugly cookies. She made an exception a few weeks ago and tried to talk me out of moving to Sandcastle. She and Dad both think I'm wrong to be here—but then, they haven't been happy with my decisions in the past, so it's nothing new."

"I thought she was okay with you living with Sam and that it was just Uncle Jefferson who threw a fit about it," Tabby said.

"Not many folks understood that our rela-tionship was purely what they call platonic. We were best friends and work partners, and we never dated." Ellie Mae kept working on her cookie without looking up. She and Sam had kissed one time, but it felt like she was kissing her brother, and he'd said it felt weird to him, too—like he was kissing his sister.

"How about your parents, Tabby? Did they try

to talk you out of coming down here in hurricane alley?" Alex asked as he worked on a completely round cookie that he'd cut out of the last bits of leftover dough.

"I'm paddling the same canoe as Ellie Mae," Tabby answered. "I walked away from a job as vice president of a bank to come to Sandcastle and run this old family B and B. My folks tried to get me to see a therapist or, at the very least, come to work at their law firm if I was burned out with the bank job."

Cleo turned to Ellie Mae. "Were you a banker, too? Were you and this Sam work partners in a big corporation?"

Ellie Mae shook her head. Her feelings paralleled Tabby's very closely: she'd suffered a terrible loss when Sam died, and this was a chance for a big change in her life. "Much to my folks' dismay, I took woodshop in high school. It was mainly in protest to it being an all-boys' class."

And probably because I was going through a rebellious stage after my mother moved back to Ireland, leaving me with my dad instead of even giving me a choice about going with her or staying in Arkansas, she thought.

"That class," Ellie Mae went on, "taught me that I liked working with my hands. When I graduated, I got a job in a nonprofit business that built houses for needy folks all over the lower

111

forty-eight states. Sam and I did that for five years; then we went to work for a private business doing finish-carpentry work in northwest and central Arkansas. My parents have both been disappointed in my decisions, but that's probably the only thing they've agreed on in the past twenty years."

"Hey, there's nothing wrong with carpentry work," Homer said with a serious expression. "Me and Frank did lots of that after we got out of the army. For years we did house-framing, and then we got jobs putting up fast-food stores all over Texas and Oklahoma. Frank was a supervisor when we retired and invested in our little convenience store–gas station combination. We miss our store and sometimes wish we had stayed with it until they carried us out feetfirst."

"Yep," Frank agreed with a nod.

Ellie Mae flashed a smile across the table. "Where were you when I needed someone to stand up for me?"

"Probably pumping gas, but I would have sure enough had your back, girl," Homer said.

Ellie Mae wondered what path she might have taken if she hadn't had that rebellious streak. Would she have been a lawyer now, a partner in her father's firm? Would it have been tougher to leave that kind of job to move to Sandcastle than it had been to simply walk away from construction? If Sam were still her roommate and hadn't died so suddenly—her chin quivered—would she have made a different choice?

"Dammit!" Tabby swore under her breath that afternoon when she flipped the light switch in the pantry and got nothing but more darkness.

She felt a presence behind her before she even turned around and saw Alex in the doorway, holding up a lantern. Every time he was close by, a little jolt of electricity struck her heart and told her that he wasn't far away.

"Old habits are hard to break. I've been trying to turn on lights all day, too," Alex said. "Can I help you find something?"

"I need flour, yeast, and sugar," she answered, very aware that she and Alex were in the dimly lit closet-size pantry together. His shaving lotion—something woodsy, with a hint of vanilla—wafted toward her across the cramped space, and when he spoke, the warmth of his breath on her neck sent shivers down her back.

"That'll all be on the back shelf where Charlotte kept the baking supplies." He turned the lantern around toward the back wall of shelving. "What are we making?"

"Yeast rolls for supper," she answered.

He brushed against her shoulder and hip as he maneuvered around her, sending hot sparks dancing around the room. The feeling couldn't be a result of a lingering desire left behind by their one and only kiss, because at the time, she'd been disappointed and had wondered what the supposedly big deal about kissing boys was all about. It was just dry lips touching, and he'd just eaten a hot dog with onions. Besides, she had no idea whether he was romantically involved with someone or not. They'd been stuck in a darkened house, with very little access to the outside world, so there could be a girlfriend or someone he was in a serious relationship with out there, waiting for his call. Still, she couldn't deny the electricity she felt anytime he was nearby—but even if it was possible, she would never be able to do anything about it.

The vibes had to come from the fact that she hadn't so much as gone out with a man since she and James had split up. For that matter, they hadn't shared much intimacy for several years. Then their daughter's death had driven a wedge between them that had just gotten wider and wider with each passing day before Tabby finally filed for divorce.

Alex set the lantern on a shelf and picked up the canisters containing flour and sugar, then stacked smaller ones labeled "Yeast" and "Salt" on top of them. "What did you have in mind to go with these hot rolls?"

"Maybe, since I'm using yeast anyway, cinnamon rolls for dessert." She grabbed the light and lit the way back to the kitchen for him. "I'm planning on a nice pot roast with potatoes and carrots."

"If it wasn't for the damage, I'd say that I love hurricanes," Alex said.

"Just because of pot roast?" Tabby asked.

"That, and hot rolls," Alex said with a smile as he set the canisters on the counter. "And the company. I see people almost every day, but they're only there a day to go out on the fishing boat, and we mostly talk about fish all day. This is kind of like family."

"Yes, it is," Tabby said, remembering the days when she had a family, back before it had been ripped away from her in a single minute. Her heart caught in her chest, and for a very brief moment, she relived when the police came to tell her that her sixteen-year-old daughter had been killed in a car accident. She took a deep breath to clear her head and changed the subject. "Have you been up to Cleo's room to get your fortune told?"

"Yep," Alex said with a nod. "I'm going to live a long life, find love in a strange place, and enjoy grandchildren. Typical fortune. Have you ever had yours told?"

"Nope, but now I think I know what to expect." Tabby measured warm water and poured it into a big bowl, then added yeast and sugar. Her past had been so devastating that she wasn't sure she wanted to know what the future held—

especially if it was going to deliver more pain and heartache. "I hope that I will live to be an old woman, but I don't expect to find love or to ever have a grandchild."

"Is that another long story?" Alex asked.

"Have you ever read a book series that has like, maybe six or seven novels in it?" she asked, not even sure if she wanted to drag up everything that had happened since Natalie died two years ago. Alex wouldn't want to hear all about how from her childhood she had felt so much like a nuisance to her parents, or that she'd let a man manipulate her life so that her daughter would never have to feel like she had.

"Of course," he answered.

"Then consider that story to be told in the fourth or fifth book," she told him and changed the subject again. "It sounds like the rain has about stopped. If the sun comes out this afternoon, do you think we can take some of the boards off the windows? This darkness is depressing."

Alex took a while to answer but finally said, "I suppose we could uncover the windows even if it's still cloudy. I was able to get a call out to Ricky this morning. He's my friend who's in the construction business, and he says that most things on the east side of town got hit pretty hard. That includes my house—my boat is completely gone. The center where the old folks lived is demolished. The concrete foundation is still there, but it's covered in water. The rest is just a pile of rubbish. I've kept the news to myself because they're having so much fun, and I didn't want to spoil the day for them."

Tabby shook her head in disbelief, and her chest tightened. She didn't need Cleo to tell her what her future held—at least for the next couple of weeks—because there was no way she could just throw the four seniors out of the B and B. She finished adding the rest of ingredients and plopped the ball of dough out onto the cabinet. Kneading it didn't do a bit of good to ease her frustration. "What will we do with them now?"

"Give them a few days to figure things out, I guess," Alex said with a shrug. "Whoever built that center should have realized that a frame building wouldn't withstand a hurricane. I wonder if Cleo had good insurance. And why are you so angry?"

"I'm not," she protested, then shook her head. "That's a lie. I am upset. I hate change, and even though I knew coming to Sandcastle was a good move for me, it hasn't been easy. Ellie Mae and I got busy with our remodeling plans, and we didn't have any of that done when"—she waved her flour-covered hands around the room—"this all happened. Too much change, and there's nothing we can do but accept it." She picked up the dough ball, plopped it into a bowl, threw a towel over it, and set it to the side to rise. Then she washed her hands, dried them, and sat down in a kitchen chair.

Alex poured a glass of sweet tea and set it in front of her. "You ever stop to think that maybe the universe is working out something in your life?"

"Thank you for the tea and that thought," Tabby said with a sigh and, for the first time in a long while, hoped that he was right. "I needed both."

"Everyone else has had their fortunes told except for you and Maude, and just between me and you, I don't expect her to want to deal with Cleo. Are you going to tell me what your future looks like when Cleo looks into her crystal ball?" Alex asked.

Bless his heart—and she meant that in a good way—he was trying to divert her attention from all the thoughts chasing through her head about the changes in her life.

"Sure, I will"—Tabby turned up her tea and took several long gulps—"but I'm still trying to deal with the past, so I'm not so sure I want to know what the future holds."

"Aren't we all? But I'm sure her fortune-telling is all just a fun thing." Alex pushed back his chair. "After all, no one really knows what tomorrow holds, do they?"

Tabby shook her head. "No, we don't—and thank God or the universe or whoever keeps it in the dark for us for that. If we knew some of the things that are headed our way, we'd just want to climb into bed with the covers over our heads." The completely empty and desolate feeling that had drained her when the policeman told her about her daughter began to pull at her again. If she'd known that evening what the future held, she would never have let Natalie leave the house. She would have never let James talk her into moving in with him and taking complete control of her life for those seventeen years.

And I would have fought with James harder about giving Natalie a car for her sixteenth birthday, she thought as she finished off her tea and put the glass in the dishwasher.

"Ready to go find out about a tall, dark, handsome man that will sweep you off your feet?" Alex offered his arm to her.

She tucked hers into it. Her heart skipped a beat, like she had expected it to when Alex kissed her out in the barn all those years ago.

"Cadillac or pickup truck?" Alex asked when they reached the bottom of the stairs.

Tabby wondered if she'd been so deep in her own thoughts that she had missed whatever he had said before. "I'm sorry. What's a Cadillac or truck got to do with—"

Alex chuckled and pointed to the lift chair. "Cadillac." Then he pointed toward the stairs. "Pickup."

"I've always been partial to a truck," she finally said with a smile.

"Me too." Alex covered her hand with his free one, and together they climbed the stairs. When they reached Cleo's door, he let go of her hand and said, "In six months, you'll look back on this time and think that the path this hurricane picked you up and set you down on was a miracle."

He brought her hand to his lips and kissed her knuckles, and the rush that she had expected with that first kiss was there—arriving a few years late, but there all the same. He dropped her hand, and Tabby watched him disappear down the stairs.

"I hope that's what Cleo tells me about the future," she whispered as she pushed a curtain of multicolored beads covering the door to the side and entered Cleo's room. A filmy red scarf covered the lantern on the dresser, where more beads hung from the mirror as well as from the door into the bathroom. Chakra symbols on a brightly colored tapestry covered the bed. Cleo sat on a bright purple velvet pillow on the floor. A shiny gold base held a lighted crystal ball the size of a basketball on the floor in front of her, and soft music played in the background.

Cleo motioned toward a row of pillows on the other side of the ball. "Have a seat, Tabby. You look like a person who would love yellow, so sit on that pillow." She lowered her voice to a whisper, almost as if she were trying to hypnotize Tabby. "Let the music soothe your soul and take you to a peaceful place. Listen to the gentle waves washing up on the shore. Not crashing, like they're doing now, but bringing peace and happiness to you. My ball tells me that you are too full of fears and regrets for me to get a good reading, so close your eyes, and together, we will empty all that from your vessel."

Good luck with that, Tabby thought as she sat cross-legged on the yellow pillow and closed her eyes. At first, she couldn't shut out the idea of how they were going to deal with these old folks for weeks instead of days. Then her mind jumped tracks, and she thought about Alex and wondered if his business was destroyed, too, and if he would be staying on to help at the B and B. The idea of him being there with her to help take care of things soothed her as much as or more than the music. The soft, ethereal music evoked Natalie going through a meditation phase when she was about fifteen. Her daughter had listened to similar music and sat cross-legged, her middle fingers and thumbs touching as she meditated. During that time, the television had to be turned off, and the house had to be totally quiet. Tabby touched her thumbs with her middle fingers and imagined her beautiful daughter sitting on the third pillow beside her.

James's voice popped into her head, and she felt her body stiffen. *Go away,* she thought. *I don't want you here to spoil my memory.*

You have always been too uptight for anyone to live with, and you've never learned your place in our marriage. I wish we would have buried you today instead of Natalie. His words stung now as much as they had the night after Natalie's funeral.

That had been the beginning of the end of their marriage—his words, the last nail in the coffin. Was remembering that part of "emptying her vessel"? She mentally took the thoughts about her ex, put them in a trash bag, and carried them outside to the bin. Finally, it seemed that the music really crept into her soul and calmed her spirit.

Cleo's voice changed into something even raspier than just a whisper. "Open your eyes slowly, and look right into the crystal ball."

Tabby didn't want to leave the peaceful state she'd found, but she obeyed Cleo. At first, the crystal ball was a blur, but in a few seconds, it looked more like an oversize snow globe without the usual white flakes or a tiny Statue of Liberty or Santa Claus on his sleigh inside it.

Aunt Charlotte popped into Tabby's head. *You never know where you might prepare for a good future.*

Aunt Charlotte, who had been her rock after

Natalie's death and who had championed her divorce, was always welcome, whether it was in her thoughts, in phone calls, or in person. She had left Sandcastle and come to stay a week with Tabby during the funeral, and had called her every day for weeks afterward. She had resumed those calls when Tabby had filed for divorce and stood beside her when her own parents turned their backs on her. So whatever Aunt Charlotte had to say was appreciated.

Out of nowhere, Maude's voice broke her trancelike state, and for a split second, Tabby was aggravated, but then Aunt Charlotte's voice popped into her head again. *Don't let anger take away the happiness of this moment.*

"I don't believe in this bunk, but Duke here keeps running over to this room and whining outside the door, so we might as well get this over with so he'll be happy."

Cleo winked at Tabby. "If it's all right with Tabby, we can have a group session. She was here first, but this means your futures are most likely tied up together."

Maybe this fortune-telling stuff was real after all, because, as Cleo had said, every one of them, including Duke, would have a future—at least for a little while—tied up together.

"It's fine with me," Tabby said with a smile. "Should we start all over? I'll close my eyes and listen to the music."

Cleo pointed to the red pillow to her right. "Maude, I want you and Duke to sit down, close your eyes, and listen to the meditative music."

"I'm not listening to that witch music," Maude declared, "and I won't let Duke listen to it, either. He's named after the tough and mighty John Wayne. I bet *he* didn't listen to voodoo music."

Tabby patted the red cushion next to her. "It's not witch music. It's what folks listen to when they meditate. My daughter used to listen to it, and I was enjoying it with my eyes closed just before you came in. It totally relaxed me."

For the first time ever, Tabby understood that Natalie hadn't just been going through a phase when she'd meditated. She had needed to rid herself of the tension in the house, where James wanted to unconditionally rule the roost. *If only,* Tabby thought, *I had realized that this could help me as well, I might have tried it with her.*

"I promise I won't hypnotize you and make you cluck like a chicken," Cleo teased.

Maude spun around and started out the door. "I'm not even taking a chance on that."

"Oh, come on back and sit down. Loosen up and have some fun," Cleo said. "Are you really that afraid of me?"

"I'm not afraid of anything." Maude stiffened and whipped back around. "This is all a big Halloween hoax anyway. Nothing you say will come true, but I'll listen to your dumb fortune-telling. If Duke gets nervous, though, we are leaving. Dogs feel it when there's anything supernatural in their presence."

"That sounds fair," Cleo agreed. "Now, have a seat, and if you're not too old and decrepit, you can try to cross your legs."

"Hmph!" Maude huffed as she sat down, stretched her short legs out, and crossed them at the ankles. "Okay, what am I supposed to think about?"

"Nothing," Tabby answered and flashed on a vision of Alex helping her prepare supper the night before. Could that have been only yesterday? Surely it was at least a week ago, or so it seemed. The soft music relaxed her a second time, and she wasn't ready to open her eyes when Cleo asked to her look into the crystal ball.

Maude opened her eyes slowly as if coming out of a slight trance or maybe the beginnings of a doze. Duke was curled up in her lap with a paw over his nose, snoring loudly for such a small little critter. Tabby stared into the crystal ball for the second time, but she didn't see anything at all.

"I see a future that involves Maude and Tabby together right here on this property, but not in this house," Cleo said. "I see sunshine—not just natural but spiritual for both of you—and I see happiness for Tabby. Sometime in the future, she will have a big family."

"Don't you see happiness for me?" Maude asked.

"Yes, but I see a bridge that crosses over troubled waters, and you will have to decide which side you want to be on." Cleo waved her hands over the crystal ball and gasped.

"What?" Maude demanded. "Is Duke going to die? I only just got him, and I don't want him to die! Is that what you just now saw? He's not a young pup anymore, and Homer has no idea how old he really is."

"Duke will live awhile longer," Cleo answered.

"I don't believe in all that hocus-pocus about bridges and darkness and sunshine." Maude groaned as she got to her feet. "But I'm glad to know that Duke will live a long time. I didn't know how much I missed having someone to talk to until today."

"You've always got someone to talk to," Cleo said.

"Not someone who will listen without arguing," Maude snapped as she carried the dog out of the room.

"What did you see?" Tabby asked. "I saw your expression change. Was it something about me?"

"No, darlin', you've had enough darkness in your life." Cleo picked up her phone and turned off the music. "You've got rays of sunshine coming to you that will be so strong, they will make you forget the sad times and only remember the good ones. It was a little glimmer of something that will have to do with me and Maude, but I couldn't get a good grasp on it. I'm hoping that the two of us will wade through these issues and come through the fog and darkness into a brighter time in our old age."

"Do you really believe this stuff?" Tabby asked as she stood up.

Cleo shrugged. "It makes for a good time, and we all need to think our future is bright and sunny, not dark and drab."

Tabby went downstairs with a sense of gloom overshadowing the sunshine that Cleo had talked about. That night after they'd had supper, she would have to tell Cleo and the others about the Sandcastle Assisted-Living Care Center. Tabby was surprised that the town police hadn't already been by to tell Cleo about the center. Telling the folks certainly would not be a bright and sunny moment.

Chapter Six

E llie Mae removed a screw from the wood covering a window and turned to look over her shoulder at the gray skies. She wondered if maybe they were taking the coverings off too early.

"What does that sky remind you of?" Alex asked Tabby and Ellie Mae. The surf was still rolling in, in huge foamy waves, but the waves weren't touching the seawall anymore, and that was a blessing.

"The smoky ceiling in an old honky-tonk back when folks could smoke inside the place," Ellie Mae answered.

"You're not old enough to remember those days," Tabby said.

"Maybe not, but Sam and I loved to watch old Westerns on television." Ellie Mae removed the last screw from the wood over the window. "You know what I just thought of? Me and Sam worked together all those years, but not once did we build a beach house for someone or even work in a coastal town. I couldn't even get him to come to Sandcastle with me. Not much scared him, but he had a phobia about drowning. I forget what it's called."

"Aquaphobia," Alex said. "Why was he so afraid?"

"His uncle thought the way to teach him to swim was to throw him out into deep water," Ellie Mae answered. "He panicked and nearly drowned before his dad swam out and rescued him. Just hearing him tell the story and seeing the fear still in his eyes made me want to knock some sense into his uncle. No one should ever do that to a child."

"That's almost child abuse," Tabby said as she helped take down that last piece of wood.

"I agree." Alex shifted the slab of wood over to one side. "My grandpa waded out into the ocean with me when I was a little kid and held me in his arms while I dog-paddled back to shore."

"I had swim lessons," Tabby said.

"Me too, and ballet lessons and piano and all those things that Mama thought a girl should have," Ellie Mae said. "I know she was disappointed in me when I blew off college and went to work as a carpenter."

"It's not letting a lot of light inside the house, but on a gray day like this, even a little bit beats the darkness we've been living in," Alex said.

Ellie Mae thought of the dark days since Sam died and nodded in agreement. Even a little bit of light in her heart and soul was better than those first couple of days when she felt as if there was a stone in her chest rather than a heart.

"We'll take whatever light we can get," Tabby said.

"Such as it is and what there is of it, like Aunt Charlotte says," Ellie Mae added.

"I hadn't thought of that saying in years, but my grandpa used to come off with it when something wasn't quite right," Alex said. "Just having light in the house, even if it is kind of dim with these gray skies, will be nice. I'll make a deal with y'all: I'll climb up the old ladder and take down the upstairs coverings if y'all will tell Cleo and the others they don't have a home to go to."

"I'd rather climb up that rickety old ladder and haul those sheets of wood out to the barn all by myself," Ellie Mae said.

"No deal from this end," Tabby answered, "but we should all three be there when one of us tells them, and it should be today. They're going to find out anyway, and we should be the ones to break the news."

"What a way to bring in the new month." Ellie Mae sighed and thought of Sam again. How could her best friend, partner in work, and roommate be dead? She still couldn't believe that she'd never see him again. Maybe if his folks hadn't banned her from the funeral, she could have had some measure of closure. Now she just had anger at Sam for leaving her without even a warning. One minute they were talking about their day; the next he was gone—or so it seemed, when she looked back on that horrible time. "Think the old folks will still be here at Thanksgiving? We can't kick them out if they have no place to go."

Alex took a deep breath and spit out, "More bad news. The house I own and run my business out of is gone, too, and my fishing boat is demolished. Y'all think I could stay here and pay rent or maybe help with all the cleanup until the insurance settles with me?"

Before anyone could snap out of their shock to answer, Tabby's phone rang. She slipped it out of the hip pocket of her jeans, saw that it was Aunt Charlotte, and answered on the second ring. "Hello, Aunt Charlotte. We survived and we're uncovering the windows today. I'm putting you on speaker with Alex and Ellie Mae."

"Whoa, girl!" Charlotte said. "I know all that already. I've talked to a couple of friends who have already been out checking the damage. I also talked to Ricky, who helps Alex when we have to fix things after a storm, and he says that you'll have top priority in anything that needs to be done, so be sure to call him when you get a better idea of the damage. I understand the railings around the second-floor balcony are a mess, and the handicap ramp took a hard hit. And call the insurance company and take lots of pictures. Also, check the house roof carefully."

Ellie Mae bit back a smile. Aunt Charlotte might have turned the place over to her and

Tabby, but she hadn't really handed them the reins just yet.

"I'll take care of things, Miz Charlotte," Alex said. "And I've talked to Ricky. He'll be here tomorrow morning to help me with cleanup and repairs."

"I'm so sorry about your house and boat, Alex, but rest assured, you and the folks from the assisted-care place are welcome to stay at the B and B as long as you need to," Charlotte said. "I'll see all of you at Christmas. I'm not coming home for Thanksgiving this year with all the damage. Bye now, and I'm glad that y'all are all safe."

The phone screen went dark, and Tabby shoved it back into her pocket. "I guess we just solved the problem of where these old folks are going to stay, didn't we?"

Alex shook his head. "Not really. You and Ellie Mae need to make the final decision."

Ellie Mae and Tabby exchanged a look, and then Tabby said, "You know how to deal with the generator and the well, Alex, and you just said you would help clean up all this mess, so you can have room and board in exchange for helping us."

"Sounds fair enough to me," Alex said, "and speaking of the generator, I should refill it with fuel when we get all these windows uncovered."

"Light! I see light!" Cleo flung open the front

door and stepped outside. "Oh. My. Goodness! Look at the mess in the yard. When will it be cleaned up enough so you can take me to check on the center, Alex?"

"We need to talk about that," Alex said. "Could you gather everyone up in the living room in a couple of hours?"

Cleo stared right into his eyes. "It's ruined, isn't it?"

"Is that what you saw in the crystal ball?" Tabby asked.

"If the assisted-care center is demolished, then that's probably what I saw in the crystal ball, Tabby. It was something dark between me and Maude. Now that the center is gone, she'll probably refuse to live in the same place with me, and any possibility of us even being friends—much less sisters—before we die will be gone," Cleo said with a sigh.

If Ellie Mae hadn't been looking right at Tabby, she would have missed the compassion in her eyes. She opened her mouth to tell Cleo that she was right about the center being nothing but a pile of splintered wood and twisted bed frames, but Tabby spoke before she could.

"Y'all can stay here until you figure out a place to live," she said.

Cleo laid a hand over her heart and closed her eyes for a moment. "Prayers answered. Thank you, and I will write you a check today for what it costs us to stay at the center each month." She quoted a price.

"That's too much," Tabby said. "Only half that is about what we would charge for the rooms."

"But you'd only provide breakfast, and we want our three meals, like you've done the past couple of days," Cleo said. "And anywhere else wouldn't let us have our pets. You know what Duke means to Maude, and I'm really fond of Julep and her babies. I reckon we can figure out another arrangement for all of us within the month. So is it a deal?"

"Yes, ma'am," Ellie Mae answered.

"Good." Cleo's grin deepened the wrinkles in her cheeks. "I'm going to go tell the others the good news. We like it here better than the center anyway. It's so much homier." She disappeared back into the house.

"Well, I guess that job is done," Alex muttered. "I can't help but wonder what the next month will hold for all of us. Y'all got any predictions?"

"I do," Ellie Mae said with a smile. "I predict that we'll carry the pieces of plywood out to the barn."

"Not me," Tabby said. "I'm going inside to make a chocolate cake for supper, and I predict that everyone is going to love having some light in the house and a delicious dessert for supper."

Ellie Mae picked up one end of the plywood, Alex got a firm hold on the other, and they took it out to the barn, where a rack was waiting for all the window coverings. While they were there, she checked the rafters and was surprised to find them all dry.

"I expected a couple of leaks at the very least," she said.

"Charlotte got tired of replacing shingles and had a metal roof put on both the house and the barn the last time we had a tropical storm. It's considered the best kind to withstand hurricanes," Alex explained.

"What did the center have on it—or for that matter, your house?" Ellie Mae asked.

"Shingles on both, but it wouldn't have mattered in those cases," Alex said as he led the way down the narrow stairs. "They didn't have what this old dinosaur has got, and that's staying power."

Staying power.

That's what Aunt Charlotte had said when Ellie Mae's folks divorced and her mother moved back to Ireland. She had told Ellie Mae that she was a Landry, and Landry DNA had staying power.

"Your parents lacked staying power from the beginning. If you hadn't come along, they wouldn't have made it as long as they did, but don't you go blaming yourself for anything. What happened between them was their choices, not yours," she had told Ellie Mae right after her mother had left.

From there, Ellie Mae's mind shifted over to Tabby and James's divorce as she and Alex went back to the house. Rather than Natalie's death bringing them closer together in their grief, it had driven a wedge between them that wouldn't heal. The Landry family might be blessed when it came to financial security and the ownership of the Sandcastle B and B, but it sure seemed that they were cursed when it came to relationships.

Maude came out of her room with Duke trotting along behind her as fast as his short little legs would carry him. "I understand y'all have offered to let us stay here for a month while we figure out what we can do about moving. I want to thank you for that and to offer to rent my room from you for even longer, possibly permanently. Most places won't let me have a pet. Seems like we're safe here from the storms as well, and it's just a short walk to the beach. Now that we can go outside, Duke and I are going to go sit on the front porch and get some fresh air."

"I'll talk to Tabby." Ellie Mae had figured she and Tabby could just break even on their remodeling expenses the first year they were in business. With what Cleo had offered, they would be doing a lot better than that.

Maude gave her a quick nod, picked the dog up, and headed for the lift chair. "Are there any chairs left on the porch, or did that evil hurricane blow them all away?"

"Nope, but there's some extra lawn chairs in the basement," Ellie Mae answered.

"I'll bring some out for y'all," Alex offered.

"We'll be waiting," Maude said with a curt nod.

Ellie Mae wished she could help Maude and Cleo figure out a way to act like sisters rather than being so hateful to each other. Natalie's and Sam's deaths had taught her that life was short and that family was important; those two old girls weren't getting any younger.

Sam's sudden death still had her in a state of shell shock. She couldn't make rhyme or reason of why God or the universe would do that to such a good man who hadn't even reached thirty years of age. It just flat out wasn't fair, and thinking about it made her angry.

That would be the second step in grieving. Aunt Charlotte's voice was back in her head.

I may never get past this step, Ellie Mae declared.

Evidently, relationships were pretty much the same in siblings as in marriages, she thought, and when neither party would budge an inch, then there was a divorce. Of course, her father had always been married to his work, so nothing much had changed there. She sat down in one of the two wingback chairs in the wide hallway to think about the pros and cons of taking on older guests on a permanent basis. They would need to hire more help. She and Tabby couldn't keep up with the laundry, the meals, taking the folks to doctors' appointments, and whatever else the caretakers had been responsible for at the assisted-living center.

"Meds," she muttered, thinking of the time when one of them might get dementia and would need assistance with their medication. That would require a nurse, federal inspections, and all kinds of legalities.

She didn't hear Tabby coming up the stairs and wasn't even aware she was in the hallway until she caught a movement out of her peripheral vision.

"What are you thinking about?" Tabby asked. "You look like you're trying to solve the problems of the whole world."

"Maude," Ellie Mae answered.

"Me too," Tabby said. "She came through the kitchen on her way to the porch and probably told me the same thing she told you. I'm not so sure I'm ready for full-time residents."

"Me either, but I can't bear to break those two sisters' hearts or see them go to different places." Ellie Mae sighed. "Cleo wants to make amends, but it seems like neither of them know how. Where's Cleo now?"

"In the utility room with her cats," Tabby answered. "I'm thinking that if they can't be friends in a month, then it isn't going to happen. So let's not give Maude an answer for a while—

or any of the others, if they ask us for the same thing."

"I like that plan," Ellie Mae said and then cocked her head to one side. "I hear more than one guy's voice out in the backyard, and it's not Frank or Homer."

"That would be Ricky Benoit," Tabby told her. "He and Alex are talking about what all they need to fix the railings on the balcony and around the front porch. That big tree out in the backyard broke one of the back-porch posts, too."

Ellie Mae listened more intently. "That's a deep Cajun accent—one even more pronounced than Frank's."

"Yep, it is," Tabby answered. "From what little I overheard when Alex asked him about his family, their place didn't get hit too hard by the hurricane. They live up near Anahuac. He seems to be multiracial. He's got dark hair and nearly black eyes. A good-lookin' guy."

"So now you have a choice of tall, dark, and handsome or tall, sexy, and blond," Ellie Mae teased.

"Neither one, thank you very much," Tabby snapped. "And I might call Ricky *dark* and *handsome* but certainly not *tall*. He's probably only a few inches taller than you are. I'll let you have your choice of them, but be warned: I've decided Aunt Charlotte was the smart one. She didn't get married for a reason."

"And that is?" Ellie Mae asked.

Tabby leaned her head back on the chair. "Because us Landrys suck at relationships."

"Speak for yourself. I was very good at a relationship, and besides, your folks are still together," Ellie Mae reminded her.

"My folks have a law firm together, and they have a house together, but they have had separate bedrooms for years, and I haven't seen them show any affection for each other since I was a little girl," Tabby whispered. "Daddy has a girlfriend. Sometimes, I think Mother knows and just doesn't care as long as he doesn't rock the boat at the firm. And, honey, you and Sam were very good at a *friendship*. A relationship involves more than being roommates."

"You're kidding, right?" Ellie Mae gasped. "I thought Uncle Kenneth and Aunt Gloria were the . . ." She struggled to find the right word.

"Ultimate happy couple?" Tabby asked.

Ellie Mae nodded. "We are all cursed with more than just clumsiness, aren't we?"

"Yep, we're bad at relationships, but my Natalie didn't get the Landry DNA. She was as graceful as an angel," Tabby said.

"Are you telling me you and James were having issues before . . ." Ellie Mae laid a hand on Tabby's. "Before Natalie was killed? I thought that's what caused the divorce."

Tabby shook her head. "Looking back, I think

we started having trouble on our wedding day. He and his family were old-school. The man of the house had the final word on everything, and he didn't need to consult with the wife on anything—even if she worked and brought in as much of the bacon as he did. The husband made the decisions, and the wife lived with them and counted herself blessed to have a hardworking partner. I just brushed it under the rug, so to speak, and learned to live with it, but I had not been happy in a long, long time. The house was so full of tension that Natalie did meditation exercises. I didn't realize that she felt it so much, but looking back . . ." She shrugged. "Well, hindsight is twenty-twenty, isn't it? Enough of this depressing talk, though. It's snack time, and you know how Frank and Homer look forward to their little midday 'pick-me-up,' as they call it."

Ellie Mae followed her cousin down the stairs and into the kitchen, where Alex and Ricky were now sitting at the kitchen table with a notepad between them.

"Hey, Ellie Mae, come and meet Ricky," Alex said before making the introduction. "He'll be helping out with repairs and cleanup around here. We've taken stock of what we need, and maybe if he gets up to the lumberyard in Anahuac before too many other folks get in ahead of him to buy supplies, he can get everything we need."

Ricky stood up and stuck out his hand. "Nice to meet you, Ellie Mae."

"Glad to meet you, and thanks for helping Alex get this place put back together." Ellie Mae looked into the blackest eyes she'd ever seen and eyelashes that most women would sell their souls to have.

"No problem. I always put Alex at the top of the list when he needs help. He saved my brother's life in Kuwait when they were deployed over there, so he's family now," Ricky said.

Chalk up another story in this dysfunctional group of folks staying at the B and B, Ellie Mae thought.

"Hey, hey!" Homer called out as he and Frank came in from the porch. "We're here to offer our help with the cleanup. We might have to take more breaks than you guys, but we can sure do more than sit on the porch and listen to those two old women bicker."

Alex nodded. "Thanks for that. We'll sure take you up on the offer. The first thing we need to do is cut up that tree that fell against the back porch. Think y'all could throw a few branches over on Ricky's flatbed truck so we can get it out of here? We'll get busy on it tomorrow morning."

"You bet we can," Frank said with a grin.

Ellie Mae headed to the pantry to bring out the container of peanut butter cookies Tabby had made the day before. She met Tabby in the doorway and whispered, "You were right about Ricky, but he's taller than you said."

"Was I wrong about the *dark* and *handsome?*"

Ellie Mae fanned her face with her hand. "No, ma'am. You were not."

"I ain't never seen anything like this," Frank said as he looked around the yard. "I'm not surprised that Delilah took out the center where we lived."

"Yep, you have seen something even worse than this," Homer corrected him.

"Not storm as in hurricanes." Frank sat down on the porch steps.

"Want to talk about it?" Alex asked.

"We saw some ugly stuff in the war," Homer said. "We thought we were best friends when we enlisted together and got sent to the same posts, but we wouldn't have got through what we saw . . ."

"And what we had to do," Frank whispered, "if it hadn't been that we had each other to lean on when we got home."

"I feel sorry for guys who came home to relatives who didn't understand. Remember, back then we didn't have the resources you guys have," Homer told Alex.

"Did you two ever disagree on anything?" Alex asked.

"Yep. Pretty often, we argued about who was going to get a date with a certain woman," Frank chuckled. "Folks didn't look too kindly on interracial relationships back in the late sixties, not like they do now."

"But he was always pinin' after some busty blonde"—Homer sat down beside Frank—"and I kind of liked the same type. If it wasn't for our skin color, I would've sworn that we were twins who got separated at birth."

"Yeah, right, since *that's* the only thing that's different about us," Frank chuckled again.

Homer laughed so hard that tears came to his eyes. "Guess you got a point there."

Alex propped a hip on a railing. "Ricky's brother was my best friend during my time in the war. I wish he had lived to come back to this area so we could have talked things through like you guys."

"It helped," Frank said.

"Yep, and now we're old, and we should, all of us, forget those days and think about what good times we're going to have in the next few days," Homer said. "Don't tattle on me to Cleo, but I'm kind of glad the center is gone. I like it here so much better, but I'm right sorry that you lost your business and house."

"Thanks for that." Alex pulled a hankie from his pocket, wiped his forehead, and dried his eyes at the same time. Losing both his home and business wasn't easy for him, especially when he thought about all the good times he'd had out there on his boat, *Life Is Good*. His grandfather used to say that all the time. Every time he heard the song "Toes" by the Zac Brown Band, he thought of that saying. "I'm just glad this old place is still standing so we all have a place to stay until we figure out what we're going to do."

A vision of Tabby with flour on her nose and hands flashed through his mind and put a smile on his face.

Chapter Seven

Ellie Mae was more than glad to see sunlight streaming through her bedroom window on Thursday morning when she awoke. She made a quick trip through the bathroom and dressed in a pair of old jeans and a T-shirt.

That Ricky guy is pretty sexy. You could put on something a little nicer. Her mother's voice with her Irish lilt popped into her head.

"You don't get to tell me anything about guys. Not after you left me to figure out things on my own," Ellie Mae whispered as she stepped out into the foyer just in time to hear the first argument of the day.

"Sweet Lord," she said with a sigh. "Can't they be civil with each other at least until after breakfast? I might as well be living with Dad and Uncle Kenneth."

"I told you to keep that evil cat in the utility room," Maude hissed.

Cleo pointed toward Duke, who was in a stand-off with the mama cat, the hair on both their backs standing on end. "You're supposed to keep that yappy little dog upstairs or hold it in your arms."

Julep looked like a Halloween cat with her back arched, and between deep hisses, she bared her

146

teeth and didn't blink. Duke was on point as if he'd just squared off with an alligator. He wasn't moving a muscle except for his low growl, and his brown eyes dared the cat to make a move.

Maude popped her hands on her hips and glared at Cleo. "Pick up your cat before she scratches my dog's eyes out."

"*You* grab *that dog* before he kills my cat and leaves three babies motherless," Cleo snapped. "If he does, I'm going to make you get up for the night feedings for the little orphans."

"*You* will not make *me* do anything." Maude raised her voice above the din of a growling dog and a hissing cat.

Before either of them could say another word, the door swung open, and Alex stepped into the melee. Julep chose that opportunity to dash out of the house, and Duke started after her. Maude scooped up the dog when he ran past her, and Cleo took off after the cat as fast as her legs would carry her.

"What's going on?" Homer asked from the stairs.

"Looks to me like we just walked in on a double catfight," Frank replied.

Tabby came out of the kitchen and raised an eyebrow at Ellie Mae, who shrugged. "Frank called it right: it was a double catfight. Y'all can figure out how to soothe Maude's ruffled feathers. I'm going out to help Cleo."

She sure didn't want to have to get up every two or three hours through the night to feed three abandoned kittens. Lord have mercy! When she and Tabby said the seniors could continue living at the B and B, they sure didn't reckon on having to do night feedings for kittens or having a funeral for a mama cat.

"You can't leave," Maude called out. "I thought you were on my side."

"I'm not on anyone's side, but if we don't find Julep and bring her back, we'll all take turns bottle-feeding a litter of kittens—and that will include you," Ellie Mae answered.

If Maude and Cleo were going to act like petulant little girls, then she would treat them as such. Living with hormonal prepubescent kids couldn't possibly be worse than with this group of senior citizens.

Maybe they're reverting back to childhood. Aunt Charlotte's voice popped into her head. *I'm told that some old people do that.*

"Well, I hope they hit adulthood in a hurry," Ellie Mae muttered as she ran outside, pushed away tree limbs, and made her way across the muddy yard toward the barn.

"Cleo, wait up," she yelled.

Cleo either didn't hear her or didn't want to slow down. She ran across the wet ground and through mud puddles like they weren't even there. The legs of her overalls were a mess when she reached the barn doors and threw one open.

When Ellie Mae stepped in a deep puddle and dirty water splashed halfway to her knees, she realized that she'd dashed outside in her bare feet and wished that she could put Maude and Cleo side by side on the sofa and make them hold hands. That's what her nanny had done when she was a little girl and argued with her best friend, Jolene.

"Hey, Cleo, where are you?" Ellie Mae yelled as she let her eyes adjust to the darkness in the barn.

"Back here in the corner with my Julep," she hollered. "She's curled up in a bed of loose hay. I bet that's where she planned to have her babies—behind this old wood-burning stove—but she couldn't get in here. Why would Charlotte have hay back here?"

Ellie Mae followed the sound of her voice, stumbled over the ladder, regained her balance before she fell, and finally made it to the back of the barn. "I have no idea, unless she got a couple of bales to decorate the porch with for fall. When we came for Thanksgiving, she always had everything all prettied up."

Cleo sat down on a hay bale and started petting Julep. "Damn that dog for scaring my pretty girl. Look, her feet are all muddy from running through the mud puddles."

"So are ours," Ellie Mae pointed out.

"Yes, but we don't have to wash our jeans or our feet with our tongues," Cleo said and then laughed out loud. "Look at us, Ellie Mae! We look like two little girls who waded in mud puddles on the way home from school."

"Did you ever do that?" Ellie Mae asked, sitting down on the other end of the hay bale.

"Oh, yeah, and it made Mother and Maude furious. They were both so uptight, it was downright pitiful," Cleo answered. "Did you ever wade in mud puddles?"

"No, ma'am." Ellie Mae shook her head. "My nanny would have made me clean myself up and then stand in the corner or made me wash woodwork or do some other kind of housework that involved a bucket of water. I hated housework, so I minded her like she was a general and I was a recruit in the army."

"Your nanny?" Cleo asked.

"Mother and Daddy both worked long hours. I had a nanny until I was thirteen. That was the year of the divorce, and Mother went back to Ireland to live. Believe me"—Ellie Mae could feel her eyes bulging—"that last nanny scared the bejesus out of me. I was convinced that she was a witch after the sun went down. She had a long, sharp nose, and there had to be eyes under that dark bun she wore at the nape of her neck because I couldn't get away with any- thing."

"You poor darlin'," Cleo crooned. "Since we're already in a mess, we will stomp in the puddles between here and the house on our way back. You have been deprived of one of life's greatest pleasures."

"I would love that." Ellie Mae did not want to wake up to another catfight—human or animal—and since they were going mudding together, maybe Cleo would be in the mood to listen to her idea about the cats. "What if I ask Alex and Ricky to take all the boards off the windows of this barn before they start their other jobs this morning, and we move Julep and her babies back out here? You can come out and feed her and visit with her every day. That way, she won't try to move the kittens somewhere else. They'll grow up wild if we don't tame them from babies."

"Maude would gloat." Cleo squinted and looked around the huge, open space. "But I suppose that would be a good idea. Just how big is this place, anyway? Is that a twenty-foot ladder in the middle of the floor? If it is, then the barn must be at least sixty feet long—maybe even longer."

Ellie Mae nodded and reached back to pet Julep. "Yes, ma'am, it is a twenty-footer, but we're not going to use it again. One of the rungs broke when we were climbing down it before the hurricane hit. I think it might have been around when the Landry family went into the boatbuilding business. They built the boats somewhere else but hauled them up here to do the finish painting, varnishing, and all that in a dust-free building."

"I see some possibilities." Cleo stood up and studied every corner of the darkened barn by the light coming through the door. "We'll talk about that later. For now, would you please go bring the babies and Julep's food out here? Then we'll see what she does. We'll know right away if she's happy with them being here. Damned dog, anyway, but I wouldn't mind coming out here where it's quiet to visit her every day. I like a little alone time once in a while. I could bring my sketch pad, and . . ." She paused. "You know something . . . I'd like to do that right now. I need to see what my idea looks like on paper. Maybe we could stomp in the mud puddles later."

Ellie Mae stood up. "You draw?"

"Not as in people, fruit, or landscapes, but I had to sketch out the plans when we set up the carnival. Sometimes we had five acres to use, but more often, it was a couple of town lots or maybe even a stretch of Main Street. I had to figure out where to put the rides and the booths, and where to set up our trailers," Cleo said.

"And what are you going to sketch out here?" Ellie Mae's eyes had adjusted to the dim light now.

"An idea for my future," Cleo answered.

● ● ●

Tabby looked up from the waffle iron and raised an eyebrow when Ellie Mae arrived without Cleo or Julep. After that little spat this morning, she was all for telling Maude that she would need to have a place lined up to move into by the first day of December. A ruckus like that could sure be bad for business if there were folks other than the current residents in the B and B.

"Did you have to tackle Cleo in a mud puddle?" Tabby asked. "Please tell me that she's okay and the cat hasn't headed for Houston."

"I did not do any mud wrestling. Cleo is fine and so is Julep," Ellie Mae answered. "Cleo and I have made the decision to take the babies and Julep's food to the barn."

"Thank God!" Alex said as he drained bacon on a paper towel. "That will put some distance between those two animals."

"Are we talking about women or cats and dogs?" Ellie Mae asked.

"Both," Tabby answered.

"Cleo has agreed to take care of them out there, but we would like to ask that the first job Alex and Ricky do tomorrow is take the coverings off the windows so that the cats will have some light." She set the bowl of food in the basket with the tiny kittens.

"Gladly, if it will help put a stop to those old ladies' arguments," Alex said.

"Would you please take one of those plastic lawn chairs out to the barn when you finish helping Tabby with breakfast?" Ellie Mae asked. "I'm going to stay out there with her for just a little while, and she says that she's going to come inside and get a sketch pad to do some drawing. Don't ask me what she's going to draw, because she was all secretive about it. But the only place she has to sit right now is on a bale of hay."

Alex nodded. "Will do. I'll follow you out with a couple of chairs right now, and we'll get to taking the wood off more of the windows as soon as Ricky gets here. Some time alone will be good for both Cleo and Maude."

"That's what Cleo said," Ellie Mae said.

Maude came into the kitchen without Duke and asked, "What did Cleo say? Was she talking about me?"

"No, ma'am," Ellie Mae answered. "She said that she just needed some alone time with her cats. I'm taking the kittens out there right now."

"Well, as soon as I have breakfast, Duke and I are going to sit on the porch for *our* 'alone time,' " Maude said.

"You be careful out there. We don't want a tree limb to fall on you," Ellie Mae said.

"We will," Maude said as she sat down and helped herself to a double waffle.

"Where are you going, Ellie Mae?" Homer

asked as he came around the end of the house with Frank right behind him.

"Out to the barn," Ellie Mae answered.

"Looks to me like you might ought to spray some of that mud off before she hits the shower, or me and you will have to put our plumbin' skills to work." Frank grinned.

"Our 'skills' in that area means we know how to use a plunger," Homer told Ellie Mae as she carried the basket around the edge of the biggest mud puddle.

Homer and Frank fell in behind her and followed her to the barn. Once inside, Homer whistled through his teeth. "Wow! This is four or five times bigger than our convenience store and apartment in the back of it."

"Must've been some big boats they brought in here," Frank said. "Too bad it's just sittin' here and ain't bein' used."

"Want for us to go into the boatbuilding business?" Homer asked.

"No, I was thinkin' maybe we could live in this place." Frank continued to look around.

Ellie Mae took the kittens back to where Julep and Cleo waited and set the basket down. The mama cat hopped inside and started washing her babies.

"It's got a woodstove we could use for cooking and warmth, and we could throw out some sleeping bags on the floor," Homer said.

Cleo shook her finger at them. "You two stop that kind of talk. We're all too old to sleep on a bare floor."

"Speak for yourself." Frank chuckled. "Me and Homer is tough as rusty nails."

"On that note, Ellie Mae and I are going into the house and having us some breakfast. You two can babysit Julep and be sure she don't try to move the babies," Cleo told them.

Ellie Mae had a sudden flash of nervousness when she thought about Maude still sitting at the table having her breakfast. They sure didn't need those two old gals to start throwing food at each other.

"You look worse now than you did earlier," Tabby said when Cleo and Ellie Mae came into the house looking like they'd just taken a mud bath, both giggling like little girls.

"We really did wade in the mud puddles, and it was liberating," Ellie Mae said. "You should try it sometime."

"We didn't just wade. We stomped and danced and sang 'Lizzie and the Rainman.' Did you hear us?" Cleo asked and belted out a few lines of the old song by Tanya Tucker.

"Didn't hear a word, but I wish I had," Tabby said with a grin. "Better yet, I wish I'd videoed it."

"Maybe we'll do it again next time a hurricane washes up half the Gulf into our yard," Ellie Mae

156

said, "but for now, we're going to get cleaned up. Is there enough batter left for us to have a waffle?"

"Yes, and there is sausage and bacon on the stove. When y'all come back, I'll have a couple of waffles ready for you. Did you get Julep all settled in?"

"Oh, yeah," Cleo said with a nod, and the two of them headed out of the kitchen, leaving muddy footprints in their wake.

"And I thought raising one kid was tough," Tabby muttered as she mopped up the mess.

Cleo was the first to make it back to the kitchen. She poured herself a cup of coffee and carried it to the table. "Julep seems to like it out there in the barn. That is one huge building."

"Yes, it is, but I guess the Landrys before us needed a big one to finish up their boats," Tabby said. "About all we use it for these days is storing a few things, like the wood coverings for the windows and doors when we get a hurricane warning."

"Have you got a tape measure in the house?" Cleo asked.

"Probably in Aunt Charlotte's toolbox in the basement, but I would imagine Ricky has an extra one or two if you want to borrow one. What are you going to measure?" Tabby asked.

"After I finish eating, I'm going to measure the entire length and width of the barn, and then

I'm going to do some sketching while I talk to Julep," Cleo answered. "I don't want her to think I've abandoned her."

"Why would you see exactly how big the barn is?" Tabby asked.

"Because I've got an idea for something, but I don't want to say too much until I see if it's even possible," Cleo answered.

Ellie Mae's hair was still wet when she arrived in the kitchen. "Where's Maude?"

"She and Duke are on the front porch." Tabby removed a waffle from the iron and set it in front of Cleo.

"I hope she stays away from the beach." Cleo slathered her waffle with butter and then covered it with maple syrup. "I could hear the waves hitting the shore. I'd guess they are probably still rough. As mad as I was at that mutt for scaring my Julep this morning, I wouldn't want Duke to be washed out to sea."

Sam's fear of water came to Ellie Mae's mind. Sam had been a big guy, and if she hadn't seen him shiver at the sight of a pool in a backyard where they were doing carpentry work, she would have never believed he was afraid of anything.

"What about Maude? Would you feel bad if she got washed out into the deep water?" Ellie Mae asked.

"The jury is still out," Cleo answered and shot Ellie Mae a sly wink.

Alex had had sore muscles before, but not even a day out on his fishing boat wore him out like working on that ancient live oak tree. The roots that were sticking up out of the ground towered above his head, and he was over six feet tall. Some of the limbs were as big around as his waist. He wished for a deep bathtub, or maybe a hot tub with lots of jets, as he stood under the shower that evening and let the hot water work on his shoulders.

"I shouldn't stay in here too long, or I'll have to refuel the generator, and we're getting low on gasoline." He turned off the water and stepped out into his small bathroom. He dressed in a pair of loose-fitting pajama pants and a baggy tank top and eased down the stairs as quietly as possible. He poured himself a glass of sweet tea and carried it out to the back porch. The sound of waves slapping against the beach and rocks filled the air, but the surf was a lot calmer than it had been even that morning. He took a deep breath to get a salty whiff of the ocean—or the Gulf, as some people would argue.

"If it's salt water, it's ocean." He repeated his grandfather's words.

"That's what Aunt Charlotte says," Tabby said from the far end of the porch. "If a hurricane forms out there in the ocean and hits us like this one did, then what we're smelling tonight is salt air, and therefore, we are hearing an ocean surf."

Alex stood up and moved his lawn chair down to where she was sitting. "Why did you choose to sit way down here?"

"The breeze is better in this area," she answered. "You can't sleep, either? What's keeping you awake? After the day you guys put in with that tree, I figured you'd be so tired that you'd be snoring as soon as your head hit the pillow."

"I've got decisions to make about whether I want to stay in the fishing business or take my insurance money and do something else. Ricky would like for me to go into the construction business with him, but as sore as all my muscles are tonight, I'm not sure I'm still young enough to do that kind of hard labor indefinitely," Alex said. "What about you and Ellie Mae? Are you going to let Maude live here permanently? And if you do and the others ask for the same thing, are you going to say yes to them?"

"Don't know," she answered. "Like you said, we've got some decisions to make, but we've got a month to make them, so we have time to think about it."

Alex hadn't felt so comfortable with a woman in his whole life, and he wanted to know more about her. "Since we can't sleep, could we maybe talk about chapter two of our life stories?"

"You go first. I believe you were telling me about staying with your grandpa when your mother remarried. Does she still live in Atlanta?" Tabby asked.

"No, she and my stepdad moved to Memphis and then to Washington, DC. That's where they are now. And I do love her—she's my mother. But she's more like a stranger. I'm actually closer to Miz Charlotte than I am my mother," Alex answered. "Grandpa died the week after I finished high school . . ."

"I'm sorry," Tabby said. "You don't have to remember those rough times."

He took a long drink of his tea and then set the glass on the porch. "I want to get through this chapter so I can hear *your* story. I was an only child who got to roam the beaches, so all those kids at school overwhelmed me, and their games were silly to me. I hated shoes and long pants and wanted to be home with Grandpa. High school wasn't much better, but I did learn to love to read when I reached that level."

"Did you read a lot?" Tabby asked.

"Yes, I did, right up until Grandpa died just after I graduated," Alex answered. "He must've realized that I was too young and immature to take over the fishing business, so he had put everything into a trust for me, but I couldn't touch it until I was twenty-five. The house and his business were sold, and I was given a small allowance that would barely pay rent on a tiny apartment. I was angry at first, but looking back,

I realized that he was one smart cookie, forcing me to work and learn the value of a dollar."

"Did you go on to college that fall?" she asked.

"Nope, I walked into the recruiting office and joined the army . . . left for basic training the first of August that year. I planned to make a career out of it and show the world and my grandpa that I'd made something of myself." He remembered that day as clearly as if it had been yesterday.

"*Did* you make a career of it?" she asked.

He shook his head. "No. I didn't reenlist after I'd done my six-year stint—it ended when I was twenty-four. I grew up a lot during that time, made some friends, and came home to Texas after my second deployment to Afghanistan. Ricky's brother, Travis, was my best friend, and I really missed him. I saved his life once . . ." He paused and swallowed the lump in his throat. "But I was sick and confined to quarters the next time it needed saving . . ." The feeling he'd had when they came to tell him that Travis was gone washed over him again.

He took a deep breath and went on. "When he was gone, I didn't have the heart to reenlist. I went to work on a fishing boat—not like my grandpa had, but one that I took a crew out for a whole day to see what they could catch. Turned out that I liked the job. When I got my inheritance, I bought my own boat and named it *Life Is Good*. Now it's your turn. Did you go to college?"

Tabby twisted the cap off a bottle of water and took a drink. "I did. My folks were determined that I would be a lawyer, so I started out in prelaw. Then, my junior year, I met James. He was a senior majoring in business finance, and my parents came close to disowning me when I changed my field of study. Then, when I dropped out and eloped at the end of that year, they were *really* angry. James—now my ex—and I both went to work in a bank and had a daughter, and sixteen years later we divorced. End of chapter two."

"What caused the divorce? If that's too personal, you don't have to answer," he said.

"I told James we weren't buying our daughter, Natalie, a car for her sixteenth birthday." Tabby's voice had a hollow sound to it. "He bought her one anyway, without even discussing it with me, which shouldn't have surprised me."

"Why?" Alex asked. "Didn't he always spoil your daughter? I would think he would since she was an only child."

"Not at all. Very seldom, as a matter of fact," she answered. "But James was one of those head-of-the-house-type men, and since I told him not to buy the car, he was bound, damned, and determined to show me who was in charge and had the power. I should have known better than to buck against anything he suggested, because it just made him more determined to do whatever he wanted so I could learn my 'place' in the marriage."

"And that caused the divorce?" Alex asked.

"The first night Natalie had her license, she drove to her friend's house, and on the way home, a drunk driver ran a stop sign and hit her. She died on the way to the hospital. A woman who has lost her husband is called a widow. Children who lose their parents are orphans. But there is no word for mothers who lose children, because the grief is too hard to put a name on it. Our marriage hadn't been so good anyway, but that put it on the rocks," she answered.

Her voice was so full of pain that Alex wanted to take her in his arms and comfort her, but he was afraid that the timing would be all wrong. "I'm so sorry," he said. "I cannot imagine losing a child. The grief would be overpowering."

"It was," Tabby whispered. "I've been divorced for two years, and I jumped on the chance to come down here to run this B and B. I needed a change, but I've got to admit, I didn't think it would lead to babysitting two old ladies who seem to despise each other."

Alex chuckled. "They remind me of their pets. Think they'll ever get along like sisters, or just stay fighting like cats and dogs?"

"I have no idea how sisters get along, so I can't answer that," she answered.

"Doesn't it feel like you and Ellie Mae are

sisters?" he asked. "You sure act more like siblings than cousins."

"Not really, and if all sisters act like Cleo and Maude, I don't want us to be." Tabby covered a yawn with her hand. "I'm going back inside."

"I think I'll sit out here awhile longer," Alex said.

"See you at breakfast, then," she told him, then disappeared into the house.

Alex pulled his phone from his pocket, scrolled down through the caller list, and looked at the name and picture that popped up for a long time. She would know about the hurricane since it had been all over the news, and she'd be worried about him. Bless her heart. She was an old soul, and as a military child raised mostly by a single mother, she'd had to grow up too fast. He hated to think of her worrying about him having no home or business. With a long sigh, he finally hit the call icon and waited for her to answer.

"Dad, are you all right? Why are you calling this late?" his daughter, Jazzy, asked.

"I forgot about the time change from here to Maine," he answered. "I just wanted to hear your voice tonight. How were your first weeks of college?"

"I was actually still up and studying for a test tomorrow," she said, "and I could use a little break. I hate psychology, but I love my science

165

classes. And, Daddy, I miss Declan so, so much. I wish I'd gone to Baylor in Waco with him. How are things in Texas?"

"We got hit by a hurricane, and I lost my house and my boat," he said. "Now I have to decide what I want to do."

"Come to Maine. You can get another boat and take crews out to fish for lobster," she said. "You know I'd love for you to be closer so we could see each other more often."

"It's an idea," he said, "but Texas is home, Jazzy. When are you coming to see me?"

"Thanksgiving," she answered, "like always. You still get me on Thanksgiving, and Mother gets Christmas."

"How is your mama?" When he thought of the mother of his child, he still wondered if they could have made a long-distance relationship work, but that bridge had been burned to nothing but ashes a long time ago. There was no sense digging up those old bones.

"She's decided not to retire with twenty years' service but to stay in for the full thirty. She won't be getting out until long after I finish college," his daughter answered. "I don't have any idea what she'll do with herself. She's been married to the army since she was out of high school."

"Don't I know it!" Alex said. "You better get on back to studying. I love you, girl."

"Love you, too, Daddy," she said.

Alex was afraid that it was too late to call Charlotte, so he sent a text: Why didn't you tell me about Tabby's daughter?

One came back within seconds: That's her story to tell, not mine. Does she know about Jazzy?

His thumbs were a blur as he typed: Not yet.

Charlotte's reply: That's your story to tell, but don't wait too long. It's easier to open the door of opportunity and ask it to come in for a glass of sweet tea and some brownies than to chase it a mile down the road.

He smiled and looked down at his empty tea glass and then wrote: Thank you.

Chapter Eight

Ellie Mae stared out her bedroom window at a quarter moon holding court for the millions of stars twinkling around it. The past few days seemed to have lasted a month or maybe even a year. *Do all hurricanes cause time to stand still?* she wondered. *Death sure enough does.*

When she thought about Sam even now, after a couple of weeks, minutes seemed to take hours, and a day felt like a year, and yet looking back, it went by in a flash, leaving her with nothing but a ball of anger in her gut. Aunt Charlotte had called every day, and when she offered to step down from the B and B, Ellie Mae had jumped on the chance.

"Hey, are you awake?" Tabby whispered as she eased the door open a crack.

Ellie Mae turned away from the window and motioned her cousin toward the rocking chair in the corner. She crossed the room and sat down on the floor, propping her back against the footboard of the bed. "Do you feel like it's been a month since it was just you and me in this big house?"

Tabby sank into the chair as if the weight of the world was sitting on her shoulders and pushing her down. "I really do. We've been so busy that the days have sped by, but it seems like these people have been here forever."

Her voice sounded almost as hollow as it had that night when Ellie Mae finally reached her house in Sallisaw after getting the call about Natalie. Ellie Mae had been working just over the border in Arkansas that month. Those had been the longest two hours she had ever lived. The only other time she'd felt so empty was when Sam's parents told her to leave the hospital. When Ellie Mae arrived at Tabby's house, her cousin had collapsed into her arms and said, "What am I going to do without Natalie?"

Just thinking about the devastation in Tabby's voice a little over two years ago made Ellie Mae get misty-eyed. "You've been talking about Natalie, haven't you? Did James or your folks call you tonight?"

"No. I told Alex about her, though, a-and . . ." Tabby stammered. "Oh, Ellie Mae, I still hurt every time I even think her name. Every time I see a shell on the beach, I think of the times when she would get so excited to find one."

"I understand," Ellie Mae said, her voice cracking. "I see Sam—not on the beach or near water, but . . ." She put her hands over her eyes and sobbed. "I shouldn't do this now. I need to be strong for you."

"Maybe we both need to get it out every so often until we are healed. It's the little things that make me turn into a weeping woman. Like walking past a candy store and seeing peanut butter fudge, which was her favorite." Tabby sat down on the floor beside her cousin, wrapped her up in her arms, and they cried together for the dozenth time. "I really thought"—she wiped her eyes on the sleeve of her shirt—"that I'd made progress and gotten past all the anger, but evidently I haven't gotten as far as I thought."

Ellie Mae clung to Tabby. "Me either. Please tell me that it gets better with time. Like you said, it's the little things, like buying food and not needing to pick up a quart of chocolate milk for him. Lord, I miss him so much. Does it ever go away?"

"It gets better, but then it comes back to slam against me again—like a hurricane," Tabby said. "I thought moving to this area would help, but it's going to take more than changing places where I live and work to make this horrible emptiness go away."

Ellie Mae scooted away from Tabby. "We've got to stop crying."

"Do you think the tears will ever stop when I think about her . . ." Tabby slammed a hand across her mouth. "You loved her, too, so you've got that grief and then Sam's on top of it."

"Natalie wasn't even my child, but I felt like she was more than a cousin. I still get"—Ellie Mae paused and swallowed several times—

"angry that God let her be taken from us so early." She paused again and then went on. "I've got a confession: I'd planned to buy a new truck two years ago and give my old one to her. Then James bought her that little compact car, so I just kept my old vehicle. I'm glad that she wasn't driving something I'd given her that night. I could have never forgiven myself if she had been."

"I would have told you no, just like I did James," Tabby whispered. "Natalie was a sweetheart and a wonderful daughter, but she was fearless, and I didn't think she should be turned loose with a vehicle until she had finished college. I told James a brand-new car would be a wonderful graduation present. But he had to be the boss."

"I remember when she was thirteen and wanted to do the zip line in Branson." Ellie Mae patted Tabby on the knee. "When we all reached the bottom of the ride, my heart was in my throat, but she wanted to go back and do it again. Her wreck wasn't because she was fearless or careless. It was because a drunk driver ran a traffic light."

Tabby wiped another tear away with the back of her hand. "Is it wrong for me to be glad that he died, too?"

Ellie Mae raised up on her knees and handed Tabby a tissue that she pulled from a box on her dresser. "No, it's not wrong, but I would rather have seen him suffer in prison for the rest of his life. Do you ever play *what if* in your mind?"

"I think we all do that, but what's it got to do with Natalie?" Tabby asked.

"Bear with me here, and I mean no disrespect, but this is the way I've been able to deal with Natalie and Sam being gone from our lives." Ellie Mae laid a hand over Tabby's. "What if that horrible accident hadn't happened, and the next month Natalie had been diagnosed with terminal cancer? We would have had to watch the life drain out of her day by day until there was nothing but a shell left of our fearless and precious girl. What if, in the end, she was on life support, and you had to make the decision to end it? And what if the same thing happened to Sam and I had to make that decision because his folks had passed away?"

"I couldn't do it," Tabby said. "James would have had to sign the papers for that."

"What if he couldn't do it, either?" More tears rolled down Ellie Mae's cheeks and dripped onto her nightshirt. "Maybe God was sparing Natalie and you of all that by taking her so fast that she never knew what happened. One minute, she was probably listening to her favorite radio station—maybe keeping time to the music on the steering wheel with her thumbs, maybe even singing at the top of her lungs to whatever song was on, and the next, she was an angel, singing in heaven's choir with her sweet soprano voice like she did in church on Sundays."

She remembered Sam clutching his head and then falling to the floor. Everything had happened so fast that getting him into the car and driving like a maniac to the hospital was a blur when she thought back on it. The ER was only a few blocks from their house, and she had thought in the moment she could get him there faster than an ambulance could come and go. Now she wondered if she'd done the right thing.

Tabby knotted one of her hands into a fist and slammed it into her other palm. "I just want her back in my life. I want to go shopping with her for her prom dress and help her fix up her dorm room. I want to someday see her in her pretty white satin bridal gown and plan her baby shower when she starts a family."

"We all do." Ellie Mae patted Tabby's hand again and then pulled out a couple of tissues for herself. "We have her and Sam in our hearts and in our minds. We have all those wonderful memories of that amazing child that we need to keep alive by talking about them and reliving them, and of the best big brother a girl could have, even if we didn't share a drop of DNA."

She wondered where Sam was that holiday. He'd loved Halloween so much. He would dress up, sit on the front porch, and hand out candy to all the kids in their neighborhood. She swiped a tear from her eyes and then took Tabby's hand in hers and stood up. "Let's take a walk on the beach like we did that last Thanksgiving we were here with her. Remember how Natalie begged to stay for the festival, so we went out in the middle of the afternoon and built a sandcastle before we had to leave? We'll pretend she's with us, and we might even make a sandcastle."

"People will wonder what we're doing," Tabby said, "and building a sandcastle won't bring her back to me."

"No one will even see us, and even if they do, who cares what they think?" Ellie Mae assured her cousin. "I'm the one who stomped in a mud puddle this morning with Cleo. People would have a whole bunch of opinions about that, too, wouldn't they? We won't even get dressed or put on shoes. We'll go as we are in pajama pants and faded T-shirts. We'll be as fearless as Natalie."

Tabby put her hand in Ellie Mae's and let her pull her up. "No bras? No shoes? Just us on the beach, trying to figure out a way to move on without Sam and Natalie, right?"

Ellie Mae nodded. "I can hear Natalie laughing at us and feel her pushing us out the door."

"And I can see Sam's bright smile, telling me that you're right—some of the time," Tabby said with a chuckle.

Ellie Mae laughed with her. "You got that right. Some of the time."

Ragged red flags flew from a pole set back from the edge of the water, warning people that it was too dangerous to be out in the surf. The sand was wet and cool on Tabby's feet, and the waves were still tall enough to crash against the sandbar instead of just lapping along at a sweet little speed.

Tabby pointed toward the flags. "This is how I feel."

"Natalie wants you to explain that statement," Ellie Mae said. "We're pretending she's here with us, remember?"

"The waves are the turmoil in my heart and soul. The beach is the peace I feel in this place. It's like an oxymoron of feelings. On one side, it's like heaven, but the other is hell," Tabby answered. "Parents shouldn't lose their children. It's against the laws of nature."

"Natalie agrees, but she wants to build a sand-castle." Ellie Mae sat down and began to scoop the wet sand up into a pile. "Natalie says to make it just big enough for one person because she intends to live in it. When you want to visit her, you have to come to the beach where it is peaceful and remember all the shells that she used to turn a shoebox into a jewelry case for you one Christmas."

Tabby sat down beside Ellie Mae. "I still have that jewelry box. I keep pictures of her in it. Why build a sandcastle? The tide will wash it away, or else some kids will come along and knock it down, so how will I visit her?"

Ellie Mae had already shaped a mound and picked up a piece of driftwood to use as a detailing tool. "She says that she's a free spirit, and that anytime you build one, she'll come live in it for a while."

Tabby finally smiled. "That sounds just like something she would say. She's talking to me now, and she wants to play *what if* with you. What if you hadn't been rebellious in high school and insisted that they allow girls to take wood-shop?"

"I would probably be a lawyer and maybe even be married to one of the partners in Daddy's firm, but I'm glad I didn't go down that path," Ellie Mae answered as she continued to work on the castle. "What if you hadn't taken that business class where you met James?"

"I'd be a lawyer myself, and would probably not have gotten pregnant and had a baby at twenty-one."

Ellie Mae stopped working and cocked her head to one side. "I kind of already knew that."

Tabby raised an eyebrow. "How did you know?"

"Premature babies don't usually weigh eight pounds, and you were showing way earlier than you should have been," Ellie Mae answered.

"I've never admitted that little bit of the past to

anyone. We always celebrated our anniversary in March and just kind of brushed the one in June under the rug," Tabby said with a sigh. "I wonder if everyone else figured it out as well."

"Don't know, but I doubt it. Both your folks and mine didn't pay much attention to us, especially when we both went against their wishes," Ellie Mae said.

"I've always wondered if James married me just because he thought it was the right thing to do," Tabby said. She shrugged. "That would go along with his thoughts about being the head of the family and the king of his castle."

"Did you keep it secret to protect Natalie or to keep your folks from fussing?" Ellie Mae asked.

"The folks," Tabby answered as she helped build a section of wall around the small sand-castle. "I'd planned to tell Natalie when she graduated from high school and went off to college. Someday she would have found our marriage license and figured it all out anyway, so that seemed to me like a good time to tell her."

Ellie Mae turned and looked at an imaginary dark-haired teenager. "What do you think, Natalie? Would that have upset you?" She pretended to listen for a moment and then giggled.

"What are you laughing at?" Tabby demanded.

"Natalie says that she figured all that out years ago when she was digging around in the shell box she made for you and found your marriage license. She says she is a liberated woman," Ellie Mae answered.

Tabby frowned. "That's exactly where my marriage license was."

"And she really found it," Ellie Mae said. "She told me about it and swore me to secrecy because she didn't want to embarrass you."

Tabby almost smiled. "I was so dreading the moment I had to tell her."

"She was about fourteen when she found it. She wasn't upset at all. She told me that she would live with her boyfriend for at least a year before she married him, and maybe would even have had a child or two to be sure that she wanted to commit to a lifetime with one guy." Ellie Mae stuck the piece of driftwood on top of the castle.

Tabby's smile faded, and she shivered. "James would have had cardiac arrest."

"Right now, she's whispering in my ear that she likes this castle very much, and we need to build one more often, and that we need to invite her to come with us when we do," Ellie Mae said.

"My mother-in-law would have abducted Natalie and put her in a convent if she thought her granddaughter was living with a guy and not married!" Tabby said. "But then, she'd probably have both of us committed if she knew we were on the beach, talking to Natalie as if she were here."

"Then we won't tell her. I never did like that

woman. She pretended to be all submissive, but she was really very good at manipulation." Ellie Mae stuck another slender piece of driftwood on top of the sandcastle. "That's Natalie's own personal cell tower, and that finishes our sandcastle. Think we should go back to the house and try to get some sleep?"

Tabby lay back on the sand and stared up at the stars. "Natalie and I did this one year, but it was during the day, not the middle of the night. We made sand angels that day. I wish I'd taken a picture of them."

Ellie Mae stretched out beside her. "You did. You snapped a photo with your mind that you can go back and look at anytime you want."

"James was angry with me for getting sand in the car," Tabby said, her voice going flat.

Ellie Mae swallowed three times to get past the lump in her throat. She hoped that someday he'd find a woman who backed him into a corner so he would know how Tabby felt all those years. "Tear *that* picture up and throw it away. You do realize that he was abusing you?"

"He never hit me, and seldom raised his voice," Tabby said.

"It was mental abuse," Ellie Mae told her. "I'm glad to see you can stand up for yourself now."

"It's still not easy," Tabby whispered. She sat up and gently laid a hand on the castle like Ellie Mae had seen her do when they visited

Natalie's grave. "Do you think we should build one for Sam? You might like to talk to him. It's cathartic."

"Not tonight." Ellie Mae sat up and then started to stand but stepped in a hole and fell backward. She landed on the west side of the castle, destroying half of it and leaving the other half in bad need of repair. She threw a hand over her face and started to cry. "I'm so sorry. I've ruined Natalie's castle."

Tabby rushed over to her side, grabbed her hands, and pulled her up out of the surf. "Don't worry about the castle. We can build another one. Are you okay?"

Ellie continued to sob. "Yes, but I could feel Sam's fear of drowning when I fell into the surf."

Tabby held her close, patted her back, and cried with her. "It's okay. Let it all out."

The sobs turned to giggles. "This is one of those laugh-or-cry moments, and Natalie is laughing at us."

Tabby took a step back and started to laugh with Ellie Mae. "Our fathers would say that we are crazy. There's nothing funny about this."

"We may well be." Ellie Mae pulled up her T-shirt and wiped her eyes on the tail of it.

"But ain't it a nice place to be?" Tabby said and began to sob again.

Ellie Mae took her by the hand and pulled her down beside the wrecked castle. "We can laugh or cry or do both. We are strong. We are Landrys. We will survive."

"Thank you," Tabby said, "and thank God we've got each other."

Cleo was sitting at the kitchen table the next morning when Tabby and Ellie Mae came in to start breakfast. "Well, hello to y'all," she said with a wide grin. This morning, she was dressed in baggy overalls, a long-sleeve red knit shirt, and cowboy boots. Her long fiery-red hair was piled up on her head in a bun and held in place with a yellow pencil. "You both look like crap this morning. Coffee is made. It's strong because I'm not used to making it in a pot on the stove. Please tell me you didn't have a drinkin' party without me."

Tabby had slept well after her late-night trek to the bench, but the morning had come too soon. "Good morning to you. And we just had an emotional night. No drinking involved"—she covered a yawn with the back of her hand—"and thank you for making coffee. I need a cup to get me going this morning."

"I heard y'all coming in after midnight," Cleo said. "Don't worry about keeping me up, though. I was working on my sketches, and I couldn't sleep anyway. I've never been one of those folks who need eight hours of sleep a night. Six hours is enough for me, and I can make do with four for a week or two. I was excited about my sketches."

Alex entered the kitchen from the foyer and went straight to the counter and poured coffee into two mugs. "Good morning, ladies."

"Mornin'," all three chorused.

"What have you been sketching, Cleo?" Alex asked. "Since you were in the barn most of yesterday, I figure it has something to do with it or Julep and the kittens."

Cleo flipped open the cover of the sketch pad. Tabby carried her coffee over to see what she'd drawn and was surprised at what looked like blueprints of a building—but not the B and B or anything she had ever seen before.

"I want to buy the barn," Cleo blurted out.

Tabby almost choked on a swallow of coffee. "You want to buy *what?*"

Alex peeked over her shoulder. "What are you going to do with it? That looks like you're planning on making it a two-story house."

"I am," Cleo said.

"I'm sorry," Ellie Mae said, "but Aunt Charlotte says that this property has to stay in the Landry family, and that includes the barn."

Tabby kept staring at the page. There was a rectangle that was marked "Pool Table" over at one end and a round circle with the words "Hot Tub" in another area. Why would Cleo want to turn the barn into a recreation center? Was she going for a weird honky-tonk, like they'd teased about? Was the hot tub for lady wrestlers in Jell-O?

Cleo took a deep breath and let it out slowly before she began. "Here's the deal: I might be an eccentric old lady, but I'm also rich as Midas. I don't want to live in a retirement center anymore. I just want the four of us who are staying here to have a place. Here, we can walk on the beach when we want. We have more freedom and a hell of a lot less people around us. So I want to buy the barn and remodel it. This is the sketch of what I want done on the bottom floor." She flipped the page over. "This is the four bedrooms upstairs. I will hire the supervisor we had at the center to work for me, as well as a full-time cook and housekeeper. When we are all four dead, you can do whatever you want with the property. It will never actually belong to anyone but the Landry family."

"That takes a lot of faith," Tabby said.

"Money isn't anything but dirty paper with dead presidents' pictures on it," Cleo said. "It's only good for whatever you can buy with it, and you can't buy happiness or peace. When we came here a few days ago, I felt peace when I walked into the house. I'm not asking for an answer today, but if you decide to let me do this, I will have my lawyer up in Anahuac draw up the legal papers saying what I just told you. She'll throw a hissy fit, but it's my money, and it's what I want to do."

"Are you sure that you would trust us that much? You've only known us a little while." Tabby thought maybe she was dreaming, so she turned to Alex for a bit of reality.

"It's your barn and your property, but it looks like a good deal to me," Alex said.

"I want Julep and her babies"—Cleo looked around the kitchen and lowered her voice—"*and* that yappy little dog to have a nice home. But don't tell Maude I'm doing this for her as well as myself. I know my sister doesn't have the money to live in a good retirement center. Mother had a long illness, and there was no money left after the doctor bills."

Tabby took a sip of her coffee and studied the sketch. Cleo had thought of everything from a small bathroom in each bedroom suite to a larger one at the end of the hallway that had a walk-in tub. She flipped back to the first page and pointed. "Is that a hot tub?"

"Yep, and right here"—Cleo pointed to another area—"is a pool table. You and your guests would be welcome to come out and join us anytime they want. They could even have lunch or supper with us if they wanted." She winked at Tabby and Alex. "Old people like Frank and Homer love to visit and tell stories." She quoted a figure, then went on to say, "I'm willing to hire Alex and Ricky to do all the remodeling for us. But if you think that's unfair, then we can negotiate."

"What's the catch?" Tabby didn't expect to make that much money in ten years with what she and Ellie Mae would charge for the four B and B rooms—and that was if they kept them all rented every single night.

"The catch is that we would have to live in the B and B until it is finished. I'm hoping we could be moved in by April Fool's Day because I think that would be a hoot, and y'all weren't planning on reopening until spring anyway," Cleo said. "I'm going to put this away. I don't want to get the old guys' hopes up or listen to Maude fuss and fume about living in the same place with me. You think about it for a few days, and let me know what you decide." She headed out of the kitchen at the same time Maude arrived.

"Wow!" Tabby gasped.

"That's a lot to think about, and even more to turn down," Alex whispered.

"Amen." Tabby was totally overwhelmed. She and Ellie Mae would have to take a walk on the beach after supper that evening and talk about the pros and cons for sure.

Chapter Nine

The pounding of hammers and screech of drills echoed all through the B and B that Friday afternoon. Every few minutes a fresh gust of wind made the tree limbs shiver, and palm fronds were still strewn about the yard toward the beach. Tabby could hear voices and laughter outside, but with all the commotion, she couldn't understand what they were saying. There was no doubt, though, that Homer and Frank were glad to finally be able to get out of the house, and that even with the hard work, Ellie Mae, Ricky, and Alex were enjoying themselves.

Tabby was very happy they were having a good time, but she would rather be inside, puttering about in the kitchen. She had never liked anything that had to do with outside work—lawnmowing, digging flower beds, raking leaves. Her folks had always had all those jobs done by a local gardener, and when she'd married James, he considered it "men's work." At first, she thought his old-fashioned ideas were sweet, but after a while, they soured. She was deep in her own thoughts when Maude came through the kitchen with Duke in her arms.

"All that noise is upsetting Duke," she grumbled.

"I realize it has to be done, but this poor baby hates all that noise."

A bright yellow ribbon was tied in a bow to the pink plastic collar with a gold buckle around his chubby neck. The poor little dog tucked his head, and Tabby was pretty sure that his face was scarlet down under all that reddish-brown fur.

"What have you done to him?" Tabby asked. "Would John Wayne wear that? It can't be comfortable for the little guy."

"Until I can get to a pet store and buy him something nicer, this will have to do. I made him a collar out of one of my old belts. You wouldn't remember when narrow belts were all the rage, but a few years ago they were, and I saw a picture of one of the princesses in England wearing one the other day, so they must be coming back in style. The ribbon is his leash," Maude answered.

"You think you can teach an old dog new tricks?" Tabby asked, thinking of what Aunt Charlotte had said about the next generation of Landrys. Tabby would be the "old dog" if she started all over with another baby at her age. She still remembered the baby, toddler, and teenage phases, and she wasn't sure she wanted to actually live through them again.

"If I can survive living with Cleo, Duke can learn to use a leash." Maude kissed the dog on the top of his head. "Come on, darlin'. This will protect you from getting swallowed up in the surf."

Duke's tail didn't even attempt a weak wag, but he did open one eye as if he were begging Tabby to do something. She figured he had been praying that there wouldn't be any dogs, cats, or even seagulls out that morning. Maude had barely cleared the room when the back door slammed and Cleo came into the kitchen. "I'm spittin' dust, darlin'. Is there any sweet tea made up, or do I just need to grab a bottle of water?"

"Tea and lemonade, both in the fridge," Tabby answered. "Help yourself. I was about to take a pitcher of each out to the porch for everyone. Thought they might be wanting a little morning pick-me-up."

Cleo filled one of the disposable red plastic cups with tea and took several long swallows. "Are the guys outside? And where's Maude and that pesky little dog of hers?"

Tabby smiled. "Frank and Homer are sitting out in the yard supervising the work going on up on the balcony. The storm damaged the railing in several places. Maude just took Duke out for a walk." She went on to tell Cleo about the collar and leash.

Cleo took a sip of her tea and then picked up a cookie from the plate on the counter. "I wish she and I could be like you and Ellie Mae."

"How's that?" Tabby asked as she set the two pitchers on a tray along with half a dozen red cups.

"You like and respect each other even though it's evident you didn't travel down the same path of life," Cleo answered. "Is it all right if I put some of these cookies on the tray? Homer and Frank love anything sweet. I know that they mentioned buying the barn, but if you sell it to me, I'll hire a full-time cook so the boys will always have homemade cookies."

"Go right ahead with the cookies. And I really think they were teasing about buying the barn," Tabby answered. She started to say more, but her phone rang.

Cleo picked up the tray and headed across the kitchen, then stopped. "Thank you so much for all you do to make us feel like we're at home. And, honey, I'm dead serious about that barn."

Tabby gave her a thumbs-up, slipped her phone from the hip pocket of her jeans, saw that it was Aunt Charlotte, and sat down at the table before she answered.

"Hello. Can you hear all the noise in the background?" she asked. "I'll send pictures as soon as Alex, Ellie Mae, and Ricky get the repairs all done. Did you get the before pictures I sent this morning before they started to work?"

"Got them, and we're lucky there wasn't more damage," Charlotte said. "I've been on the phone with Ellie Mae and Cleo. That's quite an offer she's making. I've often wanted to do something with that old barn but didn't want to shell out the money to do it, and we can't sell it. What's your thoughts on her idea?"

"Ellie Mae and I are going to think on it until Monday, but I can't help but wonder why four old folks would want to live in our backyard."

"My opinion is that they all want what they've basically never had," Charlotte answered. "None of them have ever been close. Frank and Homer are good friends, but neither of them ever married or had kids. In the past few days, they've seen what it would be like to have family around them—sitting down to family meals and living in a house rather than a glorified nursing home."

"So, you think we should do this?" Tabby asked.

"If I was still running the B and B, I would, but you and Ellie Mae need to make the final decision, not me," Charlotte said. "I just wanted to touch base with you this morning. I can always tell by the sound of your voice—and Ellie Mae's as well—if something is wrong."

"And how are things this morning?" Tabby asked.

"You sound better than I've heard you since Natalie left us. Ellie Mae is still struggling. She needs to mourn and to talk more about Sam. She won't say much to you because she knows you're still dealing with Natalie's death," Charlotte said. "I'm hoping she opens up to one of the old folks there."

"I loved Sam, too." Tabby told Charlotte about

the sandcastle she and Ellie Mae had built. "He was kind of like the brother she never had."

"I'm just glad he knew how to cook," Charlotte said. "What they had was more than just siblings, though. They were best friends, and even more than that. It was like their two hearts blended together. I kept waiting for them to take their relationship to the next level."

"So did I," Tabby said, "but their love just wasn't that sort."

"Maybe it's best that it wasn't. Her grief would have been even deeper if it had been," Charlotte said. "I've got to go now. Dolly, my neighbor, and I are going into town for a lunch date with a couple of other ladies. I'm so glad I moved. I miss my friends in Sandcastle, but the ones that moved up here are some that I've had since I was a little girl. Reuniting with them and not being tied down to the B and B is pure freedom. Watch Ellie Mae. Don't let her spend too much time alone. She needs people around her. It would probably be a good thing to have those old folks living in the backyard. They'd be like grandparents to you girls."

"Whether we go along with Cleo's plan or not, this change has been good for both of us," Tabby said. "So thank you for giving us this chance to move on with our lives."

"I knew it would be. Bye now. Hugs and love."

Tabby laid the phone on the table, made up

her mind how she was going to vote on the barn issue, and stood up to go outside. If having the old folks living in their backyard would help Ellie Mae, then she was all for it. She knew how hard it was to lose someone close to the heart, whether it was a child or a best friend.

She'd just opened the back door when she heard a humming noise. When she realized that it was the sound of the refrigerator motor starting to run, she let out a squeal and flipped the light switch on the wall. The whole kitchen lit up, and the wallpaper didn't even look as old and faded as it had when she'd first arrived.

"We've got power!" she yelled.

"What did you say?" Frank hollered from the yard.

Tabby stepped outside and pointed to the porch light. "We've got power!"

Cleo did a dance that looked like something between a belly dance and a Texas two-step all around the yard and sang "I Saw the Light" at the top of her lungs. By the time she got to the second line, Homer and Frank were both singing with her. Tabby was glad Maude had taken Duke for a walk, or she might have dropped down on her knees in the still-wet grass and begun to pray for the two old guys' souls. Tabby knew Maude well enough to know that she didn't care if Cleo went to heaven, so she wouldn't even get a mention in her sister's prayers.

"What's going on?" Ellie Mae yelled from the balcony.

"Lights! We've got power!" Cleo stopped singing and dancing, pointed to the porch light, and dropped down hard into one of the lawn chairs. "Whew! I'd forgotten that I'm not twenty-one anymore."

"You might be, if you used the Celsius thermometer instead of Fahrenheit," Homer told her.

"I like that idea, but I'm not so sure my body will listen to me when I tell it that." Cleo panted. "Soon as I catch my breath, I'm going back out to the barn to draw some more."

"What are you working on?" Frank asked. "Are you a famous artist? Are you drawing Homer in one of them Speedo bathing suits?"

Cleo shot one of her sly little winks toward Frank. "I'm not a famous artist, but I am pretty good at logistics. I'm working on an idea that I hope works out into a permanent plan. I should be able to show it to you after the weekend."

Homer swatted at Frank. "You shouldn't tease an old woman like that, man. In three days, we might not even be here."

"What I'm going to show you will be even better than Homer in a Speedo," Cleo said with half a giggle. "Three days without power isn't bad for a little community this far out."

"You're right," Homer said. "Frank, do you remember the last hurricane that came through here? We didn't have power in our store for a week—and we were up in Winnie, not right on the beach."

"I remember," Frank said with a long sigh. "But I'll kind of miss using the lanterns. They reminded me of walking home in the dark with just an old camp lantern to show us the way after we'd closed the café."

"Not me. I won't miss them one bit, and if I have my way, there will be no more hurricanes ever in Sandcastle, Texas," Ellie Mae yelled down.

"I can breathe easy now," Alex said. "We were about out of fuel for the generator."

"I'm glad to have it, too," Ricky said. "These tools are great, but we need electricity to charge the batteries when they run out of juice."

Tabby went back to the kitchen, picked up her phone, and called Aunt Charlotte. "We've got electricity, and everyone is happy. Cleo was so excited that she did a little song and dance," she said on a laugh when her aunt answered.

"I remember dancing around in the kitchen when the power came back on after the last storm," Charlotte told her.

"Did a storm ever hit when you had a house full of customers?" Tabby asked.

"Oh, yeah. We had a tropical storm about twenty years ago that took out the power lines for a week. All the rooms were full, and two little rowdy boys were in the house, along with several whiny women who kept asking why God had done that to them since they had no electricity for their curling irons, and lights for their mirrors to put on their makeup."

Tabby giggled. "Why didn't they just leave?"

"Roads were closed due to the floods," Charlotte answered. "I almost told those women that they'd do well to keep their mouths shut. If the townsfolk figured out that God had knocked the power out and closed the roads because of them, they might just storm the B and B, take them outside into the muddy streets, and stone them to death."

Tabby's giggle turned into laughter. "By the time they left, you might have thrown the first rock."

"Yep, I would have," Charlotte agreed. "And I might have thrown the second one at their bored husbands, who had come to Sandcastle to fish while their wives laid out on the beach and worked on their tans. Thank God for Alex. I would have sent all of the guests to the barn if he hadn't been there to help me." Charlotte paused. "Let me know when you decide something about Cleo's offer?"

Tabby nodded. "Yes, I have been giving it some thought. But before I answer that, tell me this—when you get tired of Colorado and want family around you, are you coming back to southern Texas?"

"No, darlin', I am not," Charlotte answered. "If I did, I would probably ask Cleo if I could live in the barn with whichever old folks were still alive. Our lawyer has my final wishes for when I die. He will read them to you at that time—but basically, I want to be cremated, and I want my ashes thrown out into the ocean. Mama and Daddy wanted the same thing, and I took care of it just like they wanted. The truth is, I always wanted to move away from the beach, but I felt a responsibility to keep the Landry name alive with the B and B. I will not be coming back there to live—maybe to visit a few days at Christmas, but not to stay."

"Then why do you want to have your ashes thrown out in the water?" Tabby asked.

"Because it's peaceful—and like eternity, never-ending," she said. "But now, it is Ellie Mae's and your responsibility to produce another Landry to carry on when you are gone. I'm done with my part."

"Aunt Charlotte!" Tabby gasped. "I am thirty-nine years old!"

"My mother was thirty-eight when she had me," Charlotte told her. "A baby might be the very thing you need, and Lord only knows it's time for Ellie Mae to put down her hammer and find time to get pregnant. Bye now, and you be thinking about all this."

A rush of emotions that felt the same as when

she gave birth to Natalie rushed through Tabby. Maybe Aunt Charlotte was right: a baby might just fill the void in her life.

"But, sweet Lord, a baby at forty?" Tabby muttered before she realized she had been cradling her phone in her arms like it was a baby. She was still staring at the blank screen when Alex brought in the tray with two empty pitchers on it.

"Disturbing phone call?" he asked as he set it on the counter. "You look a little pale."

"Aunt Charlotte isn't planning to come back here, even when she gets too old to take care of herself," Tabby answered.

Alex sat down beside her. "Want to talk about it?"

"She says that Ellie Mae and I have a responsibility now to keep the Landry name alive and to have offspring so the B and B can . . ." She paused and thought about how much Natalie loved the beach. Would she have lost interest when she reached adulthood, or would she have been eager to take over the business?

A wide grin covered Alex's face; then he chuckled, and soon that turned into a guffaw. He pulled a paper napkin from the holder in the middle of the table and wiped his eyes, then laughed again. "And you think you are too old to think about another child? Haven't you heard that today's forty is the new twenty?"

"That's not a laughing matter," Tabby said

through clenched teeth. "You're forty. Do you want to take on the responsibility of a baby?"

"Are you asking me to be your baby daddy?" Alex wiggled his dark eyebrows. "If so, I do not intend to go down that road again. I'm either all in with the vows and matching gold bands or nothing."

Tabby locked eyes with him and frowned. "Again? Are you speaking from experience?"

"That's a next-chapter story," he said as he stood up and headed back outside. "Maybe if we have time, we'll share some more tonight. Say, over a bottle of wine on the beach at sunset?"

"I'll bring the glasses," she agreed with a nod. "Should we meet just before sunset at that old log?"

He waved over his shoulder. "See you then."

Curiosity killed the cat. Her mother's voice popped into her head.

"And satisfaction brought him back," Tabby muttered.

Ellie Mae hated to admit it, since she'd been so against the old folks coming to stay at the B and B, but she had really begun to love every one of them, especially Cleo—probably because she could relate to her eccentricity. But that evening, she needed some time to think about the barn issue.

She had to make a decision, but her thoughts kept driving back to Sam. He had come to her again the night before in a dream. He'd been in silhouette, in front of her bedroom window, and the scent of bacon had wafted across to her. She felt like she was looking in from outside and couldn't get to him, but what he was saying was clear in her mind: "Let me go, Ellie Mae. Move on with your life."

She had woken herself up saying "I can't" over and over again.

She pulled her sweater across her chest to ward off the chilly night breeze coming off the water. When she reached the spot where she and Tabby had built the sandcastle for Natalie, she removed her shoes and sat down close enough to the surf that when the waves washed up on shore, the cool water splashed over her toes. She remembered a song, "No Shoes, No Shirt, No Problem," by Kenny Chesney. She and Sam had loved country music, and whenever that song played, he would shiver and say that he would rather be anywhere but a beach.

She pulled her phone from her hip pocket and found the song, turned the volume up as high as it would go, and sang along with the lyrics that talked about having toes in the water, ass in the sand, and a cold beer in hand. She wouldn't win a prize for her singing voice—and heaven knew, she'd never make it on a show like *The Voice*, but she had to agree that, like the lyrics said, life really had been good that day.

"Sam, you'd hate it here," she said, "but if you were still alive, I probably wouldn't have let Aunt Charlotte talk me into this. I wouldn't have left you behind—not any more than you would have left me if you'd gotten that chance to go to Nashville."

"Am I the first one at your concert?" Ricky set a six-pack of longneck beers on the wet sand. "I'll share my beers if I can join you."

"There's lots of sand and no shortage of water, so cop a squat, as they say in the movies. And thanks for the beer." Ellie Mae removed a bottle from the carton, twisted off the lid, and took a long drink, but it didn't cool down the heat she felt just being near him. "Good and cold. Thank you. This brand was Sam's favorite beer."

Ricky opened a beer for himself and drank down a fourth of it. "Boyfriend? Husband?"

"Roommate for more than ten years, and my very best friend. I loved him like he was my brother," Ellie Mae answered.

"And your roomie didn't want to come to Sandcastle with you?" he asked.

"He was not a water person. He loved the mountains and snow, and he was an excellent skier," she answered, "but what he loved most was country music. He always said when he retired, he was moving to Nashville so he could be right at the heart of all that talent."

"Was? I take it that Sam has passed away?"

Ricky patted her on the shoulder. "I'm sorry if I'm opening up old wounds—we can change the subject if you want."

For the most part, Ellie Mae had simply put the grief in a box and buried it deep inside her heart. She and Tabby had talked a little about it, but Ellie Mae always felt guilty for bringing up death and sadness when it was so evident that Tabby was still dealing with Natalie's passing.

Ellie Mae's father had thrown such a fit when she and Sam moved into a travel trailer together right out of high school that she didn't even dare bring up his name when she went to visit him. Not mentioning Sam didn't run the elephant out of the room, though, and she seldom stuck around for more than an hour. Her paternal grandparents had shared her father's feelings about Sam, so she drifted apart from them, also. She hadn't even told her father that Sam had died—couldn't bear to hear what he would say about her best friend.

"It's like this . . ." She went on to tell Ricky about taking a woodworking class the last two years of her high school career. "Sam was super tall, had wide shoulders and arms as big as hams. Everyone thought he should play football, but he didn't care a thing about any sports other than skiing. He just liked country music and building things. Like I did. From day one, he took up for me when the other boys picked on me for taking woodworking, and we became fast friends."

Ricky finished off his beer and opened another one. The moonlight lit up his unbuttoned white shirt, which covered a white tank top that hugged his brown skin. His shoulders and arms reminded Ellie Mae of Sam's—only in a much smaller way. Like Sam's, they were proof that Ricky worked hard in his construction business.

"When we had the opportunity to travel around and build houses for needy folks," she went on, "we jumped on it, but our choices weren't easy for either of our folks. We kind of had to lean on each other for support over the years because of the way our parents felt about us living together." She tipped up her bottle and took another drink. "Sam was Black. His grandfather came over here from South Africa, settled in Louisiana, and then moved up to Arkansas long before Sam's dad was even born. His folks didn't want him getting mixed up with a white half-Irish girl, and my dad sure didn't want me living with him. I didn't realize Daddy had a prejudiced bone in his body until then. I mean, it's not the fifties or even sixties anymore. But Sam and I were just best friends. He dated—a lot—but not . . ." She paused and wiped a tear from her cheek.

"Little white half-Irish girls, right?" Ricky asked. "And you dated a lot?"

"Not as much as Sam," she said with half a smile. "We ate ice cream out of the carton when our hearts got broken. If one of us was sick, the other one took care of him or her. When we lost our paychecks at a gambling table in Vegas, we both ate ramen noodles until we got paid again."

"I've never had a friend like that," Ricky said. "What happened to him? I knew Miz Charlotte fairly well. I don't think she would have told you that he couldn't come to Sandcastle with you. She didn't have a prejudiced bone in her body, and I'm saying that from experience."

Ellie Mae swallowed twice trying to get rid of the lump in her throat, but it wouldn't budge. Finally, she drank the rest of her beer, put the bottle back in the carton, and opened another one. "He was as healthy as the old proverbial horse, and we were working eight to ten hours a day. We had a little house rented in Alma, Arkansas, and one morning he woke up with a headache. He started slurring his words and then passed out. I was afraid he was having a stroke, so I rushed him to the hospital, but it was too late. They tried to revive him, but nothing worked. They told me that a blood clot had gone to his brain."

The moon hung in the sky out there above the water. Ellie Mae remembered the last night she and Sam had sat on their porch and watched the sunset and the moonrise. The sky had been surreal as the sun dipped lower and lower until all the trees looked like dark blobs. That night they thought they had all the time in the world, and they had talked about the days when they would each get married and when their grandchildren would play together.

"I'm so sorry. It's tough losing a friend, a loved one," Ricky said. "Did you stay with him until . . ."

She held up a palm. "They met me at the car with a gurney and rushed him back into the ER. I thought that since we were at the hospital, they would revive him, figure out what was wrong, and cure it. That's what doctors and hospitals do, but that was the last time I saw him." Her voice broke again, and she covered her face with her hands. Sobs shook her shoulders, and tears dripped from her cheeks, leaving spots on her T-shirt.

Ricky picked up the remaining beers and set them behind her, then moved over and wrapped her up in his arms. "It's okay to cry. It's part of the grieving process. When did all this happen?"

"Three weeks ago," she answered.

"I'm so sorry. That was just a short while ago. No wonder you are still so sad." Ricky raised his shirttail and dried her tears. "Did Tabby go to the funeral with you?"

"Thank you," she murmured. "No. I wasn't even allowed to go to his funeral."

She stared out at the waves that kept slapping the shore. The tides didn't care what went on in the world. They came in and they went out. Sometimes in hurricane situations; most of the time, calmly, like that night. The world just kept on going, so why did her heart hurt so badly when she even thought about Sam?

"But you had been . . ." Ricky's voice faded as he pulled her in closer to his side.

"It was a private family memorial service, and his parents sent word through a text on his phone that I wasn't welcome. They took his things from the house after I moved out and came down here," Ellie Mae said with a shrug. "I can't blame them. If it had been me that died, my dad wouldn't have let Sam come to the services, either."

"In today's world, that seems strange," Ricky said.

To have Ricky's arm around her shoulders was comforting. Sam used to hug her when she cried about guy problems, and parent issues, and all kinds of other things, but this felt different.

"I'm betting . . ." Ellie Mae stopped and took a long drink of her beer.

"Betting what?" Ricky asked.

"That your mama . . ." She didn't quite know how to say what was on her mind. What she wanted to say was that she'd bet that his mama had raised him right, and that from what she'd seen already of Ricky Benoit, he came from a pretty diverse family. But how did she say the words?

"My mama is a tall blonde with blue eyes and freckles across her nose. My dad's own mama was Black," he said. "I guess that's what's on your mind, right? I wasn't brought up in a prejudiced household, so if I brought a red-haired Irish girl home to meet my folks, they wouldn't throw me out."

Ellie Mae looked up at him and smiled. "That's good to know. If I run across a good red-haired Irish girl looking for a handsome dark-haired guy, I'll send her your way."

"So, you think I'm handsome, do you?" He returned her smile. "And, honey, she doesn't have to be one hundred percent *good*. I don't mind a little bit of wild thrown in to balance out all that sweetness."

"Sweetheart," she said in a slow southern drawl, "a woman would have to be stone-cold blind not to think that you are handsome or sexy, or whatever other word people our age use today. Thanks for listening to me and for the beers. I should be getting on back to the B and B, though."

"Don't go just yet," Ricky said. "You don't want to disturb Alex and Tabby, and I'm enjoying talking to you. Never have had the opportunity to visit with a red-haired Irish girl, and I, for one, am having fun."

"What's that about Alex and Tabby?" She scooted away from him a few inches so she could see his face clearly.

Ricky pointed down the beach toward the B and B, where light flowed from every upstairs window as well as the living room and kitchen. "About halfway between here and there, Alex and Tabby are enjoying a bottle of wine. He says they're covering chapter three tonight, whatever that means."

"Oh, really?" Ellie Mae *would be* going to Tabby's room later to talk about more than just whether they would sell the barn to Cleo. "Well, in that case, since I've poured my heart out to you already, then let's talk about you."

"Nothing much to talk about," Ricky said with a shrug. "I'm just your basic twenty-seven-year-old carpenter who does odd jobs for a living. My brother Travis was thirteen years older than me, and he died in the last one of his deployment tours when I was just a kid. Alex was his buddy, and they were in the same unit. My other brother, Dillon, is fourteen years older than me, is married, and has five daughters. He and his wife, Poppy, wanted a son, but after the fifth daughter, they gave up."

Ellie Mae finished off her second beer. "You're the baby, then?"

Ricky handed her another bottle, but she shook her head. Two was enough, or she might do something she would regret later. After all, Ricky really was downright sexy, and she could almost drown in his big brown eyes—plus, he had comforted her when she needed it. Those were pretty good traits in her books.

"I'm the 'oops,'" Ricky said with a chuckle. "Mama was thirty-five, and Daddy was almost forty when I surprised them. Bless their hearts!"

"Is your dad a carpenter?" she asked.

"Nope. He and Mama are both retired now. She was a kindergarten teacher. My dad was the superintendent of the school up in Anahuac, and Dillon still works there as the football coach. Not only am I the 'oops,' but I'm also the oddball who didn't go to college. Guess we have that in common, don't we?"

"I guess we do." Ellie Mae's phone pinged.

She checked it to find a message from Tabby: Are you building a sandcastle without me?

She sent one back that said: Never. I'm on my way back to the house. Let's talk.

I'll be waiting, popped up on her screen.

"That's my curfew call," Ellie Mae said as she stood up and dusted the sand from the butt of her jeans.

Ricky picked up the carton with the last two beers in it. "I'll walk you to the door, and then I'd best be getting on home, too. Alex says that I'm to hold off on taking any big jobs until Monday. Do you know what that's all about?"

"I've got a good idea, but I don't want to say anything right now," Ellie Mae answered. "But it's something that could keep you very busy until spring."

"I could use a job like that," Ricky told her.

208

When they reached the porch, he laid a hand on her shoulder and said, "Thanks for a lovely evening. The sunset and the company were both beautiful."

A sweet little shiver chased down her spine at his touch. Could this be the beginning of something good, or was it just the aftereffects of the emotional upheaval that came about when she'd talked about Sam?

"Thank you for everything. See you tomorrow?" she asked.

"Only if you go to a little country church south of Anahuac. I don't work on Sunday, but I could come by, and maybe we could take a walk on the beach again," he suggested.

"Or you could come for Sunday dinner," she said. "It'll be my way of paying you back for the therapy session."

"I'll be here," he said and then disappeared into the darkness.

Chapter Ten

I brought wine, but I never have acquired a taste for it," Alex said as he and Tabby made their way down the beach until they reached an old log that had washed up years ago. Not even Hurricane Delilah could move the thing. He removed two bottles of beer from his pockets and set them beside the wine that he'd brought. "I guess I'm not a refined person. I prefer beer to wine."

Tabby set the two stemmed wineglasses she'd brought along beside the bottle of wine. "I like beer better, too, but you've gone to the trouble to buy the wine, so we should at least have a—" She stopped and read the label on the bottle. "Oh. My. Goodness. This isn't just wine. It's champagne. Is this a celebration?"

Alex hoped it would be more like a celebration than a funeral for any future relationship. After talking to Charlotte, he had decided that he had to tell Tabby about his daughter before the attraction between them could take even one step forward.

"The last group I took out on a fishing trip was all women, and they brought a case of champagne. Every time one of them caught a fish, they popped open a bottle," he explained. "At the end of the day, they threw back everything they'd caught and were drunk as sailors on leave. That bottle was left over, so I stuck it in my truck. We've been too busy to go to a liquor store up in Anahuac or over in Winnie for a bottle of actual wine. I hope you aren't too disappointed."

"Not one bit." Tabby handed the bottle to him. "If you'll pop the cork, we can toast the sunset. It would be a sin to waste good champagne. We can twist the tops off the beers afterward."

Alex managed to work the cork out of the top of the bottle with his thumbs, and the bubbly flowed down the sides. "I don't know if the tiny bubbles mean that it's a good champagne or a cheap one, but there's lots of them."

Tabby held up her glass. "I've only had this stuff a couple of times in my life. James's family were teetotalers, so we didn't even have beer in the house. If we wanted to toast something, we did it with a bottle of that nonalcoholic stuff. My folks had champagne, but only a glass for each guest, at their twenty-fifth anniversary, and they had some at my high school graduation party. I'm not sure if they were glad to see me graduate or if they were happier to know that I'd be moving out of the house and into a dorm room."

Alex filled both glasses and set the bottle in the sand at the base of the log. "To the sunset and the future." He clinked his glass with hers.

"Hear, hear!" she said with a smile and took the first sip. "This is pretty good."

Alex downed half of what he'd poured into his glass. "Not bad, and we can always chase it with beer." He sat down on the sand and used the old log for a backrest.

Tabby kicked off her sandals, rolled up the legs of her jeans, and sat down beside him. She stretched her long legs out far enough that the water covered her feet when it rolled in on the beach. "I love this time of year. The beaches are almost deserted, and it's so peaceful. Come on in; the water is fine."

Alex followed her lead and was surprised to see that his legs were only a little longer than hers. "You're right. It really is fine. I've got something I want to tell you, Tabby."

"You're engaged or in a serious relationship?" she asked.

"No," he answered, "but I was in love with a woman about nineteen years ago. We were both twenty-one, both in the military, and on our first deployment."

"And?" She finished off her champagne and reached over her head for a bottle of beer.

Should I go into detail or just blurt it out? he wondered as he set the wineglass in the sand and grabbed the second bottle of beer.

"And she got pregnant," he answered. "I asked her to marry me, but she said no. She had gone into the military with the idea of making a career of it, and marriage was not an option for her. She didn't believe in abortion, so she kept the baby. She was sent to Maine after deployment. My orders sent me to Oklahoma, then to California for the rest of my time. She had the baby in Maine and has been a single mother. I'm not a deadbeat dad, though. I've been a part of my daughter's life through the years and have done all I can to support her."

Tabby stared out across the water at the sunset and didn't say a word for what seemed to him like forever. "You have a daughter?"

Her tone was so flat that Alex didn't know if she was angry at him for not telling her sooner or if she was thinking about her own child that she'd lost. "Yes, I do," he finally said. "Her name is Jazelle, and we call her Jazzy. The name comes from her mother's grandmother. I see her two or three times a year, and she always comes to Texas for a day or two at Thanksgiving."

"And her mother's name?" Tabby still didn't look at him.

"Lorena Parsons. Major Lorena Parsons. She's climbed the ranks very well and plans to stay with it until she reaches her thirty years. Jazzy has my last name, and right now, she and her mother are back in Maine, where Lorena could possibly finish up her career," he answered, but somehow, he didn't feel much better now than he had before he'd told Tabby about his daughter. His hands were clammy, and he felt as if someone had chained a rock to his heart.

Tabby turned up the bottle of beer and took a long gulp. "I admire Lorena for standing up for what she thought was best for her and her career. I wish I had done that, but I was too worried about what people would think of Tabitha June Landry being a single mother. So I let the worry of what others would think of me dictate my life. We kept it a secret by saying that we eloped three months before we did, but I was pregnant when James and I actually got married at the courthouse."

Alex didn't realize he was holding his breath until it all came out at once. "Lorena's been an awesome mother, and she's never kept Jazzy from me. I'm not throwing shade on your situation, Tabby, because I try not to judge, but to tell the truth, I don't think our marriage would have survived if we had tied the knot for the baby's sake."

"Why's that?" Tabby asked.

"Long distance. Different posts. But most of all, different views on everything—from religion to politics to what's important in our lives except Jazzy." He expected Tabby to ask more questions, but she just watched the sun slowly drop lower and lower behind the edge of the water out there on the far horizon.

This could be the end of what might have been,

and that made Alex sad. He liked Tabby a lot, and there was chemistry between them, but any relationship or friendship was built on trust. A solid foundation couldn't be built on anything else, and that first cornerstone had to be honesty.

She drank more of her beer and finally said, "Aunt Charlotte is coming at Christmas. And now, your daughter at Thanksgiving. We're full up already in the B and B. Where are we going to put them?"

That wasn't at all what he was expecting to hear from her. He'd hoped that she would say that she would like to meet Jazzy someday and feared that she would say that she didn't even want to start something with a man who had a daughter that age. Even dating could be a nightmare if Jazzy didn't want the father she'd had all to herself all those years to suddenly take interest in a woman.

"You kind of jumped ship, there," he said, "but I'm more than willing to sleep on the sofa or crash on the living room floor with a pillow and a blanket so that Jazzy can have my room."

"It might come to that," Tabby said.

"Sleeping quarters isn't exactly what I thought you'd want to talk about," Alex said. "I've worried all day about how to tell you about Jazzy—especially since you lost your daughter."

"The past is the past. We can't undo it," Tabby said after a long sigh. "What you did almost two decades ago can't define the future any more than what I did about that same time can determine how tomorrow looks for me. We'd probably all choose to do things different if we could go back, but then we have to ask ourselves if we would be the same people we are today if we could do that."

"That's pretty deep thinking," Alex said. "Have you ever thought of being a counselor or therapist?" He thought about the help the Veterans Administration had given him when he lost his best friend, and even after he came home. Adjusting to life outside the military had been tough, and he couldn't have done it without them. He wondered if she'd tried a therapist after her daughter died. But then, she'd had family to support her. Alex had had no one.

Tabby shook her head and then finished off her beer. "Not me. I can barely sort out my own feelings and find my own footing in this world of being single again. Knowing you have a daughter doesn't change who you are, and it doesn't change my feelings for you. But we could talk about something else for a while."

"Like what?" Alex asked, and then a picture of all seven of them around the supper table flashed through his mind. "Maybe about the barn and Cleo's idea? What's your thoughts on whether Maude will move into another place with her?"

"Who knows how anyone else will ever act in

any given situation," she answered. "How did you think I'd respond to you having a daughter?" She clamped a hand over her mouth.

He had a little emotional zing at her reaction. Was she sad that he had a daughter and she'd lost hers? "Evidently, we're not through with the conversation after all," he said. "To tell the truth, it worried me because I wasn't sure how you'd react, and I like you, Tabby. I didn't want you to think badly of me for not moving from one place to another just to be near my child. After you'd told me about losing your daughter, well . . ." He shrugged.

"I like you, too, Alex, but . . ." She couldn't seem to get the rest of the words out.

"Hey, there are no buts in a good relationship, and nothing has to go fast. We may only have tonight to live, or we may have fifty more years, but we can take things one day at a time and see where it goes," he said.

Tabby picked up the half-full bottle of champagne. "That sounds like a great plan. Now, what are we going to do with the rest of this?"

He wasn't at all surprised when their fingertips brushed together and sparks seemed to dance across the sand and float on the surface of the water. He poured the rest of the champagne out on the beach, picked up a couple of shells small enough to fit into the neck of the bottle, and then added some sand. After several tries, he popped the cork back into place and heaved the bottle out into the Gulf.

"Is this like that movie about a message in a bottle—only it's shells in a bottle?" she asked.

"Yep, it is. When we find it washed up on the beach someday in the future, we'll remember this night and see how far our friendship or our relationship or whatever other 'ship' has come to pass since I tossed it."

"What if it never washes up?" Tabby asked.

"Oh, ye of little faith." Alex stood and extended a hand. "It will come back to us. I just know it will."

She picked up her sandals and put her free hand in his. "Wouldn't it be something special if it came back at Christmas?"

"Or even at Easter, which is about when I think we'll have that barn ready for the folks to move into, if you and Ellie Mae give us the go-ahead. We'll have lots of memories to share by then," he told her as he tucked the two empty beer bottles back into his pockets.

Ellie Mae stopped at Tabby's door and raised her hand to knock.

It's none of your business if Tabby had a date with Alex. Aunt Charlotte was back in her head.

"I don't care if she had a date with him," Ellie Mae muttered. "I'm glad she's trying to move on, but I'm angry because she didn't tell me."

Whoa, Eleanor Mason, Aunt Charlotte shot back, second-naming her. *You haven't been telling her everything, either.*

Before Ellie Mae could lower her hand, the door swung open. She gasped. "What's this about 'chapter three' and a bottle of wine? Have you been holding out on me? Why didn't you tell me you had a date with Alex?"

Tabby's eyes narrowed, and her mouth set in a firm line that reminded Ellie Mae of Aunt Charlotte when she'd had enough of her two nephews throwing barbs at each other. "Don't act all high and mighty and accuse me of holding out on you. And it wasn't a date. There was no good-night kiss."

"Good grief!" Ellie Mae hissed. "We're acting like Maude and Cleo. Maybe this is a sign that we don't need to let them have the barn, if their attitude is rubbing off on us like this."

"Or maybe it's a sign that we need them in our lives to referee for us." Tabby left the door open, crossed the room, and sat down on the edge of the bed. "Come on in." She patted the place beside her. "We can't get this straightened out if we don't talk about it. I'll go first. Alex and I have been sharing our life stories, in what we call a chapter at a time. Tonight, we watched the sunset and shared a bottle of champagne. It wasn't bad, but the beer was better."

Ellie Mae sat down beside Tabby. "Do you like

him—as in *like* him, like him—or is he a Sam in your life?"

"I'm not sure," Tabby admitted, "but I want to see where this goes. He's easy to talk to, and he doesn't try to make all my decisions for me like James did. I know it's not right to judge one person by another's half bushel, as Aunt Charlotte used to say, but . . ." She raised a shoulder in a half shrug. "And he's got a daughter who is about the age that Natalie would be if she was still with us. Am I making any sense here?"

"More than you realize," Ellie Mae answered. "Ricky brought beers, and we talked about Sam, and I cried like a big old baby, just like I did when we built the sandcastle for Natalie. When he put his arm around me, it was like Sam was right there, but it wasn't the same."

"Was there electricity? Chemistry? Vibes, or whatever the new word is for attraction?" Tabby asked.

"A few, but I was crying, so maybe it was just comforting. With Sam, there was never a little devil sitting on my shoulder thinking about kissing him." Ellie Mae's voice quivered, but she sucked it up and refused to start crying again. Tabby didn't need that. Not when she was trying to find her way back from the grave—quite literally, even if it was her daughter's and not hers—and had just realized that she could enjoy a man's company again.

"Maybe I'm looking for the same thing, but that same little devil is whispering in my ear, too. He's saying that it's time for me to move on," Tabby said. "I've been hearing it more and more since we built that sandcastle."

"Time will tell for both of us," Ellie Mae said, and gave up trying to keep her emotions in check. Tears rolled down her cheeks, and she reached for a tissue from the nightstand. "You weren't—and still aren't—over Natalie's death, so I didn't want to put all my grief on your shoulders, too. But talking about Sam and remembering little things about him helps so much."

"Girl, we are the last of the Landry family. We need to lean on each other. And speaking of that business . . ." Tabby gave her a hug and then said, "You'll never believe what Aunt Charlotte told me this morning." She went on to tell Ellie Mae about their aunt saying they needed to have children so that the B and B could have a future.

"Is she losing her mind?" Ellie Mae gasped. "This started off as a fancy house, and Aunt Charlotte only turned it into a B and B after her mother died, so why should we feel responsible to have babies just to leave this old place to them? With all these twelve-foot ceilings . . ." She got up and began to pace back and forth. "And the fact that it had so many bathrooms built in a hundred years ago, it could be a museum.

I'm not getting married and having babies just so . . ." She stopped and took a breath.

"I hear you, sister!" Tabby said. "But, honey, if there's going to be more in the Landry family, it's up to you to bring them into this world. I'll be forty next summer, so I'm not in a hurry to start all over with a baby."

Ellie Mae sat back down on the bed and then threw herself backward. Feet still hanging off one side, she stared at the ceiling. "I'd be afraid to have children. With my background, I would be a horrible parent."

"Don't sell yourself short." Tabby fell backward, too, and turned her face toward Ellie Mae. "You were so good with Natalie that I think you'd be a great mama."

"Look at us," Ellie Mae said with a sigh, "talking about babies and relationships when all we've done is share a beer and a bottle of wine with a couple of hardworking guys. They're probably only interested in being friends."

"I don't think so," Tabby said. "We haven't known each other long enough to declare a relationship, but I think Alex wants more than to be just friends."

"Well, I guess time will tell." Ellie Mae yawned. "Alex could be gone as soon as he settles with the insurance company, and who knows where or what he'll do with his life next. Seems like he does what he wants and isn't hurting for money.

Ricky might have a girlfriend, for all I know. We shouldn't count our chickens before they're hatched."

"You got that right," Tabby agreed. "Are we good now?"

"Oh, yeah, we are." Ellie Mae bounced up off the bed and headed through the bathroom to her own room. "And, Tabby, I think we should take Cleo up on her offer. She'll make us laugh and bring joy in our lives."

"I was thinking the same thing—we could definitely use a lot of that joy and laughter," Tabby said.

Chapter Eleven

I like for things to be even and in balance," Maude said as she set the table with officious care that Sunday for dinner. "We always called the noon meal *dinner* and the evening one *supper.* Mother said it was presumptuous to call it *lunch* and then *dinner* for the evening meal. She said we weren't queens and princesses." She cut her eyes to Cleo.

"My family said *lunch* and *dinner,* but Aunt Charlotte has always called it *dinner* and *supper,* and I liked that better. Less formality," Tabby said.

"It really is nice to have eight people around the table today, no matter what we call it," Cleo said. "Kind of makes everything even, doesn't it?"

"We won't have any empty chairs today," Homer said from the kitchen table, where he, Frank, and Ricky were having a glass of sweet tea and visiting until dinner was ready. "And we called it *dinner* and *supper* at our house, too."

"We had *dinner* and *supper,*" Frank said, "and I loved Sundays when Mama cooked at home. She always fried a chicken, and my brother and I fought over the legs."

"I'm glad to fill a chair and keep the balance any Sunday," Ricky said with a smile. "Fried chicken is my favorite food. Is this always the Sunday dinner here at the B and B? If so, you could think about opening up a restaurant . . . maybe out in the barn. We could turn that into a really nice café."

"That would be a solid no." Ellie Mae threw up a hand in protest. "Running a B and B is enough for me."

"Aunt Charlotte said that the Landry Sunday dinner was fried chicken, and I'll add my no to the idea of a café, too," Tabby answered.

"My mother always made fried chicken for Sunday dinner," Maude said. "She would peel the potatoes and have them ready to boil when we got home from church, and she would get down the cast-iron skillet, and—"

"Roll the chicken in flour," Cleo said, "then put it in the sizzling grease to let it cook while she made biscuits."

"Don't finish my sentences for me," Maude snapped.

"Don't make me think of times when *my* mama did the same thing as *your* mother," Cleo shot back at her.

"You didn't have a mother. You were spawned by the devil or feral wolves, and the woman who raised you was sorry she ever brought you into her home," Maude smarted off.

"That's not what *my* mama told me. She said she loved me and that I got my wild nature from my aunt. Of course, she hated Aunt Nellie and refused to let her come in the house after Daddy died," Cleo said.

"That's because Aunt Nellie worked in a bar and drank like a fish." Maude left the dining room and glared at Cleo. "Mother couldn't have that kind of influence in a Christian home. How did you know about that, anyway?"

"How do you think?" Cleo answered. "Aunt Nellie kept in touch with me and even worked a season in the carnival for us."

The tension was so thick in the kitchen that Tabby didn't figure she could cut through it with even the knife she had been using to prepare the tomatoes for a salad. "Thank you for setting the table, Maude," she finally said, in hopes that she could turn the tide of the conversation. This was Ricky's first meal, and she sure didn't want to scare him off.

"My mother used to make pot roast every Sunday, but here lately, we've been going to a café after services. Mama says it's biblical," Ricky said.

He had a big smile on his face, and his dark eyes twinkled. Tabby was just glad, for Ellie Mae's sake, he hadn't pushed back his chair and made a beeline for the door.

"How's that?" Alex asked.

Bless both of their hearts, Tabby thought.

"She says it's right there in the Good Book," Ricky answered. "It says, 'Blessed are they that hunger and thirst after righteousness.' Mama says that we've been to church, which is like getting a shot of righteousness, and that we are hungry and thirsty, so we should be fed."

"Well, we haven't been to church, but I *am* starving. We never got fried chicken at our house." Tabby remembered the formal meals that the cook had prepared for the family. "And everything is on the table, so come and get it while it's hot. Mashed potatoes aren't good when they get cold."

Frank was the first on his feet and to make it to the dining room table. "You don't have to call me twice. Man alive, I sure like living here. Wish me and Homer would have discovered this place before we did the center. We could've been stayin' here for the past year."

Homer was right behind him. "You got that right, and you don't have to ask a fat man twice if he's ready for fried chicken, either."

When they were all seated, Maude said a quick grace, then picked up the basket of biscuits and passed them to Homer.

"Thank you, ma'am." He took one and handed them off to Frank.

"I'm right sorry that the hurricane ruined the center—and your business, Alex," Frank continued. "But I got to admit, I like it here a lot better. If you'd let me and Homer live here permanently, I'd give you what I paid the center. I bet that would work out to be more than you'd make on renting my room every day of the month. We all know that every room won't be full every single day at a B and B."

Tabby inhaled and let the air out slowly. She had never—not even in her wildest dreams—thought she would be running a retirement center, or have even been a part of one. But Ellie Mae had hit the nail right on the head when she said that Cleo made them laugh. These four fantastic old folks had brought a lot of life into the B and B, whether it was through their arguing or telling stories.

"Cleo, do you have something to discuss with the folks?" Tabby asked.

Cleo laid a hand over her heart. "Are you saying that you are accepting my offer? Please tell me that you've reached an early decision."

"I believe we have," Ellie Mae answered. "Should you call a meeting this afternoon?"

"I'm too excited to wait until then." Cleo stood up and tapped her tea glass with a spoon.

"She's always been dramatic," Maude grumbled. "I hope she doesn't wake Duke. He was sleeping soundly when I came down for dinner. If I get to stay here permanently, I hope that the other guests aren't noisy."

"I'll show you my sketch pad after dessert, once we get the table cleaned off. But I would like to announce that I'm not building a new retirement center," Cleo said.

"Are we buying a bar?" Homer asked.

Maude threw up both palms. "If you are, count me out."

"I considered it," Cleo said with a chuckle, "but we're too old for that business, and"—the chuckle turned into a giggle—"Alex refused to come work for me. So I gave up on the honky-tonk. A bar needs either a sexy man or a scantily clad woman, and at almost eighty, none of us can fill that bill."

"Speak for yourself," Frank said and took a chicken thigh from the platter.

Maude rolled her eyes toward the high ceiling. "Thank you, Jesus, for answering my prayers."

Tabby hoped that she and Ellie Mae had made the right decision. She had given up a life of tension when she and James divorced, and she sure didn't want to live in that kind of world again. Yet if Cleo and Maude didn't stop their bickering, she would have to put them in time-out chairs.

"Okay, then," Homer said. "I don't care what it is, I'm in. I don't even care if you're buying a carnival. I figure I can run the throw-the-baseball-at-milk-bottles game. Frank here can dress up like a clown, and we'll have a grand old time."

"I might have considered that," Cleo said with half a giggle. "But Maude is too stubborn to help us with it, and I can't uproot Julep and the babies from her home here in Sandcastle."

"Duke is getting up in years, too," Homer said with a sideways glance at Maude. "You know what they say about teaching an old dog new tricks."

Maude lowered her chin and glared at him. "Are you talking about me? If you are, I'm not an old dog."

Frank chuckled. "Well, you ain't a young pup."

Cleo set her glass and spoon back on the table. "Here's the deal: I'm buying that old barn out in the backyard and remodeling it into a place for the four of us to live. Since I won't have to hire as much staff, I figure I can cut the cost down by a third for each of you. I've gotten the basic plans drawn up. We'll each have a little place of our own, with a small sitting room, bedroom, and bathroom on the second floor." She paused and glanced over at Maude. "And there will be a lift chair. The first floor will be our living, dining, and recreational area."

"Count me and Frank in," Homer said.

"Whoa!" Frank held up a hand. "I can speak for myself—but I dang sure call rights on one of those upstairs apartments."

Alex leaned over and whispered into Tabby's ear, "Does that mean I've got a room here at the B and B until the barn is finished?"

His warm breath on her neck shot shivers down her back that had nothing to do with the cool afternoon. The universe had to be telling her that it was time to move on, but she wasn't sure that she was ready for that step. She had been so involved with getting through the grieving process of losing Natalie and the death of her marriage at the same time that she was afraid she would cave in if she let go of all those feelings at once.

"Well?" Alex asked.

"Yes," she said quickly. "I'm sorry. I was deep in my own thoughts."

"Be careful of rabbit holes," Alex said.

"I hear you loud and clear. But yes, please stay on with us. I should've talked to you before I told Cleo that we'd go along with her plan. I'm not sure we could do this without your help," she said.

"Is this the job you've been hinting at?" Ricky asked. "If it is, then when can we get started? And when can I see the plans so I can get a rough estimate of materials, labor, and time drawn up? And, Alex—can I depend on you to help me and Ellie Mae to chip in when she has time?"

Homer finished off his food and leaned back in his chair. "I ain't too old to fetch and carry, so count me in, too. I'm just grateful that we get to stay right close here."

"Me too," Frank added, "and we'll be glad to help any way we can."

Everyone turned their eyes toward Maude.

"I like living here on the beach, and this place has proven that it will stand up under a hurricane. So Duke and I would like to live in the new place," she said. "Now, would you please quit hoggin' the gravy, Cleo, and pass it down here to me?"

At least three conversations were going on at once around the table: Ricky and Ellie Mae were talking in low tones about two-by-fours and support beams. Homer and Cleo were all into something about a hot tub. Frank was telling Maude that they needed a pool table because all that bending and using the arms was as good as going to a gym.

"I'll even teach you how to play," Frank said.

"I don't gamble," she said.

"We don't have to play for money," Frank informed her. "We can play for pieces of candy or even just bragging rights."

"Then I just might learn." Maude finally smiled. "I'd like to learn so I can beat Cleo."

Alex nudged Tabby on the shoulder. "Let's bring out dessert. If you'll get the ice cream and bowls, I'll bring out the blackberry cobbler," he said. "It's going to be bubbly hot right out of the oven, and that cast-iron skillet will be heavy."

Tabby pushed back her chair. "Seems like I've been saying this a lot, but thank you for everything you do to make life easier around here."

"You are so welcome," Alex said and then lowered his voice. "And thank you for letting me keep my room. We should have that barn up and ready within six months, and by then, I will have figured out what I want to do next in my life."

If you are lucky, whatever he decides might even have something to do with what you are doing with your life. Aunt Charlotte was back in her head.

James had been her first serious relationship, and then she had married him, so it was impossible not to compare what she'd had with him to the thoughtfulness that Alex showed her. James would never have helped her with anything domestic and had very seldom extended a hand to help her with anything beyond those terms the way Alex had done. James had never even picked up his own towel and underwear from the bathroom floor after his shower or put away the toothpaste. Those were all things that a woman did for her husband, including cleaning and cooking. He mowed the lawn and sometimes took out the trash—those kinds of things were what he considered man's work.

He hadn't been like that in the first days of their relationship; the change had been so gradual and subtle that she didn't even realize just how he had molded her until Natalie was a toddler. *No wonder I loved my job at the bank so much,* she thought. That was one place where she had a little bit of control.

How he slipped through the cracks of the nineteenth century, where he belonged, into modern society made me believe in time travel. Few in today's world treat their wives like James treated you, Aunt Charlotte whispered.

"Amen!" Tabby muttered.

"Are you agreeing with me about the cobbler being too hot and heavy for you to carry?" Alex took a couple of oven mitts from a drawer and slipped his big hands down into them. "Or are you fighting with the voices in your head?"

"Maybe both," Tabby answered, "but how did you know?"

Alex opened the oven door, releasing a rush of blackberry-cobbler aroma that flowed throughout the kitchen and into the dining room. "You would not make a good poker player, Tabby Landry. Whatever you are thinking shows on your face."

Good Lord, I hope not! Tabby fought against a blush. If Alex knew the picture that had flashed into her head when he'd said "hot and heavy," he wouldn't want to ever play cards with her.

"Aunt Charlotte and I were having a mental discussion, and I agreed with her," Tabby said as she brought eight dessert bowls down from the cabinet and set them on the counter. Then she took the ice cream out of the freezer, glad to have a little blast of cool air to help with the slight burn on her face. "I'm ready if you are."

"Are we still talking about dessert?" Alex teased.

"You tell me," Tabby flirted. "You can read my face so well; what does it tell you?"

"That you are confused about your own feelings." Alex headed for the dining room with the cobbler in his hands.

She followed him and set the bowls and ice cream on the table. "You got that right. Maybe you should be the fortune-teller."

"What did he get right? And no, ma'am, he does not get my job," Cleo teased.

"He said I'm confused about my feelings," Tabby answered.

"We're all in that boat right along with you," Maude agreed with a nod.

Wow! Tabby almost said out loud. *There's something we can all agree on, even if it's confusion about the way we feel.*

Alex picked up a bowl and said, "I'll serve, but y'all will have to tell me whether you want ice cream and when."

"I haven't heard that expression since my mama passed away," Frank said. "Just fill up the bowl, and then top it off with a big scoop of ice cream. I love cobbler."

"He eats so slow that it'll be midnight before we get to see Cleo's plans for the barn," Homer grumbled.

"Got to savor the good stuff when we can," Frank said with a grin. "And it don't matter what Cleo cooked up anyway—I already said that I'm in. I didn't like it so good at the assisted-care center. I felt like I was just waiting for the undertaker to come get me."

"Well," Maude huffed, "I'm glad she's not buying another carnival. Duke and I would pitch a tent on the beach before we joined one of those things."

"My plans aren't set in stone just yet, so I'll be open to any ideas that you all might have to make it better," Cleo said.

"Are you serious?" Maude eyed her suspiciously. "You'll listen to my ideas?"

"I am very serious," Cleo answered. "But I thought you'd refuse."

"Not me," Maude said. "I'd rather not live with you, but this will allow me to take Duke for walks on the beach, and I like it here better than that center. Please make sure there's pink wallpaper in my bedroom."

Cleo held up a hand to let Alex know he had dipped out enough cobbler for her. "Do you think pink-rose wallpaper will offend Duke's self-image? You have to think about him, Maude."

"I'll ask him. And if it does, then maybe we can just do the bathroom," Maude answered.

As soon as they finished dessert, Cleo brought out her sketch pad and laid it out on the kitchen table. "Right here is the little area where the hot tub will be housed, and this is the pool table area." She pointed to different areas on the page labeled "First Floor." "Back here is the kitchen and dining area."

Maude peered over Cleo's shoulder. "I've never been in a hot tub."

"They're wonderful," Homer said. "Sometimes Frank and I would get rooms in a hotel over in Beaumont for a night just so we could use their hot tub."

"I've never been in one, but I might try it." Maude pointed to the kitchen. "Is there going to be a problem with inspections if we have animals? That's why we couldn't have them at the center."

"Don't need inspections. This particular place will be a private home," Cleo answered. "You can have whatever or however many pets you want as long as you clean up after them and they don't stink up the place. I would probably draw the line on a pet skunk or a rat. I don't like rats."

If you want to see someone who doesn't have a poker face, take a look at the joy in Cleo's expression right now, Tabby thought as she helped Alex clean off the table.

"I told you before that I'm in, but this is even better than the carnival," Homer said with a big grin. "We'll be close enough that me and Frank can walk up to the senior citizens building and whip all of them old men at dominoes. We go when we can, but sometimes the shuttle is needed to take someone to the doctor, so we don't get into town as often as we'd like."

"We could get more chances to take their money in a poker game if we can get someone to watch for the cops." Frank hadn't taken his eyes off the sketch since he sat down.

"I'm not going to get into an illegal poker game with you guys, but I might walk up to the senior citizens center and make friends with some of the ladies." Cleo's eyes twinkled. "Think you might go with me, Maude?"

"Sure, I would. I wanted to go to the center when Mama was alive, but she wouldn't have any part of it, and if I had gone alone, she would have made me feel guilty," Maude answered, then turned the page to show the second-floor plans.

"That means we get to have Thanksgiving here, right?" Homer asked.

"Yes, I guess we will all be spending the holiday together," Ellie Mae answered. "Tabby and Alex can cook, and I will eat."

Alex loaded the dishwasher while Tabby put the leftovers away. "I'll be glad to help with the cooking," he said.

James had not only never helped her cook a meal but also probably didn't even know how to turn on the dishwasher when she moved out of the house. Tabby scolded herself for thinking that all men were like her ex—and her father, who didn't do anything around the house, either.

"Thank you," she said with a nod toward Alex. "Aunt Charlotte always cooked the Thanksgiving dinner. She'd let me help a little, but she ran my mother and Aunt Dara—that would be Ellie Mae's mama—out of the kitchen. Neither of them minded all that much since they wouldn't have known a teakettle from a skillet anyway."

"Where did you learn?" he asked.

"Lots of trial and error," she answered.

Ellie Mae whipped the tablecloth off the table and carried it to the utility room. When she returned to the kitchen, Ricky was leaning over the plans and making a list. A little thrill tiptoed up her spine at the sight of him.

He looked up with a broad smile. "This is going to keep me busy until spring. I'm glad for the job. Will you be helping us?"

"If she wants to spend her time out there with a hammer or a saw in her hand, it's fine by me," Tabby answered as she dug the last of the cobbler out of the skillet and put it in a container. "We'll be putting our redecorating on hold in here, anyway, so she's free to do whatever she likes. She'd be bored to tears in the kitchen."

"I'd like to help out, then," Ellie Mae said. "Seems only fitting since Alex will be helping some with the cooking here. It'll be like a trade-off, but I will be here to help with laundry and cleaning, too, so I won't be in the barn all day."

"Does that mean you don't cook?" Ricky asked.

"That's exactly what it means," Ellie Mae told him. "I'm dangerous in the kitchen. How about you?"

"Yep. I can cook and clean and do all that stuff. I'm no gourmet, but I can make a mean fried-bologna sandwich, and I know how to open a can of soup. I'll even volunteer to make the turkey and dressing for Thanksgiving if anyone needs me to. I can get the recipe from my mama. She makes it in the slow cooker. And FYI"—he placed his notepad on the table and nudged it exactly parallel to the edge—"I'm also a neat freak, so my house is spotless all the time."

"Looks like we've got another Sam in the house." Ellie Mae didn't have a lump in her throat when she said his name—for the first time since he had passed away.

"I'll take that as a compliment," Ricky said, "and I'm serious about helping out any way I can."

"It's meant as one." Tabby finished up in the kitchen and looked over Cleo's shoulder at the sketches. "She loved Sam more than anyone."

"Not more than you," Ellie Mae argued, "and I'll help, too. If Aunt Charlotte left a detailed recipe, I'll even try making the dressing."

"Aww, thank you, Eleanor Mason. You know I'd never turn down help for the holiday meal, but I've got Aunt Charlotte's recipes for everything, including the dressing."

"If you need me, all you have to do is yell," Maude offered. "I'm a good cook."

"And I'm good at cleanup," Cleo said.

Frank held up a hand. "I'm going to volunteer to say grace and bring a healthy appetite. Can we go out to the barn and look at it? Me and Homer might have some ideas to add."

"I'll take any suggestions y'all want to throw out," Cleo said. "I'm just glad that you're agreeing with my plans."

Homer pushed back his chair and stood up. "Girl, I haven't been this excited about anything since me and Frank bought the convenience store. Who'd have ever thought that a hurricane could bring joy into our lives?"

"You can call me *girl* anytime you want." Cleo fluffed back her hair in a flirty gesture.

"That don't mean you're young." Maude stuck her nose in the air and rolled her eyes. "It just means you ain't a boy."

Ellie Mae nudged Tabby on the arm and whispered for her ears only, "I'll keep them busy and out of your way on Thanksgiving. You'd have a riot going in the kitchen if they all got involved."

"I'm holding you to that," Tabby said with a

sigh. "Think we'll ever get around to bringing this place out of the dark ages and getting it up to date?"

"If we don't, then it was meant to stay the way it is," Ellie Mae answered. "Which is fine with me. I wouldn't change anything in it, except for those ugly bedspreads. When I come here, I step back in time."

"The wallpaper is growing on me, but I'm with you about the bedspreads, and all those doilies on the dressers and nightstands need to go," Tabby said. "Every time a guest leaves, they'll have to be washed and done up."

"The way you said 'done up' sounded just like Aunt Charlotte," Ellie Mae said. "That's a compliment in my book. I want to grow up and be just like her. Maybe not in the kitchen but in attitude. I'm headed to the beach to walk off my second helping of mashed potatoes."

"I'll go with you." Ricky headed for the back door. "Thanks for giving me the job, Cleo. I've got a general idea of what we'll need to get started, and I'll put in a couple of calls to see where I can get the best deal."

Ellie Mae slipped out the back door with Ricky right behind her. When she headed for the barn, he asked, "Aren't we going to the beach?"

"In a minute or two," she answered. "After looking at those sketches, I want to look at the barn. How about you?"

"I'm game, for sure." Ricky started toward the door. "She said she'd measured the building, but she's got a lot going on in her drawings."

When Ellie Mae opened the barn door, Julep came running from her place at the far end and rubbed around Ellie Mae's legs. She stooped down and petted the cat, crooning, "Are you lonely, sweet mama cat? Cleo will be out in a little while, so you'll have some company soon."

Ricky looked up at the rafters and then all around the foundation and walls. "The bones are good—practically petrified, as solid as the stones covering the outside of this place. There are plenty of windows already in place, most likely because the painters back in the day needed as much light—and possibly ventilation—as they could have to do a good job finishing the boats."

"Looks that way to me, too." Ellie Mae followed the cat back to her bed.

"The cat might have a fit when the work starts," Ricky said as he made his way toward the far end of the building.

Ellie Mae pointed to the bed of hay where Julep and her three kittens were curled up. "Julep was a stray that Aunt Charlotte took in, and now Cleo has claimed her. I'm not sure how the cat and kittens will handle all the noise when we start this job, but I trust Cleo has already got something up her sleeve."

Ricky sat down on the bale of hay and reached

down to gently pet the cat and each kitten. "So, her name is Julep. Are the kittens named, too?"

"Not yet, but I've got a feeling that once the house is finished, everyone will be fighting over who gets to play with the kittens more. Maude says she hates cats, but I'd bet dollars to doughnuts that she is the first one to buy cat toys."

"Mama has an old cat that is about fifteen years old." Ricky kept looking around the barn. "Her name is Queen, and she rules the whole house. I might beat Maude at buying cat toys for the babies. Reckon she'll keep them all in this place or let them roam the beach?"

"She told me that she has found a small vendor wagon and is working out a deal to buy it for Julep and her babies," Ellie Mae explained. "She plans to park it out back of the barn, and part of the remodeling job is to run electricity into it so that she can heat and cool it for her cats. According to her, it will be like the playhouse that she never had as a child. It was an old cotton-candy wagon, but she's got plans drawn up to strip the inside and fix it all up with a recliner, a television, and a cat-tree thing she's been looking to buy online."

"Wow!" Ricky said. "She must really love these critters."

"Oh, that's not the best part," Ellie Mae went

on. "She's having it repainted with a calico cat and three black kittens on the outside, and an elaborate sign above the window that says THE CAT HOUSE."

"Are you kidding me?" Ricky said and then laughed. "I bet Maude will have something to say about that."

"Probably so. I can hear it now." Ellie Mae raised her tone an octave to sound more like Maude. "This is the craziest thing you've done yet, and it's a waste of good money."

"To which Cleo will say, 'Holy crap on a cracker, woman! I will have my own cat house or else I'll let Julep scratch Duke's eyes out, and then you'll have a blind dog to deal with.' I didn't do as good as you did with Maude's voice, but the words are true, right?" Ricky asked.

"Sam used to say that about crap on a cracker all the time. He said he got it from his mother, who didn't like to use swear words. I bet Cleo is making the cat house thing just to irritate Maude." Ellie Mae stood and headed toward the door. "Those two are like the cats and the dog. They can never agree on anything, but down deep they want to be sisters."

Ricky was following her one minute, but then he stopped in his tracks. "Are they sisters for real?"

"Yes, but don't tell Maude that you know," Ellie Mae said. "She kind of disowned Cleo years ago when she ran off at sixteen and joined a carnival." She waved her hand to take in the whole place. "So, we're in agreement that what she's got drawn up is even doable."

Ricky looked up at the rafters in the ceiling. "It was built to last and has a sturdy floor. I can work with her blueprints. They're actually really good, and I've worked with far less. How about you? What's your thoughts on this idea as a project—not as in those four folks living so close to y'all, but on what this will look like when it's finished?"

Ellie Mae would rather have talked about whether Ricky was in a committed relationship. As forward as she was, she got tongue-tied at the thought of asking him. She could ask Alex, but that sounded like something teenagers would do, not a woman who was almost thirty.

"My thoughts on the project?" She paused before she went on. "Like you said, it could work, and with three of us out here every day, we could probably get it done by spring, barring any more hurricanes."

"We'll take Thanksgiving off and a couple of days at Christmas, but six months could be enough time to do what she wants done," Ricky said. Then he blurted out, "Are you in a relationship with someone?"

Ellie Mae was so shocked at the sudden change in subject—from construction to relationships—

that it took a minute to even register that she wasn't just hearing things.

"No," she finally answered. "Are you?" She sucked in a lungful of air and held it.

"Nope. Haven't been in a couple of years," he said.

She exhaled slowly, elated that they were in the same place as far as relationships went.

"I'm not one of those guys who assumes, and I'm damn sure not one who steps into another man's field. But since we're both unattached, I'd like to ask you for a date."

"Okay," Ellie Mae said.

" 'Okay' I can ask, or 'okay' that you will say yes?" Ricky asked.

"You'll have to ask to find out," she teased, but she knew that she would say yes without a moment's hesitation.

"I will figure out a time and call you," he said, "but for right now, would you take a walk on the beach with me? Pretty soon, we're going to be either too busy or too tired for lazy afternoon strolls on the beach like this."

This is real. Ellie Mae's pulse raced, and her heartbeat jacked up a few notches. Was she ready for a relationship?

Yes, you are, Sam's voice whispered in her ear. *Go for it.*

Sam had always supported her no matter what, so she wasn't surprised to hear his advice.

Besides, she knew he would really like Ricky.

She slipped her hand into Ricky's and hoped he didn't realize how nervous she was. "Maybe we'll even build a sandcastle to practice for the festival."

"I'd like that," he said with a smile.

Tabby wasn't Ellie Mae's mother or even her sister, but she had been looking out the kitchen window all the same that afternoon when she saw Ricky and Ellie Mae walking toward the beach, hand in hand. Construction partners or even good friends didn't hold hands like that. By the time supper was finished later that evening and dark had settled in, Ellie Mae still wasn't home. Tabby had begun to worry and was about ready to go upstairs to Alex's room and ask him to go with her in search of Ellie Mae and Ricky.

Before she could take a step toward the stairs, Ellie Mae came in the back door.

"Where have you been?" Tabby asked and popped her with a towel.

"Hey!" Ellie Mae swatted it away. "I'm home before the midnight curfew. Ricky and I went for a long walk down the beach, and we built a sandcastle. He talked about his brother that got killed, the one that Alex knew. I invited Sam to visit the castle."

Tabby hoped that a little jealousy didn't show in her face. "So, you were on a date?"

"No, just a walk. He has to kiss me good night at the door for it to be a date. At least, that's what you said when I asked if you were on a date with Alex," Ellie Mae told her. "Has Alex asked you out yet?"

Tabby took a plate of food out of the refrigerator and stuck it in the microwave. "No, and I'm not so sure I want him to—and you can't change the subject to keep from talking to me. I made you a plate to heat up."

Ellie Mae poured herself a glass of sweet tea and carried it to the kitchen table. "Why? There's chemistry between y'all, and it's been two years since you and James ended things. It's way past time for you to move on—unless you plan to be like Aunt Charlotte and be the old maid who runs the Sandcastle B and B."

"Maybe that would be the best course for me," Tabby said and removed the plate as soon as the timer dinged. "I'm angry at Alex. I have no right to be, but I am, and until I get over that, I don't see any reason to start something up with him."

Tabby set the plate of food on the table and handed Ellie Mae a fork and knife. "Aren't you going to ask me why I'm mad at him?"

"Thank you for fixing this for me—and no, I'm not asking, because you're going to tell me or else I'm going to pour this tea on your head," Ellie Mae answered.

"You wouldn't dare!" Tabby gasped.

"Yep, I would, and then I might throw a fistful of mashed potatoes at you," Ellie Mae said with a giggle. "We're not too old for a food fight."

Tabby sat down across the table from Ellie Mae. "You've been hanging around Cleo too much."

"I probably have, but isn't it fun to have her and Maude in the house?" Ellie Mae took a sip of tea. "But, alas, you are beating around the bush, trying to divert my attention to something other than your anger at Alex. Time to fess up."

"I lost my precious Natalie," Tabby said with another long sigh, "and she was the light in my world. She left a hole in my heart that nothing will fill."

"Still beating around the bush," Ellie Mae told her. "What's the connecting thread between Natalie and Alex? He had never even met her."

Tabby knew she should have told Ellie Mae about Jazzy the night she found out that Alex had a daughter, but she was still trying to sort out her own feelings about their chemistry. She took a deep breath and started talking. "When he was in the service, he dated a girl who had enlisted about the same time as he did. They broke up, and then she found out she was pregnant. As Alex put it, however, she was 'married to the military,' and that's what broke them up to begin with. He wanted a future with a family in it, and she didn't. She had a daughter, who is about the same age as Natalie would have been. Her name is Jazelle, and they call her Jazzy for short." Tabby couldn't force herself to go on until Ellie Mae raised an eyebrow.

She sucked in more air and then let it all out. "I don't even know how to begin. I feel like I'm on an emotional roller coaster. One minute, I like Alex and would love to move on and date him. The next, I'm mad because he's still got a daughter and I don't, and neither he nor his girlfriend even wanted a baby to begin with. It's not fair that they get to keep Jazzy and I had to give up Natalie." She stopped long enough to draw in more air. "Then I feel guilty because I wouldn't want anything to happen to that girl, and I sure wouldn't want Alex to feel the pain I've had to endure since I lost Natalie."

"Life isn't fair," Ellie Mae said between bites. "If it was, Sam wouldn't have died. Natalie would have left the house five minutes later than she did, and that stupid drunk driver would have already been on down the road. James wouldn't have been a controlling son of a bitch. My dad wouldn't be prejudiced. And we wouldn't have gotten hit with a hurricane when we'd only been here for two weeks."

"But . . ." Tabby started.

Ellie Mae held up a hand. "As for that big old empty hole in your heart, I've got one, too. I vote that we start filling them with wonderful memories instead of just leaving them like a big old black abyss that draws us into the center every waking moment of every day."

"That's a big order." Tabby went to the freezer and took out a container of pecan-praline ice cream. She removed the lid, laid it aside, got two spoons from a drawer, and stuck them in the top.

"Must be a really tough pill to swallow, if you are setting out the good ice cream." Ellie Mae picked up a spoon and dug deep. "Think you can put one sweet memory of Natalie in that hole each day?"

"How'd you get to be so smart?" Tabby asked. As if on cue, a picture of Natalie as a newborn baby flashed into her mind. She had been so tiny, with that full head of dark hair and those piercing blue eyes. That would be the first thing she filed away in that hole in her heart.

"I can't take credit for the idea," Ellie Mae said. "That's the way Ricky said he dealt with his brother's death. He had such a hard time accepting that his hero was gone that his mother told him to fill up the hole in his heart with happy memories. She said that was the only way a parent could survive the loss of a child."

Tabby filled a spoon with ice cream and said, "Someday, I want to meet this woman." Then she put the ice cream in her mouth and let it melt slowly. There was another memory—Natalie saying that ice cream should be savored, not eaten fast, and that this was her favorite kind. Tabby hadn't thought of that in years.

"Are you going to hate this Jazzy when you meet her?" Ellie Mae asked.

Tabby swallowed the bite before she wanted to. "No, I can't hate her. She didn't ask to be born, and FYI, she's coming to visit Alex sometime over the Thanksgiving holiday. He says he'll crash on the sofa and give her his room."

"Too bad we're the only B and B or even hotel in Sandcastle," Ellie Mae said. "But if there was another one, we'd have to fight competition. What does Jazzy look like? Is she blonde like Alex and have his blue eyes? How old is she?"

"I have no idea what she looks like, but I guess she's about eighteen or nineteen since she's in college. Not so very different from what Natalie would be if she hadn't . . ." Tears filled Tabby's eyes.

Ellie Mae handed her a paper napkin from the holder in the middle of the table. "It's a little scary how everything is twisting and turning in our world, isn't it?"

"Yes, it is, but I suppose we have to face the past if we're going to have any kind of future," Tabby said, getting up to put the ice cream back in the freezer.

"I would have never thought we'd get hit with a hurricane *and* the past all at once," Ellie Mae said.

"Thank God I've got you to talk to and help me through this." Tabby wiped her eyes and blew her nose.

"Right back at you." Ellie Mae took the spoons to the dishwasher and then gave Tabby a hug.

Chapter Twelve

E llie Mae leaned on the front-porch railing and watched the rough surf rolling in and out at its own speed. Ominous dark clouds moved angrily about in the sky, and even the seagulls had gone off somewhere to find shelter. All the signs said that a storm was brewing out there, even though the sun was shining brightly to the north of town.

Cleo brought two bottles of water out of the house and handed one off to Ellie Mae. "Do you believe in omens?"

"Thank you," Ellie Mae said as she twisted the top off the bottle and took a drink. "Depends on whether I like them or not. Do you see one right now?"

"Yes, I do. There's a storm brewing in all our lives, but we *will* all weather it and come out with a blessing on the other side," Cleo answered.

"Is the storm coming into our lives today, like the one we can see in the sky right now, or later?" Ellie Mae asked with some skepticism.

"Today is all but gone, my child, and it's been a good day." Cleo sat down in one of the lawn chairs that had been left on the porch. "You've gotten all the work done on this place, and Ricky assures me come Monday morning, lumber will be arriving to start my project in the barn."

"What did your lawyer say about all that?" Ellie Mae asked.

Cleo narrowed her eyes and looked out over the huge waves smashing against the beach. "She was not a happy camper—but it's my money, not hers. I've got enough in reserve to take care of the barn. That's before the insurance comes through on the center, so . . ." She shrugged.

"I want to grow up and be like you: smart, independent, and living my life to the fullest," Ellie Mae said.

Cleo's expression changed from aggravated to happy in an instant. "Be careful what you wish for, darlin'. You just might get it and then not know what to do with it. And besides, you've already got all those things in your life, and you are beautiful to boot, as my old daddy used to say."

Ellie Mae blew off the compliment with a wave of her hand. "Thank you, but it could be time for you to buy some good strong glasses, Miz Cleo." She pulled a rubber band from her pocket and gathered her hair up into a ponytail. "Looks like it's about to hit us."

"Yep, I just saw a little streak of lightning out there," Cleo said.

"Oh. My. Goodness!" Maude gasped when she came out of the house. "I was going to take Duke out for a walk down the beach, but maybe we should just take a stroll out around the barn."

"If you get caught in the rain, don't go in the barn with that dog. Julep wouldn't like that one bit," Cleo said.

"And I would have to kill the cat if she so much as raised a paw at my dog," Maude declared.

Before Cleo could come back with a smart answer, a fat mouse ran out from under the porch and scurried down the handicap ramp and then out to the beach. Duke growled down deep in his throat and took off after the varmint like he was a hundred-pound Doberman instead of a Chihuahua. When he got to the end of the ribbon leash, he jerked it so hard that Maude lost hold of it, and the race was on. By the time Maude made it to the end of the ramp, Duke was nothing but a tiny blur going east.

"Oh, no! Do something, Cleo and Ellie Mae. Go get him," Maude moaned as she tried to catch her breath.

"Neither of us are fast enough to catch that critter," Cleo said. "He'll come home when he gets hungry, or if he catches that rat, he can wrestle it to the ground and have it for supper."

Maude sat down at the end of the ramp and put her head in her hands. "He's going to be washed away by big waves. I'm never having another pet. I've only had him a little while, and it hurts my heart to lose him."

Cleo stood up and eased down the ramp, sat down beside her sister, and draped an arm around her shoulders. "He'll come home. He knows you love him."

"*You* didn't," Maude whined. "You ran away and never came back."

"I couldn't," Cleo whispered. "Mama caught me packing my bags that night I left and told me that I had to sleep in the bed I was making. She said that if I walked out the door, I couldn't come back in it. I started into your room to tell you goodbye, and she told me that I couldn't do that, either. So about a week later, I wrote you a long letter and asked you to join me and Lewis."

"I don't believe you." Maude stopped weeping and stared at Cleo. "Mother moaned and cried and even went to bed for a week when you left. Then Daddy died, and she went into an even worse depression. I never got a letter from you, and even if I had, I couldn't have left her."

Cleo shrugged, removed her arm, and scooted away from Maude. "Mother was a master at manipulation. She wanted you to feel sorry for her and wait on her hand and foot. She probably burned my letter to you. It's your choice whether to believe me or not, but you knew Mama as well as I did. Or maybe you just had your head stuck in the sand all those years."

"I did not!" Maude protested. "I don't need this. I'm going inside to mourn the loss of my dog." She stood up and stomped across the porch and into the house.

"Was that all true?" Ellie Mae asked as she sat down beside Cleo.

"Every word of it," Cleo answered.

Thunder rolled out there in the distance, and Ellie Mae remembered what Cleo had said about omens. "Duke ran away, and I'm guessing that was the storm. You and Maude talked, even if it was just a little, so that was the blessing. I guess I'm beginning to believe in omens."

"Good for you." Cleo snuggled in closer to Ellie Mae and laid her head on her shoulder. "But I told her the truth, and I wanted her to believe me. Mother was manipulative, and that made it hard to communicate with her. I could see that things weren't right at home, and so could my dad, but she always had Maude snowed."

Ellie Mae patted her on the back. "Baby steps. Give her time to think about what you said, to sort it all out in her mind."

"At our age, we don't have much of that time stuff left in our lives," Cleo said.

"Would it help to talk about what happened that night you left?" Ellie Mae asked.

"I never even told Lewis what Mama said to me, and I was married to him for more than fifty years. I hoped that she would get over her snit in a year or two," Cleo said, "and I sent a Christmas card with money in it every year until she died.

I never got an answer, so I guess she burned them—maybe without even reading them."

Ellie Mae thought about her own father's attitude the day she had brought Sam home after school to work on the blueprints for a house they had to design for a class project. That evening, after Sam had left, her dad told her in no uncertain terms that she was not to be friends with that boy, nor was she ever to bring him into their home again.

"Well, then, we'll just go to his house when we have a team project," she had smarted off.

They never got around to making that threat a reality, though, because when Sam's folks found out he was friends with a white Irish girl, they told him the same thing. Ellie Mae couldn't understand why her friendship with a Black boy was such an issue in today's supposedly modern world, but there hadn't been much she could do about it until she graduated and left home.

"Did she ever meet Lewis?" Ellie Mae asked.

"No, she did not." Cleo's face registered several different emotions, from anger to sadness, one after another, for a few moments. "Mama forbade us to go to the carnival when it came to town. Daddy was a long-distance truck driver and was gone a lot of the time, so her word was the law, the gospel, and probably written in a stone propped up against the Pearly Gates of heaven.

Maude was the good child. Mama called her an angel. I was the wild one. Mama used to say that my attitude was her punishment for all her past sins, or that it wasn't fair that she had to pay for Aunt Nellie's sins."

Ellie Mae was suddenly glad she'd never had a sibling, or her father might have felt the same way about her. "Did you go against your mother very often?"

"Just every chance I got," Cleo answered. "Sometimes I would get caught, and Mama would make me spend hours on my knees, supposedly praying for forgiveness. Things were different sixty and seventy years ago. Parents didn't get in trouble for spanking kids or disciplining them however they saw fit. Mama never hit me, but I'd have rather taken a whipping than a tongue-lashing from her. Her words and her tone cut like a machete through a stick of soft butter."

"Did Maude ever get punished?" Ellie Mae asked.

Cleo managed a giggle at the same time a streak of lightning zigzagged down between the dark clouds and thunder rolled over their heads. "Angels never sin. They are pure and perfect and do everything they're told to do."

"It must've been tough growing up in that kind of house," Ellie Mae said.

"Yes, it was, but I didn't even realize how restricted it was until I was free from all of it. You asked if I took Lewis home to meet my mother. No, I didn't. I knew better. Go back sixty-two years, back about the time that some Texas and Louisiana schools were integrating. Back to a time when if a girl got pregnant, her parents could take her to an unwed-mothers home and force her to give the baby up for adoption. Girls couldn't wear pants to school, and we were even limited as to how much jewelry and makeup we could wear."

"That's so different from today," Ellie Mae said.

"Yes, it is. With that in mind, think about what would happen if I took a guy home that looked a lot like Ricky to meet a mother like mine. He had a white father and a Black mother who were never married," Cleo explained. "When the schools integrated in Arkansas, my Lewis had tried going to the white school, but it didn't work out so well for him, so he quit at sixteen and joined the carnival staff."

"Oh my!" Ellie Mae exclaimed. Time didn't matter so much in some instances because she would have gotten the same treatment if she'd told her dad that she and Sam were getting married. "Did your mama know that Lewis's mama was Black?"

Cleo nodded. "I was upfront and honest with her when she caught me packing to leave. I told her exactly who I was leaving with, and I could almost see fire coming out of her eyes. I don't expect you to understand, but times were so different back then."

"Not really," Ellie Mae contradicted with a shake of her head, then explained her situation with Sam, up to and including his death. "Some folks haven't moved forward as much as you think."

"That's too bad," Cleo said. "Folks should look at the heart, not the color of skin."

A yipping noise filtered in between the flashes of lightning and the blasts of thunder. Ellie Mae stared down the beach but couldn't see anything in the twilight. Then, suddenly, there was Duke, running toward them with a dead mouse hanging out of his mouth. He ran a few feet, then laid the mouse down and barked; then he picked it up and went a little farther before repeating the same. When he reached the house, he didn't stop but ran around the house.

Cleo was on her feet and running after him in a split second. "I left the door to the barn cracked so Julep could get out if she wanted to prowl around."

Ellie Mae didn't know a woman who was nearing eighty years old could run so fast until she tried to keep up with her. Cleo cussed the dog all the way to and inside the barn, then stopped so fast that Ellie Mae almost knocked her down trying to stop herself.

"What's happening?" Ellie Mae bent forward and put her hands on her knees.

"Look!" Cleo pointed.

Duke had taken the mouse close to the hay nest where Julep had her babies and laid it down. Julep came out and rubbed noses with the dog as if she were thanking him, then carried it back to the nest.

"Would you look at that . . . They're friends. How did this happen?" Cleo's tone suggested that she was totally flabbergasted. "They hated each other in the house."

"Maybe they were just having a spat," Ellie Mae suggested. "Julep was angry because of the hurricane, and Duke was used to hunting and running wild, so he didn't want to be cooped up." She tiptoed down the length of the barn and peeked over at the kittens. Even with their eyes just starting to open, they were some ferocious little animals, hissing and spitting at each other as they fought over the mouse as if it were a favorite toy.

Duke stood over to one side, tail wagging, and watched the whole foray as if he were a proud uncle. Then he turned around and went back to where Cleo was still standing in shock and yipped at her.

"What do you want?" she asked.

He barked again, and she picked him up. He put his paws on her chest, laid his head down, and closed his eyes.

"I can't believe this," she said.

"I think he's telling you that he trusts you to take him back to Maude," Ellie Mae told her. "We should do that right now because it's starting to rain."

"Will you come with me?" Cleo asked.

"Of course," Ellie Mae agreed. "Want me to lock the door? It's your barn now."

"Yes, please." Cleo held on to Duke like he was a baby and hurried outside.

The little dog didn't move a muscle when they crossed the yard, went into the house, and climbed the stairs. He had begun to snore when they reached Maude's door and Ellie Mae knocked on it. Maude flung it open, and Cleo handed Duke over to her.

"Oh, my precious pet!" Maude said in a high-pitched voice. "You *did* come home to me. I didn't think you would. I thought the waves would take you away from me."

"May I come in?" Cleo asked.

"Of course." Maude stepped to the side. "Did you rescue him?"

"No, but you've got to hear this story," Cleo said and then mouthed, "Thank you. Talk later?" to Ellie Mae.

"Baby steps, one at a time," Ellie Mae whispered and then backed out into the hallway and went down to the kitchen.

"Where have you been?" Tabby asked. "I heard

you and Cleo talking on the front porch, but when I went outside, both of you took off around the house like the devil was chasing you."

"Good thing you missed that." Ellie Mae chuckled. "Duke chased down a mouse, killed it, and carried it back home—*for the cats!*" She then told her the story about Duke's return and that Maude had invited Cleo into her room.

"Maybe that's the first step toward them making up," Tabby said, but her tone suggested something else was on her mind.

Ellie Mae wondered if maybe Tabby and Alex had had words about how she felt about him having a daughter, but then Alex came through the kitchen, and Tabby smiled at him.

"Want to watch some *Longmire* with us guys?" he asked. "Homer and Frank say it's their favorite all-time Western."

"Next to *Justified*, it's probably mine, too," Tabby answered. "I'll be in there in a few minutes. Go ahead and get it started. I won't be long."

As soon as he cleared the room, Ellie Mae asked, "What's got a bur under your saddle? Don't say you're just glad that you didn't have to look at a dead mouse or baby rat or whatever that varmint is. Something is wrong. I can feel it in my heart, see it in your face, and even hear it in your tone."

"*You* are what's wrong." Tabby wrung her

hands. "And I don't even know how to talk to you about it."

"What'd I do?" Ellie Mae asked.

"I'm worried about you and Ricky starting up a relationship, and it's been on my mind all day long." She picked up a dish towel and twisted it while she talked. "How are you going to work on the barn every day with him if things don't work out? We're committed to selling the barn, and Ricky will be supervising the whole remodeling job. It would be like you were sleeping with your boss, and that could be a disaster."

"There is no Ricky and me, and I think this is jealousy on more levels than just one. You are mad because you can't move on and go out with Alex even though he's made it clear he is interested in you. And you're jealous because I might fall for Ricky, but . . ." Ellie Mae stopped for a breath, wishing she hadn't said those things.

"You need to figure out what you want— friendship or relationship—and remember that he's younger than you." Tabby paused. "Do you want to have problems with your dad all over again? It would be a good thing if we could make peace with our folks, don't you think?"

Ellie Mae had never—not one time—been really upset with Tabby, but the very mention of her father caused her anger to flare up. "What does a couple of years between us have to do with anything at our age? And I don't care what my father thinks of Ricky. I love you, Tabitha June, but you are not my mother."

"No, I'm not, and I'm glad for that. I can't imagine trying to raise a daughter as rebellious as you were and still are." Tabby stood up and moved over to the kitchen. "You would have driven me up a wall like James did."

Ellie Mae balled her small hands into fists. "Don't you compare me to that bastard."

"Then think about your choices and the consequences." Tabby's tone was scolding. "Don't use Ricky as a substitute for Sam."

"I need time away from you for a few hours, too." Ellie Mae whipped around and stormed into her room, slammed the door behind her, and fell back onto her bed. "Now I believe in omens because that was one ugly storm between me and Tabby," she muttered. "I just hope there's a silver lining in that dark cloud, because it's our first-ever argument, and I don't like fighting with her. Maybe the omen is that there's only so much peace and love that can exist in this house. Cleo and Maude took a step forward, so Tabby and I had to take a step backward to maintain balance."

That's a load of horse crap, Aunt Charlotte said very loudly in her head. *You need to listen to Tabby, and you damn sure need to take care of your emotions about Sam's death before you move on to someone else—friend or boyfriend.*

"Okay, okay!" Ellie Mae sighed and then

268

stood up, peeled off her clothes, and went to the bathroom for a long hot shower. "I hear you both, and I promise I'll take it into consideration. But I make my own choices. Like that song says about living and dying by the choices we make: I'll live with the consequences of mine—and I'll do it without whining."

Chapter Thirteen

M ore has happened in a month than should in a year," Tabby muttered that Saturday morning as she stirred up a date-nut cake. With a long sigh, she thought back over the past four weeks and wished she hadn't even brought up the situation with Ricky and Ellie Mae to her cousin. "I just didn't want to see her, or Ricky, hurt—or for them to be in an awkward situation."

Her phone rang. When she saw Charlotte Landry's name on the screen, she answered. "Good morning. What are you doing today? I'm putting you on speaker because I'm cooking, but there's no one in the kitchen with me."

"I'm playing canasta in a few minutes with my Sunday-school class. I'm hosting today, but we're having a potluck lunch in between our games, so I only had to make a peach cobbler and a salad. What's the matter with you?" Charlotte asked.

Tabby filled the Bundt pan with batter and slid it into the oven. She thought about denying that anything was wrong, but she'd learned in the past that there was no such thing as fooling Aunt Charlotte. "Ellie Mae and I had an argument a week ago, and nothing's been the same since."

"Well, it's about damn time," Charlotte said with half a giggle.

Tabby was speechless for a moment.

"Are you still there?" Charlotte yelled.

Tabby took the phone off speaker and held it to her ear. "Yes, I'm here. Why did you say that about it being time?"

"Tell me about the argument."

"It's a long story." Tabby was in no mood to go over the details again. She'd already beaten that old proverbial horse to death more than once during the past week by going over and over what they had said to each other.

"I've got half an hour and a cup of hot peach tea in my hand. Start talking," Charlotte told her.

"You know that Ricky is working on the barn . . ." Tabby went on to unload her burden to her aunt, ending with, "It hasn't been the same since that night. It's like a cold blast of air has come between us."

"Best news ever," Charlotte said. "You've been in a submissive state of mind ever since you were a little girl. You wouldn't speak up to your parents—not until James came into your world. Then you took a back seat to whatever he wanted or demanded of you. Ellie Mae has been a spitfire her whole life. She plows right into a problem like a bull in a china shop. Both of you are insecure in your own way. *You* keep everything inside. *She* bluffs her way through whatever obstacle comes up. I knew there would be disagreements between you, but those are the very things that will make each of you grow."

"Aunt Charlotte, I am almost forty. I'm a grown woman." Tabby could hear the exasperation in her own voice. "And Ellie Mae is pushing thirty."

Her aunt chuckled again. "Age has nothing to do with anything."

Tabby remembered what Ellie Mae had said about Ricky being a little younger than she was. "How can it not? I've been through rough times, and Ellie Mae could learn from my mistakes."

"And she's been through some, too, and *you* could learn from *her* mistakes," Charlotte reminded her in her listen-to-me tone. "In any relationship—whether it's cousins, friends, or lovers—we can learn from each other. Should I talk to Ellie Mae?"

"Lord no!" Tabby spit out without a split second's hesitation. "I don't want to add talking about her behind her back to the iceberg already between us."

"Okay, then, but you two need to talk this out and move on. You can't run a business or live in the same house together with an elephant in the room. Look, Tabby, my first friend is here to play cards, so I have to go now. But let me know how things are going in the next few days," Charlotte said. "Bye now, and I love you—both of you!"

Tabby disconnected the call and slipped her

phone back into her pocket, set the timer on the oven, and went out to sit on the porch for a few minutes. Maybe the smell of salt in the air would ease her mind, she thought, but a blast of cold wind sent her back inside for a sweater and reminded her again of the chill between her and Ellie Mae.

The noise of saws and hammers going nonstop in the backyard drew her to the back porch. Julep joined her when she sat down on the top step. The old cotton candy–vendor's wagon Cleo had purchased had been delivered the day before, and even though the outside of it hadn't been repainted, the cat and kittens seemed happy to move right into it. Right then, Homer and Frank were sitting just inside the doors of the barn, and Cleo was in the cat house.

In spite of the heavy feeling in her heart because of the argument with Ellie Mae, Tabby smiled at how fast they'd all started calling the small wagon by that name. The back door squeaked when it opened, and Maude came outside with Duke at her heels. Since he had come home last week after chasing down the mouse, Maude had been more comfortable letting him go on his own little adventures down to the beach.

"I smell something heavenly baking." She eased down on the top step beside Tabby.

"That would be date-nut cake," Tabby said. "It's from one of Aunt Charlotte's recipes."

"Well, my mouth is already watering just thinking about it." Maude pointed to the dog and the cat, who were touching noses. "I thought for sure they'd be enemies, but it looks like they were just having bad days with the hurricane and all."

After a couple more nose bumps, Julep meandered back toward her new home, and Duke went out to check on what was going on in the barn.

"Do you think you and Cleo will ever be more than enemies?" Tabby asked.

"I have to love her because Jesus says I do, but it's tough to even like her," Maude said. "I've been praying that I will learn to do that, at the very least. A couple of times—like when she asked me to live in the new place and when she brought Duke to me—I almost thought I could. But there's a lot of history there."

"Oh, really?" Tabby raised an eyebrow.

"We used to be sisters," Maude whispered, "but don't tell her that I said that. She never could follow orders, and Mother was a little bit of a temperamental person. Living with both of them in the house was a good bit like living with an earthquake and a hurricane hitting me every minute of every day."

Maude didn't know they knew. But Tabby was not surprised at her revelation. She could relate. Sometimes, she had felt the same way living with James. She never knew what demands he would make or how long the silent treatment would go on if he didn't get his way. "I lived with a controlling husband, who thought a wife should be so submissive that she didn't even question whatever he decided to do."

Maude let out a long sigh. "That was my mother. Daddy was a long-distance truck driver. Looking back, I think that he hated the time he spent at home and was always eager to get back in that big rig and leave—she bossed him around so much when he was home that I kind of felt sorry for him. But . . ." She paused. "Cleo is coming out of that abominable wagon, so I'd better hush. No, wait a minute—she's going into the barn."

"You were saying?" Tabby asked.

Maude touched her cheek with a forefinger. "Where was I? Oh, yes. I was the child that Mother kind of liked. She tattled to me about Cleo and reminded me almost daily that I should never get married or else I might have a child just like her. Then Cleo ran away, and Daddy died, and I was responsible for taking care of her. No matter how she behaved, she was my mother, and I owed her that much, but Cleo cheated me out of a life of my own. It's hard to forgive her for doing that," Maude said. "She doesn't deserve forgiveness after the mess she left me with."

"We don't always pardon a person to make *them* feel better," Tabby said, but she wasn't sure if she was talking to Maude or to herself. "We let them off the hook to take the hardness out of our own hearts. I'm trying to get over the way James treated me in order to even take one baby step forward. If I keep all that bitterness in my heart, it will ruin my life."

Maude seemed to be letting that settle for a moment, and then she asked, "How has that worked out for you?"

Tabby slung an arm around Maude's shoulders and gave her a sideways hug. "I'm still working on forgiving my ex-husband for buying our daughter the car I didn't want her to have. The first time she drove it, she was hit by a drunk driver and died instantly. Between that and his constant demands, our marriage fell apart."

"I'm sorry for your loss. I guess we've both got a lot of praying to do," Maude said. "Mother always preached to me that we should take our problems to God."

Tabby just nodded in agreement, but she wondered if maybe Maude needed to listen to what God had to say about a solution to her problems when she unloaded her problems on Him.

How about you? Aunt Charlotte's voice popped into her head so clearly that she twisted around to see if she was standing on the other side of the screen door. *When you get an answer to a problem, do you apply it? Or do you ignore it?*

"Thanks for listening." Maude's knees creaked

when she stood up. "I'm going to go out to the barn and sit with Homer and Frank for a little while. Never know how many pretty days we'll have, so we might as well"—a broad smile deepened the wrinkles around her eyes—"make hay while the sun shines."

"Anytime." Tabby stood up and headed into the house about the same time the timer went off in the kitchen.

Ignore it and it will go away.

That's what Ellie Mae thought all day as she fought off a bit of nausea. She attributed it to nerves. After all, this would be her first official date in more than a year, and the first one since Sam had died. She always came home from a date—especially a *first* date—to find Sam waiting up for her so they could talk about what had happened. She did the same whenever he went out with a girl, but tonight, he wouldn't be there.

Tabby will be, the voice in her head reminded her.

"Yes, and I don't know if she wants to talk about my date," she whispered as she dropped the last of her clothing on the bathroom floor and stepped into the shower.

No way would she admit that she didn't feel well—especially to Tabby. Thank God she and Ricky were going to supper so she would have an excuse not to eat with everyone that evening. She stood under the pulsating water for a long time, but not even that helped. Then she dried her hair and curled it and dressed in a pair of skinny jeans and a forest-green sweater that matched her eyes. She had just finished applying lipstick—the taste of it gagged her—when the doorbell rang. Before she could get out of her bedroom, she heard Tabby telling Ricky to come on in.

Awkward was the only word that described the situation when she walked out into the foyer. She caught the disapproving looks from her cousin. On the other hand, Ricky's eyes said he sure liked what he was seeing.

There are two sides to every coin, Sam reminded her in that quiet way he had of speaking. *Both are equally important.*

"You look beautiful," Ricky said.

"Thank you." She tucked her arm into his and said, "Don't wait up, Tabby. We might be late."

"Don't wake me," Tabby said. "You know I'm an old bear if I don't get my rest."

"Amen to that." Ellie Mae let go of Ricky's arm and picked up her purse on the way outside. There was no doubt in her mind that Tabby was still mad at her—the look in her eyes and the set of her jaw testified to as much. That made Ellie Mae sad, but not sad enough to make her tell Ricky she couldn't go.

Ricky had changed from the faded bibbed

overalls he wore to work every day into a pair of jeans, a light-blue-and-tan plaid shirt, and cowboy boots. A soft breeze brought a whiff of his shaving lotion right to her. Any other time, she would have inhaled deeply to enjoy more of the sexy scent, but that evening, she turned her face away from him.

"You really do look nice," he said as he ushered her out to his truck with his hand on the small of her back and then opened the door for her. "But you didn't have to get all 'fancied up,' as my grandmother says. We're just going to a burger place up in Anahuac, and then I thought we'd take a walk through a little park up there where Mama and Daddy used to take me to play. Unless you would rather drive to Beaumont and catch a late showing of a movie."

"The park is fine with me. Do they have swings?" She assured herself that by the time they arrived at the burger place, her nerves would have settled, and she would be starving. But even the thought of swinging made her stomach do a flip-flop.

Did the universe really have two sides to every coin? For the life of her, she couldn't fathom what the other side of her father's prejudicial coin would have.

Her hands went clammy, and her focus blurred when she looked out the truck's window at the backside of the B and B. She took a long, deep breath, and her vision cleared up, but her stomach cramped, and she felt faint. No amount of ignoring the feeling was going to make it disappear.

She had no doubt that she would never make it twenty miles up the road without her either needing a bathroom or having to hang her head out the door to upchuck.

"I'm so sorry," she said, "but we're going to have to put this off until another time."

"Are you sick?" he asked.

She nodded. "It just hit me, and . . ." She gagged. "I've got to get into the house. So, so sorry, Ricky." She bailed out of the truck and jogged across the yard and into the B and B, then barely made it to the bathroom in time to drop to her knees and hug the toilet.

"Tab . . . beee," she whined, but no one answered. When she finished dry heaving, she washed all the makeup off her face, peeled off her clothing, and left it on the bathroom floor. Then she put on an oversize T-shirt that had belonged to Sam and crawled into bed.

"Which side of the coin is this?" she muttered. "Do you not like Ricky? Are you jealous of him, Sam? Why did you do this to me?"

I didn't do this, Sam scolded her. *It was probably those unwashed grapes you ate. I've told you a million times not to eat anything until you wash it.*

· · ·

Tabby left for a walk down the beach just seconds after Ellie Mae and Ricky closed the front door. The feelings that seemed to be widening the gap between her and her cousin were constantly on her mind, and she planned to wait up for her that evening—even if Ellie Mae had explicitly told her not to do that. She did not intend to get to be the age that Cleo and Maude were and live with an iceberg the size of an elephant still sitting between them, growing bigger with the passing of each day. This whole thing was going to be settled tonight, she was determined, even if it took until the break of dawn to get done.

With her mind on Ellie Mae and her hands in her hair, trying to pull it up into a ponytail, she didn't even see the piece of driftwood right in front of her. It wasn't all that big, but she still tripped over it. She grabbed for something to break her fall, but all she got was an armful of night air. Her first thought when she fell into the shallow surf was that the Landry women really *had* been cursed with clumsiness. There she was, lying on her side in the foamy surf that smelled of salt and fish. She pushed herself up to a sitting position, then stood slowly and began to laugh.

Laughter is far better than tears, Aunt Charlotte often said. *Tears make wrinkles, and laughter puts joy in your face.*

She brushed what sand she could from her wet clothing and took a couple of steps, only to find out that her ankle was already getting sore.

"Nothing to do but hobble home," she said as she started back toward the B and B.

She was halfway there when she saw Alex coming toward her. He had been walking, but when he saw her, he began to jog. Her pulse sped up in concert, and her heart threw in an extra thump at the sight of him caring enough to race toward her.

"Good grief! What have you done?" Alex quickly wrapped an arm around her shoulders and helped her limp to the house.

"I wasn't watching where I was going, and I tripped over a piece of driftwood. I've had ankle sprains before, so I know this isn't a bad one. It's just going to be tender for a day or two. Maybe you should know right now, before we go any further in whatever this is between us, that I'm not known for gracefulness," she replied.

"You make up for what you lack there in beauty," Alex said with a grin. "Can you walk up the stairs to the porch, or should we use the ramp?"

"Let's go around back," she said. "My pride is hurt worse than my ankle. Let's just take a moment and sit out there in the lawn chairs in front of the barn before we go inside. I don't want all the folks in the house to treat me like an invalid. If I sit for a little while, I'll be able to walk better, and maybe they won't even notice."

"They love you. And besides, you're the primary cook, now that I'm working in the barn." Alex pulled up a chair for her and got her settled before he sat down. "They sure wouldn't want to have to live on canned soup and sandwiches, although I bet Homer and Frank wouldn't mind, if they had a choice between staying here and going to a nursing home. Sorry I haven't been more help this week."

Tabby raised a hand in protest. "Hey, you don't owe anyone an apology. Everyone has been pitching in and helping clean up the kitchen after meals. Have you noticed that even Maude and Cleo haven't been biting at each other as much lately? I think they might be friends someday, if they live long enough."

"If they live to be a hundred, maybe." Alex chuckled. "But yes, I have noticed, and so have Homer and Frank. We've decided to sit back and let it all play out rather than interfering and trying to talk to them."

"Smart move." Tabby wished that James would have had that kind of insight instead of always wanting to control every issue. His job as a bank president fit him well: he had lots of folks to boss around and a position that made him feel superior.

"Are you all right?" Alex blurted out. "I'm not asking about your ankle but about whatever has been worrying you."

"Why are you asking?"

"You've been off this whole week. Did I say or do something to offend you?" he asked.

James had never noticed when she was having a bad week or even a horrible day. Not once in their married life had he asked if he had upset her in any way.

"Ellie Mae and I had an argument," Tabby answered, and then she told him what she had said. "I felt like it was something she needed to hear and think about, but . . ."

Alex reached across the distance and covered her hand with his. "You did it out of concern for her feelings, and, honey, there are no *buts* in love. It doesn't matter if it's love between siblings or between a man and woman. There should never be a *but*—only *ands*. *But* means there's something negative; *and* means there's just more positive on the way."

"Thank you." Her mouth went so dry at his touch that she was surprised she could utter a single word—much less two.

"Ricky hasn't dated a lot and has only been in a couple of semiserious relationships, but he seems to like Ellie Mae a lot. He was all psyched up about tonight," Alex said with a grin. "He was worried about making a good impression and

284

wondering whether he should kiss her good night on their first official date."

"Do guys worry about that?" Tabby asked. "I mean, I just thought guys would be so macho that—" She stopped herself, deciding right then that she had to start being more open-minded and do a lot less comparing of James and Alex.

"Oh, yeah, we do, and we probably worry more about what we'll wear than girls do." His grin turned into a chuckle. "If *we* go out, you can bet I'll show up in my best jeans and an ironed shirt, and I'll even polish my Sunday boots."

"Oh, *are* we going out someday?"

Alex gave her hand a gentle squeeze. "Yes, we are. But I'm a patient man, and I can wait until *you* are ready. You've still got to get over Natalie's death—and the divorce."

"It's been two years," she told him.

"Each person grieves at their own speed, darlin'." He brought her hand to his lips and kissed her knuckles.

"Thank you for understanding," she said.

This feeling must be what people are talking about when they say they can feel the chemistry and electricity sparking between them, Tabby thought. She had never felt like this—not with her teenage boyfriends or with James. Why couldn't the universe have put Alex back in her path earlier?

"Hey!" Cleo yelled as she came out of the cat

house. "I've got the babies all to sleep, so I'm going in the house for another piece of that cake and a big glass of milk. Y'all want to join me?" She didn't even slow down as she headed straight for the back porch.

"Love to," Alex said, getting to his feet and helping Tabby stand. "How's the ankle feeling now?"

"Already better," she answered.

Just as the door slammed behind Cleo, Tabby lost her balance and started to fall for the second time that evening. Alex caught her and pulled her tightly to his chest. Then he tipped her chin up with his fist and stared right into her eyes for a long moment before he bent his head forward to kiss her.

She barely had time to moisten her lips when his mouth closed over hers. At first the kiss was sweet, but then it deepened, and Tabby's whole world stood perfectly still. When Alex took half a step back, a falling star shot through the sky behind his head.

"Oh my!" she gasped.

"Was it that good?" He brushed a soft kiss across her forehead.

"Yes, it was," she answered honestly. "But there was a shooting star right afterward."

"What are you going to wish for?" he asked.

"One more of those kisses." She was surprised at her own brazenness.

"Your wish is . . ." He tipped up her chin again and kissed her once more.

This one left her breathless, but there were no more stars falling out of the sky, and she didn't have time to wish again because he drew her in for another kiss.

Chapter Fourteen

Tabby eased her bedroom door shut and went straight to the bathroom for a shower. "What the devil? This is just their first date. Are they already in bed together?" she complained as she stepped over Ellie Mae's jeans, sweater, and shoes. The sweet memory of Alex's kisses disappeared in a fog of the slightest sickly smell that hung around the room.

A groan from the other side of the bathroom door brought it all home to her—those were groans not of passion but of pain. Tabby didn't knock but instead marched right into her cousin's bedroom and sat down on the edge of the bed. "What's going on? You're supposed to be out with Ricky."

"Didn't make it out of the driveway," Ellie Mae whispered.

Tabby laid a hand on Ellie Mae's forehead. "Why didn't you call me? You've got a fever, girl."

Ellie Mae swiped a tear from her cheek. "I did, but it went to voice mail, so I thought you were too mad at me to answer."

"I'm going to get a cold cloth, an aspirin, and some nausea pills. You lay still." Tabby started for the door and then turned back. "Alex kissed me."

"Was it good?" Ellie Mae asked.

"Amazing." All the thoughts of their angry words came back to Tabby, and she felt guilty.

"At least one of us had a good time," Ellie Mae groaned; then she slung off the covers and headed to the bathroom with her hand over her mouth.

Tabby followed and kicked Ellie Mae's clothing over to the other side of the bathroom. She raised the toilet lid and held her cousin's curly red hair back when she bent over. "Bless your heart. Did this come on suddenly, or have you been sick all day?"

Ellie Mae moaned and stretched out on the cool tile floor. "All day, but I thought it was nerves. First-date nerves and that argument with you. But I think it was those unwashed grapes that I ate before you put them in the sink. They just looked so good, and they tasted fine, but . . ." She moaned. "Just let me lay here for a while to be sure it's all over."

Tabby wet a cloth with cold water, sat down on the floor, and washed Ellie Mae's face. "How are you ever going to date anyone, if it wasn't the grapes and this is just what happens every time?"

"Never happened before, but if this is what it's like going forward, I'll be an old maid all my life," Ellie Mae declared.

Tabby tucked Ellie Mae's hair behind her ears.

"Please, tell me this isn't morning sickness."

"I haven't had sex in six months, so I think we're good on that issue," Ellie Mae answered. "I'm going to try to get from here to the bed. Thank you for being here for me, and I hope you don't get whatever this is."

"Me too, but I hope even more that our guests"—she pointed to the ceiling—"don't come down with it. We're miles from a doctor or a hospital. I hope you haven't gotten the flu!"

Ellie Mae sat up and grabbed her head. "That would be horrible. This is too miserable to have to endure it for more than a day, and Maude would be a blister if she got it. But I think it's food poisoning. I had it once before, and I heard Sam fussing at me in my head about eating unwashed fruit. I hope I don't have the flu and infect anyone else."

Tabby laid a hand on Ellie Mae's head. "I just hope that whatever it is won't need a trip to the hospital. When James came down with acute appendicitis, he spiked a fever that wouldn't go away."

"My side doesn't hurt, so rule out appendicitis. We haven't been anywhere in a month for us to catch anything." She stood up slowly and made her way back to bed. "It's either something I ate or a twenty-four-hour bug."

Tabby tucked the bedspread up around her cousin's shoulders and then headed out of the room. "I've got something that will calm that stomach right down. It tastes awful, but if you'll lay real still for five minutes, you'll feel better."

"Anything you say," Ellie Mae muttered. "And, Tabby, I'm sorry for what I said about—"

"Me too," Tabby butted in before Ellie Mae could finish her sentence.

Ellie Mae opened her eyes slowly and lay very still, not wanting to move for fear that her stomach would rebel against any kind of jiggling. She felt as if she was suffocating, so she threw off the covers and eased out of bed. Her stomach seemed to be fine, but she was as sweaty as if she'd worked all day in the blistering-hot sun, so she took a cool shower. Then she dressed in a fresh pair of pajama bottoms and a T-shirt and wandered out to the kitchen. She poured herself a glass of sweet tea, added ice, and took a sip. It felt good going down, so she carried it into the living room and sat down on the end of the sofa.

A lovely crescent moon hung in the window, with stars dancing all around it. *If an artist could capture that scene on canvas, it would probably make him famous,* she thought. She stretched her legs out on the sofa, used the arm as a backrest, and sent up a silent prayer of gratitude that whatever sickness had hit her was passing.

At first, she thought the sound of someone weeping was coming from across the foyer—

maybe in Tabby's bedroom—but then she realized the noise was coming from upstairs. When she heard a deep voice mumble, "Run! Run fast!" she sat up a little straighter. Then there was the sound of footsteps and Cleo's unmistakable voice saying, "Shh . . . wake up . . . it's okay, Frank."

Ellie Mae started to head that way, but then she heard Cleo talking softly as she and Frank came downstairs. Remembering that she could be contagious, Ellie Mae just sat back and waited.

The kitchen light came on, and Cleo said, "I'm going to make us some hot chocolate and get out a plate of those peanut butter cookies that Tabby made today. Then you can tell me about that nightmare."

Ellie Mae eased her half-full glass of tea down onto the end table and wished it had been Maude who'd had the bad dream. Maybe that would help her realize that Cleo really wanted to make amends and be a sister to her.

There was the sound of the microwave door closing, a humming noise, and then a *ding* when the instant hot chocolate was finished. Ellie Mae waited for Maude to say something, but it was Frank's deep southern voice that she heard next.

"No sense in talking about a dream that's kept coming back for more'n fifty years," he said.

"You won't ever get rid of it if you keep it all bottled up inside of you," Cleo said. "So tell me what it is that makes you want to run. That's what you were yelling in your sleep."

Ellie Mae started to get up to tiptoe back into her room, but she couldn't seem to force herself to leave, and she didn't want them to know she could hear every word. Eavesdropping, or just flat out being rude, she was drawn to their conversation.

It's like watching a horrible car wreck, she thought. *But instead of not taking my eyes off it, I can't shut my ears to it.*

"I've never talked to anyone about the dream," Frank said.

"Is it about the war or something else?" Cleo asked.

"It changes from time to time," Frank answered. "There's two nightmares where I wake up yelling 'Run.' One is about when Homer got shot, and the other is . . ." He paused.

Ellie Mae got up and tiptoed into the foyer, where she could stay in the shadows of a ficus tree and peek around the corner. She'd done that often when she was a little girl and had eavesdropped on her dad and Aunt Charlotte's conversations in the kitchen.

Cleo set two mugs of hot chocolate and a container of cookies on the table, and then she sat down across from Frank and laid a hand on his arm. They looked like an old married couple sitting there together. Cleo was dressed in bright red satin pajamas, and her hair hung to her waist. Frank wore plaid pajama pants and a red sweatshirt.

"Which one is it tonight?" Cleo asked.

Frank picked up a cookie and dipped it into his hot chocolate.

I know you're stalling. Ellie Mae forgot all about being sick and slid down the wall to sit on the floor. She pulled her knees up and wrapped her arms around them.

"It's about my cousin. He was just younger than me. He grew up in the city, and I was just a country cousin," Frank finally said. "It was during Halloween in Louisiana. Mama took me over there to visit with her people during that time of year. Quinton—that was my cousin's name—and I went to a haunted house the last night that it was going on."

"And you got into trouble and had to run away?" Cleo asked. "That's what you were saying when I woke you."

"We were only thirteen that year, and that haunted house scared the hell out of us." Frank's deep voice sounded hollow. "When we came out into the alley back behind the place, there were a couple of boys in a fight. I recognized one as the kid who had taken our money to get into the haunted house, but I didn't know the other one, who was brandishin' a gun and demandin' that the kid who worked there give him the money."

"What happened?" Cleo asked.

"It wasn't our fight, and when a shot got fired, I yelled at Quinton to run. I took off as fast as I could, thinking he was behind me. That boy always won the races we had at family reunions. It wasn't until I got home that I figured he had taken a shortcut and beat me to Aunt Rosie's house. I shouldn't be tellin' you this. It's not something that can be helped by talkin' about it."

"Yes, it can," Cleo disagreed. "What happened? Was Quinton hurt?"

"My daddy and uncle went back to where I'd left him, and he was layin' there in a puddle of blood. He was still alive then, but he didn't make it through the night. The police came and said it was a robbery that went bad. Both of the other boys had gone, and it was just my story. At first they thought I'd shot him, but when they found the gun, my prints weren't on it," Frank answered and then sighed. "If I would've made sure he was behind me, I might have gotten help to save his life—but I ran. I've never forgiven myself for that night, and it comes back to haunt me."

A lump the size of a grapefruit grew in Ellie Mae's throat, and tears welled up in her eyes. She wanted to go into the kitchen and hug Frank, tell him that it wasn't his fault, but that would create an awkward moment. Besides, Cleo was taking care of things very well.

"Did they find the boy that killed him?" Cleo asked.

"To tell the truth," Frank said with a shrug, "I don't think the authorities put a lot of effort into it. Things were different back then. Wasn't like it is today."

Cleo stood up and rounded the table. She wrapped her arms around Frank and hugged him tightly. "You have got to forgive yourself, Frank, or the dreams won't ever stop. Quinton should have run instead of trying to stand up to those bullies. With that gun, the numbers were against y'all, even if you were both scrappers."

Ellie Mae took Cleo's advice to her own heart. She needed to forgive herself for not getting Sam to the hospital sooner, for not realizing that something was seriously wrong and that his ailment was not just a common headache. Until she did that, she wasn't going to truly move on with her life.

"How do I do that?" Frank asked.

"Come on." Cleo took him by the hand and headed toward the door. "I'll show you how."

"We can't go outside barefoot," Frank protested.

Cleo tugged at his hand and said, "Yes, we can. We ran around barefoot when we were kids, and we can do it now. Don't you know that when we get old, we get to revert back to being kids and enjoy the simple things in life?"

"I heard my mama say that my grandmother was in her second childhood before Big Mama passed away." Frank finally smiled.

"Big Mama?" Cleo kept his hand in hers and led him outside.

"That was my maternal grandmother. Daddy's mama was Mam-Maw. Big Mama lived right next door to us. We had to obey her just like we did Mama," Frank explained.

Ellie Mae waited until the back door closed, and then she followed them. She had to know how Cleo was going to make Frank forget the trauma that had plagued him since he was a teenager.

"You are a heck of a woman," Frank chuckled when they left the handicap ramp and their feet hit the sand. "How does this help a nightmare?"

"Trust me," Cleo said.

"Are you a witch?" Frank asked. "Big Mama's sister did spells and believed in that kind of thing."

"Then this will work." Cleo walked right up to the edge of the water, picked up a handful of sand, and handed it to Frank. "This is your nightmare. Each little grain of sand represents one of those nights when you woke up in a sweat, with tears running down your face as you thought of your cousin."

Frank held the sand in his hands. "What do I do with it?"

Ellie Mae slumped down behind the log.

"You give it to the sea," Cleo told him. "Throw it out there as far as you can, and let poor little Quinton finally rest in peace. His spirit has been uneasy all these years because you have been so troubled about that night. It's a nice, still night, so the wind won't bring the sand back to you. The ocean will carry it way on out there and out of your life. You and Quinton will both be at peace."

"This sounds *couyon*," Frank whispered. "That's Cajun for *insane*. But I'll try anything, so here goes." He put all the sand in one of his big hands, drew back like he was throwing a baseball, and let it fly. A north wind picked up about that time and carried it out even farther than his expert toss could have taken it.

"Rest in peace, Quinton," Cleo said. "And you are forgiven, Frank."

"Strange, but I do feel better," Frank whispered.

Cleo stooped down and got another handful of sand and put it in his hands. "Of course you do. But before we leave, I want you to get rid of whatever it is that causes you to have nightmares from the war."

Frank took the sand and said, "I told Homer to run, and he did. Sometimes it gets all mixed up in my head, and I don't know if it's Quinton or if it's Homer—but I keep dreaming that the bullet went into his heart and killed him."

298

"Give it to the sea," Cleo said. "Homer says you saved his life."

Frank repeated his last throw. The sand seemed to hover in the air as if it were moving in slow motion; then it settled into the water. "One more thing," he said as he got his own handful of sand. "This is for the guilt I feel about poor old Homer never getting married and having a family."

"Why would you feel guilty about that?" Cleo asked. "You didn't get married, either."

"But I didn't want to. Homer, though, fell in love with a woman when we was about thirty, and, well . . ."

"Well, what?"

"Things didn't work out, and he never trusted another woman for anything other than a fling now and then after that," Frank answered.

"That didn't have anything to do with you, did it?" Cleo asked.

"It kind of did. I didn't like her, and several of our friends told him she was cheating on him. He didn't believe them, so I told him what I knew. He believed me." He took a deep breath. "I feel guilty about that. Maybe if they'd given it more time, things could have worked out between them. Thank you for this, Cleo. Now, can we go back in the house? I believe I'll be able to sleep now."

"Yes, we sure can," Cleo answered.

Ellie Mae waited until she saw the kitchen light

go out, and then she made her way across the beach, up the seawall and porch steps, and into the house. She was sure glad that Cleo hadn't locked the back door, because she'd forgotten to pick up her phone when she left her bedroom earlier. She slipped back inside, tiptoed across the foyer, and eased into Tabby's room. Before she even reached the side of the bed, Tabby sat straight up and started rubbing her eyes.

"Are you going to be sick again? Do you need me?" she asked.

"No, I need you to come with me." Ellie Mae drew back the covers and took Tabby's hand in hers. "We need to do something right now. It might have to do with the crescent moon. I don't know that—but it could, and I don't want to miss this chance or wait a whole month for another moon like it."

"Are you sure you're all right?" Tabby let herself be pulled up to a standing position.

"Don't put on shoes," Ellie Mae said. "That could have something to do with it, too. I want this to work as well as it did for Frank."

"Are you delusional? How high did your fever go?" Tabby asked.

"I don't think I ever had a fever." Ellie Mae tugged on her hand and led her across the foyer and the kitchen, out the back door, and down to the beach in front of the old log.

"You do realize that it's the middle of the night, don't you?" Tabby asked.

"Yep." Ellie Mae picked up a fistful of sand and told her all about the ritual Cleo and Frank had performed. "We've got to move on past our argument and past Sam's and Natalie's deaths, Tabitha June, so we're going to do this. Natalie can't rest until you let her, and Sam can't until I let go of him. We're going to give all the pain to the sea and only remember the good times we had with them. Then you are going to throw away all the resentment you have in your heart for James."

Tabby covered a yawn with her hand. "That's—"

"*Couyon*, according to Frank, and that means *insane* in Cajun. But if it works, just think how blessed we'll be, and when we get done, I'll tell you what Frank threw away." Ellie Mae put a fistful of sand into Tabby's hand and said, "Throw it as far as you can. Think of it like this—you are setting Natalie's spirit free."

Tabby heaved the sand into the water, then picked up a second handful and threw it out over the water as well. "I do want to be rid of these feelings so that I can move on. I'll try anything twice."

"Me too," Ellie Mae said and did the same. Then she sat down with her back against the old log.

"So, we're staying out here for a while?" Tabby asked as she sat down beside Ellie Mae.

"Yes, we are," Ellie Mae answered. "I feel so much lighter. It's hard to explain. How about you?"

"You feel like a weight has been lifted because you threw up so hard earlier this evening," Tabby said. "But I do feel like a burden has lightened a bit. Maybe it's just the physical act of doing something stupid like this that brings a spiritual peace. Do you think Cleo is a witch?"

"Nope. Just a very wise woman."

Tabby picked up another handful of sand and let some of it sift through her fingers; then she stood up and heaved the rest of it out into the ocean as a big wave came to shore. "That one is throwing away the argument we had. You were right—but I'm hoping that now I can be ready to move on to a relationship."

"Me too," Ellie Mae said. "It might not be with Ricky, but with someone. After all, I'm the one who'll have to produce a Landry heir to run this place when we're too old, if there's going to be one."

"Hey, now," Tabby said with half a giggle. "Lots of forty-year-old women have a child. You told me that yourself."

Ellie Mae moved over and gave Tabby a hug. "That's the spirit!"

Chapter Fifteen

D o you think we'll ever get a do-over on that date?" Ricky asked when Ellie Mae showed up at the barn that morning, even though they'd decided to take the rest of the week off for the Thanksgiving Day holiday.

Ellie Mae climbed up the ladder to the second floor and sat down on the bare boards. "Maybe. But if I get sick again on the day of the date, I'm taking it as an omen that we shouldn't be seeing each other." She crossed her fingers behind her back like a little girl in hopes that she didn't turn up sick again. She really did want to get to know Ricky better.

Ricky followed her up and plopped down beside her. "Will you be my date for the festival on Saturday?"

"We can give it a try," she agreed. "But we'll be building a castle most of the morning."

"That, and a visit to the taco wagon could *be* the date," Ricky said.

"I'll meet you at the beach at nine o'clock," Ellie Mae said with a nod. "The spot for the B and B's sandcastle is right behind the old log." A visual of hiding in that spot just a few nights before popped into Ellie Mae's head. Crazy—or *couyon*—as it was, she felt more at peace after Cleo's sand ritual.

Ricky covered her hand with his and gently squeezed. "I'll be there, with my red plastic cup to use to build the turrets on our castle."

"I'll bring a putty knife to shape your turrets," Ellie Mae said. "And I'm sure Tabby will gather up some kitchen tools for us to work with. How big is our castle going to be?"

"At least six bedrooms and a huge living room for the kids to play in," he answered.

"Are we talking about a sandcastle or a future?" Ellie Mae frowned. "*Six* bedrooms?"

"That should accommodate a dozen kids, right?" Ricky teased. "I don't think each kid needs a room of their own. Sharing with a sibling teaches them not to be selfish. What do you think?"

"I've never had a sibling, so I can't pass judgment on that," Ellie Mae answered. "But right now, I think we should go back to the house and help Alex and Tabby get things prepped for the Thanksgiving dinner tomorrow. I promised I'd try to keep some of the folks out of the kitchen." A dozen kids meant that whoever Ricky married would be pregnant for the next fifteen years, and Ellie Mae couldn't even begin to think in those terms.

"Scared you, didn't I?" Ricky said with a chuckle.

"Terrified me so badly, I'm not sure there will be another date," she said as she stood up and headed toward the ladder. She gripped the sides tightly as she descended, remembering the day Tabby fell.

Ricky followed her. "Good, because I want a family—but only two kids. That's enough in today's world. See there? Now two doesn't sound like such a big deal, does it?"

"And that's something we should discuss on the twentieth date, not before the first one." Ellie Mae reached the bottom without a mishap and started toward the door.

Ricky stayed right beside her. "Why not? Why even start something if there's no finish line in sight? That would be wasting both of our time. I'm in no hurry for a permanent commitment, but a family is on my bucket list. What's on yours?"

"Right now, the top thing is getting in the house to run some interference for Tabby or else she's going to make me sleep on the porch," Ellie Mae teased.

Ricky slung an arm around her shoulders. "Not to worry, darlin'. I'll cuddle up with you and keep you warm."

Tabby could say or believe whatever she wanted to, but Ellie Mae never got the vibes from Sam when he put his arm around her shoulders that she got when Ricky did the same thing. Not once had Sam ever sent little shots of heat scooting up her backbone. They had been best friends—this thing with Ricky had to be so much more.

Tabby shot a look of pure dismay at her cousin when Ellie Mae came into the kitchen through the back door. "Help! Please!" she mouthed.

Cleo and Maude were both bustling around her like a couple of bees. Homer and Frank were sitting at the table, throwing out comments about Thanksgiving dinners of the past.

"Hey," Ricky said right away. "I've got some cold beers out in my truck, and it's a beautiful evening. Won't be long until it's too chilly to sit on the porch and watch the sunset. You guys want to come out and have a beer with me? I could sure use some advice on a guy problem I've got."

"Sure," Homer agreed. "You comin' with us, Alex?"

"I should stay in here and help get things ready," Alex answered.

Frank stood up and patted him on the shoulder. "Come on with us. These ladies can take care of the rest of the job. We've given them plenty of good ideas."

When Tabby rolled her eyes toward the ceiling, Ellie Mae piped up with, "I was thinking that maybe Maude and Cleo would come down to the beach with me and figure out exactly where we're going to build our sandcastle," she said. "And Alex is Tabby's right-hand man in the kitchen, so he should stick around and finish helping her. When they get done, maybe he could join you on the porch for a beer, and Tabby could come on down to the beach and help us plan our castle."

"Thank you," Tabby mouthed.

"Sounds good to me. But don't take too long," Frank said. "This young'un"—he pointed toward Ricky—"might need some advice that two old bachelors don't know how to give him. Today's problems are a lot different than what we faced when we was young whippersnappers."

"Amen to that," Homer agreed.

Maude removed her apron, grabbed her pink sweater from the back of a chair, and headed for the door. "Maybe by the time we get through talkin' about the sandcastle, Duke will be back. I hope he didn't roll in another dead fish that washed up on the shore again like he did yesterday. By the time I finished his bath, my knees were killin' me. The way Duke smelled reminded me of that stinky salve Mother rubbed on her knees and elbows at night. I swore that I'd never use that stuff no matter how much I hurt."

Ellie Mae bit back a giggle when Cleo shot her an eye roll that rivaled Tabby's from minutes before. Cleo pulled on a bright red hooded sweatshirt, zipped it up the front, and slipped her feet into a pair of purple rubber boots she kept tucked under the ladder-back chair in the foyer.

Maude frowned at her sister and clucked like

an old hen gathering in her chicks before a storm. "All you need is a grocery cart, and folks would think you're homeless."

"Oh, get that stick out of your butt, Maude," Cleo said. "We came from the same family, so stop pretending you're all that and a bag of chips."

"At least I didn't run off to the danged old carnival," Maude smarted off.

Cleo's boots made a squeaking sound with every step until she reached the sand. "Be careful. Saying *danged* is just glorified Sunday-school cussin'. And you could have joined the carnival with me. I tried to get you to go, but you chose not to, and it was your choice to leave college and come home when Daddy died. You just enabled Mama into depending on you. It made you feel all superior. And don't give me those dirty looks."

Maude whipped around and glared at Cleo. "I'll look at you any way I want."

Ellie Mae stopped at the old log and sat down. "Cleo, did you ever take your own advice about the sand trick?"

Cleo chuckled and then said, "Have you tried it?"

"Yep, and it worked," Ellie Mae said. "Maude needs to give it a shot, and it wouldn't hurt you to do the same."

"Maybe later," Cleo said.

"What trick? Or do I even want to know?"

Maude sat down beside Ellie Mae and kept on talking before either of them could tell her about throwing sand out into the ocean. "I think we should build our castle behind the log. That way, it will be sheltered from the surf and tide for a little longer than the other ones. We should make it with a wall around it, like a real castle would have, and we could use driftwood for a little drawbridge."

"I've got battery-powered lights to put around the top of the wall," Cleo said, "and we'll need a flag to fly at the top of one of the turrets."

"I can make that," Maude offered. "I've got a scarf I can cut a triangle out of, and . . ." She stopped and bent forward to stare at her sister. "Castles didn't have Christmas lights strung around them."

"Depends," Cleo said with a giggle. "Ours can have whatever we want. We're building this thing, and we can make it whimsical like the ones in the fairy tales if we want to."

Maude sat up straight and slapped a hand over her mouth. "You aren't going to put up Cinderella or Snow White wallpaper in our new bedrooms out in the barn, are you?"

"No. I'm using G.I. Joe in the guys' rooms; Elsa from *Frozen* for your room because of your old, cold heart; and Rapunzel for mine because I haven't cut my hair in fifty years," Cleo told her.

"You wouldn't dare," Maude gasped.

"Don't test me, Sister," Cleo whispered.

"Don't call me that," Maude snapped.

Cleo jumped up and sang as she danced around the log, "Sister! Sister! Sister! She ain't a nun, but she's my sister all the same."

"Sit down. You're an embarrassment!" Maude yelled.

"Maybe so, but I've lived life to the fullest, and you've never lived a day." Cleo kept singing, twirling, and dancing. "Come on, Sister, wade out into the water with me. Ellie Mae can baptize both of us. We'll bury our old lives and rise up to a new one where we are friends."

"I was baptized when I was ten years old. You should remember that day," Maude said.

Cleo stopped dancing and plopped down beside her. "I'll never forget that day. Mama wanted me to be baptized, too, and I threw a bawling fit at the edge of the pond where the preacher had already dunked about a dozen people. Mama was always telling me how evil I was, and I just knew she had put that extra dollar in the collection plate that morning to pay the preacher to drown me."

Maude made a few clucking noises. "She made you sit on a hard chair for two hours that afternoon. I got to admit that I was too afraid of what she would do if I *didn't* get dunked under the water, but I have already been baptized, so I'm not doing it again. Besides, Mama would rise up out of her grave at this sacrilege if we did something as blasphemous as getting baptized by a woman that hasn't been ordained."

If they would just stop being so hateful to each other, Ellie Mae would gladly wade out there in that chilly water and do a baptism even though she wasn't a preacher. She smiled at the thought of holding each of them under just a few seconds longer than necessary to be sure their pasts were buried forever.

"It can't be sacrilege and blasphemy both," Cleo argued. "Choose one or the other."

You owe me big-time, Tabby, Ellie Mae thought. *I hope you get at least another kiss or two from Alex—or maybe even that the two of you make out for a while in the pantry. You're going to need some sweet, sexy memories when I refuse to help with cleanup after Thanksgiving dinner.*

A visual of her father and Tabby's folks sitting around the table flashed through her mind. She envisioned Ricky showing up around the time dinner was finished—or maybe, if he could get away, in time for dessert. The look that she imagined would be on her father's face sent icy chills down her spine that had nothing to do with the weather.

Maude laid a hand on her shoulder. "Are you all right, child? Are you getting sick again? You're not"—she lowered her voice to a whisper—"pregnant, are you?"

"I wish she was," Cleo said. "I can't wait for

her and Tabby both to find good men, get married, and have babies for us to spoil. I do wish I could have had children so there would be grandchildren for me to play with when I get old."

"I'm not pregnant," Ellie Mae answered. "I was thinking about my father." She told them about Sam and her father's issues with her rooming with a Black guy.

"My mother would have felt the same way," Maude said with a nod. "It don't make it right, but she disowned Cleo for that very thing. I wasn't allowed to even speak her name out loud."

"I guess he'll have a fit if you date Ricky, won't he?" Cleo asked.

"No doubt about it." Maude's tone was dead serious. "But don't you worry, darlin' girl. We'll all support you. Me and Homer and Frank—and Cleo will, too." She shot a squinty-eyed look at her sister. "Say you will or else I'll drown you. I'm bigger and stronger than you are, and I bet I can hold you under the water until the bubbles stop coming up."

"Of course I'll be there for Ellie Mae and for Tabby both, but you can't drown me," Cleo said with a smirk. "I'll kick you in one of your bum knees and swim away from you. I've always been a better swimmer than you."

"Maybe so, but I'll pull you under by all that hair you've got and then sit on you. I'm bigger than you are," Maude said.

"Hey, time-out?" Ellie Mae made the referee sign with her hands. "Tomorrow is Thanksgiving, and Aunt Charlotte always made us go around the table and tell one thing we were most thankful for in the past year. Y'all need to stop this bickering and figure out something to say."

"What are you planning to say, Ellie Mae?" Cleo asked.

"That I'm thankful for the closure I've found with Sam and that I'm trying to let his spirit go so it can rest in peace. That's what he would have wanted," she answered. "What about you?"

"That I'm grateful for the hurricane because it brought us together and gave us a family," Cleo said and then held up a finger. "And for Julep and the kittens for making me smile."

They both turned to look at Maude.

"I'm going to pray about it and think before I answer. But how can you be thankful for a hurricane, especially one that destroyed our home?" Maude asked, though her tone wasn't bitter or biting.

"When one door closes, another one opens," Cleo answered. "Sometimes what's behind door number two is even better than what has been behind door number one. I'm speaking from experience, Maudie. I just couldn't live in that house with Mama any longer, and door number two was my salvation."

"You called me Maudie." Maude smiled. "You

called me that when we were children and you had a secret to tell me."

"Yes, I did. And you called me Cleopatra," Cleo said.

Duke trotted down the beach like an egotistical little king, hiked his leg on the end of the log, left a wet spot, and then barked up at Maude and wagged his tail. She picked him up and held him close to her chest.

"I *am* thankful to have you in my life," she said. "Having something to love, and that loves me unconditionally, is wonderful."

Why couldn't you say that about your sister? Ellie Mae thought.

Rome was not built in a day. Aunt Charlotte's voice in her head answered the question for her.

You are so right, Ellie Mae agreed with a nod. *Everything seemed to happen one little step at a time—all our parents coming to Thanksgiving dinner, the situation with Ricky, and remodeling the barn so we can get on with the business of running a B and B.*

"Think of this as just another dinner," Alex said as he removed the pecan pie from the oven and set it on the counter to cool. "Our senior citizens out there"—he nodded toward the door—"would eat hamburgers and potato chips for a chance to sit around the table like a family."

"They might, but my parents will be here by

noon, and they're used to having a spread that Aunt Charlotte lays out," Tabby said with a sigh. "They'll leave by six o'clock, stay in a hotel in Beaumont, and fly back to Oklahoma the next day."

"They'll only be here for about six hours. If we can survive Maude and Cleo's barbs for weeks, we're tough enough to get through this. Besides, I promise to run interference for you," Alex assured her.

"That's a big promise," Tabby said. "They sided with James when we got the divorce even though they were mad at me for marrying him. I can't win where they're concerned, and they never miss a chance for a subtle snotty remark."

Alex draped an arm around her shoulders and led her to the table, then went back into the kitchen and took two beers from the fridge. He twisted the tops off both and handed one to her before he sat down across from her. "They sound a lot like my mom and stepdad, so I've got experience in handling people like them. We will survive this Thanksgiving."

"Only if I don't burn the turkey, put the right amount of sage in the dressing, and make the pumpkin pies just like Aunt Charlotte's." Tabby sighed again.

Alex covered her hand with his. "Honey, if we can put up with them for a few hours, then they can damn well suck it up and enjoy this awesome dinner we are making. Why would they want you to stay in a marriage that wasn't working?"

"Security, for one thing, and Daddy never quite forgave his brother for putting what he considered a blight on the Landry name by divorcing his wife." Tabby took a long drink of her beer and then went on. "Uncle Jefferson met Aunt Dara in college. She had come to the States from Ireland to study at Oklahoma University. They fell in love and got married right out of college, and then she went back to Ireland to her cousin's wedding several years later, and an old flame stepped into the picture. She came home, but . . ." Tabby shrugged.

"The writing was on the wall," Alex said. "But why would your folks get angry about that? It's really none of their business."

"Nope, it really isn't. But it was the first divorce in the Landry family history books, and then I put the second one in there. I'm their child, so all that cussing they gave Uncle Jefferson kind of came back to bite them on their butts. Does that make sense?" Tabby asked. "Sometimes, I feel like I could be walking on a barbed wire fence like it was a tightrope, singing my folks' favorite songs, and taking homemade fudge to them, and they'd still find something wrong with what I'm doing. I didn't become a lawyer like they wanted, and they've never forgiven me for that, either."

Alex nodded. "It makes more sense than you

realize. I can see why you jumped at the chance to come to South Texas and put some distance between yourself and them. My granddad used to tell me that everything happens for a reason. Maybe this is just the path the universe has put you on so you can find true happiness. I was upset when my house and boat were destroyed, but then I heard my grandpa telling me not to sweat the small stuff. He used to say that all the time. He also said the sky is darkest just before the dawn. I'm trying to believe that although all my material possessions are gone, it's a sign that something better is right around the corner."

"Aunt Charlotte likes to say that home is where the heart is," Tabby said.

Alex brought her hand to his lips and kissed her knuckles. "My heart is right here, Tabby, and maybe it was time for me to move on to better things than being a guide for fishermen. We just have to believe what is happening now is for a good reason, and what brought us to this day has shaped us into the people we are."

Tabby flashed him a smile that seemed to brighten the whole room. "Does that mean that based on that first kiss we shared when we were young, we might not have made it for the long haul as a perfect married couple?"

"Oh, honey." Alex chuckled. "That little boy wasn't worthy of you, and I'm not so sure this grown man is, but I'd like to give it my best shot."

"Anybody home?" The front door opened and closed, and a feminine voice floated down the hallway. "Daddy, are you here? Where is everyone?"

"Jazzy?" Alex knew his daughter's voice but couldn't believe she was in the house.

He was on his feet and had stepped around the table when Jazzy came through the door.

"Surprise!" She hurried across the room and wrapped Alex up in a hug. "How's that for a Thanksgiving Day bear hug?"

"It's wonderful. Come on over to the table and meet Tabby. You are early. How did you get here?" He turned around to find Tabby right behind him.

Jazzy stepped back from Alex, took a long stride, and hugged Tabby. "I'm so glad to finally meet you. Daddy talks about you every time I call. I've got another surprise . . ." Jazzy spun around and pulled a tall dark-haired young man into the room with her. "This is Declan Morris, Daddy. You've heard me talk about him for the past couple of years."

"Well, I'm glad to finally meet you." Alex stuck out his hand. "Jazzy has told me all about you. Welcome to Sandcastle."

"Thank you, sir," Declan said.

Alex's mind spun in circles so fast that it made him about half-dizzy. "I hope you brought sleeping bags. We've got a full house."

Jazzy tucked her hand into Declan's. "No problem, Daddy. I flew into Waco. Declan picked me up, and we brought our tent. We thought we'd pitch it on the beach and watch the sunrise in the morning. We have to drive back tomorrow evening after dinner because Declan needs to study for finals that are coming up in two weeks. He doesn't want to blow his 4.0 average." She took a deep breath and went on. "Mother has taken a two-year position in London, and I don't want to stay in Maine without her there, but I don't want to live in England and be so far from Declan, either. This long-distance thing is killing us, so I finished up my courses in Maine two weeks early, and I've moved to Waco. Declan and I are going to live together in his apartment, and I'll be finishing my education at Baylor." She pumped her fist in the air. "Go Bears!"

"Has your mother already left for England?" Alex asked. His mind kept spinning with that daughter download.

"Yep, two days ago," Jazzy answered. "I think she was relieved that I was moving down here closer to you. She was going to get in touch with you to talk about me moving, but I wanted to surprise you."

Alex started to say something, but words would not come. This wasn't what he would have wanted for his only child, if he'd had a choice. He would have wanted her to have the college

319

experience of being fancy-free, cramming all night for tests, and friends all around her in a dorm room. But Jazzy had always been an old soul. Declan was a good kid with goals. The most important thing was that he adored Jazzy, and that went a long way in Alex's book.

"I'm so glad you'll be in the state so we can visit more often," Alex said.

"You kids can have my room, and I'll bunk with Ellie Mae," Tabby offered.

"Thank you, but we are excited about staying on the beach."

"Well, if it gets chilly out there, you kids can take up as much floor as you want in the living room or pitch your tent out in the barn—either one. It's not heated, but at least it would have protection from the wind," Tabby said.

"Thank you," Declan said with a smile, his eyes still on Jazzy, "but we've got a down-filled sleeping bag, so we'll be plenty warm."

For just a minute, Alex went into daddy mode, and then he remembered the kids would be living together.

"Have you had supper?" Tabby's mother mode kicked in after she'd gotten over the initial shock of having to prepare for an extra person for dinner the next day. For a second, she wondered if she'd said the words out loud. When she figured out that she had, she pasted on a smile and said,

"Welcome to Sandcastle and to the B and B. We're so glad to have you. It's wonderful that you are going to be living a lot closer than Maine, but it would be even better if it was Houston instead of Waco."

Jazzy left her dad's side, crossed the room, and hugged Tabby again. "Thank you so much, and we haven't had supper. We just grabbed a snack from a convenience store," she answered.

"There's a pot of chili still in the slow cooker," Tabby said.

"Got corn chips and cheese?" Jazzy asked.

"We do," Alex answered. "And mustard."

Tabby wondered how in the world Alex could be so calm. If Natalie had come in from her first semester of college and said she was moving in with her boyfriend, James would have gone through the roof—and for one of the few times in their marriage, Tabby would have agreed with him. Right out of high school was way too young to be living with a boyfriend, but this wasn't her *bailiwick,* as Aunt Charlotte would probably say.

"There's sweet tea, water, and . . ." Tabby paused. "And beer if . . ."

"Neither of us drink," Declan said. "I'll just have water. Thank you."

Tabby kept track of Jazzy from the corner of her eye as she headed for the refrigerator. The girl—young woman—was almost as tall as her father and had the same blue eyes. Her flame-red hair hung down past her shoulders. Did she not drink beer because Declan told her she couldn't, like James had told her what she could and couldn't do? If she was letting a boyfriend tell her what to do, then someone needed to flip her around and head her down another pathway.

"You and your father have a lot to visit about." Declan kissed Jazzy on the forehead. "I can make two chili pies for us. I'll top yours with your favorites and pour you a glass of sweet tea. Oh, look!" He pointed to the counter. "Pecan pies. They're my favorite."

"We've also got pumpkin pies cooling in the pantry," Tabby said as she fetched her vibrating phone from her hip pocket.

"My second favorite. But back east, we don't get pecan very often, so that's what I'm having tomorrow." Declan opened cabinet doors until he found the bowls and then set about putting together a couple of chili pies.

He's not James, Aunt Charlotte's voice whispered softly in Tabby's ear. *James would have sat down and demanded that you bring him supper.*

I don't even want to think about him again tonight, Tabby thought as she looked at the text from her mother: **Set an extra plate. We're bringing someone with us.**

"Bathroom first," Jazzy said. "I'll only be a minute, and then we can talk, Daddy."

Alex pointed. "Top of the stairs, at the end of the hallway."

"Thanks, Daddy." Jazzy disappeared.

"What do you think of her?" Alex whispered as he put ice into two glasses.

"She's definitely your daughter," Tabby whispered. "Are you okay with . . . you know?"

"They've been together since they were freshmen in high school. She has her head glued on pretty good. I was surprised she didn't follow him to Baylor in the beginning," Alex answered.

Men! They sure looked at things from a different viewpoint. Maybe that book that came out years ago about the two sexes being from different planets was right.

Chapter Sixteen

A thousand butterflies flittered around in Tabby's stomach on Thanksgiving morning as she and Alex worked together to make the cornbread dressing. The rest of the crew was in the living room watching the Thanksgiving Day parade on television. When that was over, they had plans to take in the afternoon football game and had already made their bets as to who would win. Tabby was the bank, and she had declared that five dollars was the head of any bet they could make.

"You're as nervous as a long-tailed cat in a room full of toddlers," Alex said. "Is it because Jazzy and her boyfriend are here?"

"No, it's because my dad and Uncle Jefferson are coming, and, well . . . it's like Cleo and Maude on steroids. I like Jazzy. She seems very mature for her age."

"She's had to be, as an army brat all these years," Alex said. "We talked last night, and she's got things planned. She says she's going to finish her master's degree in nursing and then go to work while Declan finishes his medical degree. Then they plan on doing some of that Doctors Without Borders stuff for a couple of years."

"Marriage? Kids?" Tabby asked.

"Somewhere down the line on both—but according to Jazzy, forty is the new thirty, and that's plenty of time to start a family." He grinned.

Tabby stopped and stared at him with eyes so wide, they began to ache. "How can you be so calm about this?"

"Do I like that she's living with her boyfriend when she's so young?" Alex shook his head. "No, I do not. I would rather she be out having a good time with her friends. But Declan is a good kid, and he adores her. I might not agree with her decision, but I can support her in it, and that keeps the lines of communication open between us. Calm comes with peace, and peace comes with admitting when we can't do anything about the situation and letting it play out however it will."

"That's a good way to think but not an easy one." Tabby wondered if she'd be able to ever let a situation between her father and uncle play out however it could without letting it unnerve her.

"Hey, what can we do to help?" Declan asked as he and Jazzy came through the front door.

"We've pretty well got things under control right now. Are you hungry?" Tabby asked, remembering that her daughter had only wanted to down a glass of milk or some god-awful green smoothie each morning before she chased off to school.

"Yes, ma'am," Jazzy answered. "We ate a

granola bar and had some juice while we watched the sunrise; then we took a long walk on the beach. A little Chihuahua dog followed us home and is flopped out on the porch. Cute little thing that acts like he owns the place."

"He and the mama cat and kittens in their own little house out back probably do run things," Tabby said with a big smile. "The dog belongs to Maude. His name is Duke, and he arrived during the hurricane. The cats are Cleo's, and they showed up at the same time Duke did."

Jazzy picked up a cinnamon roll with her fingers and bit off a chunk. "I love animals," she said between bites. "I thought about being a vet, but I decided to be a nurse instead. Declan and I think that helping people, especially those who are needy, will be rewarding. When I finish this, is it okay if I take a shower?"

"You're right," Tabby said with a nod. "People come first. And, honey, it's fine if you take a shower. Please make yourself at home. Towels are stacked on a ladder-back chair beside the tub. I guess you've been in this house before?"

Jazzy flashed a brilliant smile—one that reminded Tabby of Natalie—toward her and nodded. "Lots of times. Daddy always brought me to see Miz Charlotte when I came to Texas, but I never went upstairs until last night. Miz Charlotte makes the best pecan tarts and snickerdoodles in the whole world."

"Yes, she does," Alex agreed. "Since we've got things under control in here, I'd love to show you what we're working on out in the barn, Declan."

"Lead the way," Declan said. "I grew up in a military house, so I follow orders fairly well. I'm happy to help."

As soon as they were out of the kitchen, Tabby grabbed a pencil and notepad and began to figure out a seating arrangement. The dining room table only seated six. Seven could be squeezed in, but there was no way she could fit everyone around it.

"What are you working on?" Maude asked as she pulled out a chair and sat down beside her. "You look worried."

"I'm trying to figure out seating for the big dinner this afternoon. How can you know that it's making me nervous?" Tabby asked.

"My mother was always on edge, always worrying about what other people might think or say," Maude answered. "I can see the signs from a mile away. I lived with them, tried to control everything to keep her from having what she called 'a spell,' and prayed every morning that she would have a good day. So what's got you all in a tizzy? Did you and Alex have an argument? I knew we should have stayed in the kitchen with y'all last night. Men don't do so well when it comes to cooking."

"Alex and I are fine—and he's really a better cook than I am," Tabby said. "My folks are coming and bringing an extra guest. They wouldn't tell me who it is—just said it was a surprise. I'm hoping they're not trying to set me up on a date with one of their colleagues. Adding a stranger in the mix doesn't help. They probably won't like Alex. They've said that I don't have any sense when it comes to men, and they blame me for the divorce. That's enough to make me nervous. And then Jazzy and her boyfriend are here, and I want them to like me."

"Well, don't you worry your pretty head about it. I've got your back, honey." Maude patted her on the shoulder.

"Thank you." Tabby managed a smile but thought she would far rather that Cleo had Maude's support.

"The pool table will be right here," Ellie Mae whispered as she wandered around the barn. Sam would have loved this place—and the senior citizens who would be living here. He could sit for hours on end and listen to the older guys tell their stories on work sites.

She felt a presence behind her, but when she glanced over her shoulder, it still startled her to see Cleo standing there.

"Who are you talking to?" Cleo asked. "You've got kind of a haunted expression on your face."

"I was talking to myself but thinking of my friend Sam," Ellie Mae answered.

"Memories are a good thing," Cleo said. "My best ones come around when I'm out in my trailer with Julep and the kittens. Lewis and I lived in a little place like that our whole married life. A bed at the back, a rocking chair, and a small television. We didn't need a big screen since we were only a few feet away."

"No kitchen?" Ellie Mae asked.

"Nope." Cleo shook her head. "We had communal meals. Our cook, who also operated the Ferris wheel for us, had a small kitchen in his trailer. He died just a couple of weeks before Lewis did. We all had a good run, but it was time to sell out and retire."

"Regrets?" Ellie Mae asked.

"For a while I had some. But not now," Cleo answered. "I love what we're doing here, and it seems like Maude and I are slowly finding our way to some semblance of family. I'm not so sure it'll ever be what you and Tabby have, but it's a start."

Ellie Mae's phone rang, and she fished it out of her shirt pocket. "Excuse me just a minute. This is my dad. It could be my lucky day."

"How's that?" Cleo asked.

"Maybe he's decided to stay home." Ellie Mae smiled as she answered, "Hello, Daddy. Happy Thanksgiving."

"And to you as well," Jefferson said. "I'm on my way, and we should be there in a couple of hours. I called to let you know I'm bringing an extra with me this year."

"Mama?" Ellie Mae asked, startled.

"No, it's a surprise," he said. "See you soon."

She hung up, slipped the phone back into her pocket, and rolled her eyes. "Not lucky. He's bringing a guest, and he says it's a surprise. Thanksgiving was never as much fun as other times in the year when I could come stay a day or two with Aunt Charlotte without my folks. Thanksgiving was always tense because my dad and uncle do not like each other so much, and my mother and Aunt Gloria were catty with each other."

"Life can sure get messy," Cleo said.

"Oh, yeah!" Ellie Mae agreed. "I should get on back in the house and tell Tabby. There's no way we can all fit around the dining room table."

Cleo motioned toward the windows. "Look at that beautiful sky out there. Big white clouds, a mild temperature for this time of year, and the smell of salt air. Why don't y'all put small tables on the front porch and serve the dinner buffet-style in the dining room."

Ellie Mae grabbed Cleo in a tight hug. "You are a genius. That's a wonderful idea. This is our first Thanksgiving at the Sandcastle B and B, and we can do it our way."

Cleo burst into the old song "My Way" and danced around in the barn as if she were on a stage and thousands of people were looking on.

Ellie Mae stayed to watch a few minutes of the show and then ducked out to jog to the house. She was out of breath by the time she reached the back door. When she stepped into the kitchen, wadded-up paper was all over the table, and some had fallen to the floor. Tabby was bent over another sheet and writing something down on it while Maude watched her silently from the end of the table.

"You writing a book?" Ellie Mae asked. "If you are, I've got fodder for another chapter. Daddy is bringing a guest, and he says it's a surprise, but it's not Mama. Who do you think it might be?"

Tabby ripped the sheet of paper from the notepad, crumpled it up into a tight little ball, and tossed it over with the others. "What am I going to do? Even if we set the kitchen table against the end of the dining room table, there's no way we can seat fourteen people around them."

Ellie Mae sank down into a chair across from Tabby. "At least it's not thirteen! That's an unlucky number, isn't it?"

"Yep, it is. I got married on the thirteenth. Natalie died on the thirteenth. This is going to be a disaster of a day." Tabby groaned.

"No, it is not, because we won't let it be." Ellie Mae put her hands on Tabby's shoulders and looked her right in the eyes. This was going to be a good day, no matter what day it was. Ellie Mae was determined to make it happen, and she felt good about her determination. "We control what happens in this B and B. Remember that! This is our first Thanksgiving in Sandcastle, and no matter what, it's going to be a good one. Cleo had a good suggestion: Aunt Charlotte has several little folding card tables in the attic. Remember when she used to bring them out for us to play board games on when it rained on Thanksgiving and we had to stay inside?"

Tabby covered Ellie Mae's hands with hers. "I remember playing games around one of those tables. Are you suggesting dinner on the porch?"

Maude clapped her hands like a little girl. "What a wonderful idea! It'll be like having dinner at one of those fancy restaurants."

"We'll get Alex and Declan to bring five of them down to the porch," Ellie Mae said, "and we'll put a colorful cloth on each one, set up chairs around them, and serve the dinner from the dining room table, buffet-style." Ellie Mae still had high hopes that her dad and his surprise guest would decide to stay away from Sandcastle. "After all, this is our party, and if anyone doesn't like it, he, she, or they can go home and eat hot dogs."

"We only need four tables," Tabby said.

"Five will be better. If I have to sit with Daddy and Ricky comes for dessert, you can bet your sweet soul that Daddy will need a place to move to, and we sure don't want to put Uncle Jefferson and my dad at the same table," Ellie Mae assured her.

As if on cue, Alex and Declan came into the house. Ellie Mae told them the plan, and Alex nodded. "We'll go bring down the tables right now. Y'all seen Jazzy?"

"She just left to go out to Cleo's trailer to see the kittens. You probably just missed her," Tabby answered. "She told me she never could have a pet because she and her mother moved too much." She thought of her own daughter, who had always wanted a puppy, but James was allergic—or so he said. Tabby had never seen him sneeze one time when they visited his folks, and they had two corgis.

"Yep, that's the life of an army brat," Declan said. "Where are these tables? Let's go get them brought down so I can go play with the kittens, too. I've got to admit, Duke has stolen my heart, though. I'd take him home with me if the apartment complex allowed pets."

"I could never give Duke away"—Maude pushed back her chair—"and we're all going to enjoy eating outside on the porch so much. I'm going outside to tell the men what's going on."

Declan and Alex disappeared up the stairs.

Ellie Mae gathered up all the balls of paper and put them in the trash. "Now, what other problem can I solve for you, and who do you think your folks are bringing? Have they picked out a second husband for you?"

"God, I hope not!" Tabby groaned. "If they bring someone with that in mind, I'm sitting at the table with Alex, Declan, and Jazzy."

"If you're smart, you will anyway." Ellie Mae poured two cups of coffee and carried them to the table. "Now that we've got a minute alone, what do you think of Jazzy? Does she remind you of Natalie?"

Tabby took a sip of her coffee. "Not one bit. Natalie was all into her friends, doing her nails, going to the mall. This girl seems to be a thirty-year-old in a nineteen-year-old body. Natalie would have never been ready to move in with a guy at that age."

"I was." Ellie Mae smiled. "Not with benefits, but Sam and I moved into our first trailer together when we were right out of high school."

"You've always been an old soul, too," Tabby told her, "And I mean that as a compliment. To answer your question, I like Jazzy. She seems to be comfortable in her skin. But if Declan were twenty years older, I might give her a run for her money. That boy is a keeper. He's exactly the type of long-term boyfriend I would have wanted for Natalie."

Cleo came waltzing into the kitchen through the back door and got herself a cup of coffee. "We need centerpieces for our little tables. Since we're eating at four o'clock, the sun will be setting by the time we get finished with dessert— so how about candles? I've got jar candles in my room that I use when I'm telling fortunes, and I'll ask Maude to help me work up a centerpiece for them."

"That would be wonderful," Tabby said. "We'll put the cloths on, and y'all can light them just before we call everyone to dinner. This is going to be a wonderful first Thanksgiving, even with all the surprises. I refuse to let anything spoil it."

Ellie Mae sure hoped that her cousin meant that with her whole heart and not just wishful thinking.

Chapter Seventeen

I love Thanksgiving," Alex said that afternoon as he brushed past Tabby to wash his hands in the kitchen sink. "I love the aroma of turkey baking in the oven and fresh bread, and everything about the holiday."

That simple remark put a smile on Tabby's face—and once again, his touch put flutters in her heart. To have something as simple as the smell of fresh bread wafting through the house be appreciated meant more to her than he'd ever know. "Thank you. I'll take whatever compliments I can get today—anything to bolster my courage. My folks will be here any minute."

Alex slipped his arms around her waist and kissed her on the forehead. "You are beautiful. You are amazing. You are strong. Remember those three things and that I'm here to help you with anything from washing dishes to toasting you for preparing this meal."

Tabby leaned into his embrace. "I couldn't have done it without you."

Somehow, she was enjoying the warmth and comfort that Alex always seemed to give her so much that she didn't even hear the front door open or close. She felt a presence and looked over into the shocked expression on her parents' faces—and the disgusted one on the face of her ex-husband, James, who was standing not ten feet away, with her mother on one side and her father on the other.

"What are *you* doing here?" she gasped and took a step back from Alex. She blinked several times, thinking that surely she was seeing things—but every time she opened them, James was still there.

Alex stepped forward and extended his hand. "Hello. I'm Alex LaSalle."

Her father shook with him. "Kenneth Landry, and this is my wife, Gloria, and . . ." He turned to James.

"I'm James Cassidy," he said. "I'm Tabitha's ex-husband."

"What the hell?" Ellie Mae's voice went all high and squeaky when she entered the kitchen through the back door. "Uncle Kenneth, have you lost your mind? Why would you bring James to Thanksgiving?"

Gloria shook her finger in Ellie Mae's direction and growled, "Don't you talk to your uncle like that, young lady."

"Don't *you* talk to Ellie Mae in that tone," Tabby said through clenched teeth.

James sneered. "You've let this renegade cousin of yours influence you, haven't you?"

"I'm sure you all have things to talk about, so

I'll go out and help Cleo and Maude with the tablecloths and centerpieces," Alex said.

Tabby grabbed hold of his hand before he could take the first step. "You don't have to leave. Whatever they've got to say can be said in front of you. Without you, Ellie Mae and I couldn't have managed this place during and after the hurricane."

James had the audacity to go right to the bar, where Tabby had laid out snacks, and load a chip with guacamole. "We have some things to talk to you about. In private. So tell this man"— he looked at Alex like he was something he had tracked in from the barnyard—"and your cousin to go away for a little while." He didn't even spare Ellie Mae a glance.

White-hot anger rose from Tabby's heart, turning her face scarlet. Her hands knotted into fists, and she gritted her teeth so hard that words couldn't get out past them.

Ellie Mae popped her hands on her hips. "Tabby and I are a team, and unless she tells me to leave, I'm not budgin'. And neither is Alex."

"Have it your way," Gloria said with a flick of her hand. "We wanted to tell you in person that we've hired James to be a member of our firm. We feel like . . ."

All Tabby heard was *blah, blah, blah* for the next several minutes. Without Ellie Mae beside her and Alex's hand in hers, she might have told all three of them to turn around and leave the house.

Honey, not vinegar, Aunt Charlotte's voice whispered in her ear.

When the three of them had each had their say, something between awkward and the calm before a storm hung over the room. Tabby wanted to say something, but her mind was blank. The tension was so thick that she could hardly breathe, much less force words from her mouth. How could they hire her ex-husband after the way he had treated her all those years?

"Well?" Kenneth asked. "Are you going to say anything or not?"

"What y'all decide to do with the firm is your business, not mine. James talked me out of going down that pathway years ago." Tabby's voice sounded hollow in her own ears. "Now, Alex and I have got some finishing touches to put on the dinner. You are welcome to go in the living room and watch the parade on television in there, or you can take a long walk on the beach. The day is lovely, but right now . . ." she said without a hint of a smile, "you can all three get the hell out of my kitchen. I refuse to let you ruin my Thanksgiving."

Gloria spoke up. "We thought maybe now that you and James have had a couple years of cooling-off time that—"

Tabby's palms raised without thinking, as if she

339

were deflecting a physical blow. With eyes wide open, she glared at her mother. "Don't even go there. It's not happening. I've moved on." Maybe she should have thrown a whole bucket of sand out into the ocean when she and Ellie Mae did their ritual under the crescent moon. "I've found out that living with a controlling man like James is misery, not marriage, and I'm never going back to that life. Why on earth would you even think of hiring him or bringing him here?"

"He's an amazing accountant, and he's been president of a bank, so he understands business. We needed someone to fill a spot, and *he's family*." Kenneth shifted his eyes from his daughter over to Alex.

"Not anymore. He's an ex, not a son or even a son-in-law," Tabby argued. "But if you want him to be part of your family, then count me out. I'm not so hateful as to send you home after you've traveled down here today, but don't you ever pull a stunt like this on me again."

"You've been around Ellie Mae too much. She never did know her place. That's why she's still single." James started out of the room with Kenneth and Gloria right behind him.

"You are a real piece of work," Ellie Mae growled.

James turned around and shot a nasty look over his shoulder. Tabby's hands knotted into fists as she took a step toward him with full intentions of decking him; then a little voice in her head gave her a better idea. She backed up, raised up on her tiptoes, wrapped her arms around Alex's neck, and kissed him—long, hard, and passionately.

"Thank you, darlin', for not leaving me alone," she said.

"Anytime," Alex said with a grin. "But I think you could have taken him down with one hand tied behind your back."

"And I would have helped her with that." Ellie Mae paced from the middle of the kitchen floor to the table and then made circles around it. She hadn't been this angry since her father told her she couldn't bring Sam back into his house all those years ago. "What in the world were they thinking? Why would they bring that bastard down here to Thanksgiving dinner?"

"Everything happens for a reason," Alex said. "We might not even know what it is today or why this happened, but—"

"It's to prove to me that whatever I had with James is over and done with," Tabby said, butting in. "That he's just a stranger—or better yet, just a person who works for my folks."

"Then it was worth it," Ellie Mae spat out.

"He has no idea what he's getting into." Tabby removed anything that James might have touched and tossed it in the trash. "He thinks women should walk two steps behind him and one to the

341

right. He thinks they should run, not walk, when he beckons. That's how he treats the ladies at the bank he manages. My mother is so controlling that she could make the pope lose his religion, so James is about to find out just how it feels to have someone—especially a woman—hold all the cards."

"Does that mean I can't poison him or at least trip him when he walks past me?" Ellie Mae asked.

"Oh, honey." Tabby pulled her hand free. "He's about to get all the poison and falling on his face that he can stand."

Ellie Mae stopped pacing and popped a chip into her mouth. "You are a stronger woman than I am."

"Hello, house," Jefferson Landry yelled from the back door in his deep voice. "Ellie Mae, where are you? I've got a surprise for you."

Ellie Mae rolled her eyes. "Let's run away right now, Tabby. No one can handle another surprise. Alex, go get the truck and bring it around back. We won't even peek in the rearview mirror at whatever surprise my father has, and we won't come home until they're gone."

"Too late. We couldn't run fast enough or far enough," Tabby whispered.

Face your fears, and if necessary, smash them with whatever tool comes to your hands or mind. Aunt Charlotte's words popped into Ellie Mae's head.

When her father strutted into the kitchen like a little bantam rooster that afternoon, she remembered Aunt Charlotte saying that Jefferson Landry was afflicted with "short man's syndrome." He must've gotten contacts, because he wasn't wearing glasses, and his hair was styled in a feathered-back cut that was longer than he usually wore it.

He had a big smile on his face that Aunt Charlotte would say was "like a possum eating grapes through a barbed wire fence," and he was holding the hand of a woman who looked vaguely familiar. The blonde towered above him in her four-inch heels. Her baby-blue off-the-shoulder sweater matched her eyes. A name played on the tip of Ellie Mae's tongue, but she couldn't spit it out.

"Who's this, Daddy?" she asked in a voice she didn't recognize as her own.

"I told you I was bringing a surprise. Surely you remember Kayla Simmons?" Jefferson's tone was all spicy, and his posture again reminded her of a little fighting rooster.

"Of course," Ellie Mae said. "We went to the same high school. We had a class or two together. Have you hired her at the office?"

He held up Kayla's left hand, where a huge diamond sparkled in the sunlight pouring in through the kitchen window. "We're engaged. We're planning to get married the Saturday before Christmas. Surprise!" His grin got even bigger.

"I'd rather have had a new pickup truck," Ellie Mae said and then wondered if she'd said the words out loud.

"Holy smoke!" Tabby gasped. "You've got to be kidding us, right?"

"This is not a time for jokes from either of you. I knew it was a mistake for you two to move down here together," Jefferson growled.

Tabby, you better stand beside me like I did you, she thought.

"Who said I'm joking?" Ellie Mae said.

"Why do you have to be so hateful?" Kayla muttered.

"That's enough out of you, Kayla, and, Uncle Jefferson, springing this on us at Thanksgiving is terrible," Tabby said.

Alex moved over until he was standing between the two women.

Ellie Mae thought of what Aunt Charlotte had told her about a three-cord rope being hard to break. She, Tabby, and Alex made a virtual rope like that together, and no one, not even their biological families, would break them.

"Darlin', she's just shocked." Kayla bent slightly and kissed her fiancé on the cheek before glaring at Ellie Mae. "I've already picked out six bridesmaids from my sorority sisters. But I would love for you to sit at the guest table, Ellie Mae."

"Holy hell!" Ellie Mae felt the color go out of her face. Kayla Simmons was only twenty-eight, and her father would be fifty-six on his next birthday. That meant his bride-to-be was half his age and a year younger than his own daughter.

"Congratulations," Alex finally said after a moment of awkward silence.

Ellie Mae almost gagged when her father brought Kayla's hand to his lips and kissed the ring.

"We met at the coffee shop at the beginning of summer and fell in love. I proposed on our six-month anniversary," he said.

Kayla snuggled up closer to his side. "But we moved in together on July Fourth."

She was the absolute stereotype of a trophy wife, with her blonde hair, big blue eyes, lots of makeup, skintight pants, and an expensive leather coat. There was no way, Ellie Mae vowed to herself, she was going to be any part of their wedding—not even if her father promised her half his kingdom. Speaking of that, she sure hoped her father had the good sense to draw up a prenup, or there very likely wouldn't be anything to inherit. Kayla would strip him of everything he had and leave him naked on the curb. She'd had that kind of reputation even in high school.

Aunt Charlotte's old adage came to her mind: *What will be will be, and what won't be might be anyway.*

"Aren't you going to say anything, Eleanor?" Jefferson asked.

"Not right now. I need a little time to process this, but I do hope you don't have to eat and run. I have someone I want you to meet, too, and he can only be here for dessert." She glanced down at Kayla's shoes. "Why don't y'all take a nice little walk on the beach while we finish up the meal?"

"Oh, darlin'." Kayla shot a look across the room that warned Ellie Mae to stay out of her way. "It would be so romantic to take a walk on the beach before we have to fly back to Arkansas. We can both take our shoes off and roll up the legs of our jeans, and we can write our names in a heart in the sand."

Ellie Mae glanced down at their skinny jeans. "That'll be a trick."

"Be nice," Jefferson said.

Ellie Mae glared at him. "I will if you will."

"What's that supposed to mean?" he asked. "We *will* leave if you've invited Sam."

"I would rather have him here than you, but he couldn't make it," Ellie Mae said. "He died a few weeks ago, Daddy."

"Who is Sam?" Kayla asked and then clamped a hand over her mouth. "Oh, I remember now. We should talk later about getting you some therapy, sweetie."

Jefferson tugged at Kayla's hand and led her

outside. "She's always been like this, darlin'. I don't think therapy will help. For now, let's go take that walk on the beach."

Tabby crossed the room and gave Ellie Mae a hug. "One thing's for sure: We'll both remember this Thanksgiving, won't we? Did you really go to school with that woman? That would make her about half his age, right?"

Ellie Mae shrugged. "She's always been a gold digger, but hey, it's his decision to get fleeced. He couldn't talk me into giving up my friendship with Sam. I'm not even going to try to talk him out of the decision to wear skinny jeans for a woman a year younger than I am."

Cleo peeked around the doorjamb. "Am I interrupting something? Y'all look like you could chew up railroad ties and spit out toothpicks. Do I need to put a spell on some of those people who just walked past us like we weren't even there and headed to the beach? Three in one group and a man and his daughter in the other."

Ellie Mae giggled, which quickly turned into a laugh and then a guffaw that was so infectious, everyone was wiping their eyes before they got things under control.

"What is going on . . . on?" Cleo hiccuped. "I'm laughing at y'all, but what's got you so tickled? Is everyone slaphappy because it's Thanksgiving?"

"Yes, we are," Alex said. "And that guy with

the young woman was Ellie Mae's dad—and she isn't his daughter but his fiancée."

"Sweet Lord!" Cleo's hand went to her heart. "So he's trying to go back in time, is he?"

Ellie Mae crossed the room and wrapped her arms around Cleo. "I'd settle for him just leaving."

"Were those other folks Tabby's family?" Cleo asked. "Homer spoke to the first three, but they were too busy saying something about Tabby not being in her right mind. Made us all mad as hornets. Frank stretched out a leg to trip the short guy, but he just stepped over it."

"As bad as I hate to admit it," Tabby said, "those are my parents, and that particular short guy is my ex-husband, James."

"Holy crap on a cracker!" Cleo's voice went so high that she sounded like Maude. "Why would they bring that man to a holiday dinner—or any dinner, for that matter?"

"Just to mess with me," Tabby said.

"This is going to be a fun day." Cleo's eyes twinkled. "I've got some stuff up in my room that could show them a little trip for saying that about you. Shall I put it in their sweet tea?"

"No!" Tabby said and then smiled. "But, on second thought, that might be a good idea."

Ellie Mae took a step back. "I would gladly let you sprinkle some of whatever you've got in my future stepmother's sweet tea."

"I guess it's either laugh or cry, isn't it?" Cleo said with a sigh. "Why did they even come for the holiday if they're only here to cause a ruckus?"

"Tradition," Tabby said. "Landrys always come to Sandcastle for Thanksgiving and then bitch about it all year. But next year, the tradition changes. After what they've pulled this year, they can have frozen pizza for their holiday meal."

Ellie Mae heaved a sigh of her own. "When they're gone, we might all celebrate their leaving with some of whatever it is up in your room."

"That really sounds like they're the ones who aren't in their right minds," Cleo said.

"The truth is stranger than fiction!" Ellie Mae declared.

"It always is, darlin' girl," Cleo said. "I'll go right back out and warn the others. Don't y'all worry. We're here, and we'll take care of this. No wonder you wanted to move to Sandcastle. And, honey, you know I'm a sharing person, so just let me know if you want some of my special oregano." She winked. "Or if not, maybe we'll all just get drunk after they leave."

Chapter Eighteen

Tabby slid the hot rolls in the oven and basted the turkey while she had the oven door open. Then she brought the cranberry salad out of the refrigerator, dished it up into a fancy bowl, and set it on the table. She had to keep herself busy to ease the anger, and so that she wouldn't tear into her folks again.

"It's a whole hour until we'll be ready to serve dinner," she muttered. "I wish it was right now so they would all leave. I'll enjoy the leftovers more later tonight than I will the actual dinner. I wonder how Aunt Charlotte ever managed to get through the time she had to spend with her nephews."

Ellie Mae straightened the already-perfect orange cloth on the dining room table and made sure the ceramic turkey centerpiece in the middle was right under the chandelier. "I never thought I'd feel like this, but I wish we were having dinner with just the family—and by that, I mean our regular crew. They're more like relatives than the ones who are kin by blood."

Alex filled the teakettle and set it on a burner. "This way, it will be ready to make another gallon if we need it. I usually had Thanksgiving dinner during the holiday with Jazzy. She tells me now that we can expect her for Christmas, too."

"That's awesome," Tabby said. "And maybe spring break, if they don't have other plans. After the folks move out to the barn, we'll even have more room for them when they can come see us."

"Okay, everyone." Ellie Mae finally threw up her hands. "We're all doing busywork to keep from talking about what's going on."

"No, we are trying to convince ourselves not to strangle some folks and throw their sorry bodies in the ocean for the fish to eat for Thanksgiving dinner," Tabby told her.

Ellie Mae leaned on the bar separating the kitchen from the breakfast nook. "This feels like a nightmare," she said. "Alex, wake me up, please."

"Sorry, but I can't," Alex apologized. "Tabby and I are right in the middle of the dream with you."

"Where are these troublesome guests that are trying to ruin our holiday?" Maude asked as she and Cleo came back inside the house. "Cleo told me all about them, and we've got a plan."

"We're going to make seating cards," Cleo said.

"Why would you do that?" Alex asked.

"Because we want to have some fun. I'll be on the table with your folks and your ex, Tabby." Cleo gave Tabby one of her famous winks. "That way I can brag on the way y'all have taken four old strays in and then let us buy the barn to remodel."

"And Frank and Homer have agreed"—Maude giggled—"to entertain Ellie Mae's dad and his new young little fiancée with stories of the war. That should bore her into wanting to leave quickly and never come back."

"At some time during the meal, Cleo and I are going to pick up our plates and switch, like playing musical chairs." Maude giggled again. "I'll go to the table with the ex, and I just can't wait for my time there. Cleo and Homer are going to take the gold-diggin' trophy-wife table, and Frank will join y'all three at your place. By then Ricky should be here."

"Sounds complicated," Alex said. "What about Jazzy and Declan?"

"They will have the table close to y'all so you can visit, but when we all do our musical-chair turnabout, you and Tabby will join them, and Ricky and Ellie Mae will have a table of their own for desserts," Cleo said. "If you get confused, I'll help you out. By the time they all leave, their minds will be scrambled so badly that they will be glad to break tradition next year."

"And if not, we'll still give them plenty of fodder to feed their griping mill for a while each year," Maude said. "Too bad I didn't think to take up for myself with our mother like these girls have done."

"This keeps y'all from having to deal with these people while we eat," Cleo said as she pulled Maude toward the door. "After Ricky gets here"—she threw a glance over at Ellie Mae—"make sure your dad sees you as a couple. Maybe you could even hug him when he arrives." Cleo grabbed Maude's hand. "Come on. We've only got a little while to get this job done. It's going to be so much fun. I've got stories of my carnival days all lined up."

"Cleo!" Ellie Mae gasped. "That's not fair to Ricky!"

"Well, it would surely make things more interesting. Us old folks need a little excitement to keep our blood flowing," Cleo said, and then she and Maude disappeared together.

Their giggles, one high-pitched and the other a bit lower, echoed all down the stairs. Tabby chalked another incident up to the strangeness of the day. "Are they really getting along?" She couldn't imagine getting through this tough day without Alex—who had absolutely been a lifesaver—and the two sisters.

Alex stopped in the middle of the kitchen and kissed Tabby on the cheek. "It's a Thanksgiving miracle. Are you going to be all right, or should we just put the food on the table and run away? I know a little place up toward Winnie that is open on Thanksgiving, but they only serve hamburgers and hot dogs."

"I've always loved hamburgers and been a cheap date, so don't tempt me." Tabby finally smiled. "You are my hero today," she whispered for his ears only.

"Glad to be of help, ma'am. That hamburger offer is good for all day." He smiled.

"Can I go with y'all? I love turkey and dressing, but I swear, to walk out the door right now and leave the lot of them behind would be great," Ellie Mae said. "And I bet Cleo and the rest of the gang would have them running for the hills before dinner was finished."

"We can't do that to our fantastic four," Alex said.

"Fantastic four," Tabby said. "I like that nickname. We could even shorten it to Fan Four."

"Think they'd want to run away with us?" Ellie Mae asked.

"Do what to who?" Jazzy asked as she came through the back door.

"And who's running away?" Declan followed right behind her.

Alex explained about the new guests who had arrived while the kids were out in the cat house.

Jazzy's eyes grew wider with each word her father said. "Does your Fan Four—that's a perfect nickname for them, by the way—need any help?"

"Just do whatever Cleo tells you to do. She and Maude are taking care of things right now," Alex answered. "At first, you and Declan will be at a table alone but close to Tabby and me."

"Whatever it takes," Declan said with a nod. "If we see an opening, we'll step in and help all we can. I guess you guys have had enough surprises for a while."

"We've each had one," Alex agreed, "but mine has been the only good one."

"Amen," Tabby and Ellie Mae said at the same time.

"Maybe we could just take our plates out to the barn and leave them on the porch to fight it out," Ellie Mae suggested. "Daddy and Uncle Kenneth can get all surly with each other, and Aunt Gloria can wear the queen's crown as usual."

"And Kayla can get catty with Gloria like a spoiled teenager. The next couple of years should be a hoot. Ellie Mae, did you think about the fact that Kayla and my mother are going to be sisters-in-law?" Tabby asked.

Ellie Mae giggled and then laughed out loud. "I have a whole new appreciation for Aunt Charlotte for putting up with family on this holiday. No wonder she finally ran off to Colorado and isn't coming home until Christmas."

"That's the gospel truth." Tabby crossed the distance between them and gave Ellie Mae a hug. "Hey, when Ricky arrives, it could cause a rift between your dad and Kayla. When she finds out how he feels about people of color, you just might not have a stepmom after all. I bet she's a lot more liberal than he is."

"Pretty green dollar bills dancing around in her big blue eyes could change any liberal into a radical conservative." Ellie Mae popped a chip into her mouth.

"Are we still putting everything on the table at four o'clock?" Cleo asked as she and Maude breezed back through the room with Duke at their heels.

"That's the plan," Alex said. "We're going to gather around the table, say what we're thankful for, and then I'll carve the turkey. Ellie Mae and Tabby have volunteered to help serve."

"Then we'd better get our place cards done and put around the tables." Maude's eyes were twinkling. "This is going to be just a little payback for all y'all have done for us." She practically floated out of the kitchen.

"So, are you two going to make up and be sisters?" Tabby whispered to Cleo.

"We are coconspirators today. Maybe that's on the way to being sisters, but I'm not holding my breath. We're just having fun in the moment, and tomorrow will take care of itself," Cleo answered as she followed Maude.

"Maybe that's the way we should all feel today," Alex suggested. "Have fun today and not worry about tomorrow."

"Yes!" Ellie Mae pumped her fist in the air. "If

we let your ex and my father spoil our day, then they have power over us. If we treat them like we'll treat guests who stay at our B and B in the future, then they're just strangers or sojourners who are stopping by for a short time and then going on their way." She stopped for a breath and went on. "I've looked forward to the turkey and dressing and a slice of pumpkin pie all week. I refuse to let Miss Bimbo Gold Digger or James Cassidy ruin my day."

"That might be easier said than done," Tabby said.

"Cassidy?" Alex asked.

"I took my maiden name of Landry back when we divorced. I didn't want anything to do with him or his name," Tabby answered.

Alex draped an arm around her shoulders. "Just keep your eyes on me, and don't look at him or give him the satisfaction of thinking he's upset you. How long has it been since you've seen him, anyway?"

Tabby removed the turkey from the oven. "Not since divorce court two years ago."

"And how did you feel when you realized he was in the room?" Alex shifted the turkey from the pan over onto the traditional holiday platter.

"Anger at my folks for bringing him but relief that I wasn't with him," Tabby replied. "What makes me mad is that my folks brought him to our family gathering. He's not part of the family—and I am, so they should have asked me."

Ellie Mae removed the pumpkin pie and whipped cream from the refrigerator and took it to the dining room table. "And Daddy should've given me a heads-up about Kayla, like maybe told me back in the summer that he had moved her into the house with him. Cleo was right: we are lucky that Aunt Charlotte is the sane one in the bunch and that she gave us her DNA along with this B and B to get us away from all that, and . . ." She inhaled and let the breath out in a whoosh. "After the way Daddy sprung Kayla on me, I've changed my mind about hugging Ricky when he gets here. Heck, I may even kiss him."

"That really wouldn't be right," Tabby told her.

"Why not?" Ellie Mae asked.

"Because it would be using Ricky," Alex answered, "and it would be kissing him for all the wrong reasons. He likes you a lot, Ellie Mae, and when you kiss him, it should be for something other than getting even with your father."

"You're right," Ellie Mae said, "but that hateful comment about Sam made me *so, so mad*."

"Don't get mad, get even," Jazzy said with half a giggle.

Tabby pulled the pan of hot rolls from the oven and basted the tops with melted butter. "Out of the mouths of babes . . ."

"Comes forth wisdom," Ellie Mae finished for her cousin.

"Never considered myself a babe or wise, but I'll take the compliment. Thank you," Jazzy said. "Looks like it's ready to put on the table. Want me to call everyone, or is that someone else's job?"

"No one has claimed it yet," Ellie Mae told her. "Give us five minutes to get the ice in the tea glasses, and then go gather them in."

Ellie Mae had memories—both good and bad—of always wanting to stay longer when her folks said it was time to leave Aunt Charlotte's place. Good because of the love that her aunt showered upon her and Tabby. Bad because of the tension that followed them all the way back to Arkansas.

Her favorite memory was of that summer when her folks had let her stay a whole week with Aunt Charlotte. That had been the only time she had truly felt free as she ran up and down the beach whenever she wanted, collected shells, and even built several sandcastles. She tried to keep that feeling in her heart when everyone gathered around the table.

"We have decided to keep up with Aunt Charlotte's Thanksgiving tradition," she said. "Each one of us will tell one thing we are grateful for, and then we'll fill our plates and go to the front porch. As you may have already noticed, Cleo and Maude have made place cards, so sit where they have planned, please. Sometime during the meal, some of us will be moving—kind of like musical chairs—so everyone can get to know everyone else."

Alex raised a hand. "I'll start. I'm grateful for good friends and for Tabby."

Homer was standing beside Alex. "I'm thankful for Hurricane Delilah."

"Same here," Frank said. "And pecan pie."

"I'm thankful for today." Maude glanced over at Cleo.

"Declan and my daddy." Jazzy smiled.

"Just Jazzy," Declan added.

Kenneth shot a look across the table at Tabby. "James coming to work for us."

Ellie Mae wished that she had told Cleo to bring down some of her special oregano to put in her uncle's cornbread dressing. There was no doubt that barb was intended for Tabby, and from the look on her cousin's face, she was having trouble staying civil.

James gave a one-shoulder shrug. "A new job."

Gloria's little tight smile was the prelude to a snide remark. "That Ellie Mae didn't cook anything on this table."

"Me too," Jefferson agreed.

"Be careful," Ellie Mae said with a sarcastic grin. "I've been reading about the seasoning power of hemlock."

"Ellie Mae and Tabby for taking us in," Cleo

said before anyone could respond to Ellie Mae's comment.

Kayla moved so close to Jefferson that air couldn't have passed between them, and she shot a dirty look toward Ellie Mae. "I'm thankful for my sweetie here, Jefferson Landry."

"I'm thankful for our new B and B members, and for Ricky," Ellie Mae said.

Tabby finished the round with one word: "Alex."

"Thank you, darlin'." Alex leaned over and kissed her on the cheek. "And if Ricky were here, he would tell us that he's thankful for you all for giving him a job that will last until spring and for Ellie Mae. Now, line up and tell me which part of this big beautiful bird you want me to carve off for you folks."

"I hope the turkey is better than Aunt Charlotte's," Gloria said. "Hers was always too dry."

"I told her for years that she should come to our house and our cook would make dinner," Jefferson said.

"Or ours." Kenneth held out his plate for Tabby to put a spoonful of cranberry sauce on it. "There was one of her, and yet we all had to make the trip to this godforsaken place for the holiday. Thank God the almighty Landry family didn't have a Christmas tradition."

Ellie Mae felt another wave of anger. "This

is the last year that the Landry family will have Thanksgiving here at the B and B."

"But it's tradition," Kenneth argued.

"Tradition ends after we have dinner," Ellie Mae said. "And speaking of Christmas, Sam made an amazing turkey for our Christmas dinner. I'll miss that this holiday, but I do love all the sweet memories he and I made through the years."

"Amen!" Tabby said.

Jefferson looked like smoke could start coming out his ears at any moment.

Kenneth's expression said that he might explode at any minute.

For once, the two brothers were pretty much on the same page—too bad it was in anger and not love.

"First time for everything," Tabby whispered for Ellie Mae's ears only.

"What's that?" Ellie Mae asked.

"Our fathers are agreeing on something," Tabby replied.

Kayla held out her plate to Alex. "A thin slice of white meat, please. No dressing. I have to watch my carbs, even on holidays."

Gloria heaped up her plate with a thick slice of turkey and all the trimmings. "I've never had an informal holiday meal before in my life. I guess next year we can host the dinner, and the following year it will fall on Kayla and Jefferson since we are finally breaking with the Landry tradition."

"Thank God," Kayla said.

"We like things done kind of Bohemian here," Cleo said. "Seems more down to earth and family-style than sitting all prim and proper around a table."

"And having this new family around us is nice." Maude put two hot rolls on her plate. "For years it was just me and Mother, and we usually shared a Cornish hen."

"I like that we're all a team now and not those old homeless people from the assisted-care center."

Frank dipped deep into the sweet potatoes. "Maybe they'll make a movie about us, and Morgan Freeman can play my part."

"I want Tommy Lee Jones to be me, and the movie can be called *The Sandcastle Hurricane*," Homer declared. "How about you, Cleo?"

"Swoosie Kurtz," she answered without a moment's hesitation. "And Shirley MacLaine is Maude."

"She's way too spicy for my character," Maude protested loudly. "I want to be Angela Lansbury."

Just listening to them lifted Ellie Mae's spirits. "Then we don't even need a casting call, do we? The title is set in stone, and all the actors have been chosen."

"And you are Molly Quinn," Cleo said, "and

Tabby is Jennifer Garner, and Alex has to be Matthew McConaughey. There now. We are ready for the first scene, when the hurricane hits."

Ellie Mae could feel Kayla's aggravation—her aura, as Cleo might say—filling the dining room because no one was saying *she* looked like a movie star. She made a mental note to look up Molly Quinn. She couldn't quite place her in the grand realm of movies. Then it hit her that Molly had played the daughter on the television series *Castle*. She sure didn't agree with Cleo on that call—but then, it was all just a game, and it made the group happy to play it.

"Looks like I'm the fifth wheel today," she said as she loaded her plate.

"Not for long," Alex told her. "I got a text from Ricky a couple of minutes ago. His family ate a little early, and he's on the way. He said he'd sent you a message, too."

Ellie Mae set her plate on the table and fished her phone out of the pocket of her jeans. Sure enough, there was a text saying that he had left and would be at the B and B in twenty minutes. That had been ten minutes ago, so he would be there soon.

"Y'all go on out," Ellie Mae said. "I'm going to sit at the kitchen table until Ricky gets here."

"What do we tell Jefferson and the new step-mom if they ask where you are?" Tabby asked.

"Tell them that I'm a bit temperamental, as some movie stars are, and I'll be out as soon as I get through meditating," Ellie Mae teased. "Or just say that I'm eating in the kitchen because I've got a surprise on the way, and they should get ready for it. If Daddy can drop his little bombshell on me, then I can drop Ricky on him."

"Is it too much to ask that you do that literally?" Tabby asked as she and Alex headed out of the dining room.

"Nope, just figuratively, although I wouldn't mind pushing either one of those two into the surf right after a hurricane makes landfall—or maybe just Daddy. If he sucked in enough salt water, maybe it would clear out his case of midlife craziness," Ellie Mae answered.

Thank you, Jesus, for a moment of quiet, she thought before she took the first bite of her turkey after everyone had gone outside. She could hear the conversations going on out on the porch, even if she couldn't make out the individual words. The bored, almost yawning sounds had to be coming from Aunt Gloria and Kayla. The deep southern twang was Alex for sure, and the rather high, squeaky, totally unsexy voice had to be coming from James.

"I never did like him," Ellie Mae whispered. "He was the male version of Aunt Gloria. All full of himself and expecting Tabby to jump at his beck and call."

"What did you do that you have to sit in the kitchen all by yourself? Have you been a bad girl?" Ricky teased as he entered the house by the back door and sat down beside her. "I parked out at the barn so I wouldn't have to move my truck for folks to get out."

"Smart man," she said. "Maybe we could go right back out there and leave as soon as I finish eating."

"Your wish and all that," Ricky said with a broad smile. "You needin' to run away—far from the madding crowd?"

"Yep," she answered and, between bites, told him all about Kayla and her father, then about Tabby's folks bringing her ex to the traditional dinner. "I wouldn't blame you if you didn't stick around."

"I'm not going anywhere." Ricky's tone turned serious without a bit of humor in it. "I'll be right beside you. And if those people don't like me because I'm Black"—he leaned over and kissed her on the cheek—"then that's their problem. If you like me, that's all that matters to me."

"Thank you, and I do like you—a lot." Ellie Mae reached across the table and laid her hand on his. "Never worry. I'll protect you from them."

Ricky chuckled. "I can take care of myself."

Ellie Mae heard Kayla's high heels tapping out a beat on the foyer's hardwood floor, and then there she was, glaring at Ellie Mae.

"I wanted a moment alone with you, but I see that's impossible. Your daddy is going to throw a fit over . . ." She nodded toward Ricky. "Why do you have to rile him up like you do?"

"Why does he have to rile *me* up by moving a woman younger than I am into the house? You and I both know what you are." Ellie Mae didn't let go of Ricky's hand.

Kayla popped her hands on her hips. "What is that supposed to mean?"

"It means that you have always been a gold digger, even back in high school. Only the rich boys were good enough for you, and then just until someone came along with a little more money," Ellie Mae told her. "I hope he's got the good sense to make you sign a prenup."

"I love him, whether you like it or not, and we don't need a prenup. I would never hurt him," Kayla snapped, but she didn't make eye contact with Ellie Mae.

"Yeah, right." Ellie Mae stared right into her face. "Have you thought about the road ahead of you? When you are fifty, he'll be almost eighty."

"Shut your mouth!" Kayla raised her voice. "You've always been a troublemaker. Living with Sam, and now this." She pointed at Ricky. "Your father will never accept him, and you know it."

"Never accept me, why?" Ricky asked. "I'm a hardworking guy who has been brought up in a good home by Christian parents who worked in the school system in Anahuac for years. I treat women with respect, and I really do like Ellie Mae. What's not to like about me?"

"You are at least half-Black." Kayla had more venom in her tone than a ten-year-old rattlesnake.

"A quarter, to be exact, but what does that have to do with anything? The heart doesn't see the color of a person's skin," Ricky said.

"But Jefferson Landry does," Kayla said through gritted teeth. "And so do I." She spun around on her spiked heels like a ballerina onstage and started for the door.

"Hey, did you tell Daddy darlin' about Malachi Johnson?" Ellie Mae called out.

Kayla did a one-eighty so fast that she popped a heel right off one of her shoes. "I have not, and don't you dare say a word," she said in a hoarse whisper as she hopped and shoved her shoe back together. "Or better yet, go right ahead. He would never believe you over me. That was just rumors."

"Want to test that theory?" Ellie Mae asked. "How do you think he'd feel about you going out with Malachi, our Black quarterback? I believe I can find my old yearbook with a picture in it of the two of you hugged up at a bonfire."

Kayla's hand doubled into a fist, and she took a step forward.

"Sam and I happened to be the one who caught the both of you under the bleachers one evening, if you will remember," Ellie Mae told her. "Malachi was Sam's cousin, and we were far more worried about what his family would say about him being with a white girl than what it would do to your reputation."

Kayla moved forward, and her trembling forefinger almost touched Ellie Mae's nose. "You better not say a word . . ."

"Say a word about what, sweetheart?" Jefferson came inside the house and wrapped an arm around Kayla's shoulders.

"Nothing, darlin'." Her tone was suddenly sugary sweet. "But I could never lie to you. I was going to have a piece of pecan pie in secret, and I didn't want Ellie Mae to say a word about it."

"You will always be beautiful to me," Jefferson whispered, "no matter what size you are." Then he noticed Ricky, and the smile on his face faded. "Who is this, and why would he be here?"

Ricky got to his feet and extended a hand. "I'm Ricky Benoit. I take it you are Ellie Mae's father?"

Jefferson looked at his outstretched hand as if it were an alligator about to bite him. "I am Eleanor's father, and she should know my opinion on guys like you. Kayla and I will be leaving now."

Ricky dropped his hand and sat back down.

Ellie Mae pushed her chair back so hard that it tipped over and hit the floor with a bang. She marched forward until she was nose-to-nose with her father. "My opinion on you marrying a gold digger who is half your age doesn't seem to matter to you, so your opinion of the man I'm dating doesn't matter one tiny rat's ass. If you want to marry a bimbo that's a year younger than your daughter—that would be me, unless you're going to disown me for liking Ricky—then have at it. She'll likely put you on a financial roller coaster ride that will leave you penniless. But Aunt Charlotte has provided for me, so I don't need any inheritance from you, *Daddy*." The way she emphasized that last word made it sound more like a curse than an endearment.

"You look and act just like your mother." Jefferson sneered.

"Good!" she told him as she backed away and sat down at the table again. "You won't listen to me, but I knew Kayla very well in high school. Zebras do not change their stripes, so you'd do well to have a prenup. If you don't—"

"He doesn't need a prenup," Kayla said as she walked up beside Jefferson. "I love him so much that I will never leave him."

"Let's talk about all the guys you hooked up with in high school." Ellie Mae counted them off on her fingers. "Johnny, Dillon, Eli, Matthew, Chris . . . *Malachi*. That's just our sophomore year, and they all heard the same thing out of your mouth."

Trained tears began to flow down Kayla's cheeks. "She's lying to you. I was a shy person in high school—I seldom ever had a boyfriend."

Jefferson took Kayla by the hand and pulled her toward the foyer. "We'll be leaving now, and we won't be back, Ellie Mae. When you are ready to apologize to Kayla, I might talk to you again."

"The devil will put up a snow-cone stand in hell before that happens. And, Daddy, if my boyfriend isn't welcome in your house, I won't come around," Ellie Mae said.

"That might be a blessing," Jefferson said and pulled Kayla close to his side. "I won't ever put you through this ordeal again, darlin'."

Kayla shot a smirk over her shoulder and limped pitifully out of the house on her broken shoes.

"Two down, three to go," Ellie Mae whispered.

"Does his attitude toward you hurt?" Ricky asked. "I'm a grown man, but if my dad treated me like that, I'd cry like a little kid."

"I've had twelve years to grow scar tissue around my heart where my dad is concerned. Yes, it pains me that we can't have a decent relationship, but it's his choice, not mine, and there's nothing I can do about his opinions. How do you feel about my father being a racist? Is that going to affect whatever this is between us?"

"It's his loss." Ricky shrugged. "I like you, Ellie Mae. If our relationship ever goes that far, I wouldn't be proposing to him—just you."

"That's awesome," she said with a grin. "Let's take this out to the porch and enjoy visiting with the folks."

Ricky picked up his plate with one hand and his coffee with the other one and carried it out to the table set aside for them. He set his pie and coffee down and then pulled out a chair for her. "I really like these folks. They are funny and downright fascinating. The stories they can tell would make a good book. Can I go get you some dessert?"

Ellie Mae followed him out of the kitchen. "I'll have dessert later, but you're right: those stories could even make a movie."

"Do you care if the new stepmom doesn't like me?" he asked.

Ellie Mae couldn't hold back the huge burst of laughter. "Her? Double nope, maybe even not a no, but a hell no with six exclamation points behind it. Do you care that I'll have that awful person for a stepmom?"

Ricky seated her with a grin and then pulled his chair around closer to her before he sat down. "I don't give a tiny rat's rump about either one. Like I said before, all I really care about is whether you like me or not."

"I do." After what had happened with her father, she had a flash of nerves about whether his folks would like her.

"Am I really your boyfriend?" he asked.

"Do you want to be?" she asked, hoping that his family was as kind and sweet as he was.

"Oh, yes, ma'am," he said with a grin. "Do you want to be my girlfriend?"

She leaned over, moistened her lips, and kissed him. She could have sworn she heard Aunt Gloria gasp and Cleo giggle, but the kiss wasn't to show off for any of them; it was sincere—and hotter than blue blazes.

"Yes, I do, with all my heart," she whispered when the kiss had ended.

"Then this is the best Thanksgiving ever," he said.

Chapter Nineteen

Tabby awoke early on Friday morning and watched the slow daybreak out the bedroom window. With her hands laced behind her head, she let the previous day's events replay scene by scene, like a movie in her head.

When Jefferson and Kayla left so abruptly without even saying goodbye to Kenneth and Gloria, Cleo and Maude's plans to switch tables were upset. Then Ellie Mae and Ricky joined the crowd, and the temperature dropped twenty degrees on the porch. The chill from Kenneth, Gloria, and James, especially when Ellie Mae kissed Ricky, was probably felt all the way to Houston.

A whiff of bacon wafted across the room, and she sat straight up and inhaled deeply. Someone was already up and making breakfast. By the time she got dressed, she could also smell coffee and something sweet like cinnamon. She threw back the covers and got out of bed. She was pulling on a pair of jeans when Ellie Mae eased the bathroom door open and peeked inside.

"Have we survived?" she asked.

"Yes, but I wish I would have decked James and then kissed Alex," Tabby answered.

"Do you think Aunt Charlotte will be disappointed that we're not carrying on the traditions?" Ellie Mae sat down on the edge of the bed.

Tabby pulled on a T-shirt and then a pair of socks. "I talked to her late last night, and she says we did the right thing. According to her, we were too nice. I should have thrown James out of this house on his ear, and you should've done the same thing to your dad and his woman."

"That's good news," Ellie Mae said. "From what I'm smelling, I expect Alex is making breakfast for us."

"Yep, he is amazing," Tabby said with a smile. "Let's go eat and then hit the beach and build a castle. Wouldn't it be something if we got a ribbon?"

"We deserve it after yesterday." Ellie Mae looped her arm through Tabby's, and together they headed for the kitchen.

"Good morning," Alex and all the other folks chimed in when Ellie Mae and Tabby entered the room.

"We're waiting on Ricky to get here," Homer said. "You four kids are going to do the building. Us four are going to be the gofers."

"We'll *go for* sticks or shells or whatever you need," Frank explained.

"And Cleo and I have a tote bag full of stuff you can use to decorate," Maude added.

Alex poured two mugs of coffee, handed them to Ellie Mae and Tabby, and started another pot.

"Everything will be ready to serve when the eggs are done," he said. "Did you sleep well?"

Tabby kissed him on the cheek. "Better than I have in a long time, thanks to you and all the folks here for helping us through the day."

"You are welcome. You were here for us, and we've become a family. Now, let's get after this good food," Cleo said. "Alex made cinnamon-apple muffins for breakfast-dessert. That's what I'm having first. When you get to be my age, you eat dessert first because you never know when your next breath might be the last."

"Bull honky," Maude snapped. "You'll live to be a hundred and ten just to give me misery."

"I guess the sister act from yesterday has finished?" Alex whispered to Tabby.

"Maybe this is the way they show that they really love each other," she said out of the side of her mouth.

"What is 'bull honky'?" Homer asked. "I've heard lots of ways to use *bull* in creative cussing, but that's a new one on me."

Cleo winked at him. "It's Maude's way of saying something that would have gotten her mouth washed out with soap when we were little girls. And, darlin' sister, I will gladly live to be over a hundred just so I can argue with you. It's what I live for. I just hope that neither of us ever have problems with short-term memory and get to where we don't know each other."

"Hmmph," Maude snorted. "Mother was lucid until she took her last breath, so I reckon we'll both have our senses about us until we die."

"What time does the festival begin?" Ellie Mae carried the bowl of scrambled eggs to the table.

"Ten o'clock," Alex answered. "At nine thirty, everyone who's paid their entry fee takes something—stakes, shells, flags, or whatever they've got—and marks out their area on the plot map. Then, at five till the hour, the fire chief or the mayor or the minister of the church will welcome everyone, do the countdown, and ring the bell for the festival to begin. The carnival music will start and then—"

Cleo butted in. "We will build our sandcastle, and then I'm going to the carnival. This is the first time it's been close enough for me to go see my old friends since I sold it."

"You mean your carnival came here?" Maude asked.

"Yes, it did," Cleo said.

Maude laid a hand on her chest. "Somebody tape her to a chair and watch her all day. If she gets a taste of that life, she'll run away again, and then who will finish building our new place?"

"Is that all you're interested in?" Ellie Mae asked.

"Of course." Maude almost smiled. "What else could there be?"

"I thought you'd go with me," Cleo told her. "If you meet my friends, you might want to run away with me this time."

"I believe they just might be friends after all," Alex whispered to Tabby.

"The jury is going to be out on that verdict for a while. Maybe come spring, when the barn is finished, we'll have a decision. Have you decided whether you're going into business with Ricky?" Tabby picked up a muffin and slathered it with butter.

"I'm committed to the barn job until spring," Alex said. "A lot can happen between now and then, but I'm happy working with Ricky and Ellie Mae. And I'm even happier working with you right here at the B and B. I've got a place to live, a beautiful woman to talk to every day, and friends all around me."

Tabby's face turned a faint shade of red. "Well, you got two out of three right."

"I didn't know women in today's world still knew how to blush," Alex teased. "And I was right on all three counts. You really are a beautiful woman, and you're also very smart and kind, and you have an amazing smile."

The blush deepened, and a smile broke out across her face.

"What are y'all talking about?" Ellie Mae asked. "I haven't seen Tabby's face turn all red or seen her eyes look that big in years."

"I just told her that she was beautiful and smart," Alex admitted.

"Always has been, except when it came to James," Ellie Mae agreed as she put a scoop of eggs and three strips of bacon on her plate. "I'm going to ask Ricky to ride the Ferris wheel with me."

Alex handed Tabby a plate. "Will you ride with me?"

"I'd love to," she answered.

"First, we pile up sand, right?" Ellie Mae said when they reached the spot behind the old log that they'd staked out for their sandcastle. Excitement was in the air all around them as folks from all over the county gathered to work on sandcastles. For the next three hours, she and Ricky, along with Alex and Tabby, would be building the first-ever entry for the Sandcastle Bed-and-Breakfast.

"Yep, and there looks like there's plenty of sand," Frank teased.

Homer chuckled. "I doubt that you and I will have to steal any from the folks on either side of us."

"What's the biggest one you've ever made?" Ricky asked.

"About a foot high, but I don't think size will matter as much as how fancy it is," Alex answered. "A couple of years ago, the winning castle was only about knee high."

"Knee high on you or on me?" Ricky teased.

Alex nudged him on the shoulder. "Probably on you."

Ellie Mae got a little misty-eyed when she looked around at the seven B and B occupants and Ricky. Eight of them in all, and even Cleo and Maude seemed to have called a truce for the day. Then she remembered the dream she'd had the night before. She and Ricky were building a house. That didn't take a rocket scientist to interpret since they had been working on making the barn into a retirement home. What had her puzzled was that they were arguing when she woke up, and it was about what type of flooring to put in the kitchen. Cleo had already picked out the tile for the bathrooms and kitchen, as well as the carpet for the rest of the place. So, even in a dream, why would they be talking about what style vinyl planks to lay in the house?

There was chemistry between them; every time their hands touched, Ellie Mae felt something she hadn't felt before in all her twenty-nine years. Ricky told her that he felt it, too, and when their hands got tangled up in the sand again, he jerked his back dramatically and blew on it as if it were on fire.

"What's that all about?" Frank asked as he piled up sticks of driftwood in various sizes.

"Heat." Ricky smiled. "Evidently, we're working so fast that every time Ellie Mae's hand touches mine, sparks fly."

"That ain't weatherwise heat, boy. That's what you young'uns call *vibes*." Homer chuckled.

"Young'uns?" Ricky said with a laugh. "I'm kind of past that stage."

"Depends," Maude told him, "on whether you are looking eighty in the eye or if you haven't even reached thirty yet."

"*Vibes* mean that both parties feel the heat." Ricky's eyes locked with Ellie Mae's across the pile of sand.

She pulled her hand out, dusted it off, and blew on it. "Had to get the sand off first because when sand gets hot, it turns to glass. I wouldn't want to end up with some sort of superhero hand."

"Now, that's vibes for sure," Cleo said. "Maybe y'all need to make a trip down to the surf and dip your hands in the water to cool them off."

"Humph." Frank almost snorted. "That might cause the ocean to boil."

Ellie Mae giggled and said, "The sand is kind of cold. Maybe if we are careful, we can get this castle built without turning it into glass."

"Maude and I are anxious to fly the flag that we made special with the Sandcastle B and B logo on it. So more work and less talk," Cleo said.

Tabby packed down the pile of sand until it was solid and ready to mold into a castle. "I didn't know we had a logo."

Maude pulled out the tiny flag and held it up. Glitter letters on a dark blue background sparkled in the sunshine. "Sandcastle Bed and Breakfast, or SB&B."

"Ain't it beautiful?" Cleo asked.

"It is, and if we win the trophy, I think we should keep it in the barn when it's finished," Tabby said and turned to Alex. "What are you doing with that putty knife?"

"Building a wall around the castle. We have to protect the beautiful dark-haired princess who lives there," he answered.

"And who would that be?" Tabby teased.

"I won't call any names, but her initials are *Tabby Landry*." Alex stopped long enough to kiss her on the forehead and then went back to work.

Ricky pulled his knife out of his pocket and began to cut sticks into the right length for a drawbridge. "Got to have a drawbridge to keep the red-haired princess's evil stepmother from coming in and hauling her off to a convent for liking the stable boy."

"Thank you." Ellie Mae nudged him on the shoulder. "My Irish ancestors will accept you in their pubs and not even care that you are the stable boy."

Maude laid out their decorative materials on the ground. "These will be here when y'all are ready to choose what you need. Cleo even had a set of battery-powered lights that she put around her door at the center last Christmas."

"It'll look like the castle has candles in the

windows if you situate them just right and cover the white wire with sand," Cleo said. "Which reminds me, do we get to put up a Christmas tree at the B and B?"

"Of course we'll put up a tree," Ellie Mae answered. "Let's plan to do it a week from Saturday night, and everyone can help trim it and put up decorations."

Maude's head bobbed up and down. Her blue eyes twinkled even brighter than the sun sparkling out on the calm waters that morning. "I love Christmas. It was the only time of the year that Mother was almost happy."

"We were at our winter quarters, so we always had a tree," Cleo said with a long sigh. "We drew names, and our presents couldn't cost more than ten dollars."

"We should do that this year, but to allow for inflation, let's make it twenty dollars." Ellie Mae knew exactly what she would buy Ricky if she happened to get his name—she'd seen a tiny sandcastle that could be engraved with names or initials across the base.

Homer set his mouth in a serious line. "I like it. Me and Frank ain't had a tree since we was in Vietnam. Frank's mama sent us a little fake tree that was about a foot high, and we set it up in our barracks. We didn't have any decorations, so we made some out of paper. And on Christmas morning . . ." His voice broke.

"That was the day we both got injured," Frank finished for him. "We ain't had a tree since, but we'd love to help fix one and draw names with y'all."

Homer pulled a red bandanna from the bib pocket of his overalls and wiped his wet cheeks. "Them are some tough memories, but what we've been makin' at the B and B is kind of pushin' them to the back of our minds."

Ellie Mae scooted back and threw her arm around Homer's shoulders. "You're making me all misty-eyed. Can I borrow your hankie?"

Homer didn't hand it to her; instead, he wiped her tears away gently with the unused corner. "I appreciate this, child. Y'all have done so much for us. Giving us not just a place to live for a little while but a home, and then selling Cleo the barn so we will always be close to y'all. If I'd had grandkids, I couldn't have asked for better ones than you and Tabby, and Alex and Ricky."

"That's enough." Frank grabbed the hankie and dabbed his eyes. "We got a castle to build and a carnival to go to. Let's talk about what we're going to do rather than what we had to endure to get to this time of our lives. I'm going to hit the corn dog wagon first, then the cotton candy one, and after that, I might have some tacos."

Maude reached out for the hankie, used it, and then passed it over to Cleo.

"Y'all are so sweet," Tabby whispered, "and I'm glad to be your grandchild."

"Me too," Ellie Mae said. "I think I even look a little like Cleo."

"Yes, you do, darlin'," Cleo agreed with a nod. "Our Irish shines forth."

Before anyone could comment on that, a gull floated in from the sky and landed on top of the castle they were building. Homer used his damp hankie to shoo it away, but then half a dozen more came to rest all around them. Duke had been sleeping in Maude's lap, but when the first bird squawked, the little guy woke up, growled deep down in his throat, and took off so fast, his tiny body was nothing but a blur. He ran at the gulls like he was King Kong and they were hummingbirds. The winged critters must have believed that he was meaner than he looked because they flew away.

"He's got his bluff in on them." Homer laughed.

Frank smiled so big that his wrinkles deepened. "He ain't named after John Wayne for nothing."

"I'd like to see your cats do that," Maude taunted Cleo.

"If Julep came out here, she would kill those birds, not just chase them away," Cleo shot back. "And then she would carry one back to the barn to share with Buddy, Venus, and Daisy."

"Where did you get those names?" Alex asked without looking up from his work.

"There's one boy and two girls, and the names came to me in a dream. Buddy, because he's the only boy; Venus for me, because my head is in the stars; Daisy for you, Maude, because the two solid black kittens are sisters, and you have always liked daisies," Cleo answered.

"If they were real babies, I might come to the christening since you named one for me," Maude said.

"We can have a christening," Cleo said. "I'm an ordained minister by the authority of the internet, so I can take care of a service for them."

"*You* are a preacher?" Maude gasped.

"No, I'm not a *preacher*. Heaven forbid!" Cleo shook her head. "I got my license so I can marry folks. We needed someone who could do that legally at the carnival. I've performed several weddings in the past few years. I'll get a little basin of water ready."

Ricky burst out laughing. "Can I come watch you baptize your cats?"

Cleo slapped his arm. "I'm not going to duck them under the water. That would traumatize my babies. I will just let a couple of drops fall on their little heads as I formally name them. You are all invited. We'll have the ceremony Sunday at the cat house."

"What time?" Alex asked.

"Midafternoon—say, two thirty—after us *old folks* get our naps," she answered with a smile.

"I'll have snacks in the kitchen after the ceremony to make it official," Tabby said. "And, honey, none of you four will ever be old."

Ellie Mae's thoughts drifted away from the conversation everyone else was having and wandered over to the dream she'd had the night before. Maybe she would ask Cleo if she could interpret dreams as well as tell fortunes. With words flying around like the gulls, both from her own group and those on either side of their plot, Ellie Mae didn't realize that another team had stopped and was watching them put their castle together.

"You sure are working hard, son." A deep voice startled her and jerked her from her thoughts and back into the present reality. She looked up over her head to see a tall dark-skinned man with a little silver in the temples of his dark hair and the deepest brown eyes she'd ever seen. He looked like a taller, older version of Ricky, and he had his arm draped around a short blonde lady with clear blue eyes and freckles across the white skin of her nose.

"Dad!" Ricky rolled up on his knees and then stood up. "I was hoping y'all would come today." He made introductions and then announced to the group, "This is my dad, Richard Benoit, and my mama, Betsy."

"We've heard so much about you all that we feel we already know you," Betsy said.

"Especially you, Ellie Mae. You should come to church with us on Sunday and then have dinner with us at our house."

Ellie Mae glanced up to see Ricky smiling like the Cheshire cat. Meeting the parents was supposed to be a tenth-date kind of thing, not a before-the-first-official-date thing.

He's met your dad and your prospective new stepmom, so you should go spend some time with his folks. I've got a feeling it will be far different than yesterday, Aunt Charlotte reminded her so clearly that a vision of her aunt wearing her signature jeans and plaid shirt popped into Ellie Mae's head.

"Thank you, but we have plans for a christening . . . ," Ellie Mae started to say.

"Whoa!" Cleo butted in before she could finish. "We can put off the ceremony until four o'clock and then have supper afterward. You go on with these folks. I don't think you've been off the property except to come to the beach since the hurricane hit us."

"It will do you good to get away for a little bit," Maude added.

"Thank you, to both of our new grannies," Ellie Mae said.

"Then you'll say yes?" Ricky asked.

"Of course she says yes," Cleo said. "Now, get back to work on that drawbridge, and Ellie Mae, you and Tabby have a turret to finish."

"Yes, Granny," Ellie Mae said.

"I'm not old enough to be a granny. You can call me Gigi," Cleo said.

"And I'm Mamaw," Maude said. "That's what Cleo and I called our grandmother."

Ellie Mae shifted her gaze from Ricky to his mother. "Thank you for the invitation. I would love to join you for services and for dinner. Which church do you attend, and what time do I meet you there?"

"Ricky will pick you up about ten thirty. Services start at eleven," Richard chimed in. "We're off to the carnival now. I just love gyro sandwiches and have been looking forward to getting one all week."

"We'll talk more Sunday," Betsy said.

Ricky dropped back down on his knees to finish the drawbridge. "See y'all later."

Betsy tucked her arm into her husband's. "Text us when you get home so I don't worry."

"Sure thing," Ricky said without even looking up.

Ellie Mae couldn't remember a time when her father asked her to let him know that she had arrived home safely. The realization didn't make her angry—just sad.

Tabby had just covered up the last of the wires with sand and lit their castle when the bell ringer rode down the beach in a four-wheeler. She stood up, and all eight of them took a step back to wait for the judging.

Maude picked up Duke and held him in her arms. "You can't growl at the judges, sweetie. You've done a good job of chasing those birds away from our castle, but now it's time for you to wag your tail and be real nice."

Alex slipped an arm around Tabby's shoulders and said, "That was so much fun."

Ricky whipped out his phone and took a picture. "Would all y'all stand on the other side of the log? We need a picture of you with the castle. Y'all worked hard at being gofers."

"Maybe we should be called the Gofer Four?" Frank said with a deep chuckle.

"Do I have to stand beside Cleo?" Maude asked.

"No, we can put her between me and Homer," Frank told her.

"Never thought I'd see the day that a woman would come between us," Homer teased.

Frank took his place and pulled Cleo over next to him. "You're getting senile. Have you forgot about Millie back when we were in our twenties? And later on, Bobby Sue?"

Homer's smile and the twinkle in his eye said he had not forgotten. "Who are you talkin' about?"

"Millie, that we both fell in love when we first came back from Nam, and then . . ." Frank poked

Homer in the shoulder. "You old renegade. You *do* remember, don't you?"

"Yep, I do, and I also remember that we vowed after Bobby Sue that we'd never let another woman get in the way of our friendship," Homer said. "Now, smile for Ricky. I want one of these pictures to frame for my new room. We helped build a castle made of sand today, but we will be moving into a real modern-day castle in a few months."

"And that one will stand forever because, like the Good Book says, it will be built on a rock and not upon the sand," Maude said.

"Amen!" Cleo said with a nod.

Ricky snapped the picture and then said, "Your turn, Alex and Tabby."

Tabby stepped right up into place. She wanted to have pictures to commemorate the good time they'd all had. She handed her phone to Ricky and said, "Don't y'all go anywhere. I want Ricky to take all the pictures with my phone, too. I'm thinking a collage might be nice to hang above the credenza in the foyer."

That brought out several phones from pockets among them all, and Ricky was busy snapping pictures until the judges walked by their display and made a few notes on their clipboards. Then he said, "Okay, folks, now it's my turn with Ellie Mae. Alex, will you do the honors for this one?"

"No fussing," Tabby whispered to Ellie Mae.

"But my hair is a fright, and I'm covered with sand," Ellie Mae said.

"And you are still beautiful." Ricky drew her close enough that she could lay her cheek against his chest. "This is even better than winning anything in the contest."

"I agree," Ellie Mae told him.

Tabby was busy looking through all the photos that Ricky had taken when the judges came by again and attached a third-place ribbon to the castle. One second, she was staring at the picture of her and Alex; the next, he had picked her up and was twirling her around. Cleo and Maude were actually hugging each other. Homer and Frank patted each other on the back, and Ricky was kissing Ellie Mae.

When Alex finally set her down, she was breathless and barely got out, "It's third place, not first place."

He tipped her chin up with his fist and kissed her before she even had time to close her eyes. When the kiss ended, she was even more breathless than before. *This must be what it's like to really be falling in love as an adult,* she thought. She touched her lips and was surprised to find that they weren't as hot as they felt.

"We placed on our first year. That's awesome!" Frank shouted.

"Can we frame the ribbon with a bunch of the

pictures around it and hang it in the barn?" Cleo asked.

"Yes, you can put the ribbon out in your new castle," Tabby answered.

"Right above the pool table," Homer said. "This has been the best day we've had in years, and we still get to do the carnival."

"They're going to be like a bunch of sugared-up five-year-olds who just spent the day at their grandmother's house," Alex whispered. "They'll spend half the night sitting around the living room, telling stories and eating all the desserts left over from yesterday."

She leaned her head over on his chest and slipped her hand in his. "Do you think we'll ever get them raised?"

"Probably not," Alex said. "Do you realize that, figuratively, they got dropped on your doorstep just like Duke and Julep?"

"I guess they did, and like Duke and Julep, they sure have made our lives richer," she told him.

"Does that include me?" Alex asked. "I was in the basket with them when Miz Charlotte sent them to the B and B."

"Especially you," Tabby said. "Now, let's take some more pictures of the castle with its pretty white ribbon attached to the turret."

Chapter Twenty

Ellie Mae stopped abruptly at the bottom of the porch stairs. "Are you sure about this?" she whispered.

Ricky dropped her hand and wrapped his arms around her. "I've never been surer about anything. Mama wouldn't have invited you if she didn't like you already."

"But she only met me for five minutes on the beach," Ellie Mae argued.

"My mama has never invited one of my girlfriends to sit with the family in church," Ricky whispered.

Ellie Mae took half a step back. "For real?"

"Cross my heart," Ricky answered.

Before Ellie Mae could say another word, Betsy slung the door open. "You kids come on in here. Don't just stand out there on the lawn. Dinner is almost ready."

Ellie Mae inhaled deeply and let the air out slowly; then she pasted a smile on her face. "Yes, ma'am," she said.

When they entered the foyer, Ricky's brother Dillon's wife, Poppy, came out of the kitchen and gave Ellie Mae a quick hug. She was a tall brunette with twinkling blue eyes and a quick smile that instantly put Ellie Mae at ease.

"We're huggers in this family, so you might as well get used to it," Poppy said. "Mama Benoit and I rushed out of church so we could get here and put the finishing touches on dinner, so we didn't get to visit after services this morning. We're so excited you could join us today, and we'll have time to visit over dinner. Come on in here, and help me set the table." She took Ellie Mae's hand and pulled her away from Ricky. "We can fill you in on anything you want to ask about Ricky."

"Hey, now!" Ricky said.

"Go on in the living room with Daddy Benoit and Dillon. Your jobs begin after dinner when you help us with cleanup," Poppy said.

"Yes, ma'am," Ricky said with a smile, then whispered, "See? I told you so."

"Just tell me what you want me to do, but I'll be up-front and honest: I don't do so well when it comes to cooking. My roommate, Sam, did most of the cooking," Ellie Mae admitted.

"Ricky told us you'd lost your best friend," Poppy said. "I'm so sorry. That would be tough. And to be honest, I'm not such a good cook, either. I can open a can and make a very good peanut butter sandwich, but Dillon does most of the cooking at our house. Our job is to set the table and help bring all the food from the kitchen to the dining room."

"I can manage that without getting out a 'how to' book," Ellie Mae said with a smile.

"I hope you like Mexican food," Betsy said. "I'm using up the last of the Thanksgiving turkey to make a casserole. We've got refried beans and fried rice to go with it."

"Sounds wonderful. I love Mexican food. Something good and hot will be so good on this cold, rainy day." Ellie Mae already felt more at home in this house than she had in her father's place after she'd moved in with Sam—and he had not hugged her since that day, either.

Poppy handed Ellie Mae a stack of plates. "The dining room is through that door. We'll have eleven for dinner today, but the table seats twelve."

"I always wanted lots of grandbabies, so I picked out a big dining room table when we bought the house." Betsy stirred spices into the rice that filled a huge cast-iron skillet. "I got five granddaughters—Kara, Makela, Bethany, Sarah, and Nicole—and I keep telling Ricky that it's his job to produce us a redheaded grandson."

Ellie Mae thought about the discussion they'd had while building the castle. If their relationship got even more serious, would one of their children be that little redhaired grandson?

"I tried five times for a boy, but it just didn't happen," Poppy said. "I was going to name him Nixon if I'd ever had a son."

Ellie Mae couldn't believe they were sharing such personal details with her, like they had known each other all their lives. She'd never been one of those women who had her kids named at sixteen, but she did like the name Nixon.

Travis Nixon Benoit has a good ring to it, she thought and then blushed. She shouldn't be thinking of baby names this early in their relationship.

Dinner was a lot like what every meal was like at the Sandcastle B and B—lots of conversation, memories, and teasing each other—and Ellie Mae felt right at home. Afterward, the guys all pitched in and helped with cleanup, and then it was time for Ricky and Ellie Mae to go home for the christening ceremony for the cats.

"You are a very lucky man," Ellie Mae said on the way back to Sandcastle.

"I know that because I got to sit beside you in church this morning, and you came to Sunday dinner with me at my folks'." Ricky turned south onto the highway. "And you fit right in with my family. But what makes you say I'm a lucky man?"

"You have an awesome family," Ellie Mae answered. "They accept me like I wish my dad would accept you and would have been nicer about Sam. I felt more comfortable there than I have anywhere except the B and B and in my own home with Sam."

Ricky reached over the console and laid a hand

on her shoulder. "I'm glad you didn't inherit your dad's narrow-mindedness. On another note, my dad and brother took me aside and told me that you were a keeper."

"I bet they say that about all the women you bring home, because they want you to be settled down and making more grandbabies for them," she teased.

"Honey, I have dated—and I've even been in a fairly serious relationship where we almost moved in together. But you are the first woman my mama ever invited to Sunday dinner, let alone church." Ricky moved his hand back to the steering wheel and kept his eyes on the road.

Ellie Mae was glad she wasn't driving since the rain was coming down in sheets, and she could barely see the center line in the highway. With all that going on outside, and her heart thumping like a drum inside her chest, she wouldn't be able to stay between the lines. "As close as your family is, she had to have known your girlfriends. If it wasn't for Baytown and Texas City, the county wouldn't have more than ten thousand people in it."

"You've done your homework." Ricky chuckled. "The old saying among this sparsely populated area is that everyone knows everything everyone is doing, when they're doing it, and who they're doing it with. My mother used to remind me of that when I left the house. And pretty often when I came home, she could tell me where I'd been, how many beers I'd drunk, and who I'd kissed."

"Really?" Ellie Mae asked.

"I'm exaggerating, but I'm dead serious when I tell you that being invited to Sunday dinner is a big thing in our family. Only one girl has been invited before you, and that was Poppy," Ricky said.

"Why me?" Ellie Mae whispered.

"Mama says that when I talk about you, there's something in my voice, and when I'm with you, my eyes twinkle. She says that Dillon did the same with Poppy, and that my dad looks at *her* like that even yet," he explained. "I don't want to scare you off by rushing things, but I'd really like for us to try a third date."

"Third?" Ellie Mae asked.

Ricky held up one finger but kept his eyes firmly on the road. "First date, you got sick—but I polished my boots, so it was a date." Another finger went up. "Second one was today, and I polished my boots last night." A third finger shot up. "Trying for a third one."

"So, polishing your boots is a factor in determining whether it's a date? Maybe that's what put your mama onto things. If you polish your boots, you are serious about the woman," Ellie Mae said with a smile.

Ricky put his hand back on the steering wheel

and nodded. "Could very well be, but I think it has to do with your being Irish. At the top of our family tree is an Irish lady named Martha Cummins, who married a Benoit, and besides all that, Mama has always wanted a redhaired grandchild."

"Let's try out that third date before we start having children." Ellie Mae caught a mental vision of a little boy who looked like Ricky, only with curly red hair and freckles across his nose. Then there was a little girl about two feet behind him. Her red curls bounced, and the black kitten in her arms squirmed as it tried to get free from her grasp.

Ricky parked behind the B and B, leaned over, and kissed Ellie Mae on the cheek. "Tomorrow night after work, would you go to the park with me for our third date, if this rain lets up?"

"I'd like that," Ellie Mae said.

Ricky slid out from behind the steering wheel, brought out a big black umbrella from under the seat, and popped it open. "Want me to lay my coat down so you don't get your shoes all muddy?"

"Nope." Ellie Mae pulled her high-heeled shoes off. "My feet will wash just fine, and you're not wearing a coat."

He held the umbrella with one hand and extended the other to help her. "I've got a shirt that I'll sacrifice for you."

"You can't go to a religious ceremony with no

shirt." Ellie Mae giggled. "I'll keep on the grass, so my feet should just be wet, not muddy."

"You amaze me," Ricky said as they walked together through the rain and onto the back porch.

Ellie Mae opened the door and stepped inside the utility room. "Right back at you."

A few pings on the window told Tabby there was hail mixed with the rain that had been coming down in buckets all day long. Poor Cleo had gotten soaked bringing Julep and her kittens into the house and had to change her outfit before it was time for the services to begin. When a loud clap of thunder rolled over the house, Tabby wondered if it was a sign that they were getting pretty danged close to sacrilege by christening cats.

"I heard a car door slam," Alex said. "That'll be Ricky and Ellie Mae. We need to get this over before one of those streaks of lightning shoots through the window and zaps Cleo."

"I'm not so worried about adopting the dog, but baptizing cats is walking on the edge," Tabby agreed.

Alex raised an eyebrow. "Adopting a dog?"

Tabby carried a platter of turkey-salad sandwiches made from the last of the holiday bird to the table and set it down among plates of cookies, a chocolate cake with all the animals' names on it, and a crystal bowl full of Aunt Charlotte's amaretto punch. "Turns out that Frank is a notary, so Maude is formally adopting Duke today. Cleo drew up a paper, and Maude will sign the document that says Duke is officially her dog. And since she suggested the adoption, Cleo is going to adopt Julep and the kittens, too. One of them sure can't let the other outdo her. Kids couldn't be this much trouble."

"Seventy- and eighty-year-old kids and teen-agers coming in from a date." Alex chuckled. "All we need now is a baby, two toddlers, and a kindergartner to round it all out."

Tabby hip-bumped him. "Bite your tongue, and besides, with the dog and four cats, we've about got that covered, too."

"And you thought you would be bored down here in the backwoods little beach town of Sandcastle, didn't you?" Alex teased.

"Hello!" Ellie Mae yelled as she came in through the back door. "We're here. Let the baptism begin."

"I didn't ever think I'd be bored . . . but if someone would have told me I'd be all dressed up for a cat baptism, I would have thought I'd heard wrong," Tabby answered.

"There's never a dull moment." Ellie Mae carried her shoes past Tabby and snagged a cookie as she headed toward the living room. "Do I have to wear shoes for this event?"

"Might be best, if you want to be in the pictures. Cleo says we have to have lots of photos to commemorate the day, just like we did at the beach. She's even talked Frank and Homer into wearing dress pants and sports jackets," Tabby answered.

"We've got a notary and a minister," Alex said. "Maybe we could talk Frank into going to night school to be a cat vet and Homer into being a pet funeral-home director, and we'll have it covered." He paused for a moment. "I'm sorry. That was insensitive, after what you went through a couple of years ago."

Tabby slipped her hand into Alex's and drew him into the living room. "It's okay. I'm finding a measure of peace here in Sandcastle. And the minister—that would be Cleo—can serve as the funeral-home director when one of the animals passes away. Maybe we can talk Jazzy into becoming a vet, or Declan. It would be nice to have one in this area and for them to live closer to us."

"Yes, it would. But I'm not interfering with their lives," Alex said.

For some strange, unexplainable reason, Tabby remembered something her Aunt Charlotte had said about the Fan Four the afternoon she'd called and told her Alex was bringing them to the B and B: *"They'll just eat and sleep most of the time."*

403

"Yeah, right," Tabby muttered under her breath.

"Are you talking to me?" Alex asked.

"Nope, just to myself," Tabby answered.

Alex hadn't had this much fun in years—not even when he beat Charlotte at poker or had a great day out on the boat with old guys who reminded him of his grandfather. He couldn't remember the last time a woman had made him feel so alive, and he intended to do whatever was necessary to have a permanent relationship with Tabby—not just a few stolen kisses or a date or two.

When they entered the living room, Cleo was standing in front of the windows. She was dressed in a flowing red robe with a purple scarf tied loosely around her neck, its ends hanging to her knees on either side. Her red hair was braided and wrapped around her head like a crown, and she held in her hands a book with a picture of trees and a lake on the cover.

"Come in and have a seat," she said in a serious tone. "I will begin by saying that to keep humble, everyone should have either a dog or a cat, both of which have a mind of their own and will either ignore you or make you feel like you just won the lottery. These animals we are baptizing today and adopting as our own were blown into our lives by fate."

"Hmmph," Maude almost snorted. "They were blown in by a hurricane. Fate didn't have anything to do with it. Labor pains and fear of drowning did the job."

Cleo gave her a dirty look and said, "That's enough out of you. As I was saying, fate has brought them to us, and we accept them into our lives as part of our family. First, I will baptize the kittens one at a time and give them their names."

"What's the book got to do with anything?" Alex asked out of the side of his mouth.

"I reckon it's just part of the costume," Tabby whispered.

Cleo reached into a bowl of water sitting on the coffee table and picked up the kitten with white on the tip of his tail. She touched the kitten on the head and said, "I baptize you Rufus Homer Franklin Oliver, and your nickname is Buddy." She set him down, and he snuggled up into his mama's belly and began to have supper. She grabbed the next one by the scruff of the neck and repeated the process, dipping her fingers in the water and then touching the kitten on the head. "I baptize you Venus Ellie Tabby Oliver, and you will be called Venus." She pulled the last kitten from under the sofa by the scruff of the neck and kissed the top of its little head. "Sorry, darlin' baby, but we've got to get your little soul taken care of."

It hissed and squalled at the top of its lungs the whole time she repeated the steps. "Just like my sister, you have to be difficult. I baptize you Maude Daisy Cleo, and you will be called Daisy."

"And now for the adoption." Maude held up Duke, who looked a little embarrassed at the red bow around his neck. "Your formal name is Alexander Richard Duke Dodson. You will be called Duke, and I expect you to guard me with your life."

"That's so sweet," Ricky said.

"Yes, sir, it is." Alex bit back laughter.

"And now, Julep's adoption and baptism. I wouldn't want her to not be able to cross over the Rainbow Bridge because I didn't get her soul taken care of." Cleo dotted the cat with a drop of water. "Your new name is Callie Julep Oliver, but we'll call you Julep since that's what you know. And that concludes—"

Maude threw up a palm. "Whoa! Wait a minute." She hopped up from the chair she'd just sat back down in, dipped her finger in the bowl of water, and touched Duke on the top of his head. "If your cats are going over the Rainbow Bridge, then my dog isn't going to be left behind." She touched Duke's head and said, "I baptize you in the name of the Father, the Son, and the Holy Spirit. There now; it's done. Duke is a Christian dog, and he can enjoy heaven with me."

"We're honored that you named the kitten for us—but you don't expect us to pay child support, do you?" Frank asked.

"Only if you want to see Buddy or his sisters," Cleo answered. "Child support will be in the form of babysitting when I'm busy telling fortunes."

"I reckon we can manage that." Homer chuckled. "Now, can we go eat? Those sandwiches Tabby made are calling my name. Anytime Duke or the cats need some extra love, just send them to me. I babysit animals for free—long as they're not elephants or snakes."

"Why not those two critters?" Alex asked as he watched all the kittens tumbling around in a three-way wrestling match.

"Because elephants intimidate me," Homer answered.

"And snakes of any kind terrify him," Frank finished for him.

"I can tolerate an earthworm, but just barely," Homer admitted.

Frank stood up and started for the kitchen. "When we go fishing, I bait his hook for him if we're using worms. And I'm hungry, so I'm going to eat. Besides, I feel pretty spiffy all dressed up for something that ain't a funeral. Alex, you and Ricky best keep them women close to you today. They're liable to leave y'all for me."

Homer followed Frank's lead. "Not as long as I'm in the runnin'."

Alex pulled Tabby close to his side with one hand and saluted dramatically with the other one. "Sir, yes, sir."

Ricky kissed Ellie Mae on the forehead. "Don't leave me. My mama likes you."

"Oh, really?" Tabby raised an eyebrow.

"Later," Ellie Mae mouthed.

Tabby gave her a brief nod.

Alex made a mental note to ask Ricky exactly what he meant by that statement the next day when they got a moment alone.

Tabby had only had cabin fever a couple of times in her life. The first one had come about the night before she'd moved out of the house she shared with James and into a small apartment. The second was when the hurricane had hit, and everything was dark for all those days. That night, after the ceremonies, she couldn't find the peace she usually had when she sat on the floor with crossed legs and tried to meditate. Finally, she stood up, shoved her feet down into a pair of rubber boots, put on a jacket, and then slipped out of her bedroom and headed outside.

When she stepped onto the porch, the crisp night air washed over her, bringing with it the smell of salt water. The sounds of the waves lapping up on the shore made her feel like she was listening to Cleo's chakra music in her ears. She bent forward and placed her hands on the cold railing, took a deep breath, and felt free for a moment. Then that antsy feeling she got when Alex was nearby wrapped itself around her.

She heard the front door open, and then he was standing right next to her, his hands on the railing beside hers.

"Having trouble sleeping again, too?" he asked.

"Cabin fever, and I don't understand why," she answered. "Nothing seems to be wrong in my life. I've even come to grips with the wallpaper and agree with Ellie Mae about leaving it alone."

"Wallpaper?" Alex asked. "That's what is keeping you awake?"

"Not really, but that was the only thing we've really disagreed on when it comes to the redecorating job. I've accepted our Fan Four and even realize now that Cleo was spot-on when she told my fortune," Tabby answered. "I don't know why I'm not—"

Alex turned her around and wrapped her up in his arms before she could say another word. "I think maybe you are fighting against us, just like I've been doing."

She leaned back far enough to look up into his face. "Why do you have worries about us?"

"I've never been married, and it's a little late in life to start a family. I already have a teenage daughter, and . . ."

Tabby rolled up on her tiptoes and kissed him on the mouth. "I don't know if I want to start another family or not, but I do know that I have deep feelings for you. Having a late-in-life family is something we can worry about later. I really liked Jazzy and Declan. I wish they lived closer to us, but at least they're in the same state. What I'm thinking about now is where do we go from here?"

"One day at a time," Alex said. "And maybe one date night out away from the crowd at least once a week. Does that sound like a good place to go from here? I felt something when we shared the first kiss that I have never felt since before we met again, but I just chalked it up to young love." He brushed a strand of her dark hair back behind her ear.

"So did I," she whispered. "And your idea sounds wonderful to me."

He bent down slightly, and his lips met hers for another kiss, and she realized from the heat flowing through her body that she wanted more than a make-out session. When the kiss ended, she took his hands in hers. "This is a big step for me, but . . ."

"I know." His deep voice was hoarse with emotion. "It's a big step. Are you sure?"

"I am," she said.

"My place or yours? Or shall I get a blanket for the beach?" he asked.

Only Alex would think of that, she thought as she led him off the porch. "I was thinking that maybe an old quilt in the back of my SUV in the garage. The walls are thin in both my place and yours."

"Whatever you say, darlin'." He scooped her up in his arms and carried her around the house, through the door, and into the garage, and closed it with his bare foot.

Chapter Twenty-One

Ellie Mae was not looking forward to putting up a Christmas tree that Saturday evening. Cleo had written all their names on individual pieces of paper, folded them at least half a dozen times, and then tossed them into a gold hat decorated with tinsel. Alex and Ricky had brought the tree down from the attic and were busy putting it together, with supervision from Homer and Frank.

Excitement filled the house, but not Ellie Mae's heart. On the day after Thanksgiving last year, she and Sam had bought a bottle of expensive red wine, got down the two stemmed glasses that they had saved for the occasion, and put up their tree just like they'd done every year they'd been together. She almost smiled at the vision of the pitiful little two-foot Charlie Brown–type tree with one red bulb hanging from an almost-bare limb. She and Sam toasted the season with a glass of wine and talked about Christmases past and future.

Tabby came out of the kitchen with a bottle of wine and eight disposable stemmed glasses on a tray. She set it down on the coffee table and then eased down onto the sofa beside Ellie Mae.

"I remember your story about your Christmases with Sam. This isn't what y'all had, but it is the last bottle of Aunt Charlotte's elderberry wine I found hidden in the pantry. Maybe we'll start our own tradition, since this is our first Christmas at the B and B."

"Do you know how to make elderberry wine?" Ellie Mae asked. "If this is going to be our tradition, we'd better keep it true to the original."

"I do not, but after these past few weeks, I figure I can learn. Aunt Charlotte says the elderberries grow out behind the barn and that they are ready to be harvested in early August," Tabby said. "How are you holding up? Thinking about Sam and that scraggly little tree y'all always had?"

"Yes, I was." Ellie Mae nodded. "How are *you* holding up?"

"Wonderfully well," Tabby said with a smile. "Natalie will always have a special place in my heart, but doing a little meditation each evening is helping me move on."

Ellie Mae leaned over and whispered, "I didn't know folks called it *meditation* these days."

Tabby blushed scarlet. "What?"

"I'm not sure if you and Alex are sleeping in his room, in yours, or behind the log out on the beach. I'm not even a fortune-teller like Cleo, but you've been happier than I've ever seen you since last Sunday. Tell me where y'all are having your little sessions so that I don't embarrass you by blasting into your room when I have a nightmare." Ellie Mae wiggled her eyebrows.

Tabby's blush deepened to maroon. "We're keeping things quiet for a while."

"My lips are sealed," Ellie Mae said, "but I'm happy for you. Looking back on these last weeks, I can see that he's been in love with you for a long time."

"We haven't said those words yet," Tabby said.

Cleo came into the room and leaned on the back of the sofa between them. "What words?"

"That we were dreading Christmas," Ellie Mae said, covering their tracks without skipping a beat. "It's my first one without my friend Sam, and the season is tough on Tabby because of memories of her daughter, Natalie."

Tabby could have hugged Ellie Mae for being so fast on her feet. "And now that you Fan Four are here with us, it's not so tough after all."

"It's like a good old-fashioned family Christmas," Cleo said, "and Maude is even being nice." She crossed her fingers and nodded toward her sister, who was just coming into the room. "She's humming, so that's a good sign. The best Christmas present ever would be if she would let bygones be bygones."

"You didn't start without me, did you?" Maude called out as she arrived in the living room. "Oh. My. Goodness! That tree has to be ten feet tall."

Alex and Ricky arrived with boxes in their arms and set them on the floor.

"These are the lights, according to what's written on the top of the box, but there's a lot more boxes to be brought down," Alex said. "And yes, Maude, the tree *is* a ten-footer. Miz Charlotte put it up every year all by herself. I offered to help because I didn't think she should be on a ladder, but she said that she could take care of it. She always had a group from her church come over for a gift exchange on Christmas Eve. Before that, sometime in the middle of the month, the Chambers County Historical Society had a tour of homes, and the Sandcastle B and B always kicked off the event."

Homer took a step back, cupped his chin in his hand, and studied the tree. "I heard the tour has been canceled this year because of all the damage Delilah did, but that don't mean we can't have our own special holiday. I believe it's ready for y'all to put the lights on it. Alex and Tabby should do that because they're the tallest."

"And they're still young enough to stoop down to get them on the bottom limbs," Frank chuckled.

"We'll bring down more boxes while y'all do that," Ricky said. "Ellie Mae, will you help me? None of them are very heavy."

"Sure thing," Ellie Mae answered.

Ellie Mae snapped a photo of Homer and Frank discussing whether they should pull the tree out a little farther from the wall. She sent it to Aunt Charlotte before slipping her hand in Ricky's, and the two of them started up the wide staircase.

Are you and Ricky in a relationship now? Aunt Charlotte's voice was back in her head.

Whoever said ghosts didn't exist had rocks for brains. How else could her aunt, who was hundreds of miles away, know what she was thinking and feeling?

"I'm going to make a run to the bathroom before we start bringing down boxes," Ricky said. "All that coffee this morning has hit bottom."

"I'll take a minute to call Aunt Charlotte, then." Ellie Mae sat down on the bottom step of the stairs leading up to the attic, took out her phone, and called her aunt.

"Hello, darlin' girl," Charlotte answered. "I just got the first picture. The old tree looks good, but let this be the last year you use it. It's time for it to go out with the New Year's trash, and a new one to take its place next year. I got one of those new-fangled prelit ones for my cabin, and it's so much easier to put up."

"Aunt Charlotte, I wish you were here."

"I hear confusion and sadness in your voice," Charlotte said. "This is your first Christmas without Sam, so that would be normal."

"Yes, I am sad, but I'm moving on, and I've got lots of help with Tabby here, and Ricky and the Fan Four. That's what we've nicknamed the folks who'll be living in the barn. But . . ." She wasn't quite sure how to get the words out. "I hate to admit it, but I'm also a little jealous of Tabby. She and Alex . . ."

"They have taken things to the next level, and you wish you and Ricky were there yourselves?" Charlotte asked.

Ellie Mae glanced down the hallway, looked up at the ceiling, and then back down the stairs. Didn't people have to die before they became a ghost? "How do you know these things?"

"I'm old, not blind or deaf," Charlotte said with a giggle. "I talked to Tabby earlier this morning, and she needed me to tell her it wasn't too early for her and Alex to be sleeping together."

"Did you?" Ellie Mae asked.

"Honey, true love does not abide by a clock or a calendar. I told her the same thing I will tell you, and that's to listen to your heart. It don't ever steer you wrong. Is it telling you that Ricky is the one?"

"I don't know about that, but it is telling me to give him a chance and see if he might be," Ellie Mae answered.

"Then that's enough for today," Charlotte told her. "I forgot to ask Tabby about Maude and Cleo. Are they making any progress?"

"Maybe a little," Ellie Mae replied. "Cleo *so* wants Maude to come around and for them to be sisters. It's painful sometimes to see them, at their age, being so stubborn. Did I tell you that Cleo interpreted a dream I had?"

"I've been visiting with Cleo on the phone almost every day, and she told me about your dream. I agreed with her interpretation. You were worried about the little things with Ricky—like, at the time, if his folks would like you because you knew Jefferson wasn't going to like him. Don't sweat the small stuff, and remember nearly everything is small stuff. The best way you and Tabby can help Maude and Cleo is just to continue being an example to them," Charlotte told her. "Remember to send pictures all day. I love you girls. Bye now."

Ellie Mae barely had time to say goodbye before the phone screen went dark and Ricky came out of the bathroom at the end of the hallway. "Are you all ready to get to it?"

"What is 'it'?" she teased.

He raised a dark eyebrow. "Whatever you want *it* to be."

She giggled and got to her feet. "Today *it* will have to be taking boxes of decorations downstairs."

"And tomorrow?" Ricky pulled her to his body and kissed her—long, lingering, and passionately.

"*It* can change from day to day," she said when the kiss ended and left her weak-kneed.

Ricky started up the stairs ahead of her. "Life will never be dull with you around."

"I hope not," Ellie Mae said. "Now, what do we need to haul down there first?"

"Cleo and Homer seem to be the bosses of the decorating process down there," Ricky said as he climbed the stairs, "and they said we'll need to bring down the garland and ornaments next."

"What's left after that?" Ellie Mae asked.

"There's still lots of boxes up there. One says 'Around the Window,' and another has 'For the Coffee Table' written on it," Ricky answered, taking her hand in his.

Aunt Charlotte, if I listened to my heart right now, I'd lock the attic door, and the folks could just wait for garland and ornaments, she thought.

"That's a beautiful smile you are wearing." Ricky kept her hand on the way to the door leading up the narrow stairs and into the attic.

"Thank you." Her grin widened even more. "I wore it special for you today."

When she reached the top of the stairs, she crossed over to an old rocking chair and sat down. "We should talk."

Ricky eased down onto the top of an old steamer trunk. "I'm game for whatever you want to talk about. It will take Alex and Tabby at least an hour to get the lights on the tree, so we've got plenty of time. Of course, if we take too long, or if you have dust on your back when we get back down there with the next boxes, you might get teased," he said. "Are you ready for that?"

"I think I just might be," she answered. "I want to talk about us."

"I'm planning on buying you a Christmas gift, but you don't need to feel obligated, if that's what's bothering you." Ricky leaned forward and brushed a small spider from her shoulder, then killed it with the toe of his boot. "In my book, the only good spider is a dead one."

"I've been reading the same book you have, then, but that's not what's on my mind," she told him. "Are we just flirting? Is this just a fling? Or is there a future? I'm not asking for a proposal or . . ." She hesitated and looked up to see him staring right into her eyes.

He took both her hands in his and kissed her on the cheek. "I love flirting with you. I love seeing your eyes light up, but, darlin', this is not just a fling where I'm concerned. I'm looking for a permanent relationship in the next year or two. We don't have to be in a rush, but I don't want to start something that doesn't have a goal in the future. So if this is flirting and a fling, tell me now, and we can call it what it was and move on."

Ellie Mae cupped Ricky's face in her hands and stared into his dark brown eyes. "I feel something when I'm around you that takes my breath away, so I would like to see if we can make it to that goal together." She moistened her lips and leaned over to kiss him.

When the kiss ended, he pulled her up to a standing position and wrapped his arms around her. His dark lashes fluttered and then came to rest on his high cheekbones, and his mouth found hers for a second time in a scorching-hot kiss that left them both panting.

When the bunch had finished with the tree and put out all of Charlotte's decorations, the living room looked like maybe the Landry family were descendants of the Griswold family from the old Christmas movie that Tabby and Natalie had watched every year. That quickly became another sweet memory that Tabby placed in what had been nothing but a black hole in her heart for two years.

"Time to draw names," she said as she picked up the hat and held it out for Homer to pick out the first name. He made a big deal out of fetching his piece of paper, shielding it from peering eyes as he unfolded it to see the name, and then tearing it up into tiny pieces and putting it in the trash can with a flourish.

"What are you doing?" Frank asked as he reached into the hat. "Old as we are, you're liable to forget whose name was written on that paper."

Homer touched his forehead with his finger. "Not me, buddy. I've got a mind like a steel trap. Dementia does not run in the Anderson family. We all drop with heart attacks from eating too much bacon and good food—but what a way to go."

Tabby passed the hat from one to another until there was only one name left, and she took it, slipped it into her pocket, and said, "Now, let's light up the tree and all these pretty decorations. Homer, why don't you do the honors? Ellie Mae, will you please take pictures and send them to Aunt Charlotte? Maude, you can pray that we don't blow a fuse—or worse yet, a transformer—and be thrown into darkness until the electric company can send someone to fix it for us."

Maude bowed her head and closed her eyes. Homer held the ends of the two cords in his hands until she raised her head, and then he said, "Amen. And now, the countdown begins. Ten . . . nine . . . eight . . . I'd like to say this holiday season is the best I've ever had."

"I can second that," Frank said with a nod.

The last time Tabby was this happy was the morning she'd given birth to Natalie and held her for the first time. Pure joy had filled her heart and soul. She looked at the tree waiting to be lit up and the decorations all over the place, and she wished she would have come home to Sandcastle at Christmas as well as Thanksgiving in years past.

Home! That's what I've been waiting to hear from you. Aunt Charlotte's voice in her head sounded happy.

"Seven . . . six . . . five . . . four . . ." Homer paused again. "If I'd had a blood-kin family, I'd want it to be just like this."

"We love you and everyone in this room, too, so just plug in the damn lights!" Cleo said.

Tabby slipped her hand into Alex's. "Home is where the heart is, and mine is right here."

"What brought that on?" he asked.

"The miracle of Christmas, I guess," she said.

"Three . . . two . . . one!" Homer connected the two plugs, and the whole room became a wonderland. The little train that circled the tree began to run, and all the decorations with lights added a brilliance to the room.

Alex squeezed Tabby's hand. "The children are happy."

"So are the teenagers." She nodded toward Ellie Mae and Ricky all snuggled up close together on the sofa. "Best Christmas ever!"

"Yes, it is, and it will be even better on the actual day. Charlotte will be here, and so will Jazzy and Declan," Alex said. "This will be the first Christmas Day that I've got to spend with my daughter. Usually, I fly to Maine or wherever her mother is stationed and spend Christmas Eve with her, then try to catch a red-eye back to Texas that night."

"We'll do our best to make it extra special," Tabby said.

Chapter Twenty-Two

T his is ridiculous," Ellie Mae said on Christmas Eve morning as she and Tabby put fresh sheets on Alex's bed—the last one they had to change out before going back downstairs to strip their own.

"Why do you say that?" Tabby asked. "We change sheets every Saturday. That's been the routine since the hurricane hit us, and anyway, we want everything fresh for Christmas, don't we?"

"It's not that," Ellie Mae answered. "You and Alex are spending every night together somewhere and sneaking either out of a room or out in the garage or the barn or the beach. We all know it, but no one talks about it. I vote that you two come out of the unnecessary closet y'all are hiding in and admit that you are in love."

Tabby turned the tables on her. "How about you and Ricky?"

"Let's open up that closet door together. Aunt Charlotte can stay in your bedroom. Jazzy and Declan can stay in my room, and I'll go home with Ricky while they're here," Ellie Mae suggested. "Ricky has been wanting me to spend the night with him so he won't have to drive back home at dawn, and I'm sure Alex would like to wake up tomorrow morning with you beside him. And those kids won't have to pitch a tent out in the barn or on the beach."

Tabby stuffed a pillow into a case and then fluffed it up. "What about the example we would be setting for Declan and Jazzy?"

Ellie Mae giggled. "Honey, we are not living in the Dark Ages, or even forty years ago. Jazzy and Declan live together. The only one who might blush if she catches you coming out of Alex's room would be Maude. Cleo will pat you on the back, and Homer and Frank will give y'all a standing ovation."

"Lord, but ten years makes a difference," Tabby said with a sigh.

"Ten years?" Ellie Mae frowned. "You've only been divorced a little over two."

"There's that many years between me and thee," Tabby answered, "and we have such different views on what's morally correct."

"It's not the age," Ellie Mae informed her with half a shrug. "It's the way you were living all those years. James had just come out of the cave, shaved and dressed in jeans instead of animal skins—probably skunks—when you met him. You lived under his rules so long that it's hard to shake them, but we are liberated women, my sweet cousin. We can live with our boyfriends if we want to." She lowered her voice to a conspiratorial whisper. "We can even throw our bras and underpants in the fire, if we have a mind to do so."

"You better not do that with *your* bra," Tabby said with a chuckle. "If you had to run from something or someone, you would black both your eyes."

"Probably so." Ellie Mae laughed with her. "So, what do you say about my suggestion?"

"Hey, Tabby, where are you?" Alex's voice floated up the stairs, and then suddenly, he was standing in the doorway. "Jazzy just called. They're thirty minutes from here, and Ricky sent a text saying that he has picked up Charlotte at the airport. Is there anything I can do to help?"

"I think we've got it, but I'm packing a bag to go to Ricky's after we open presents tonight," Ellie Mae told him. "Jazzy and Declan can have my bedroom, and Aunt Charlotte is taking Tabby's room."

Alex crossed the room and drew Tabby into a hug. "Does this mean what I think it does? Are you really going to move in with me?"

"I am," she answered, "and I like your room better than mine anyway because I love watching the sunrise with you out on the balcony."

"This is the best Christmas present ever," Alex said.

Ellie Mae tiptoed out into the hallway and eased the door shut.

"What's going on?" Maude asked. "Have you seen Cleo?"

"Alex and Tabby are going to live together," Ellie Mae whispered and then tucked Maude's arm into hers and led her to the top of the stairs. "And I believe Cleo is in the kitchen making pecan pies for tomorrow."

"Fifty years ago, I would have led the parade to tar and feather them and run them out of town on a rail, but today things are different, and I'm happy for them," Maude said with a sigh. "And that's the least of what I need to worry about this day."

Ellie Mae settled Maude into the lift chair and pulled out her phone to call Ricky while she waited for the chair to make its way slowly to the bottom of the stairs.

"Hey, we're just getting into Anahuac," he answered. "We should be there in half an hour."

"Jazzy and Declan will arrive about the same time you do," Ellie Mae told him. "I hope you were serious a couple of days ago when you said you'd like to wake up with me next to you, because I'm going home with you tonight."

"For real?" Ricky asked. "Are you serious?"

"If you were, then I am," she answered.

"Why did you tell me this on the phone?" he asked. "I want to kiss you so much right now."

"Because if you hesitated or hum-hawed

around, I didn't want you to see me cry," she answered. "This is a big step for me, Ricky Benoit."

"There's something I want to say to you, but not on the phone," he said. "See you soon."

"I'll be waiting right here," she told him and then followed Maude into the kitchen.

Maybe the magic of the holiday would continue and the two old sisters wouldn't find some minuscule detail to argue about. That's what Ellie Mae was hoping for when she crossed the foyer and followed the aroma of pecan pies baking in the oven with her nose.

Maude was already sitting at the table, looking as if she might start crying any minute. Cleo moved her shoulders to a tune she whistled as she poured herself a glass of sweet tea.

"Are you all right, Maude?" Ellie Mae asked.

Maude shook her head. "No, I'm not. I've wasted all these years—I can never get them back, and I feel like a fool."

Cleo left her tea sitting on the cabinet and hurried over to Maude. "You're not dying, are you? Do you have a terminal illness that you haven't told me about?"

One little tear escaped Maude's eye, then another, and soon a river flowed down her cheeks and dripped onto her pale blue sweatshirt with a snowman printed on the front. "I'm not dying, but . . ." She stood up, grabbed Cleo around the neck, and held on to her as if her life depended on it. "But I was wrong, and you were right, and we're too old to go back and start all over, and I'm so sorry. If we could have a do-over, I would run away with you to the carnival. I should have at least tried to get in touch with you—but oh, no, I was too busy trying to deal with Mother to even think of anything else, and I shouldn't have believed what she said about you."

Cleo picked up a paper napkin and wiped Maude's tears. "You've got to stop crying. You arc making me well up, too. What on earth brought all this on, anyway?"

Maude blew her nose and then began to sob again. "I opened the box that I should have burned, like Mother told me to do." She sat back down in her chair.

"What box? What are you talking about?" Cleo asked.

Ellie Mae fixed another glass of tea and took both to the table. "Take a drink, Maude, and calm down. What happened? You were fine when we were upstairs. Do I need to call a doctor?"

"No doctor. My blood pressure is up, but not to the danger level right now. There's a funny thumping noise in my ears when it reaches the danger zone," Maude answered and took a sip of her tea. "When Mother passed away, I found a shoebox all taped up under her bed. *Burn This* was written on the top in her handwriting.

I couldn't make myself open it, but something in my heart said that I shouldn't burn it without seeing what was inside—just in case she had tucked money away in the box and forgotten. In her old age, her secrecy and her paranoia got even worse," she said and then sniffled several times. "Oh, Cleo, I opened the box just now, and there it all was. More than sixty years of wasted life in a damned . . ." She rolled her eyes toward the ceiling and said, "Forgive me, Lord, for swearing, but it's the truth."

"Damned *what?*" Cleo pulled a chair up close to Maude and laid a hand over hers.

"One of Daddy's boot boxes!" Maude raised her voice. "Mother convinced me that you hated both of us, that you had disowned us, and she reminded me of that at least once a day. She even held my hand on her deathbed and said that she wished I had been her only child."

"We can't go back and undo the past, but we can go forward," Cleo said and patted her hand.

Ellie Mae considered leaving the room, but her feet were glued to the floor.

"I found the letter you wrote to me all those years ago—just like you said you'd done, and I didn't believe you. And there were Christmas cards, one for me and one for her, where you told us to buy ourselves something nice with the money enclosed, only there was no money in any of them. I guess she used it and didn't even tell me." Maude wiped her wet cheeks with another napkin. "Why was she like that?"

"Like I said, she was unwell in a way that we will probably never understand," Cleo answered. "We could analyze her forever and not get to the bottom of why she felt the way she did about either of us, but we can just put it to rest and go on. Are you going to burn all those cards?"

"I will keep mine to remind me that you loved me all those years after all, but the ones to her, I'll throw away in hopes that it will help me close the door on the past." Maude scooted her chair over and laid her head on Cleo's shoulder. "Can you forgive me? And can we be sisters?"

"I have forgiven you because I knew what kind of person Mother was, and we've always been sisters," Cleo answered.

"Don't let me be like her," Maude whispered.

"I promise I won't," Cleo said. "Now, stop your weeping, put on a happy face, and get ready for Christmas. We've got company on the way, and this is going to be our best Christmas ever."

Maude took a deep breath, stood up, and said, "Yes, it is, and I won't ever let anything come between us again. What can I do to help out?"

"Give us a smile first, and then you can help me wash the dishes I messed up. I'll wash and you can dry. You're way too slow when it comes to washing," Cleo said.

"I am not," Maude protested, but she did it with

a smile on her face. "You go too fast and miss stuff stuck in the corners."

"At least I don't try to wash the flowers off the bowls," Cleo smarted off.

Ellie Mae caught a flicker of movement in her peripheral vision and turned to find Tabby motioning for her to join her in the foyer. She left Cleo and Maude going at each other, but now their banter didn't have the bitter edge it had before.

"Do I need to go referee before Aunt Charlotte gets here?" Tabby whispered.

"Nope," Ellie Mae said and then told her what had happened. "I know I should have let them have their private moment, but it was like passing a terrible car wreck. I couldn't take my eyes off them, and my feet wouldn't let me leave the room. Finally, they are making up, and there is hope for them. Who would've thought it could ever happen?"

"It's a Christmas miracle, for sure," Tabby said.

"So, you and Alex?" Ellie Mae changed the subject. "Are you officially moving in together tonight?"

"Are you and Ricky?" Tabby asked.

"Don't know," Ellie Mae answered. "The way I figure it, this will be like a trial run for us."

Alex walked up behind Tabby and slipped his arms around her waist. "I'm ready for a permanent commitment, but I'm not rushing this beautiful woman. Whatever, whenever, and however she wants things done, I'll make it happen, even if I have to move heaven and earth to do it."

"That is so romantic," Ellie Mae said. "I hear a truck engine. Either Aunt Charlotte or the kids have arrived."

Aunt Charlotte pushed the front door open with Ricky right behind her. "I'm home, and what's romantic?"

"It doesn't matter. You're here!" Tabby was first to her aunt's side, and she gave her a big hug. "Welcome back home."

"This *was* home, but now my place in Colorado is home. That said, I'm glad you are finally feeling like this is *your* home." Charlotte took a step back and opened her arms to Ellie Mae.

Their aunt hadn't changed in the past year. She still wore jeans and a sweatshirt—this one with a picture of Mrs. Claus on the front—and boots that laced up to her ankles. But there was one change that showed Aunt Charlotte still did things her own way: she had a red streak in her gray chin-length hair.

"Your hair?" Tabby said.

"Don't you just love it? My favorite erotic romance author wears a red streak in her hair, and I copied it." Charlotte wiggled her fingers, beckoning Ellie Mae into her arms.

Ellie Mae walked into them and whispered,

"What is romantic is that Alex and Tabby are moving in together up in his room. You will have your old bedroom all to yourself while you are here."

Charlotte stepped back. "And you and Ricky?"

"We'll be staying at my place so Declan and Jazzy can have her room," Ricky answered as he rolled Charlotte's suitcase toward the bedroom door.

"Looks to me like this is going to be a perfect Christmas," Charlotte said. "Now, where's this Fan Four? I want to meet them, and Duke, and I need to see Julep and the kittens."

"Homer and Frank are on the front porch," Alex said. "Welcome back, Miz Charlotte."

"And Maude and Cleo are bickering in the kitchen, but I think they're ready to be sisters for real," Ellie Mae said.

"It sounds like this old house is full of life and fun, and, Alex, I think it's time for you to call me Aunt Charlotte," she said with a grin.

"I'm ready to do just that." Alex gave her a quick hug.

Ricky grabbed Ellie Mae by the hand, and pulled her out onto the back porch. "Merry Christmas to me!" he whispered and then kissed her.

She panted when the kiss ended. "It's not Christmas yet."

"No, but I get to wake up on Christmas morning

with you beside me," he said. "I love you, Ellie Mae, and I'm in love *with* you."

"I love you, too, but Ricky, we've only known each other for a few months," Ellie Mae said.

"I didn't believe in love at first sight until I met you, but I do now." Ricky took both her hands in his. "The moment I saw you, my heart said, 'This is the one.' I told it that it was not a brain and shouldn't be thinking, but it has kept telling me the same thing ever since then."

"Are you proposing to me?" Ellie Mae asked, not sure how she would answer if he was. Just agreeing to spend a few nights in his apartment and saying the three magic words was a lot.

Ricky dropped one of her hands and brought the other one to his lips to kiss her knuckles. "No, darlin', and when I do, you won't have to ask. For now, it's enough that you said you love me and that you're going to stay the night with me."

In that moment, Ellie Mae knew that when he did propose, she would say yes without a second's hesitation. She had found "the one," and she wanted to spend the rest of her life with him.

Epilogue

ONE YEAR LATER

T abby felt like she was seeing the past year go by in warp speed. As she straightened the circlet of white roses on top of Ellie Mae's head and then smoothed the front of her own red velvet dress that flowed from her shoulders to the floor, she couldn't help but smile. "And to think we are here today because of a hurricane named Delilah."

"I'm glad you decided to wear flat shoes, Ellie Mae. I have nightmares about you tripping over the skirt of your wedding dress and tumbling forward in high heels," Aunt Charlotte said from the other side of the room.

"If I wore heels, I'd fall right into Tabby," Ellie Mae said with half a giggle, "and with that big belly, she wouldn't stop rolling until she hit the hot tub. But it would serve her right, after the way she fell on top of me just before the hurricane hit."

"We can't have that," Cleo gasped. "We're all looking forward to a grandbaby too much to have Tabby fall down the stairs."

"I've never gotten to be a bridesmaid before

in my life." Maude wiped a tear away with her handkerchief. "This is such an honor."

"You could have been one at my wedding, if you had run away with me," Cleo said.

Maude waved her hand in dismissal. "That's all water under the bridge."

"This is my first time, too," Poppy said, "and all the girls are so excited to be flower girls. This is really a family wedding."

"My bridesmaids and flower girls are all beautiful," Ellie Mae said. "I would hug each of you, but Tabby would shoot me if I messed up my makeup. She's got a bad case of pregnant brain today."

"Yes, I would," Tabby said with a nod.

Charlotte sat down on the edge of the bed and smiled. "I'm just glad that there's going to be a baby in the family. You'd better get busy making another one, Eleanor Mason Landry."

"Why would I do that?" Ellie Mae took one more look at herself in the cheval mirror. The dress was exactly what she had wanted, and Cleo had designed and made it special for her: white velvet, with a wide scoop neck, long sleeves, and a short train that would drag behind her as she walked down the staircase and into the great room in the barn.

"Because we need two babies, or little Alexander Landry LaSalle will be spoiled too rotten for the garbage man to even take away,"

Maude answered. "His name sounds like he might grow up to be the president of the United States."

"I like that they're going to call him Xander. That sounds like a ballet dancer's name, or maybe a movie actor," Cleo said.

Tabby handed each of the bridesmaids their poinsettia bouquets. "Doesn't matter what he wants to do—whether he's a beach bum or builds boats, Alex and I will support him."

"I've got gossip." Charlotte chuckled.

"Well, then, spill the tea," Tabby said.

"Your mama called me last night. She'd had way too much to drink, and she wasn't just spilling tea—she was taking a virtual bath in it," Charlotte said.

"Go on." Tabby sat down beside her. "Don't tell me that she and Daddy are getting a divorce."

"Oh, no, darlin', it's much better than that. Kenneth has had a long-term affair with his assistant, and Gloria found out that her thirteen-year-old son belongs to Kenneth. You have a half brother that your father has been supporting all these years," Charlotte said.

"Good grief! Does he go by the Landry name?" Tabby asked.

"No, he uses his mother's name, but by the time Gloria discovered this news, she had already set Jefferson up with this woman. I guess that was back in the spring, when Kayla threw him over for a richer man. Jefferson fell in love with her and married her six weeks later—kind of a rebound thing."

"I've got a stepmother?" Ellie Mae gasped.

"Yep, and a stepbrother who is also your cousin." Charlotte giggled. "But that's not the funny part of the story. Jefferson was married to her, and she and her son had moved in with him before he found out that Ilene's—that's your new stepmother's name—grandmother was Black."

Ellie Mae got so tickled just thinking about the wild situation that tears ran down her face, smearing her makeup. "Why have you kept all this from us for this long?"

"I just found out about it all last night, when Gloria called me to fuss about the holidays. Now that she and Kenneth are having to host holiday dinners, they have to socialize with Jefferson and Ilene, and of course they bring Dallas—that's the boy's name," Charlotte said. "What goes around comes around, and after the way they all acted last Thanksgiving, they are getting to eat comeuppance pie. But I feel so sorry for Ilene and Dallas. That poor little boy didn't ask for this kind of dysfunctional family."

"I can agree for their sakes—but as for my folks, they deserve that comeuppance pie," Tabby said. "Right now, though, we've got to quit giggling and touch up our makeup, or Ellie Mae is going to be late for her wedding."

"After the way they treated our girls and Ricky that day, this story is like the icing on the cake," Cleo said. "But Ellie Mae can't be late."

"She's right," Poppy said. "Ricky is so nervous that he can't be still."

Tabby pulled a tissue from the box and got to work on Ellie Mae's face. She felt sorry for her parents and for Ellie Mae's. They had no idea what they were missing out on because of their refusal to come to Sandcastle for her wedding reception or for Ellie Mae's wedding. But at the same time, the happiness and joy in her heart overshadowed any bit of sadness.

Ellie Mae took one final look in the mirror after Tabby finished with her makeup and then turned to face a room full of women of all ages and five little girls. "Thank you all for making this day so special."

"Don't get us to cryin'," Maude said. "I don't want tearstains on this lovely red dress."

"Or me either," Charlotte chimed in. "I'm waiting to drop wedding cake on mine. Us Landry women are known for being clumsy."

Ellie Mae was ready to get the ceremony and reception over with and go on home to the house that she and Ricky had built. Alex had given them the land where his house had been before the hurricane hit so they would be closer to the B and B.

She took her bouquet from her aunt's hand and asked, "You're sure you aren't disappointed that we closed down the B and B, Aunt Charlotte?"

"It was a home before it was a B and B," she answered. "I just wanted Landrys to live in it. I'm so glad that Tabby has kept it pretty much the same as when I lived there. Besides, now I can come visit anytime I want and not have to worry about having a bed. And I understand that Declan and Jazzy like having their own room, too. It's all worked out wonderfully well." She turned to Tabby. "You will be busy with all the bookwork you are doing for the family businesses: Ricky and Ellie Mae's construction and Alex's fishing guide. You wouldn't have time for guests anyway, so now the B and B becomes a home again."

"Don't forget that she's also taking care of our finances for the Barn. I love the name we gave our place," Cleo said.

"And now she'll be a mother in a little while, so she'll be juggling all her work, plus taking care of Alexander Landry LaSalle," Charlotte said. "Now, can we get this show on the road? I'm ready for wedding cake, and I'm so tickled that you used my recipe for punch."

"Yes, ma'am," Ellie Mae said. "Give them the signal, Maude."

Maude opened the door a crack and waved a lace hankie. Poppy handed each of her five girls a basket of rose petals to strew down the stairs

441

and across the floor to the front of the living area, picked up her bouquet, and followed them out of the room.

"From This Moment On" by Shania Twain filled the barn, and Maude kissed Ellie Mae's hand and touched her cheek and then Tabby's. "Thank you, girls, for everything. They say the golden years are the best, but this past one has been the best of the best."

"Oh, get out of here." Cleo gave Maude a gentle push out the open door.

"Don't you lay hands on me." Maude shot a dirty look toward Cleo. "You'll muss up my dress, and if you do that, I might just push you down the stairs, Sister."

Cleo blew her sister a kiss and then followed her out into the hallway. Charlotte was next, and she turned at the door and flashed a brilliant smile before leaving the room. "My prayers have been answered. I am a happy woman."

"So have mine and Tabby's," Ellie Mae said.

"Now it's just me and you," Tabby said. "Like those first two weeks before the Fan Four and Alex got dropped on us. I love you, little cousin, and I'm so happy for you and Ricky. But why didn't you tell Aunt Charlotte that the glow on your face isn't just because this is your wedding day?"

"Ricky and I want this day to be *just* our wedding day. We'll announce the baby at New

Year's. Just think—Xander will have someone to grow up with, and with only six months between them, I hope they'll be as close as we are." Ellie Mae headed for the door. "I agree with you, Tabby. It doesn't matter what this little one"— she touched her still-flat stomach—"wants to be. I will support her or him."

"And the irony is that we have all these blessings because of a hurricane," Tabby said as she stepped out into the hallway.

Ellie Mae followed her out of the room. Halfway down the stairs that she had helped build, she caught Ricky's eye. He was waiting at the end of the room in his black suit, with Homer, Frank, his brother, and his father standing beside him.

"Life is good," she muttered, "and I'm a lucky woman."

Dear readers,

Sandcastles mesmerize me. I don't know if it's the sandcastles themselves or if it's the fact that I can hear the ocean waves and inhale all that lovely salty air while I'm looking at them. A couple of years ago, we had a family reunion at the beach in Florida. Fifty-two of us were able to go, and I rented fifteen condos for a week. It was the vacation of a lifetime. During that time, my grandson Seth Lemar spent a lot of time on the beach with the younger grandkids—building sandcastles and digging an enormous hole. As I looked out from my deck, I felt truly blessed that all the kids, grandkids, and great-grands had given up their vacation time to travel that far and spend a week with us.

When I thought about setting this book down on the southern coast of Texas, those sandcastles came to my mind. We went down to that area to do some research right after a hurricane had hit, and before we got back home, the characters in this book had become as real as my next-door neighbors. As usual, I thought I had it all planned, but—again, as usual—the characters took over the writing, and the story began to have layer upon layer. I hope you all enjoy reading about the Sandcastle B and B as much as I did during the time I spent there.

As always, there are so many people to thank for helping me take a rough idea and turn it into the book you hold in your hands. There is a saying about life: *You don't meet people by accident. There's always a reason—a lesson or a blessing!* Many of the people I have met have taught me valuable lessons, and many others have brought a blessing into my life. Bits and pieces of some of them are inspirations for the characters in this book.

Today, I'd like to thank those who came bearing blessings. To my developmental editor, Krista Stroever—you are truly the wind beneath my wings. To my acquiring editor, Alison Dasho—thank you for continuing to believe in me. To my publisher, Montlake—thank you for everything from covers to promotion to all the behind-the-scenes folks who work hard to make this the best book possible. To my agent, Erin Niumata—I couldn't ask for a better friend and agent. To my agency, Folio Management—thank you for taking care of everything for me. To all my readers—y'all are awesome, and I appreciate every one of you. To my family—I love all y'all. And of course, as always, to Mr. B—you've always been my biggest blessing.

Hugs to you all,
Carolyn Brown

About the Author

Carolyn Brown is a *New York Times*, *USA Today*, *Washington Post*, *Wall Street Journal*, and *Publishers Weekly* bestselling author and RITA finalist with more than 125 published books. She has written women's fiction, historical and contemporary romance, and cowboys-and-country-music novels. She and her husband live in the small town of Davis, Oklahoma, where everyone knows everyone else, knows what they are doing and when, and reads the local newspaper on Wednesday to see who got caught. They have three grown children and enough grandchildren and great-grandchildren to keep them young. For more information, visit www.carolynbrownbooks.com.

Center Point Large Print
600 Brooks Road / PO Box 1
Thorndike, ME 04986-0001 USA

(207) 568-3717

US & Canada:
1 800 929-9108
www.centerpointlargeprint.com